MW01229840

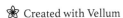 Created with Vellum

ALSO BY LINDA ULLESEIT

Flying Horse Books:

On a Wing and a Dare

In the Winds of Danger

Under a Wild and Darkening Sky

Other Historical Fiction:

Under the Almond Trees

The Aloha Spirit

The River Remembers

Innocents at Home is dedicated to

Amelia Fiona Ulleseit and the next generation

INNOCENTS AT HOME

LINDA ULLESEIT

1

Nina Churchman Larrowe
New York City, New York , November 1867

"Travel is fatal to prejudice, bigotry and narrow-mindedness, and many of our people need it sorely on these accounts."
- Mark Twain, Innocents Abroad

Nina Larrowe paused at the top of the gangway, anticipating the accolades of jostling reporters as she disembarked from the *Quaker City* after a five-month voyage. She tugged at the snug waistline of her dress and pulled in her stomach. Straightening her shoulders, she lifted her chin and adjusted her hat. But to her disappointment, only a smattering of people waited for the passengers in New York Harbor. Her husband was not among them. She shivered in the November cold. Sixty-five people had been to the Holy Land on a unique excursion of piety and pleasure. Surely they deserved a bit of fanfare upon their return. At least her husband could have been there on time.

Emma Beach and her father, Moses Beach, stood at the bottom of the gangway, having already disembarked from the ship. A few reporters gathered around them. Samuel Clemens sauntered over to the group. Mr. Beach owned the *New York Sun,* but Mr. Clemens was nothing more than an ambitious reporter from a small California newspaper. Emma was a tiny scrap of a woman with reddish-gold hair. Nina was only five years older, and next to Emma she felt ancient, clumsy, and fat.

When they boarded the ship last June, Nina hadn't known Emma Beach. Two women of a similar age became acquainted rather quickly, though, on a voyage comprised mostly of men with religious connections. Emma had caught the eye of the eminent-in-his-own-mind Mr. Clemens, and his flirting with the young lady during the trip soured Nina's impression of the man. After all, the trip was intended for pious people to visit the Holy Land. It required decorum. And Mr. Clemens was almost twice Emma's age. He was a good eight inches taller than the petite Emma, so she always had to look up at him during conversation. The attention of an older man, well-known if not as prestigious as her own father, had clearly turned Emma's innocent head.

Nina scanned the dock again, still hoping to see Marcus. He had intended to accompany her on the trip, but mere days before they were to embark he'd received a telegram from his brother, announcing the death of their father. Now, Marcus and his brother were all that remained of the Larrowe clan.

She'd missed him. This trip was supposed to be a second honeymoon of sorts, one that would reconnect them after three hectic years of marriage. Nina wanted a strong marriage like that of her parents. Instead, she'd spent their third anniversary alone. No, not alone. She'd dined with Emma, on board the *Quaker City,* anchored off the shore of Athens where they'd been quarantined by Greek officials due to a fear of cholera. She would rather have dined with Marcus anywhere in the world.

"I must go home," he'd told her on the eve of the cruise.

"And I should be there for you," she'd said, trying to keep her voice strong. She'd been looking forward to the cruise. She loved the drama and intrigue of history, and anticipated seeing evidence of civilizations she'd only read about. Still, she'd wanted to share it with Marcus.

He'd taken her hand and said, "No, you must go on this voyage. You'll be of great service to your aunt and uncle."

"They will want my help on distant shores," she'd admitted.

She didn't know her relatives well even though she referred to them as aunt and uncle. They were distant Lockwood relatives of her mother's, aging and refusing to admit their frailties.

But it was her duty to support her husband. "Shouldn't I be there for you?" she'd asked.

"No, I insist. Just be sure you behave properly," Marcus had admonished her. "One can speak clearly without shouting."

His words stung. He clearly didn't value her education in the art of elocution, but she had agreed and sailed without looking back.

Still no sign of Marcus. Descending the gangway and stepping onto the dock, Nina waved a hasty goodbye to her aunt and uncle as they made their way off the ship to catch a train to their home in Norwalk. Three reporters jostled each other as they tried to gain Mr. Beach's attention. Mr. Clemens stole the limelight with his usual caustic sarcasm that Nina never found funny but Emma always did.

"Your readers will never know what consummate asses they can become, until they go abroad," he told the reporters. "In Paris they just simply opened their eyes and stared when we spoke to them in French. We never did succeed in making those idiots understand their own language." The reporters laughed.

"What poppycock," Nina muttered.

Even though Marcus wasn't here, Nina felt her duty as his wife was to get his name in print. The more people who knew about Marcus Larrowe, the better his new business venture in memory training would do. She stepped up beside Emma and waited for Mr. Clemens to stop talking like a supporting actor in a play.

"I just wanted to say goodbye, Miss Beach. Have a nice ferry ride across the river," Nina said.

"Oh, Mrs. Larrowe, I'm sorry to see this trip end. I've made so many new friends." Emma spoke in a low voice.

Nina pursed her lips and looked at the reporters. They seemed to be wondering who Nina was. "Mrs. Marcus Larrowe," Nina said to them, carefully controlling the volume of her voice. "My husband helped Mr. Clemens book his passage on the *Quaker City* for this cruise." Her family had known Mr. Clemens in Nevada. When he'd come to New York, Marcus had been glad to assist. "Unfortunately, Mr. Larrowe was unable to join us at the last moment. He was too busy securing his family's buckwheat farm." As the veil of disinterest dropped over the reporters' eyes, she added, "Marcus Larrowe is a Yale graduate who was active in politics out West. He now holds lectures to discuss the science of memory." She added a nod of the head and wave of the hand to punctuate her words.

Ignoring her, one of the reporters called out to Emma's father, "Mr. Beach! Is it true your newest daughter isn't yours?"

Nina had heard the rumors about the affair between Emma's mother and Reverend Henry Ward Beecher. She didn't see Mr. Beach's reaction to the question, but Emma dropped her eyes to the ground.

Mr. Clemens let loose a boisterous laugh that drew attention back to him.

Emma took Nina's arm and turned away from the men. "I hate all this fuss," Emma said. "I'd be happy to arrive at home with no one the wiser. Father is a pillar of the community, though, so they won't leave him alone."

"At least people know his name. That gives weight to his words, value to his endeavors," Nina said. Emma didn't know how fruitless it was to fade into the wallpaper. Connections built prosperity, and no one made important connections sitting home waiting for the world to call on them.

"Oh, I don't know," Emma said. "It's tiresome having people inquire about every aspect of your life. There's plenty of value in a quiet life well lived."

Nina just smiled, refraining from an indulgent pat on the younger girl's arm.

Mr. Beach announced, "I'm sorry, we have no more time. We must board the ferry post haste."

Emma nodded to Nina as she turned to go.

Nina's husband had not yet arrived. Whatever was keeping the man? She tried so hard to be supportive of her husband's career the way her mother had taught her to be. But Nina had never learned how to deal with an abrupt career shift like Marcus's change from lawyer to lecturer. Sometimes she felt that she no longer knew her husband at all.

She refused to wait any longer. Nina held her head high as she moved toward the line of carriages for hire, musing on the irony of her husband, a lecturer on memory, forgetting to meet her at the harbor.

2

Emmeline Buckingham Beach
New York City, November 1867

"When red-headed people are above a certain social grade their hair is auburn."
- *Mark Twain*, A Connecticut Yankee in King Arthur's Court

Emma watched Nina walk away alone and sighed. How wonderful to be able to enjoy a homecoming without the fuss of reporters. Mama always said that Emma's red hair drew attention. Mama smiled when she said it, but Emma tried to wear a large hat and tuck as much hair as possible under it.

"This way, Emma." Her father led her away from the reporters.

Sam Clemens always wore a calm expression, as if nothing would ever bother him, but his eyes twinkled with mischief. Emma loved the way his nose wrinkled up and his eyes half closed as he spoke. And she felt a connection to the author because of his red hair, however silly that might sound. All through the Holy Land, she'd never felt self-conscious about her hair when she was with Sam.

She knew her mother would say she had a schoolgirl crush on

Sam Clemens. Sam was older than she was, a man of the world. He'd traveled, and he'd met gold miners as well as royalty. Emma smiled, realizing that after this voyage she, too, had traveled. She'd even met the Emperor of Russia on their stop in Yalta. Sam had actually spoken to the emperor, although Emma had been too shy to do more than smile. Emma gave Sam a tiny wave goodbye, but he must not have seen it because he didn't respond. She followed her father as he walked toward her mother.

Emma's eyes teared as she saw her mother, holding baby Violet, waiting to greet them as they got on the ferry. Emma had enjoyed spending time with her father on the voyage, but she'd missed her mother and baby sister, and even her other siblings. Emma wanted to run ahead and hug her mother, but a lady never ran. She blinked away the emotional tears of homecoming.

"Chloe," her father said to his wife through tight lips.

"Welcome home, Moses." Mama's voice was soft and cool. Then she turned to Emma. "My darling, it's wonderful to have you home!" She enveloped Emma in a warm hug that squashed nine-month-old Violet between them.

Emma sank into her mother's arms. "It's good to be home, Mama."

"Mr. Beach! Is that baby the preacher's daughter?" A reporter snatched a pencil from behind his ear and poised it over the pad of paper in his hand.

Mama pulled away from Emma and addressed the reporter. "This is our youngest, Violet Beach. Isn't she precious?" She looked to her husband for confirmation, but Moses had already gone to buy ferry tickets.

Emma wished she was one of the anonymous people walking past the harbor, one of the people going about business that no one knew about. She wished she was wearing a blue-gray dress that would blend in with the swirl of blue-gray water in New York Harbor instead of the green that was her mother's favorite color. Whenever the Beach name appeared in any paper other than her father's, it was ill gossip. Reverend Beecher was a celebrity in his own right, with his

abolitionist work at the Plymouth Church. Suspicions of his affair
with her mother had titillated society even though rumors abounded
about the reverend and his female parishioners. Violet's birth in
January had caused Reverend Beecher to cancel his own spot on the
excursion. In the ensuing five months, Emma had never figured out if
Papa was glad Reverend Beecher wasn't on the ship, or worried that
he was still in Brooklyn with Mama. Violet was adorable, though, and
Emma loved her. Her father, at least in public, ignored the gossip
about his wife's affair. Emma would, too. She'd never let anyone see
her embarrassment over Mama's affair with Reverend Beecher. She'd
learned it was a good idea to follow her father's lead. Emma was good
at following. It made her appear docile although that wasn't the same
as being passive when done on purpose.

The Beach family made their way onto red-trimmed Fulton Ferry.
As they crossed the East River, Emma watched the mansions on
Columbia Heights grow larger, anticipating her first glimpse of home.
The fine houses looked out over the river back toward Manhattan,
adding spots of muted color to the grayness of the river. Her father
said the houses kept an eye on the city where everything important in
the world happened. Emma disagreed. Family, not business, was the
most important thing in the world, though she would never say so
out loud to her father.

It was true Emma was glad to be home, but she already missed
Sam. Maybe she had stars in her eyes when she looked at him, but
he'd been nicer to her than anyone else on the voyage, including her
father. She remembered an idyllic moment after they'd left Alexan-
dria. The ship had steamed toward home, still several weeks away.
Emma had taken her sketchpad and sat on deck. She'd admired the
variety of color present in the waves, and the quality of sunlight that
dazzled off the water. Sam had stood at the rail, smoking a cigar.
She'd sketched until Sam had turned and seen her.

He came to inspect her work, and she tingled at his nearness.
"You have talent," he'd said.

Emma said, "To really depict personality, I need to paint it."

Sam had laughed with his entire body and soul. The memory of it made her smile. Sam was interesting and smart and funny. They'd played chess on board the *Quaker City*. He'd quizzed her at length about her own painting and praised her sketches. He made her smile, sometimes with a blush, and her heart beat faster when he was near.

Now Sam was off to Washington, D.C. to work for a senator from Nevada, and he planned to write more articles about the cruise. He'd promised to write to her, too. As the ferry reached Brooklyn, Emma imagined what he might say in those letters. Her father hired a carriage, and she daydreamed about Sam missing her every day and visiting her with bouquets of roses. The future would be full of roses.

3

Nina Larrowe
Greenwich Village, November 1867

"Keep away from people who try to belittle your ambitions. ...the really great make you feel that you, too, can become great."
- Mark Twain, "Morally We Roll Along"

"Nina! There you are!"

It was Marcus. Finally. His coat flapped open as he hurried toward where she stood on the dock. He'd always been impervious to the cold. His hat in one hand, Marcus used the other to smooth his thinning gray hair and bushy mustache as he stopped in front of her. His eyes darted left and right, as if attempting to take in every bit of the arrival and departure bustle. He put his hat on his head and grasped both her arms to pull her in for a quick kiss on the cheek. Better late than never.

"It's good to see you," Nina said. She took his hand and squeezed it as he let go of her arms.

"They didn't talk to you?" Marcus asked, waving to indicate the departing newspapermen.

"I managed to get a few words in about you and your lecturing." She beamed with pride in her husband, pleased that she'd been so forward thinking.

But Marcus frowned. He ran a hand through his hair and said, "I'd hoped to put in a word for this week's lecture." Marcus assisted Nina into his waiting carriage while the driver loaded her trunks.

Typical. He was more interested in promoting his lecture than asking about her trip. She wouldn't let him get away with that. She said, "It was a wonderful journey. So many exotic places! I wish you'd been with me, but it's good to be home."

Marcus nodded and stared out the window.

On Bank Street in Greenwich Village, the driver pulled up in front of a brick Greek Revival townhouse, one of several built by another of her New York Lockwood relatives. Marcus helped Nina out, and the driver unloaded her trunks.

The butler opened the door and stood back to allow her to enter. "Welcome home, Mrs. Larrowe." He nodded at Marcus and went to retrieve Nina's trunks.

Nina entered the house as the clocks struck the hour. Marcus loved clocks. He had them all set so they would chime one after the other, resulting in the stentorian Westminster tones of the grandfather clock in the entry giving way to the lighter chiming of the mantel clock, then the raucous cuckoo of the clock near the kitchen. Marcus had so many clocks, some of them had to be set fifteen minutes off the actual time so they'd have their own time to shine. While it was annoying to never know which clock showed the actual time, Nina did enjoy the chiming that welcomed her home.

"Tonight we'll eat in," Marcus said, "but tomorrow is the opera."

Nina smiled. "Yes, I remember." The plans for the social season had been well under way before she'd left on the cruise.

He nodded and headed upstairs. It was the most loving reunion she could have expected. Marcus's first love would always be the study of memory. She'd known that since she married him in August of 1864, but it hadn't really come up during their honeymoon in Europe, which had been a blissful suspension of reality. When they returned to Austin, Nevada, Marcus had helped to have Nevada declared a state before the 1864 presidential election. It wasn't until two years later, halfway through his term on the Nevada Supreme Court, that Marcus had uprooted Nina and moved to New York. He was determined to study memory, and claimed some amazing research was being done in New York City at the time. Nina had tamped down her shock at this change, and her reluctance to leave her family in Nevada. If maybe she wasn't desperately in love with her husband, she managed as long as she had her parents and brother nearby. It had gotten harder when they moved to New York.

So the first three years of her marriage had truly been a whirlwind, with Marcus driven by the political calendar and later the schedule of lectures. Somewhere along the line, she'd been lost. Nina understood the role of a lawyer's wife, the example set by her mother for her entire life. Nina had expected a period of her husband working long hours, then the arrival of children that would keep her days busy. Never had she anticipated Marcus's utter devotion to learning about how people remembered things. He could quote entire newspaper articles after reading them once, but couldn't seem to remember his wife. She was a married woman, though, and must help her husband in whatever career he chose. If he was a farmer or a lawyer, a dockworker or lecturer, Nina would find a way to support him. It's what wives did. She had never expected it to be so lonely.

She went upstairs to freshen up and noticed a plate on her bedside table filled with her favorite chocolate caramels from Maillard's Confectionery. She popped one in her mouth and savored the taste of home. Weariness caught up to her then, and she told the maid she'd take dinner in her room then go to bed early.

THE NEXT MORNING, Nina dug a carefully wrapped souvenir out of her trunk and took it with her when she went downstairs for breakfast. Marcus was already at the table, sipping his first cup of coffee and reading the *New York Herald*. He nodded at Nina to acknowledge her greeting.

"Here is the souvenir I brought you from Egypt," she said. "I think you'll love it." She handed it to him and took her place at the table.

Marcus unwrapped the item. Nina loved the wooden carving she'd picked up in a tomb. It was less than a foot in length, but it boasted detailed rowers with their paddles and a pharaoh figure under a canopy. "It's lovely," Marcus said, putting it on the table.

"Can't you just see an ancient master carver working on those little figures?" Nina said. She poured herself a cup of tea.

"Yes, it's lovely," Marcus repeated.

Nina gave up. "Is there anything in the paper about the voyage?" she asked.

Marcus folded the paper so it showed an article on page seven. "There's a bit about the *Quaker City,* then an article below it."

Nina took the paper. "Written by Mark Twain. That's the name Mr. Clemens used when my family knew him in Nevada. He must have written this last night." She read Sam's words, shaking her head in disbelief. "Listen to what he says. 'The people stared at us everywhere and we stared at them. We generally made them feel rather small, too, before we got done with them, because we bore down on them with American greatness until we crushed them.'" She looked up from the paper. "How can he befriend his fellow passengers then disparage them so to the world?" In her head, though, she could hear Samuel Clemens' sarcastic voice disparaging anyone he perceived as weak. Nina skimmed the rest of the article then threw the paper down on the table.

Marcus said, "He tells the world you were all impressed with your own importance, that you talked loudly and pinched pennies." He leaned toward Nina. "He's presented you all as bumptious, ignorant, and careless."

Nina said, "I remember some of the instances Mr. Clemens lampooned, but he misconstrued some actions. Not everyone was experienced in how to treat the world."

"And you were?" He raised an eyebrow. Looking pensive, he took a bite of egg. "You know, even negative attention might be manipulated."

Nina glared at him. "You will not use gossip begun by a two-bit Western journalist to further your career at my expense." If only one woman of breeding and social standing picked up on Mr. Clemens' words, the voyagers could be the butt of social gossip for months. Even worse, if the image portrayed by Mr. Clemens caught the fancy of several of society's gossips, they could embellish the story until it caused great harm to anyone associated with the journey. But it was just a short article, on the seventh page of the paper. Maybe no one would see it.

That evening, Nina donned a lavish dress of green silk embroidered with green vines dotted with beads. Her matching green hat sat well on her dark hair. Marcus, turned out in a top hat and tails, escorted her to the carriage. They were off to see *Roméo et Juliette* at the Academy of Music. Nina had missed the first month of the social season while she'd been abroad, and was conscious of the need to be seen as soon as possible to maintain her position.

The carriage deposited them at the corner of East 14th Street and Irving Place. Nina and Marcus mingled with the best of New York society as they approached the Academy. They certainly weren't members of Mrs. Astor's Four Hundred, but Nina's family wealth and connections landed them solidly in the Upper Ten Thousand. Nina smiled at women she knew and nodded at those who recognized her and waved.

A woman Nina knew only by sight walked by and said, "I'm quite sure you weren't as ignorant as the newspaper implied, Mrs. Larrowe. I look forward to hearing your stories."

She didn't stop to chat further, which Nina had no intention of doing anyway. It seemed the people who counted, at least, had not seen the article.

The plush interior of the theater created an intimate world for theater goers, even though it held four thousand seats on five levels. Nina glanced toward the private boxes, curious to see if Mrs. Astor was attending this evening, but too many people blocked her view— the men dressed somberly in black while the women's gowns ran the gamut of colors and textures.

Nina and Marcus took their usual seats just as the gaslights went down and the curtain came up. Nina sat forward in her seat, anticipating the opening scene. She was sure this would be better than their casual shipboard plays aboard the *Quaker City*, and could only hope it would be as good as the Shakespearean performances she'd watched while growing up in Nevada City, California. Her mother always said that the most intellectual, most cultured men of the East came to the West searching for gold, so of course they appreciated Shakespeare. As a young girl, Nina remembered attending the same plays over and over with her best friend, Polly Overton, seeing them performed by different companies and discussing the merits of each afterwards. Now she would see the New York premiere of Charles Gounard's *Roméo et Juliette.*

Swept up in the story of star-crossed lovers, Nina blinked when the gaslights brightened and the show was over. It took a minute for the story to leave her head and reality to return. By then the theater was buzzing with conversation as patrons prepared to leave.

In the lobby, Mrs. Clara Livingston exclaimed over Nina. "Oh, Mrs. Larrowe, your dress is fabulous." Her wide eyes and simpering tone identified her as being a part of the less-well off Livingstons, not those that were part of the Four Hundred.

"Thank you, Mrs. Livingston," Nina said. "You look very nice, too."

Marcus continued a few steps past Nina, joining the other men who were fetching their wives' coats.

Clara turned to her companion, then back to Nina. "Mrs. Nina Larrowe, I'd like you to meet my daughter, Miss Emily Livinsgston. Emily, this is Mrs. Larrowe. She's a Lockwood." This last was said in a loud aside meant to be heard by anyone nearby.

Nina graciously nodded to the girl, whose shy attitude reminded her of Emma Beach. "Enchanted." Turning back to Clara, Nina laughed and said, "Actually my mother is a Lockwood. I've only ever been a Churchman or a Larrowe." All three women laughed as if Nina had said the funniest thing they'd heard all day.

"You were on the cruise to the Holy Land, isn't that right?" Clara Livingston asked.

Nina nodded. "A pleasant excursion."

Emily's eyes brightened as she said, "Is it true you all misbehaved dreadfully?"

Clara shushed her daughter. "I'm terribly sorry, Mrs. Larrowe. We generally don't believe what we read in the papers. I'm sure it's not true." Her tone seemed to be asking for verification.

Nina could see Marcus returning with her coat. To Mrs. Livingston, she said, "We had a marvelous voyage and saw some truly inspiring places." Changing the subject, she said, "The actors did a good job tonight, did they not?"

Clara laid a gloved hand on Nina's arm and leaned toward her. "I would invite the leading players to my dinner party tomorrow evening, but I'm afraid they speak nothing but French." Her laughter trilled.

Nina smiled and excused herself. She'd had French lessons since she was a girl and would have no trouble conversing with French actors. More interesting was Clara Livingston's willingness to entertain actors in her home. It followed the example of society's elite, whose patronage of the arts had recently begun to include a closer association with leading members of the acting profession. As she accepted her coat from Marcus, Nina was glad that she'd been able to turn the conversation away from gossip before he overheard.

By the time they reached the street, Nina had spoken to more than a handful of women, expressing her delight in the performance and promising to tell them all about her travels to the Holy Land at the next dinner party.

Still tired from her trip, Nina dozed in the carriage on the way home. Marcus helped her up the steps of their home.

"Care for a night cap?" he asked when they had shed their coats and hats.

"Lovely," she said, taking a seat by the parlor fire.

Marcus poured himself a whiskey and a sherry for her. "Did anyone mention my lecture tomorrow night?"

Nina remembered Clara Livingston talking about a dinner party the following evening. "No, they didn't. Will it be at Corinthian Hall?"

She winced as Marcus's face darkened. No doubt he expected her to already know every detail of speaking engagements he'd booked while she was on the cruise.

"I'm disappointed, Nina. I rely on you to generate interest among the women so they can speak to their husbands about my memory talks."

Nina set her sherry glass down hard on the table next to her chair. "I believe I'll go to bed." She suited actions to words, stepping carefully to avoid giving him the satisfaction of seeing her stomp out in frustration. Too wound up to sleep, she wished she could talk to Emma Beach as she sometimes had while on board the *Quaker City*. After being shipmates for five months, Emma's home in Brooklyn seemed worlds away from Greenwich Village. At least she could speak to her friend in a letter.

Dear Miss Beach,

I'm sure you've read Mr. Clemens' article in The New York Herald. *Such a despicable portrayal of his fellow shipmates. I can only believe Mr. Clemens intended all along to parody us, but I don't understand a man who would sacrifice the reputation of good people for a laugh.*

When my family knew him in Nevada several years ago, Mr. Clemens was no more than a down-on-his-luck miner who wrote sporadic articles for newspapers. The Alta California *gave him his big break when they asked him to cover our excursion to the Holy Land. Even so, he wouldn't have been able to procure a ticket without financial help from my father. That makes his betrayal even more heinous. We must stand up for ourselves and not hide from any bad publicity.*

Thinking of you and wishing you the best.
Sincerely,
Mrs. Nina Larrowe

4

E mma Beach
Brooklyn, New York, January 1868

"If there is a moral to this lecture it is an injunction to all Vandals to travel.
I am glad the American Vandal goes abroad. It does him good. It makes a
better man of him."
- Mark Twain, "The American Vandal"

Emma sat in a stiff chair by the window overlooking the East River. Ships moved past, their clouds of white steam adding to the overall grayness of water and sky on this January day. Behind her, the parlor was empty of people but full of elegant chairs and cozy tables. The square grand piano waited for Emma's sister to practice. Emma had long since refused to continue torturing the instrument, but Alice was still young enough to do as Mama wished. A gigantic landscape painting hung above the piano, stretching all the way to the carved crown molding that lent a heaviness to the entire room at odds with the delicate chairs.

A letter from Sam, read so many times she no longer had to look at it to know every word, had arrived before Christmas, about three weeks after the *New York Herald* article he'd written about his fellow travelers, and two weeks after a letter from Nina Larrowe. Emma had enjoyed Sam's company on board the *Quaker City* and didn't want to believe ill of him. So Emma had not immediately responded to Sam's letter, and now wondered if she'd left it too late.

Sam's letter, dated December 5, had come to her from Washington. He referred to December 5 as Valentine's Day so that he could have an excuse to write to "a young lady whom I have known so long, esteemed so well, and met in so many continents." Emma smiled and blushed every time she read it.

He'd begun the letter, though, with a reference to his article. "I suppose I have made you mad, too, maybe, but with all my heart I hope I haven't. You weren't particularly civil to an old and defeated chess antagonist, the day you left the ship, but I declare to goodness (pardon the expression) I cannot bear malice for that. Mr. Beach told me in New York, that even Mrs. Fairbanks felt hurt about that best-natured squib that ever was written (I refer to the one in the Herald,) and Charlie Langdon has not dropped me a line. Mrs. Fairbanks has, though, and scolds hard but she can't deceive this Prodigal Son—I detect the good nature and the forgiveness under it all."

Emma was surprised to learn that her father had shared Mrs. Fairbanks' feelings as a result of the article. Nina and Emma had felt that way, too. Did Papa not know that? Or was he just protecting his daughter?

In his published article, Sam had said, "...when presented with a desert of stumps, they exclaim, 'Oh, my soul, my beating heart, what a noble forest is here!'" Emma had never said, "Oh, my soul" to anyone. She tried to tell herself that he wasn't referring to her, but she reimagined every conversation they'd had on board the ship, looking for occasions where she might have misunderstood his friendship. She wanted him to proclaim his love for her to the world, even if he hadn't yet proclaimed it to her.

How could it be that Sam, a writer, had not been inspired by the wonderful things they'd seen? She didn't believe it was too sentimental to exclaim over the vastness of the ocean, the antiquity of

Egypt, or the beauty of Naples. Besides, people who did express their wonder did not deserve to be ridiculed for it.

She looked out the window again, at Manhattan across the river. In her response, she'd have to tell Sam how she loathed such attention while he always seemed to relish it. In fact, he was more like Nina Larrowe in that. Why hadn't he chosen Nina as a chess partner? But no, he'd chosen her. And now he'd written. She owed both Nina and Sam answers.

"Emma! Are you ready?" Her father's voice interrupted her reverie.

"Yes, Papa." Her heart flip-flopped as she rose and joined her parents. Violet, ten-year-old Alice, and seven-year-old William would stay home with the nanny.

Mama frowned at Emma. "Surely you have something more cheerful to wear?"

Emma looked down at her dove-gray dress. It was an expensive cut, fine fabric. She'd never felt the need to wear a peacock's plumage. Violet loved dressing in shades of purple, especially violet, of course. Alice preferred bright patterns. Emma's tastes were more subdued. She likened herself to the understated frame that held the glory of a master's painting. No one paid attention to the framing if the picture captured their attention properly. "I like this dress," she said. Her mother shrugged and led her daughters out of the house.

Tonight they would go to a small supper party at the Beecher home. Papa would be on his best behavior because that's what Papa did. Emma would smile, hover on the periphery, and, if the conversation dragged, think of the nearly blank canvas waiting for her at home. She was beginning to paint a scene of the Holy Land remembered from her journey, and its colors and shadows were crowding her thoughts.

The Beach family still attended Plymouth Church in Brooklyn. Mama insisted they continue to include Reverend Beecher in their lives despite Papa's tightly compressed lips and furrowed brow during the services. In Emma's hearing, at least, Mama never claimed that Reverend Beecher had a right to see his daughter even though her continued involvement with the church showed she clearly believed that to be so. In public, she never claimed Violet was Reverend Beecher's daughter, and he never acknowledged it. Still, public suspicions abounded, as it did when events were true but not discussed.

As a child, Emma had been encouraged to think of Reverend Beecher as a lovable uncle who liked to give hugs. She'd long since stopped believing that. Emma had heard Mama say, "Reverend Beecher teaches that love is the center of Christianity. God loves Reverend Beecher, and if the reverend loves me, then God loves me, too. Reverend Beecher is controversial, that's all, so people point out his faults."

Emma's father had responded, "I never thought I'd be grateful that God didn't love me."

That usually ended any conversation about Reverend Beecher that Emma could overhear. Emma couldn't imagine marrying a man, having children with him, then having a child with the reverend at the church. The trip to the Holy Land hadn't eased the pain of Emma's realization that her mother wasn't just the loving person who'd raised her. Emma loved her father fiercely, but her love for her mother had become tenuous. At the very least, Mama had lost Emma's respect for not living the life of marriage fidelity she expected her daughters to maintain someday.

But nothing about supper with the reverend would make Emma's heart race. After supper, though, they would attend a lecture billed as "The American Vandals" by Mark Twain. She would see Sam again! She could look up at him from the audience and cling to his every word without drawing a critical gaze from her mother or a frown from her father. Emma did worry a bit about the content of the speech. Would he belittle his *Quaker City* shipmates while standing in front of them? She knew several were planning to attend, and she hoped to see Nina Larrowe.

The Beach family walked the block to Beecher's three-story brownstone on Willow Street. Emma had visited the Beechers before, but not often enough for it to feel comfortable to arrive there. The butler opened the door to admit Emma and her parents. They proceeded into an elegant parlor filled with people.

"Mr. and Mrs. Beach, welcome! And Miss Emma. I'm charmed," Reverend Beecher said. His clothes, as usual, were impeccable, and his smile bright. His words addressed them all, but his eyes were on her mother, and on Violet in Mama's arms.

Emma didn't like the way he tucked his too-long hair behind his ears, but she smiled. Mama would want her to be polite.

Moses Beach ignored Henry Ward Beecher and crossed the room to talk with two men standing in an opposite corner. One of them was Sam Clemens. Emma couldn't hide her delighted smile. She hadn't known Sam would be joining them for dinner. The gathering suddenly became less stuffy.

Reverend Beecher's wife sat before the fireplace talking with another woman. Emma and her mother joined them. Alice followed. Emma recognized Reverend Beecher's sister, the author Harriet Beecher Stowe, from previous visits. Emma and her mother reacquainted themselves with Mrs. Stowe while Mrs. Beecher glared at her mother.

When they went in to supper, Sam found his seat next to Emma.

"Well, if it isn't my old *Quaker City* favorite," he said, smiling at her.

"Hardly old," Emma protested even as she felt her face light up with a smile that answered his. Here with him, in person, she responded to his teasing like a flower to sunlight.

"I'm still distressed you haven't answered my letter," he said.

Glad for the dimness of candlelight that hid her blush, Emma said, "The holidays were so busy. I will write, I promise."

"Tomorrow I take the train back to D.C.," he said. "Plenty of time to think about you writing that letter."

Emma's heart melted. She smiled at him, seeing her delight mirrored in his eyes. "Are you giving your speech in D.C.?" she asked.

"I will, after I go to California." He frowned. "I've had word that the *Alta California* has plans to publish my letters as a book. I can't let them do that when I'm working on such a book myself. I'll tour there, speaking of my experiences, making them mine, right?"

She nodded, impressed with his forward thinking. "That's an excellent idea."

Henry Ward Beecher raised his voice to include the entire table. "I'd like to take this moment to thank Moses Beach for thinking of Plymouth Church while he was in the Holy Land. The wood you brought us from the olive tree in Lebanon will make a nice pulpit for the church."

Murmurs of appreciation rippled around the table.

"Let's not forget you'll also have a matching chair from that wood. If there's enough lumber, I'll have them make a table for your papers. Got to make the most of my $200 investment. Not cheap to ship a tree." Emma's father laughed after he said this, and the assembled group joined him.

Emma just gave a tight smile. Her father's attempt to impress the congregation was just as obvious as a male peacock spreading his glorious feathers to attract the female. Reverend Beecher didn't seem cowed, though. He nodded at her father and turned to Sam.

"And our friend, Sam," Reverend Beecher said, "is talking with the American Publishing Company about a book of his travels. Make sure you drive a hard bargain with Elisha Bliss, Sam."

Sam raised his wine glass. "I shall, and thank you."

Emma admired the way Sam took the praise without sinking into himself as she would have. "You'll be as famous as Mrs. Stowe when next we gather," she whispered to Sam.

"Mrs. Stowe? How about Mr. Nathaniel Hawthorne?" He grinned, and butterflies darted around her stomach.

Emma pretended to listen as the conversation swirled around her. She watched Sam charm everyone around the table as he always had. He complimented Mrs. Beecher on the meal her cook had prepared, and he enthused over Mrs. Stowe's writing. Sam asked Reverend Beecher more questions about Mr. Bliss, and listened carefully to unsolicited advice from her father. Emma finished her meal in silence, watching Sam shine, dreaming of one day showing him her finished paintings and basking in his loving praise.

Reverend Beecher had arranged for a series of carriages to convey them all to his Plymouth Church for Sam's lecture. Sam hustled into the depths of the church to get ready to speak while the rest of them took their time, mingling with others in the vestibule. To Emma's delight, she spotted Nina Larrowe and her husband alighting from a carriage. Emma walked over, but before she could say anything, Nina spotted her.

"Miss Beach! How delightful." she grasped both of Emma's hands in hers.

"I'm so glad you came, Mrs. Larrowe," Emma said. "We'll have to sit together inside."

Nina introduced Marcus, who nodded at Emma but didn't engage in the conversation. "It will be interesting to see what Mr. Clemens has to say," Nina said.

"In person, his sarcastic humor will be easier to discern than in a newspaper article," Emma said, patting Nina's hand in reassurance.

They walked inside the massive church, able to hold two thousand congregants in several levels of pews. Nina looked up to the gas chandelier and said, "It's more beautiful than some of the theaters in Manhattan!"

The Larrowes and Beaches walked up to the front of the church, where Moses Beach greeted several other *Quaker City* passengers. Nina wanted to sit right in the front row, but Emma demurred. The very first row was a little too obvious, too much in the public eye. She preferred a little circumspection. If it wasn't Sam on the speaker's platform, Emma would have chosen the very last row, hidden under the balconies above. Instead, she drew Nina to the second row. They sat together, with family members alongside them.

Samuel Clemens strode out to the pulpit, and the crowd fell silent. He waited a beat, then began. "I am to speak of the American Vandal this evening."

His voice filled the hall. Emma knew that Reverend Beecher was quite proud of the acoustics in Plymouth Church. Her heart swelled with pride in her church, and admiration for the speaker.

Sam continued, "I wish to say in advance that I do not use this term in derision or apply it as a reproach, but I use it because it is convenient; it best describes the roving, independent, free-and-easy character of that class of traveling Americans who are *not* elaborately educated, cultivated, and refined, and gilded and filigreed with the ineffable graces of the first society. The best class of our countrymen who go abroad keep us well posted about their doings in foreign lands, but their brethren vandals cannot sing their own praises or publish their adventures."

Nina frowned, and Emma squeezed her hand. It was Sam. He cared about them and didn't mean to reproach them. That was the first thing he'd said, after all.

Sam continued, "The American Vandal gallops over England, Scotland, Spain, and Switzerland, and finally brings up in Italy. He thinks it is the proper thing to visit Genoa, the stately old City of Palaces, but he only stays in Genoa long enough to gather fragments of stone from the house Columbus was born in—your genuine Vandal is an intolerable and incorrigible relic gatherer. It is estimated that if all the fragments of stone brought from Columbus's house by Mrs. Fairbanks alone were collected together, they would suffice to build another house."

Emma gasped. He'd mentioned Mrs. Fairbanks by name. She hadn't seen the woman in the audience, and didn't dare look around for her now.

"In fact, the Vandals removed so many artifacts from ancient sites that Mrs. Larrowe threw several vases from antiquity overboard to make room for treasures from the tombs of pharaohs. But I digress. We were in Italy."

Eyes wide, Emma stared at Nina, whose face had gone white as chalk. Emma didn't remember Nina throwing anything into the sea, but the damage was done. She could already hear whispers from the row behind them.

"The Vandal goes to see the ancient and most celebrated painting in the world, *The Last Supper*. It is so damaged now, by the wear and tear of three hundred years, that the figures can hardly be distinguished. A young, impressionable Vandal goes to see this picture—which all the world praises—looks at it with a critical eye, and says it's a perfect old nightmare of a picture and she wouldn't give forty dollars for a million like it (and I endorse her opinion), and then she is done with Milan."

Emma couldn't breathe. Was she the young, impressionable Vandal? She blinked to keep tears from falling, and fastened her eyes on Sam. She refused to look around the church and draw attention to herself. Beside her, Emma's father laughed along with the crowd, unaware of his daughter's connection to Sam's words. She remembered being disappointed by the condition of *The Last Supper,* but she'd never been so crass to make such a comment. Sam had embellished his tale to get a laugh.

Sam continued in a similar vein, "You could find our Vandals breaking specimens from the dilapidated tomb of Romeo and Juliet at Padua—and infesting the picture galleries of Florence—and risking their necks on the Leaning Tower of Pisa—and snuffing sulfur fumes on the summit of Vesuvius—and burrowing among the exhumed wonders of Herculaneum and Pompeii."

He hadn't named names here, but the damage was done. He'd singled out two women by name, and those would be the names the audience would associate with the Vandals. Emma said a prayer of thanks that Sam hadn't mentioned her name. Then guilt flooded her and she glanced at Nina, still white-faced with shock. The rest of Sam's talk passed in a blur.

After detailing the entire trip, Sam said, "In closing these remarks, I will observe that I could have said more about the American Vandal abroad, and less about other things, but I found that he had too many disagreeable points about him, and so I thought I would touch him lightly and let him go." Sam executed a quick bow to acknowledge the applause and left the stage.

Conversations buzzed and skirts rustled as the audience began to leave. Marcus faced Nina and said in a loud voice, "Everyone seemed to enjoy that." He lowered his voice. "I thought I told you to behave on that voyage."

Emma watched Nina's frozen face suffuse with heat. Her eyes flashed, and she pursed her lips. She turned to Emma and said, "It was truly a pleasure seeing you, Miss Beach." She nodded to Emma's parents and brushed past Marcus to access the aisle. As they walked toward the exit, Emma could see Marcus talking fast, punctuating his words with grand gestures.

SAM RETURNED TO WASHINGTON, D.C. after the lecture. Ten days later, Emma's mother brought the mail in from where the butler had placed it on a tray in the entry. "Emma, you have a letter."

Emma reached for the letter her mother held out. Her heart leapt as she recognized the scrawl on the envelope. Her mother frowned.

"This is the second letter you've received from Mr. Clemens. Your father told me how he indulged you on the voyage. Please don't go thinking seriously about him. He's much too old for you."

"It's just a letter, Mama," Emma said. She tried to sound nonchalant, but her eagerness to open it ruined the effect.

Her mother stayed in the room as Emma read the letter. Emma tried to show no emotion, but the letter from him began, "Shipmate, Ahoy!" She laughed in delight.

Her mother frowned. "Maybe it would be better for you to consider some sort of pastime. Maybe an embroidery class? A quilting circle?"

"She should keep painting, Mama. She's good at that," said Alice.

Emma smiled and turned her attention back to the letter. After a minute, her mother picked up Violet and left the room. Emma reread the playful, teasing parts of the letter. He wrote, "I did feel so ridiculous in church last Sunday for writing a Valentine to a young lady, sitting right there, who hadn't taken any notice of it! I am very grateful that the humiliation is removed, I do assure you." She giggled and vowed to answer his letters right away from now on. "You do say the *naivest* things that ever anybody said in the world, and hit the hardest possible hits, but I like it. Your reproofs are so honest, and so pleasant, that I really can't help feeling a strong desire to deserve more of them!" He teased her about being naive, and that made her blush. Emma glowed as she daydreamed.

He went on to ask her about some Old Masters paintings they'd seen on the trip. The part she read over and over again said, "I shall come without any invitation. I shall come & stay a month! ... I know I shall be doing wrong—but then I do wrong every day, anyhow." He wanted to visit again, and would do so without an invitation from her parents! Surely that meant he cared for her as more than a friend.

Toward the end of the letter, Sam wrote, "To get the right word in the right place is a rare achievement. To condense the diffused light of a page of thought into the luminous flash of a single sentence, is worthy to rank as a prize composition just by itself. Anybody can have ideas—the difficulty is to express them without squandering a quire of paper on an idea that ought to be reduced to one glittering paragraph." He went on to encourage Emma again to make the most of her own talent for painting.

Emma's father came into the room while she was staring out the window, daydreaming and holding Sam's letter. "Emma? Your mother says you have another letter from Mr. Clemens."

Emma turned to him and tried to look nonchalant. "Yes. He asks for help remembering some details from our excursion. I shall consult my diary and send him an answer."

Papa furrowed his brow. "Should I be reading these letters? Is he appropriate in his language?"

"Papa, Sam is incorrigible, you know that!" Emma's laughter just made her father's frown deeper.

"There's no use falling in love with this man. I'll never allow you to marry a Western roughneck like Sam Clemens, so get that out of your mind right now." He turned and left the room as if in pursuit of something.

Emma just smiled.

.   .   .

BY THE END OF MARCH, however, the smile was gone. Sam had stopped writing to her. She'd answered his last letter and sent one more after that. No response for over a month left her heartsick. She tried to focus on her painting but ended up painting over large sections of what she'd already done.

Her father mentioned at a family supper that Sam had once again visited Manhattan, staying with *Quaker City* friend Charles Langdon. He did not come to Brooklyn. Emma spent her days sitting in the parlor and staring out the window, not even seeing the bustle of Manhattan across the river. Her painting was not going well. She took a deep breath and refused to become more upset. She wrote to Nina instead.

Dear Nina,

Oh, please forgive me for the weeks of silence since I saw you at Sam's lecture. I hope his use of your name hasn't spread to Manhattan. I believe I love him. If you think you're in love with someone and you feel like you're in love with someone, then you obviously are; thinking and feeling is the sum total of what love is. Papa, however, has forbidden me to marry Mr. Clemens (not that he's asked!). That must mean he's not as entertained by Mr. Clemen's article as he appears.

At any rate, I've decided to focus on my painting. I always seem to think of Mr. Clemen's praise of my talent when I'm sitting in front of the canvas. I'm happiest when I can be of assistance from the shadows, where I'm appreciated without being lauded. Please continue writing to me.

Sincerely,
Miss Emma Beach

5

N ina Larrowe
Greenwich Village, February 1868

"It takes your enemy and your friend, working together, to hurt you to the heart; the one to slander you and the other to get the news to you."
- Mark Twain, Following the Equator

Marcus and Nina attended a performance of *A Midsummer Night's Dream* at the Olympic Theater on Broadway a week after Mr. Clemens' lecture in Brooklyn. For a few nights after hearing her name so casually slandered, Nina had stayed home. She didn't want to slink into a corner and confirm Mr. Clemens' false accusations, though, so she ventured out to the usual dinner parties and performances. She'd experienced some long, cold, stares and few snubs, but she refused to be deterred.

Their seats at the Olympic Theater were in the same section where most of her society friends usually sat. Between acts, Nina tried to engage one of them in conversation. "Mrs. Barton, are you enjoying this interpretation of Puck?"

The other woman frowned and slid a glance at her husband, who was focused on the players. "Mrs. Larrowe," she hissed, "word has spread about you travelers and your shenanigans aboard ship."

"Shenanigans?"

"Throwing artifacts into the sea? And I hear Mark Twain ended his talk with hints that more scandal occurred that he didn't want to reveal." Mrs. Barton leaned forward in delicious outrage.

"I'm quite sure that never happened," Nina said, sitting up straight and using her best speaking voice with scathing undertones.

Mrs. Barton turned away and refused to engage in any more conversation.

Marcus must have sensed the woman's frostiness and glared at Nina.

Nina stared at the stage but didn't see any more of the play. The gossip mongers had planted the seed of scandal. It had sprouted and was growing fast. She'd seen this before. Society grabbed hold of one shocking vision and turned it into the scandal of the year. Apparently it wasn't thrilling enough to read that those on the cruise had misrepresented Americans by talking down to foreigners in their own country. With his words, Mr. Clemens had created a picture of American travelers carelessly tossing away the history of the Holy Land. That was an image that would stay in people's minds.

After the show, Marcus and Nina went to Delmonico's for supper. Usually Nina enjoyed dining there, since so few restaurants allowed women. Marcus loved their thick steak, but Nina preferred the chicken croquette.

"Look, there's Mrs. Barton," Nina murmured.

The woman met Nina's eyes, then whispered to the other two couples at her table. They all looked at Nina, looked away, and whispered some more.

"Scandalous rumors spread like fire," Nina said. She pursed her lips and held her head high as they were led to their usual table. Soon enough, the scandal mill would have Nina single-handedly emptying the Holy Land of precious historical items. She seethed with anger at Mr. Clemens. How cavalier to damage reputations with a few sharp words intended to what? Be funny?

"Come on, Nina, smile. People are watching," Marcus said.

She tightened her lips, creating a frown. Marcus scowled. Nina tasted nothing of her dinner.

"Dessert?" Marcus asked as their dinner plates were cleared away.

Nina said, "I'd rather go home now." The temperature of the room had gotten cold enough to freeze ice cream.

Marcus frowned. "You are being too sensitive." Nonetheless, he paid the tab and they left.

TWO WEEKS LATER, Marcus lectured at a small church in Greenwich Village. Nina sat stiffly in the front row, her back straight and her head up, as she listened to the people seated behind her. For the last year, Marcus had been attending lectures and developing a memory system of his own as well as speaking to audiences, demonstrating his prodigious memory and telling attendees how they, too, could learn to remember better. Nina attended every lecture and spoke to audience members, reinforcing Marcus's ideas whether she avidly believed them or not. As a matter of course, she never turned to look at those attending her husband's lectures. She always read the success of the event by Marcus's eyes when he came onstage. Tonight, however, the church was hushed. She could hear men whispering on her left, and a chair being moved on her right. Usually she heard anticipatory chatter. In recent weeks, audience numbers had been steadily declining.

Marcus came out on stage with a forced smile on his face. Nina admired his professionalism as he began to speak.

"It is human nature to forget," Marcus said. "Every day we are bombarded with names and numbers that we simply must remember yet we do not. I assure you that this deficiency has nothing to do with a lack of mental ability, but rather a lack of training. Memory can be improved and strengthened only if you dedicate yourself to true effort."

Nina had praised Marcus's memory from the first time she met him. He was interested in memory and how it worked, but to her knowledge he'd never had any formal training. He made up for that by being a decent speaker. Tonight, however, his delivery was flat and his stage presence nonexistent. Little emotion accompanied his recitation from memory of an article published that morning in the *Sun*. As a result, the audience reaction was lukewarm. She'd have to give him tips about modulating his tone. After all, she'd taken elocution lessons nearly all her life.

When the talk ended in a smattering of polite applause, Nina rose and turned to face the attendees as she usually did. She was shocked by the sparse attendance. Two men, a group of three ladies, and two more couples in a room that could easily hold a hundred. But Marcus had done his job, and now she must do hers. She approached the three ladies.

"Good evening. I am Mrs. Marcus Larrowe. I trust you enjoyed the presentation?" she asked.

The ladies didn't turn to acknowledge Nina. They'd heard her, since their backs stiffened and shoulders were thrown back. Nina heard one say to her companion, "I hear she took liberties with artifacts on that ill-fated cruise. I cannot condone disposing of precious history." The other two murmured assent as they left the room, leaving Nina standing with her mouth open in shock. Mr. Clemens' speech had occurred two months ago. Her name had been mentioned once.

Later, in the carriage on the way home, she broached the subject with Marcus. "I've never been so completely snubbed. Usually audience members are eager to speak with me."

Marcus nodded, his eyes on the scenery.

"Trust New York scandal mongers to take an offhand comment and corrupt it into the scandal of the century!" She bit her lip to prevent any more words from escaping. When he'd been a judge and a senator, Marcus had gotten used to respect. But Marcus said nothing. She couldn't let it go. "Why do you not take my side, Marcus?"

"People are talking, my dear. As long as they are talking about a

Larrowe, I figured the name recognition would increase attendance at my lectures. That seems to have backfired."

"Then why do you persist?" Nina wasn't sure whether she should be upset that his plan wasn't working or just upset that he'd jumped at the opportunity to benefit from her distress. She pursed her lips and stared out the window, forcing herself to quell her budding rage.

FOR MARCUS'S LAST LECTURE IN FEBRUARY, Nina put on a blue gown festooned with bows atop hem ruffles. She believed the bows drew attention away from her waistline, which was always a good thing. She'd bought a new hat at Macy's to match the dress and give her confidence.

Standing by her husband had never seemed like such a trial. She knew about assisting husbands who were lawyers or judges since she'd watched her mother do the job for her father. She'd done the same for Marcus when they were first married, and he was part of the politics in Nevada. It shouldn't be that much harder to do the same for a lecturer. But it wasn't his profession that was the issue. It was his expectation that she continue to support him while he undermined her very standing in the community. Nina was hurt, angry, and confused, but most of all she was proud. She'd do her part as expected, come what may.

Once again, the lecture hall contained too many empty chairs. Marcus hurried through his talk, which lessened its impact. Afterwards, Nina braced herself and forced a smile as she greeted the women who had attended the talk. A few managed a curt smile, but most ignored her.

A couple of women spoke in stage whispers meant to be over-heard, in the way society women did so well. One said, "Do you suppose that is the icy glare she bestowed on the peasants in the Holy Land when she was trying to make them feel small?"

Another said, "How exactly do you crush someone with America's greatness? How pompous."

The first one said, "Imagine going on a cruise without your husband!"

This experience repeated itself three more times in the next few weeks. Sometimes Nina overheard barbed comments, but usually people just turned their back on her. Word had spread, too. Whether she attended charity events, appeared at dinner parties, or walked on the street, it seemed Nina Larrowe was New York's latest pariah. This was confirmed when invitations to events and parties stopped coming. She worried about what this would mean for her husband's career and wrote to her mother for advice.

DEAR MOTHER,

I find myself in a position to wonder if you ever found yourself hindering Papa's career more than helping.

SHE LOOKED ACROSS THE ROOM, thinking. Mother had spent her entire marriage supporting her husband. How had she managed to run the household while Papa was riding a circuit with other lawyers, or leaving her behind on his first trip to California to find gold, yet still be the perfect lawyer's wife when he was home? Nina had been too young to understand the machinations that made her parents' marriage work. Her mother had hosted dinner parties and attended functions with Papa, focusing only on him. Nina racked her brain. Had her mother ever done anything for herself?

FROM YOU I learned how to be the wife of a lawyer working his way up the legal and political ladder. I did well, at first, didn't I?

Marcus has become a lecturer. I struggle to understand exactly what my role is to be. After the cruise, it has become worse. I would never trade the wonderful experiences of that voyage for anything, but I fear Mr. Clemens' words on the experience has damaged my reputation, and I am finding it difficult to shine the light back on Marcus and his memory lectures. I could use the advice of someone who has experienced both a good marriage and a poor marriage. Mama, I need your perspective.

Please don't worry over the status of my marriage. This is merely a bump in the road.

Your daughter,

Nina Churchman Larrowe

NINA CARRIED the unmailed letter with her for several days. It was unlike the cheery missives she usually sent, the ones that extolled the virtues of her marriage and related amusing anecdotes from Marcus's lectures. She had no one else to help her, though, so she finally handed it to the butler and asked him to mail it. Taking a deep breath, she resolved to forget about the letter until such a time as she received a reply.

ON A CHILLY LATE MARCH evening at their home on Bank Street in Greenwich Village, Marcus poured a whiskey for himself and brought Nina a sherry where she sat before the fire. Marcus paced the room, obviously getting ready to tell her something unpleasant. Behind him, she could see the étagère holding souvenirs from her cruise. She refused to put them away even though it seemed everyone in Manhattan had cast her in the role of Destructress of Antiquities.

"I'm having trouble getting bookings," Marcus finally said. "Four cancellations over the next month, too. Even when I do have a lecture, it's not well attended." He paused, then said, "Scandal paints everything near it with a dark brush."

"Oh, don't be ridiculous," Nina said. "This whole thing will pass as soon as something else comes along."

"The pious travelers who went to the Holy Land with Mark Twain gave a poor showing of themselves as Americans. That has tainted us both."

Nina took a deep breath to stave off her anger. "You know how society works, Marcus. At the slightest provocation they drag you, and anyone standing with you, deeper into the mud. It will blow over."

"I blame myself. If I'd been with you on the cruise, I'd be able to deflect gossip like the husbands and fathers of the other women have done. They are all pillars of the community, after all. You have no one to speak for you."

Nina pressed her lips tightly together. On the cruise, they'd been a company of travelers. She hadn't felt unprotected. Even though Marcus hadn't been on the cruise, he could publicly stand by her now if he chose. New York society could be more vicious than any brigand in the places they'd visited.

Marcus stopped pacing and faced her. "Your presence at my lectures is driving people away. I cannot have you affecting my career. You'll have to stop attending."

Outraged comprehension flashed through Nina. "It's not my presence that continues to drive people away. It's your poor speaking ability! Instead of taking advantage of my skills and learning, you've chosen to use Mr. Clemens' words to stop me from attending your lectures. You could have just asked me." She believed it was her role as his wife to give him her support, but she would not fight for her right to attend this man's lectures.

"It won't be easy, but I must work to rebuild my career alone."

At least he didn't sigh and hold a hand to his forehead like some innocent damsel in a play.

Nina stood up, took a deep breath, and stalked out of the room without giving him a glance. It would do no good to scream at him. He existed in his own world where a wife who was no longer necessary could be shredded in public and tossed away. She went upstairs to her room and ate the entire bowl of chocolate caramels left by her bedside.

FOR THE NEXT FEW MONTHS, Marcus refined his memory techniques, presenting mnemonics as the Ancient Art of Memory. The newspapers painted him as a victim of his wife's mistakes, which caused Nina to toss more than one copy of the *Herald* into the fire. Marcus often went out after his presentation with colleagues or audience members and didn't arrive home until late. Sometimes he had supper with business partners before a lecture. It wasn't long before he stopped sharing any aspect of his work with Nina. Her days emptied until she was left with nothing to do but read. She loved reading, but it was a lonely way to occupy oneself. She couldn't comprehend Emma Beach's desire to be alone in the shadows.

Nina wondered why audiences didn't realize that people had practiced the Ancient Art of Memory before Jesus Christ was born. Marcus wasn't telling them anything new. Attendance at his lectures had dropped off because Marcus was a terrible speaker. Without her advice, based on a lifetime of elocution lessons, he would fail.

THE REPLY FROM NINA'S MOTHER was not what Nina expected. The butler announced a visitor on a warm summer afternoon and showed Mrs. Samantha Churchman into the parlor.

"Mother!" Nina cried. She rose from her chair, still her favorite even when the fireplace was cold. "What brings you to New York?" She waved to the butler to bring a tea tray even as she crossed the room to enfold her mother in a warm embrace.

"I thought I'd surprise you," her mother said. "The lawyers required my presence in New York to settle some drama over my brother Ezekial's estate." She raised her eyebrows. "Do you remember your uncle Ezekial?"

Nina nodded. "He was a doctor. Auntie passed a few years ago." She wrinkled her nose. "A cousin? Julian?"

Her mother nodded. "Yes, Julian. He's supposed to inherit his father's farm, but other cousins are trying to take it since Julian has lost touch."

Nina nodded. Her cousin wasn't the only Lockwood black sheep, but his inheritance of a good-sized New York farm made him important.

The butler brought a tray of tea and biscuits. Nina poured as her mother settled herself in Marcus's chair. As she sipped her tea, Nina examined her mother.

At sixty-two, her hair showed a hint of gray in the brown waves gathered atop her head. Her body had always been thick like Nina's, but now it tended toward stout. Nina felt she was looking at a future version of herself.

"Tell me about your trip," Mama said. She set her teacup in its saucer. "And don't bother with the foolishness Mr. Clemens has spouted."

"You already heard?" Nina shook her head. She shared anecdotes from the trip and soon had her mother laughing over tales of streets in Genoa so narrow that three men couldn't walk abreast, and sighing over palaces of rose-covered marble along canals in Venice. When she told the story of Mr. Clemens and his friends, after the ship was quarantined at Athens, sneaking off the ship one night to bribe their way to the Acropolis, her mother pursed her lips.

"I'm disappointed in that man. He should know the power of words to harm others. I won't speak of him," she said.

"Then tell me about Papa," Nina urged.

"His law career is going well," Mother said. After a few minutes of nibbling on a biscuit, her mother said, "Emily's twins are growing fast."

Emily, Nina's older half-sister, had never known her father. Mother's first marriage had been a mistake. That's all she'd ever said about it. Emily's twins had been born while Nina was on the cruise the year before, so she had not yet met them. She was happy for her half-sister's family, and maybe a little jealous. "Yes, named Ed and Emily for their parents. I do wish to meet them someday."

"You will," Mother said. She took her teacup into her hand, sipped, and held it for a moment before putting it back in the saucer. "Did I ever tell you that my father wanted me to marry James Churchman in New York? Before I ever went west?"

Nina raised her eyebrows. Mother had never said anything about life before marrying Nina's father. "No, you haven't." She kept her tone even, hoping to encourage her mother to keep talking.

After a moment of gathering her thoughts, Mother said, "I was young. I knew what I wanted, and that it wasn't what my father wanted for me. He sent me to my brother in Prairie du Chien, but he was no better than my father. Determined to make my own choice, I chose badly." She stopped, and Nina held her breath. "The details don't matter. I was left with your sister, just an infant. I learned that it is possible to have a heart that is broken but still full of anger."

Nina nodded.

Mother said, "And how is Marcus?"

Of course she'd noticed his absence and needed to comment. It had been easier to write about her situation than to talk about it. Nina felt tears welling and blinked them away. She would *not* cry. "His lectures seem to be going well."

"You really love him." Mother's tone rose, as if asking a question.

Nina hesitated. "I did. He's no longer the man I fell in love with, though." She was proud that her voice didn't break. "He's not home very much."

Her mother reached for Nina's hand. "A strong marriage requires two participants. You can't keep it together by yourself."

Nina reeled. What was her mother suggesting? Nina wasn't ready to slam the door on her marriage yet. "Mother?" Her voice sounded weak. She didn't know what to say.

"It's all right," Mother said. "You don't have to make any decisions or promises right now. Just consider crafting something for yourself if you plan to maintain the marriage."

"I'll be fine." Nina lifted her chin. It was true. She was strong. She could be independent. It had to be better than constantly worrying about her husband and wondering if he would be home for dinner.

"I've been happy building a life supporting your father, but I also know such a life is not for everyone," Mother said.

An awkward silence settled between them.

After a few moments, Mother said, "Have you thought about teaching?"

"Teaching?" Nina stared at her mother, mouth open in a very unladylike way.

"I'm sure there are actors in New York who could benefit from your elocution training."

Nina nodded, unsure if her mother was advocating divorce or just living parallel lives within the marriage. She'd seen other women with that sort of arrangement, but it felt limiting to Nina. She changed the subject. "Do you want to see a play while you're in New York?"

Her mother's eyes narrowed at the change of subject, but she couldn't help her smile. "Of course!"

"We can see Edwin Forrest in *Othello*." Nina knew her mother loved Shakespeare.

"That sounds perfect." Mother smiled.

For the first time in months, Nina looked forward to something.

The rest of her mother's visit was spent in a whirlwind of theater. They attended society dramas, which were a new development, and Shakespearean comedies, which were an old favorite.

"Oh, I wish I could see Fanny Kemble once more," Mother said one evening as they made their way home after a show. "She has twenty-five of the Bard's plays in her solo performance repertoire. New York has been good to her, but she chose to end her career in Philadelphia."

"I saw her once," Nina said. "She was quite rotund at the time and sat at a table with a book in front of her, reading the play with a distinct voice for each character. She had a wonderful stage presence." Unlike Marcus, she added to herself.

Her mother sat next to her in the carriage. From the side of her eye, Nina could see Mother looking at her.

"Miss Kemble was in a difficult marriage, you know," Mother said. "She left her husband even though it meant leaving her daughters behind." Mother's tone was neutral. "I never understood why she couldn't just craft a life for herself separate from her husband. Was it really worth the scandal of divorce?"

"Hadn't she already been scandalized by being on the stage?" Nina asked.

"Oh yes, but she was of a social class where performing was at least common if not completely accepted."

Nina murmured something that sounded like a noncommittal agreement, and it seemed to satisfy her mother. The carriage pulled up to the house on Bank Street, and conversation stalled.

As they entered the house, Marcus's clocks chimed in their night-time cacophony. Mother said, "I need to make sure I'm rested for the start of my journey tomorrow. Good night."

The rustling of her skirt and the crackling of the fire filled the silence when the clocks finished announcing the hour. Nina knew how hard it was for her mother to discuss real issues, and her head reeled from Mother's candid words. Nina wondered if she would have the courage to teach gymnastics or elocution.

THE NEXT MORNING was full of the bustle of departure, with no time for private conversation. Marcus had returned home late and slept in his study, but he rose to join Nina in seeing her mother off. He stood on the porch step and waved as Nina embraced her mother and helped her into the hired coach that would take her to the harbor to meet a ship headed to California. When she was gone, Marcus mumbled something about having work to do and closeted himself in his study. Nina remained plagued by indecision.

Dear Miss Beach,

My mother's visit was a mixed delight. I remember during the Civil War when Mother, a friend of Confederate president Mr. Jefferson Davis, and Father, a friend of President Abraham Lincoln, sometimes let those personal feelings leak into political disagreements. Maybe her message was to support your husband as long as it doesn't infringe on your personal strengths.

So after months of trying to rise above perceived indiscretions, I've decided to live my own life. That doesn't mean I plan to slip quietly away, though. Mother encourages me to teach the elocution I've been trained for my entire life. I am a little nervous that I lack the knowledge of how to teach what I know, though.

I think you should apply for a place at a painting school. I've found that if I want to do something, that it helps to have the structure of lessons and requirements to keep me focused.

Sincerely,

Mrs. Nina Larrowe

6

mma Beach
Brooklyn, New York, October 1868

*"I don't know anything that mars good literature
so completely as too much truth."*
- Mark Twain, Speech to the Savage Club, London

Dear Nina,

*It's been almost a year since we returned from our cruise so surely we
are on a first-name basis? I insist you address all future letters to Emma
instead of Miss Beach!*

*I'm sorry about the gossip that still swirls about you. I know about that,
even if I've not been the target of such. People seem to prefer lies spread via
their neighbors to the truth told by friends. Violet is over a year old now. I
hope the gossip surrounding her parentage fades away before she is old
enough to be hurt by it. Alice seems unaffected by it all even though she
follows Mama everywhere like a little shadow.*

*My father, too, is the subject of talk. People think he stole the patents he
acquired for the printing press. He barrels through life pretending it doesn't*

bother him, but he's sold the Sun. *When next you read that paper, my father's name will no longer be on the masthead.*

I hate that everywhere we go, people look at us and whisper behind their hands. How do you manage it yourself? Even when I'm not with my parents, people rush up to me, eager to catch up, they say. All they want is a bit of fuel for the fire that swirls around my parents. I don't want that for my life. I long to be useful. I remember on the cruise how you talked about helping your husband with his career. (I'm sorry to remind you of something that might be painful) I could never be as onstage and present as you were, but I would like to be needed like that. So far, the only one who truly needs me is Violet.

The mailman seems to have forgotten where I live. Either that or Sam has. I've received no letters from him and feel rather low. Papa says that our fellow Quaker City *passenger Charles Langdon has announced to the world that his sister, Olivia, has fallen in love with Sam Clemens, and that Sam loves her, too. Mama says Olivia is close in age to Sam and therefore a good match. She glared at me as she said it, so I know she meant a better match than I'd be. Am I foolish for wishing he would write me a letter to tell me about Olivia himself?*

Sam always said I had artistic talent, though, so I went ahead and enrolled at Cooper Union as you suggested. The school is quite intimidating! I never dreamed I'd be a student there. I'm enjoying focusing on my art, though. It keeps me out of the public eye and out of the gossips' mouths.

Sincerely,
Emma Beach

COOPER UNION HAD BEEN FOUNDED with the express purpose of providing a world-class education in art, architecture, and engineering to everyone, including women. Classes were free, and the school had no color barrier like others in the city. Emma knew she would thrive there.

Emma's first art class of the day was a basic design class, chosen because it was surely something she either already knew or could pick up quickly. On her first day, she'd entered a classroom that was bathed in light from the tall arched windows. Butterflies fluttered in her stomach even though she told herself she was there to learn. No one would expect her to already be proficient, but it seemed everyone knew where they belonged except Emma.

She'd found a place near a young woman as slightly built as Emma herself, but with dark hair to Emma's red. The woman's large brown eyes seemed too big for her face, but she smiled, so Emma sat down. The woman had introduced herself as Kate Bloede. Emma smiled back and told Kate her name.

"Are you new to the school?" Kate asked.

Emma nodded. "My parents encouraged me to come." Oh no, why had she said that? It made her sound like a child. And it was Nina's encouragement she'd taken, not her parents'.

"Oh, are they creative? My mother is a poet," Kate said. "My father is a writer. He's the editor of the *New York Demokrat.*" At Emma's blank look, Kate added, "It's a daily paper for German-Americans, especially political refugees like my parents. Politics bores me, though. I'd rather paint." She laughed.

"My father owned the *Sun* until recently," Emma said. "Maybe great painters come from writers?" She smiled at Kate, who smiled back. It was the seed of what promised to be a close friendship.

It didn't take long for her to meet other artists. Maria Oakey painted in rich, glowing color, her brush strokes confident and strong. Helena deKay and Mary Hallock spent most of their time close together, but gathered in a group with Emma, Kate, and Maria. It was a prolific, professional group. Emma was thrilled to be a part of it, inspired to paint her best and continue to improve.

ONE MORNING IN NOVEMBER, Emma's parents sat at the table in the parlor having a breakfast of tea and toast. Emma came downstairs, prepared to leave for her classes. Her father, however, stopped her.

"Emma, last night at dinner I heard that Sam Clemens has

proposed to Olivia Langdon. She's not accepted yet, but I'm given to understand it's only a matter of time."

Emma felt the blood rush out of her face, to be replaced by dizziness. She grabbed the back of an empty chair to steady herself.

"Moses," her mother chided, "that was hardly the best way to tell her."

Her father peered at Emma. "Does she still fancy herself in love with him? This engagement is just as well, then." He picked up a piece of toast and spread it with apple butter.

Emma couldn't form coherent words. She rushed out the door and into the waiting carriage. Sam must know by now how much she loved him. It was a year since they had returned from the Holy Land, and it was true that he no longer wrote to her, but Sam and her father were friends. Sam came to Brooklyn to see him, and to see Reverend Beecher as well. On almost every visit, Emma spent at least a few minutes with him. But now he would marry another woman. Every spare thought over the last year had been focused on dreams of Sam, of a future with him, even of marriage and children when she dared. Now it seemed her entire chest had been crushed, leaving her unable to breathe and her heart unable to beat.

That day in class, she chose to paint in tones of blue. Cobalt, periwinkle, midnight, navy, cerulean, indigo—the color illustrated her mood.

Kate said, "Tell me what's bothering you."

Emma put down her brush and turned to her friend, who sat there smiling as if the world was beautiful. "I just found out someone is engaged."

"Someone?" Kate peered at her. "I take it this someone is a man you care for?"

"I was in love with him all winter. It was really more of a crush." Emma's heart denied the truth of her words. When Kate waited for more, Emma said, "It's Sam Clemens. I met him on the cruise last year. I was terribly fond of him, much to my father's displeasure."

Kate nodded. Emma had told her about the cruise. "He didn't feel like you did?"

"Apparently not. He's older, though. More experienced. He said I had artistic talent."

Kate nodded. "Sounds like infatuation, but even so it can hurt. Great painters can find a way to channel their heartbreak into their work."

"I'll give it a try." Emma smiled at Kate's efforts to cheer her. She picked up her brush, but somewhere deep inside a tiny hope insisted that Olivia Langdon would turn him down and Sam would discover that Emma was, indeed, his true love.

"There's an exhibition this Saturday of student work at the Academy of Design. Do you want to go with me?" Kate asked. "It will distract you from this bounder who broke your heart." She smiled.

Emma nodded. "I'd like that."

THAT SATURDAY, Kate and Emma arrived together at the exhibition and entered the gallery arm in arm. They were impressed by the carefully placed gaslights that enhanced the colors and dramatic composition of the paintings.

"Oh, someday we'll have our work hung like this," Kate said as she perused the work of thirty students.

Awed by the magnificence of these student paintings, Emma could only nod. She walked over to a landscape that caught her eye. "It's wonderful, Kate. Look at the use of light, and the blending of colors. It's gorgeous."

"He sure is," Kate said.

"He?" Emma turned to look at her in confusion.

Kate's eyes weren't on the painting. She looked past the artwork to the reception area where light refreshments were being served. A lean man, taller than either Emma or Kate, stood with Mr. Lemuel Wilmarth, one of the instructors who'd spoken to open the exhibition.

"I'm sure you don't mean Mr. Wilmarth," Emma teased.

Kate walked over to the two men, but Emma watched from where she was. She heard Mr. Wilmarth introduce the man as Abbottt

Thayer, and she watched as Kate nearly swooned. Emma couldn't see why. Mr. Thayer had a bony face and broad furrowed forehead. But then he smiled, and the animation transformed his face, making Emma smile and wish she was brave enough to join Kate.

Kate returned to Emma with two glasses of punch. "He's quite charming," she gushed. "He won a gold medal for one of his pieces! I gather he's a favorite of both Mr. Wilmarth and Mr. Whittaker. Mr. Thayer has secured a place at the National Academy of Design for next year's term." Stars shone in her eyes.

"You learned a lot in just a minute or two," Emma said, wondering if she'd looked so starstruck talking about Sam.

The following day, the art class met at a gallery for a session of copying. Kate and Emma chose the same painting to copy so they could sit together. Helena and Mary painted nearby, as did Maria.

"How was the exhibition?" Maria asked.

"Oh, be prepared to hear very specifically about one of the artists," Emma warned.

Kate told the others all about Abbott Thayer. "The National Academy of Design is New York's best art school," Kate said. "It's hard to get in, and hard to make your place there."

"I'm happy at Cooper Union," Emma said.

"I've applied for a place at the National Academy myself," Maria said. "I'll keep an eye out for Mr. Thayer for you." She laughed.

Kate wrinkled her nose at her friend. "Did you know Mr. Thayer does animal portraits as well as landscapes?"

"I've never spoken to the man," Emma said.

"I've never even heard of him," Helena said.

Mary said nothing, concentrating on getting the lighting right on the painting she was copying. Helena gave her some advice in a low voice, and Mary nodded.

Kate continued to babble about the artist while Emma marveled at the amount of information her friend had managed to acquire in a short conversation.

. . .

LATE IN JULY OF 1869, Kate arrived at school and pulled a book out
of her bag. "Emma, it's here!" She handed a copy of *Innocents Abroad*
to her friend.

"Oh, he did it!" Emma picked up the book as if it were precious
and beamed at her friend. She saw the author's name emblazoned on
the cover—Mark Twain—and traced the letters with her thumb.
She'd known he was working on the book, but didn't know he'd
finished it. Olivia had accepted Sam's marriage proposal in February
after keeping him hanging all through the holidays. Since then, none
of the Beach family had seen him.

"He's the one who encouraged my painting," Emma said.

"Yes, I know," Kate said with an exaggerated roll of her eyes. Both
girls laughed.

Class began, and the book was put aside and forgotten amidst
chatter of painting techniques and styles.

That evening, Emma pulled Sam's novel out of her school bag.
What an accomplishment to have a published work! He must be very
proud. She wanted to read it. No, she had to read it right away so she
would be prepared for any new revelations about the cruise. She
settled into her chair and opened the cover.

She read it whenever she could over the next few days. When she
shut the book on the last page, Emma felt a strange mixture of elation
and dread. The book was very good, actually, full of the sarcasm and
wit she'd enjoyed from him on the cruise. He'd produced something
that has never been done before, a travel guide disguised as a novel. It
reminded her of the cruise, which was the most fantastic thing she'd
ever done, but it also expanded on Sam's caustic comments about the
passengers. He seemed disgruntled that prayer meetings occurred
more often than dance parties. It was a trip to the Holy Land! How
could he complain about the piety of his fellow passengers? At least
he mentioned only his buddies by name, men so scandalous that
tales of their escapades in the Holy Land were not new.

7

Nina Larrowe
Greenwich Village, January 1870

"If husbands could realize what large returns of profit may be gotten out of a wife by a small word of praise...they would bring matters around the way they wish them much oftener than they usually do."
- Mark Twain's Autobiography

"London is where all the new science is happening in the field of memory," Marcus said. He picked up a buttered English muffin and took a bite.

Nina sat across the table from him, silently eating her poached eggs with asparagus tips. Before the cruise, breakfast together had been a delightful way to begin the day. In the ensuing two years, the meal had become cold and silent.

Marcus finished his English muffin and sipped at his cup of coffee. He covered a cracker with brie and took a bite.

Nina felt the air grow thick, pressing around her, forcing her to speak, to think of something to say.

He finished several crackers before continuing. "You've become quite morose since your father's death. What's it been? A year?"

She bristled at his heartlessness. Her father had passed away from spotted fever last August, six months ago. She'd grieved, but if the truth were known his absence didn't affect her daily life. Her father hadn't been a part of her life since her marriage, not because he didn't love her but because he was so busy with his career. Besides, how would Marcus know if she was morose? He was hardly ever home and barely spoke when he was. "London, Marcus?"

"There's a scientific community there that supports each other as they learn." He didn't look at her.

She sipped her coffee, wondering how she should answer. Since he had forbidden her from attending his lectures, Marcus had become increasingly distant. She had no idea how his lectures were being received, and he had no idea how completely ostracized she felt. They'd become just two people living in the same house.

"I'm not ready to leave yet. I must continue lecturing until I know they will take me seriously."

Leave? Nina furrowed her brow, not certain what exactly they were talking about. "It sounds perfect for you."

They ate in silence for another minute. Nina took a breath several times, wanting to ask more about this trip. Every time, she stopped short of speaking. In their entire marriage, short though it may be, she'd never been at such a loss for words. She clasped her fingers around the napkin in her lap and said, "A trip to London might be what we need, a perfect way to save our marriage. Maybe we could even have a child." She shook her head, having a hard time imagining herself as a mother. "How long would we be gone, Marcus?"

His head whipped up to face her for the first time, his eyes wide. "We?"

For three years she'd been the wife of a politician, then three more years as the wife of a lecturer. She'd adapted to follow his career. Now after a scant six years, Marcus was questioning the notion of "we." She'd done everything he'd asked of her, even stepping back when he felt she was damaging his career. She'd waited at home while her social circle pushed her out and carried on without her. Nina met his gaze and didn't respond.

He dropped his eyes to his empty plate. Behind him, the butler moved to refill Marcus's coffee cup in the smooth, invisible way of butlers. The steam curled up from the cup between them. "Oh. I don't know if you would enjoy it. Very academic, a sort of boys' club if you will. I'm sure you would be bored with nothing to do." He didn't look at her.

Bored? The plays in the West End promised hours of distraction. Life in London couldn't be any emptier than her current life in Greenwich Village. She said, "I'm sure I could amuse myself if I believed it would save my marriage."

"You see, Nina, the thing is, it's rather a man's trip. I would be traveling and studying in the company of scientists. You would not be interested in their conversation."

She fumbled for something to say to her husband, something that would support exploration of his field with a solo trip to London, a trip that sounded suspiciously like it might be an extended stay.

"It won't happen for a while yet anyway." Marcus stood up in such a hurry, he had to toss the words over his shoulder as he left the room.

Nina stared at her husband's cup of coffee until all trace of heat had dissipated. The cruise had seemed such an adventure, one that none of her friends would have. Afterwards, however, it had become a problem because no one understood the reality of the trip, only Mr. Clemens' embellishments. Nina had given up trying to rewrite his fiction or to reverse her fall from favor.

In the meantime, Marcus had hitched his wagon to a couple of renowned scientists in memory research. These men had consumed her husband's time and energy. Now she and Marcus existed in parallel worlds that only intersected over an occasional meal. It left her more alone than lonely, and she found herself thinking more about her mother's suggestion to find something for herself.

That evening, Nina sat alone at the table, a supper of roast chicken and bacon potato dumplings laid out before her. As usual, Marcus's plate was put out but not used. She nibbled at the dumplings and thought about her declaration to Marcus that she could amuse herself. The idea of teaching had grown more attractive since her mother had suggested it, and the theater might be a good place to offer her skills in elocution. She'd seen many actors onstage who could improve delivery of their lines. Lost in thoughts about what such a role would look like, she startled when she heard thumping noises on the stoop.

The front door opened and Marcus came in, flustered and rumpled. The butler hurried to take his coat. Nina cut a piece of chicken and put it in her mouth. Marcus went upstairs without saying anything to her, but returned in a short amount of time with his hair damp from trying to comb it into place. His shirt and pants had been brushed in an effort to make them look better. He took his seat at the table and put a napkin in his lap. Only then did he look at Nina.

"Enjoy this meal." His hands indicated the chicken and dumplings as well as three dishes the maid had just brought. "We won't be able to afford such largesse for much longer."

Nina raised an eyebrow.

Marcus ran a hand through his hair. "My lectures are poorly attended. I invested in the stock market to raise capital for advertising. I'm afraid I'm worse off now than before."

Nina laid her fork on her plate. "What does that mean, Marcus?"

"I can no longer keep up with the household expenses and still plan a London trip."

"Surely maintaining the household is more important than a dream?" Nina felt he was being dramatic. Their landlord was a relative of hers, albeit a distant one, and they paid no rent.

He set his lips. "I have a place to live. There's an inexpensive boarding house near the hall where I usually lecture."

He had a place to live that wasn't on Bank Street? Nina composed her face so it wouldn't show shock or dismay. "And what of me?"

Marcus waved his hand in dismissal. "I've already reduced the staff here to save money. I suppose you'll have to go home to California." He'd said what he needed to say. Now he tucked into his supper as if it was, indeed, his last meal.

Nina was no longer hungry. She set her napkin on the table and stared at him. He kept his eyes on his plate. She tried for the cold, calm tone a leading lady might use. "When you married me, you acquired someone who would be loyal to you and support you through whatever career you chose. I've done my part. You blew up our arrangement, and now you don't know what to do with me so you're sending me home." She leaned toward him and stabbed a finger on the table near his plate. "I have news for you. I am not a child you can send home to Mother, and I'm not one to slink home in disgrace from a marriage I didn't break. I deserve to make a life in New York just as much as you do."

She rose with a swish of skirts and stormed upstairs without looking back at Marcus. It was a relief to have spoken to him about their relationship, even if it meant she'd failed. She felt despair welling up, threatening to overwhelm her, but she fought it back. It was true that all her relatives were in California, but she shuddered to imagine herself dependent on their sympathy, enduring their pity. Nina's life had always been one of ease, with no financial instability at all. Prosperity had been hers, but now she had fallen below the bottom rung of the ladder of success and must provide for herself. She vowed to learn self-reliance and say nothing of her situation to her family until she was successful on her own terms.

MARCUS LEFT THE NEXT DAY, taking only his clothing and personal items. Nina heard him coming downstairs and sat in the parlor chair, arranging herself like royalty, with a teacup nearby and a book she'd been reading. She was in control. Or at least she'd appear to be. She picked up the book.

Marcus stood for a moment in the doorway to the parlor.

She looked up, affecting confusion. "Oh, are you leaving?"

He stood looking at her for a moment without saying anything. She met his gaze.

"I won't have time to check in on you," he said.

Emotional control failed as rage boiled in Nina. It turned her stomach and tightened her chest, increasing her breaths until she was snorting like an angry bull. Hoping that fire leapt from her eyes, she said, "Hell and blazes! Is there no end to your audacity?"

His face paled as Nina picked up her teacup and hurled it at him. The heavy front door slammed closed behind him, and the teacup shattered at where his head had just been. Suddenly the house felt empty. Ridiculous, she told herself. She could fill her life without Marcus. It would be a pleasure. She looked down at her book and realized she'd been holding it upside down.

The reduced staff consisted of a maid, a butler, and the cook. At least the house belonged to her family, however distant that relative might be. The Lockwoods were spread all over New York state. Some, including the aunt and uncle she'd accompanied on the cruise, were quite prominent. None of them had kept in touch, though, and Nina wasn't sure any of them even knew she still lived in New York. She refused to contact them anyway because she wasn't ready to let her mother know about her failure as a wife.

Nina told herself she was made of strong pioneer stock. She muttered, "Lockwoods have always pulled themselves up by their bootstraps and gotten ahead with ingenuity and perseverance."

As if in response, the parlor erupted into noise as Marcus's clocks began to strike the hour. The cuckoo clock next to the piano, the grandfather clock in the entry, the mantle clock, even a clock on the table chimed and chirped in turn. They were Marcus's pride and joy. Nina went from clock to clock, setting them all to the same time. They would all chime at once now. Marcus hated that. It was a tiny attempt to take control of her own life.

Nina no longer had the freedom to dabble in the possibility of teaching elocution. Now it must become reality. With her knowledge of speaking techniques, she could rehearse lines with actors. In the silence of her house, it seemed a great idea. She would place an advertisement in the paper.

The next day, as she walked up to the door of the New York *Sun*, two well-dressed men barreled out the door and almost ran over her. She retreated to safety. What made her think she could do this? She took a deep breath and tried again. As she reached for the door handle, however, she panicked. Cold chills ran down her back, though, as she pictured the alternative—living off her parents' wealth. That was not a viable alternative. She forced a smile onto her face and clenched her hands together to steady her nerves. Taking a deep breath, she entered the newspaper office and placed her advertisement.

A COUPLE OF DAYS LATER, a man and a woman called on Nina at her home on Bank Street. Mr. and Mrs. Warren proved to be sensible people, very personable. They were wealthy enough to be above the vagaries of society, to do whatever they wanted to without reprisal. Apparently they now wanted to act, and be instructed in speaking by a social pariah.

Mrs. Warren said, "You are familiar with the theater? We really know nothing of stage work." She gave a small laugh that Nina interpreted as embarrassed. "I've always been drawn to the theater, maybe because it was someplace to visit while never consorting with the players. I'm interested in players, though, and now it's becoming more acceptable to dabble in acting. Of course, I have no experience."

"I have several different types of experience," Nina said.

Further conversation revealed that the Warrens belonged to the best amateur acting club in New York. That took Nina's breath away and made her nervous about taking the job she needed so badly.

"We plan to present *Honeymoon* at a neighborhood theater," Mr. Warren said. "It sounds like you would be a valuable asset to that endeavor. Would you agree to read lines with our actors? Advise them on interpretation of the roles?"

Relief melted all of Nina's trepidation. This was a play she knew. "Yes, I can help you there," Nina said. "I studied the part of Juliana with Fanny Morant, of Daly's Theater, some time ago in just such a way."

Delighted, they hired her on the spot. After they left, doubts assailed Nina once more. The actors were amateurs, it was true, but she'd never been onstage at all.

On the evening of the first rehearsal, Nina stepped into a Fifth Avenue carriage with butterflies fluttering in her stomach. Nerves and excitement had prevented her from eating breakfast. She doubted her ability to truly help these actors, and almost jumped out of the carriage to scurry home when it entered the Murray Hill neighborhood. If the wealthy lived on Fifth Avenue, the fabulously wealthy lived on Murray Hill. The neighborhood had come together years ago to ban construction of livery stables, distilleries, breweries, tanneries, menageries, glue works, foundries, or factories for the manufacture of gunpowder or vitriol. They knew exactly what they didn't want. Arriving at the Warren's grand brownstone mansion, Nina took a deep breath and forced herself to walk confidently to the front door. Luckily her long skirts hid her trembling knees.

It wasn't long into the rehearsal that Nina realized how little the troupe actually knew about the theater. Her confidence grew as she managed the business of staging the play as well as rehearsing lines. By the end of the first evening, Nina had agreed to be the troupe's stage director for the season.

FEBRUARY BROUGHT COOLER WEATHER and a letter from her mother. Mother had stopped using the usual phrases in her letter about supporting Marcus's career and having a baby. She never mentioned Nina's letter or their short conversation, either. Nina slipped a chocolate caramel in her mouth and settled into a chair.

. . .

POOR EMILY HAS PASSED *away from cholera,* the letter said. *Her husband, Ed, is bereft, left on his own with four small children. It breaks my heart to say so, but he will have to marry again, and his prospects in the little mining town of You Bet can't be good.*

MOTHER PRATTLED on about mining towns, marriages, and babies, but grief clenched Nina's heart, and she had to stop reading. Her half-sister had loved her family and didn't deserve to die. Nina couldn't bear to send news on the nebulous state of her own marriage. She folded the letter and put it on the bedside table in her room. Another chocolate caramel made its way into her mouth.

She thought of Emily's husband, Ed Williams, alone with four small children. At least Emily had known the love of a husband and children. That was something Nina would probably never have.

She spotted Emma Beach's latest letter, and she realized she had not written to her friend in a while. She pulled out a piece of stationery and began a letter to the young woman who was her most loyal friend. Putting her situation down in words made it easier to be confident in the path she'd chosen.

DEAR EMMA,

Even though it has now been months since the release of Mr. Clemens' book, I refuse to read it. I knew right away the man was no good. Why, he drank and swore. When he went on to the Quaker City, *he was a nobody and resented that no attention was paid to him. Nobody thought he would ever be anything under the sun. He knew nothing of Eastern society. Blood always tells, as long as it's blue. Enough of him.*

I'm proud of you for enrolling in the art school on my recommendation. Following your heart into a creative endeavor is brave and commendable. In fact, I, too, am moving in that direction. I was engaged as a stage director for an amateur theater company, and we gave a satisfactory performance of our play. Several of the actors engaged me for private lessons in acting and elocution. Unlike most of society, I have long held talented actresses in high esteem. Someday I might even become an actress myself! I shall become that eccentric woman whom everyone knows and admires but no one speaks to.

I hope you are so busy with your painting that your heart remains whole. I mourn the death of my sister and the death of my marriage. May we both heal through creative expression.

Sincerely,
Nina Larrowe

8

E mma Beach
Peekskill, New York, February 1870

"A marriage makes of two fractional lives a whole;
It gives two purposeless lives a work,
And doubles the strength of each to perform it"
- Mark Twain, letter to Livy

On February 2, 1870, Emma found herself at Sam Clemens' wedding. It wasn't what she'd dreamed about, mostly because she wasn't the bride. Her father had received the invitation, though, so they took the train from New York City to Elmira, home of Olivia Langdon, the woman who had usurped Emma's place beside the groom.

The Langdon's house was a large three-story Victorian mansion, quite exceptional for the town. Emma took a seat between her sisters in the elaborate parlor where about a hundred guests had gathered. The cherrywood furniture, with its gilt medallions, had been polished to perfection, no doubt by the Irish maid who had taken care of the Beach family since their arrival the day before. Emma was surprised to see Mrs. Fairbanks there. She'd been upset when Sam used her name in his American Vandal speech, but had clearly forgiven him. Unlike Nina, who hadn't been invited.

"I heard he fell in love with a picture of Olivia on the cruise," Alice whispered to Emma.

Emma nodded. "I remember her brother. Charles was one of Sam's friends on the cruise."

"Mama says she's of a better age for Sam than you are," Alice said. "Is that true?"

"She's only four years older than me," Emma said, "and still ten years younger than he is."

Reverend Thomas Beecher stepped into the room.

"He's our Reverend Beecher's brother," Alice whispered, as if Emma didn't know.

Sam Clemens came to stand next to the reverend. Emma's heart twisted at the happy expression on his face. She still wanted his happiness to be with her.

Olivia Langdon came to the doorway and paused. She was radiant. Her rich white satin dress hung in stiff folds to the floor. Its only embellishment was a scalloped neckline and a bit of lace on the sleeves that matched the long veil.

Alice leaned closer to whisper, "She's so elegant. I heard someone say she's a proper easterner who shouldn't be marrying a rugged man of the West."

"Shh," Emma said. The words Alice had overheard reminded her of what her father had said about Sam. While it was true that Sam knew how to smoke, drink, and swear, he also knew how to behave in proper company.

Sam and Olivia clasped hands, and the reverend began to speak. Emma's eyes fastened on their hands. In art school, she was learning to visualize the way a subject was illuminated in order to paint it properly. Emma tried to visualize a wall around her heart. For a moment, it allowed her to keep a smile on her face and admire the glowing bride. It wasn't long, however, before jealous grief caused tears to well up. She pulled a lace handkerchief out of her reticule and dabbed her eyes.

"I always cry at weddings, too," Alice whispered.

Emma wondered how many weddings her little sister had been to. Thankfully, the ceremony was short. The guests reassembled for a dinner feast, and Emma took her usual place at the edge of the gathering, hoping the chocolate color of her silk gown would help her fade into the walls. She couldn't escape views of the happy couple, though, and her broken heart made crying easier than breathing, even if her mother glared at her. The dinner feast was a time for celebration. While crying during the ceremony was an acceptable showing of emotion, crying during dinner was not. Emma excused herself after the soup was served, and hid in the powder room until she could breathe more easily. By the time she returned, her cold soup was being taken away.

"Are you all right?" Alice asked in a low voice.

Emma nodded. Alice reached for her sister's hand, and held it tightly for a moment under the table. The reassurance allowed Emma to move from anguish to endurance. She kept her eyes on her plate and tried to eat a few bites of every course.

After dinner, the chairs and tables were cleared away and the dancing began. Emma backed into a corner where she could watch and not be expected to socialize. She was contemplating a potted fern beside her when she heard Sam's voice.

"Shipmate! There you are! Are you trying to pirouette with the plant?"

She turned to see Sam's radiant smile. Her heart leapt, and she smiled back. "Congratulations, Sam. Olivia seems lovely."

"Livy is wonderful. I'm so glad you and your family could be here, Emma. I'll stop by later and grab you for a dance." He turned to acknowledge a shout from across the room, and then was drawn away.

Emma's smile faded. Luckily, he forgot to follow through.

. . .

BACK IN CLASS AT COOPER UNION, Emma shared details of the Clemens' wedding with her friends. Maria wanted to hear all about the dress. Helena and Mary begged to know all the details of the decorations, food, and guests. Kate waited until they'd had their fill of questioning Emma. Then she asked, "And how was Sam?"

Emma turned toward her best friend in the world, who was examining her, trying to discover the truth of her feelings. She tried to smile. "He was happy. I was happy for him."

The five girls turned back to their work. Kate snuck glances at Emma for the rest of class, like a good friend should. Emma kept smiling, trying to show Kate her heart was whole, but Kate didn't appear convinced.

"I just can't manage the correct green on these leaves," Emma said to distract her friend. Her painting was a close-up of a tree, and she was struggling with the detail. "Who knew there were so many shades of emerald and olive and forest and shamrock?"

"Anyone have advice for Emma on her green?" Kate said to the group.

"Blend them for a closer match," Helena said.

"That'll give you even more color possibilities," agreed Mary.

Kate laughed and Emma joined her. Laughter was a release of tense emotion. It was better than crying. She laughed at unrequited love and painting struggles, at friendship. Somehow laughter made it easier to experiment with blending greens to paint the perfect tree. It also made the frustration easier when the picture just wouldn't turn out right and her head echoed with Sam's words telling her she had talent. Over the next few days, she mastered the art of feeling her heart pinch but not letting it show on her face.

AS SAM'S WEDDING faded from prominence for everyone but Emma, Abbott Thayer began to appear at art exhibitions around New York. Kate made it her mission to show up wherever he was expected. Emma went with her or met her there, enjoying the displayed paintings almost as much as Kate's fumbling efforts to impress the painter.

Although Kate had introduced Emma to Abbott, Emma had not managed more than a few shy comments to him.

At a gallery opening in March, Emma found herself in Greenwich Village and thought of Nina Larrowe. She wondered how Nina fared, and what it was like living alone. The gallery was part of an increase in creative endeavors gravitating toward Greenwich Village. Emma circled the small space and didn't see Kate. She circled the room again, examining the paintings. Most of them were mediocre. To her surprise, her own paintings were better than half of what was being shown. None of Abbott Thayer's paintings were hung there, but Kate had heard from somewhere that the painter was expected to attend. Emma frowned. It wasn't like Kate to be tardy.

About ten minutes later, the artist himself came through the door. Emma couldn't decide if his charming confidence attracted attention, or if he truly had become well-known. He spotted Emma and approached. "Miss Beach?"

The warmth of his smile made women cross the room to be closer to him. Emma was no exception. She nodded her head slightly. "Hello, Mr. Thayer. Cute little gallery, isn't it?"

Abbott nodded and scanned the gallery. "I don't see your friend?"

"Miss Bloede is supposed to meet me here, but she's late."

"I'll be happy to discuss art with you, then." His smile lit the room, and he focused it on Emma. Her return smile was warm.

Emma's shyness dissipated as they moved from painting to painting. Abbott stared at a piece of art as if internalizing it. Emma learned to wait for his comment before she responded. For the most part, Abbott was aloof and superior. Emma couldn't blame him for that. He was a better painter than anyone here.

In front of one painting, however, Abbott furrowed his brow. His eyes darkened as he frowned. "This work is a travesty of the form," he pronounced.

Emma looked at the landscape before them. It was a mountain, a meadow, and some trees. Not very exciting but surely not a travesty.

Abbott lifted a hand, holding it out toward the painting as he turned away. "I cannot bear to have it in my sight."

"Let's move on to the next one," Emma said. She led him to a different landscape, this one filled with shades of gold that lightened the overall impression. Abbott's expression cleared, and he once again became charming.

"The colors in this one are designed to please, are they not?" he asked.

"They are," Emma agreed. "I like the gold tones."

It didn't take long for Emma and Abbott to explore the gallery. Even though she enjoyed his company, Emma wondered about Kate the entire time. She considered taking a carriage directly to the Bloede residence upon leaving the gallery, but didn't want to be presumptuous. She'd see her friend the next day at school.

But Kate wasn't at Cooper Union the next day. Maria was deeply involved in her work of the moment and shrugged off Kate's absence. Helena and Mary leaned forward to ask Emma about Kate. They seemed ready to hear gossip. When Emma had nothing to say, they lost interest. Emma became more worried as the day went on.

Finally, their instructor mentioned that Kate's mother had died and her father needed Kate at home. She wouldn't be returning to Cooper Union. The school year continued, less lively without Kate. Helena announced she'd finally gotten her place at the National Academy of Design, so she'd be leaving Cooper Union. Mary, always in Helena's shadow, also left the school. Maria's art career had taken off, and she had no time for friends. That left more uninterrupted time to paint, Emma told herself. Still, she missed Kate every day. Letters to her friend just weren't the same.

Emma's life changed even more when her father announced he was bored with retirement. He'd sold the *Sun* and tinkered with patenting inventions dealing with producing newspapers. Now he chafed at the idleness of retirement and purchased a farm in Peekskill, New York, right next door to the farm that belonged to Reverend Beecher. In a humorous double entendre, he named it The Beeches. "The Beaches at The Beeches, next door to the Beechers," he said to anyone pretending ignorance. Mama and Emma just rolled their eyes. Alice and Violet laughed at him. So now he would spend summers pretending to be a farmer, with William, his only son, in his footsteps. Although her father liked to refer to the estate as a farm, in reality the house and grounds were quite impressive. At least it wasn't the rambling jumble of brick that Reverend Beecher's house next door was.

Emma loved the farm's flowers and fields. She admired the range of color in the greens of summer leaves and bright hues of flowers, both wild and planted. The farm was a marvel of Nature and provided many subjects to paint.

Alice ordered books on the plants of the area and pored over them. "Look, Emma!" she said one morning. "I'm sure I've seen these roses somewhere. Want to go look?"

Emma smiled. Tramping the hills with Alice was much better than staring at a blank canvas, pining for Sam and missing Kate. "Of course," she said.

They donned their sturdiest boots and headed off past the tended gardens into the wilder parts of the farm. Emma loved the feel of the sun on her face, and let her bonnet hang down her back.

"Your skin will turn too brown," Alice warned.

Emma thought of Nina's face, tanned but not weathered by her childhood in the western sun. She lifted her face skyward and closed her eyes. "I'll use Mama's lotion later," she told her sister.

They didn't find the rose Alice was looking for, but Alice took bits of half a dozen plants she wanted to identify and examine more closely. She also brought so many flowers to Emma's studio that it soon became strewn with purple geraniums and columbine and asters, all waiting to be painted. Some days Emma couldn't even look at them. Painting reminded her of Sam and art school, two happy periods in her life that were gone. Emma preferred the fresh air and spending time with her sister. She also appreciated a time without pressure to paint or think of Sam or wonder how her art school friends were progressing.

Kate came to visit and brought Emma a beautiful silk scarf covered with a riotous pattern of pink and purple pansies with bright yellow centers. She insisted Emma wear it when she joined Alice and

Emma on a long walk. Emma complied, appreciating the colors of the scarf even though it felt like a beacon, drawing attention to her from as far away as distant stars. Kate smiled when she saw it around Emma's neck and proceeded to speak of nothing more than Abbott Thayer.

"Abbott enjoyed the exhibition where he met you," she told Emma. "He was full of compliments about your taste in paintings."

Emma beamed even as she fidgeted, uncomfortable with hearing how Abbott and Kate had discussed her. "He is quite knowledgeable," she said, and blushed as she thought of Abbott's warm smile.

"And talented. Everyone will have heard his name before long," Kate said. She punctuated her words with waves of her hands and animated facial expressions. "He's so talented, Emma. Wait until you see his work."

"I'll live vicariously through you, Kate," Emma told her. "How about you? Are you painting?"

Kate's hands stilled. "My father needs me," she said in a dull voice. "I don't miss painting, really."

Emma felt the despair emanating from her friend. Kate was never one to moan and wring her hands. She'd always been the one smiling and making others smile. "At least you have Abbott."

Kate's face brightened. "He's amazing, Emma."

Emma thought he must be, if he could inspire such devotion so quickly.

When Kate returned to her father in Brooklyn, Emma picked up a paintbrush and painted some truly awful geraniums. It was a start.

Dear Nina,

I find my greatest solace beneath the apple trees at the farm. I paint, and I write letters to you and Kate. It's a peaceful life. I've tried to interest Alice in painting, but Mama doesn't paint so Alice won't even try. She needs someone else to admire, someone whose very existence assures Alice that she can be her own person. Some days I speculate how lost Alice would be if she ever had to do anything on her own.

You say we should both use our creative expression to heal. That is an excellent idea. Currently I am painting the flowers of the farm. Their beauty soothes my soul even if my pictures of them are not perfect. Please write and tell me all about your acting, and let me know when you are in a play I can attend. I will be there!

Yours truly,

Emma

9

Nina Larrowe
         Greenwich Village, April 1871

"It isn't the sum you get, it's how much you can buy with it...that tells
whether your wages are high in fact or only high in name."
- Mark Twain, A Connecticut Yankee in King Arthur's Court

For a year after *Honeymoon* closed, Nina hovered on the fringes of
the New York theater world, gathering clients from recommendations
by actors she'd worked with on *Honeymoon*. She also attended
lectures and readings, looking for potential clients among the speak-
ers. She saw Christine Nilsson in concert at Steinway Hall and
marveled at her stunning vocal technique. Annie Louise Cary made
her debut performance onstage with Nilsson. Cary's rich, dramatic
contralto promised a wonderful future. Nina couldn't teach Nilsson's
clear voice or Cary's three-octave range, but some of their other techniques would be helpful to her clients. Those clients gave Nina access
to Jane Croly, the founder of Sorosis, a women's club. Nina attended
several of the club's weekly meetings where she met poets Alice and
Phoebe Carey as well as columnist Fanny Fern. Jane's husband was

the managing editor of the *New York World*, and through him Nina met newspapermen Horace Greely and Whitelaw Reid. It was a different social set than the one Nina was used to, different than one that had shoved her out rather forcefully. She felt more comfortable here, though, with creative people who accepted her. As her confidence grew, so did her client list and her connections. For the first time in a long while, Nina was happy. She had no one to share that happiness with except for her maid and her correspondents.

DEAR MOTHER,

I'm busy and happy! I've come to enjoy the quiet of living alone even though I'm not home much. You were right about finding something for myself. Teaching is an excellent way for me to share the skills I learned as a child. Who could imagine there were so many actors that needed instruction in speaking skills? I love the theater as you do, and becoming acquainted with the players has been delightful. I am contributing to the acting profession by motivating actors to hone their skills so that they can inspire others with their performance.

I hear nothing from Marcus. At this point in my life, Marcus may be the perfect husband for me. He is absent, allowing me freedom to pursue my life.

Looking forward to taking you to more plays on your next visit, and introducing you to the theater people with whom I've become acquainted.

Truly,
Nina

One afternoon, Nina sat in her parlor with Mirabel Cronin, a budding actress and client. Nina sipped tea as she listened to Mirabel talk of her future.

"I won't join just any stock company, Mrs. Larrowe," she said, waving her hand in the air for dramatic emphasis. "Too many companies are embracing the new society drama. I will be part of one that does not let the Bard of Avon fall by the wayside, or I will start my own."

"A Shakespearean company, Miss Cronin? Surely there are plenty of well-known troupes you could join. Starting your own seems rather...dramatic." Nina smiled into her teacup, but her humor was lost on the other woman.

"If I can find the right troupe, I might stay with them. I have a role that might be the one. James, an acquaintance of mine, convinced Miss Catherine that with him as Othello and her as Iago they could not fail." She looked at Nina out of lowered eyes. "Many women, you know, have played Iago, including the wonderful Charlotte Cushman."

Nina suspected Miss Catherine must have a fortune that would help at least as much as her talent and good name. "And your role?"

Mirabel blinked demurely, allowing her long eyelashes to brush her cheek. "I have been cast as Desdemona in their production of *Othello*." She nearly toppled her forgotten teacup as she reached for Nina's arm. "Oh, you must come to a rehearsal! I'm sure there are members of the cast who can use your services."

Nina accepted. The promise of adding clients was too good to pass up.

REHEARSALS WERE HELD in the parlor of Miss Catherine's elegant brownstone. Miss Catherine had a homely, masculine face but kind and gentle manners. She welcomed Nina, who took a seat in the back and settled in to watch. It was clear from the beginning that the principals in this troupe were no more professional than those she'd worked with on *Honeymoon*. She let her attention wander, so she was startled when Mirabel's voice rang out.

"What do you *mean* you're leaving?" Mirabel said. She stood stiff with tension, staring at the amateur actress who played Emilia, Iago's wife.

The actress, unknown to Nina, cowered under Mirabel's outrage and dashed out the door.

Mirabel stood erect, every muscle in her body tense, and stared at the door. Conversation swirled with a range of emotions.

"What will we do?" Anguish.

"We cannot go on without an Emilia!" Desperation.

"We are ruined." Fatalism.

"A waste of money!" Fury from Miss Catherine.

Mirabel whirled to face Nina. "You can be our Emilia!"

James regarded Nina thoughtfully. "Do you act?"

"I've never done so," Nina said.

"I know you'll do well," Mirabel said, "because you recite so well."

Nina reflected on how much she loved the theater and how many times she'd thought about becoming an actress. "Acting is entirely different from reciting."

James frowned. "Mrs. Larrowe, is it? Does your husband not approve of the theater?"

Nina hadn't included Marcus in any plans she'd made in well over a year. For James to ask about him now startled her. Clients who came to her parlor for lessons sometimes asked about him, and she brushed off casual inquiries about his whereabouts. Now, though, she was considering stepping into the acting world. This was her opportunity. She didn't want to continually explain where her husband was, though, and she didn't want to miss out on opportunities because he wasn't beside her. There was only one solution.

"My husband is dead." Nina pushed away guilt, sorrow, rage. "I'll take the part of Emilia."

BY THE NEXT REHEARSAL, Nina knew Emilia's part letter perfect. She must have internalized Marcus's memory tactics more than she realized. She approached Miss Catherine's brownstone with trepidation, however, knowing she had much to learn about the stage business. The professionals who had been engaged to fill out the cast shone resplendently against the amateurs. In contrast, both Othello and Iago delivered their lines in a flat monotone.

It seemed fitting that James as Othello and Miss Catherine as Iago chose to be referred to by initials—Mr. J and Miss C. Their acting certainly would never make a name for them, yet they strutted around the parlor as if they were lord and lady of all they surveyed.

James and Miss Catherine had arranged a New England tour that began in Portland, Maine. The company took a steamer from New York Harbor, setting off with a celebratory air. Nina, though, was nervous. She hadn't slept the night before, and hadn't been able to eat anything that morning. She'd focused so hard on learning her role that she hadn't contemplated until now the importance of such a big part. How would she ever get through it? James and Miss Catherine had also never acted before, and Mirabel only a few times. They would play roles that the greatest actors had played, yet the other three were cool and fearless, which made Nina break out in cold perspiration.

Until they arrived in Maine, the company had rehearsed only in Miss Catherine's parlor. They rehearsed in a theater for the first time on the afternoon of the performance. Word came that the mayor of Portland had reserved a box for the evening, and advance ticket sales had gone well.

Stage fright gripped Nina until she was on the verge of collapse. She said to James, "I'm no actress. I can't go on tonight."

"Ah," he said. "Stage fright." He waved to the professional actors, who rallied around all the amateurs and propped up their failing courage with words of praise and reassurance.

The parts of Cassio, Roderigo, and Brabantio were all played by professionals. Mindful of where their salary was coming from, they had refrained from commenting on the rehearsals. Now emboldened by their roles as mentors, they tried to take over the stage rehearsal.

Nina felt relief in following what they said, but James drew himself up as tall as he could, like a male peacock showing dominance over another male.

"You must mind your own business," James said. "Miss Catherine and I are the managers and financiers of this company, and we'll take no direction from anyone."

His statement did nothing to alleviate Nina's stage fright, especially when the professionals frowned and turned away.

That evening, the women donned rich and elegant costumes. Miss Catherine's thin legs were plumped by the addition of padding in Iago's trousers. She was looking at herself in the mirror when James knocked on their door. "How do I look?" he asked. He preened a bit for them.

Miss Catherine said, "You look splendid."

Nina felt sick. Makeup was an art, especially if it was used to turn a white man black. James's makeup had not been well done, turning him into a mottled creature who looked ridiculous.

The company played to a full house that began heckling the minute the leading characters stepped onstage. They were so loud that Othello and Iago's lines could barely be heard, upsetting those who were backstage. Nina tried to take deep breaths to calm down, but fear pressed against her chest. The professional actors took Nina and Mirabel aside.

"Please, you must use Emilia and Desdemona to arouse a proper passion."

Mirabel threw her shoulders back. "We shall do our best."

Nina just nodded, unsure about what exactly that meant.

For the first two acts Emilia silently followed Desdemona, giving Nina an opportunity to relax. Her fear gave way to anger that the audience could be so disruptive. When her lines began, she acquitted herself well, substituting anger for stage technique. The audience gave her round after round of applause as she gave an awkward bow.

The professional actor who played Cassio whispered, "You saved the entire show."

"Oh, I'm sure it was Mirabel's beauty more than my earnestness that won the audience," she said.

The crowd had been so disrespectful to James and Miss Catherine that Nina felt sympathy for the actors. No matter how badly they acted, they didn't deserve to be insulted.

The troupe left the theater in carriages arranged by James and paid for by Miss Catherine. At the hotel, the staff turned up their noses and made it clear they assisted the troupe out of duty, not respect. Religious tracts warning of the dreadful fate of actors were left on their pillows. Nina tried to laugh them off as the others did, but the scorn took her back to her experiences in society after Mr. Clemens' article about the cruise.

In the morning, Nina and the rest of the troupe dressed appropriately and behaved like ladies and gentlemen even though additional copies of the religious pamphlet were laid next to their breakfast plates.

James must have sensed Nina's disquiet. He leaned toward her, tapped a pamphlet, and said, "You might wonder how the authors of these, who think it's a sin to go to the theater, are so familiar with actors, the ways of the theater, and the supposed way we conduct our lives. Don't forget that they, as well as those who laid them out, probably attended the show last night."

His words improved Nina's spirits. The rest of the tour, a barnstorming of manufacturing towns, met a similar reaction. The outcry against acting was so great that the company performed in music halls, where they could be passed off as something other than drama. Despite the public resistance, the performances were well-attended.

In New York, Nina told herself, theaters were well thought of and dramatic performers sought after. As actors began to come from the best families, everything dramatic had risen in esteem. The thespian could hold her head up and walk with painters, sculptors, musicians, and singers. She looked forward to continuing her career.

AFTER THE TOUR, Nina returned home with a sense of accomplishment and a bit of money in her pocket. Her first acting experience had shown her that being a skilled elocutionist was not enough. An elocutionist knew oratory and platform—voice, breathing, articulation—but nothing about stage business, the crossing, grouping, working up to climaxes, knowledge of makeup, or the need for real emotion to prompt the action on stage.

She heard about Steele MacKaye, who had just returned from Paris, where he'd studied an acting system developed by Francois

Delsarte. Both men claimed the system would revolutionize the stage. The idea was to study the muscles of the face and find out which muscle controlled a certain emotion. The actor could then work that muscle. Certain movements of the arms and fingers meant certain things, from placing an arm to raising an eyebrow. Nina thought it seemed an interesting way to add emotion to an actor's repertoire.

Mr. MacKaye found a backer and hired a small theater. He selected amateur actors that he could train in his method and advertised heavily all over New York. The amateur community buzzed with excitement over the notion that years of acting lessons might not be necessary before winning a part onstage.

Nina wanted to believe it, but her limited experience indicated otherwise. Nonetheless, she attended the show. Mr. MacKay flexed this muscle, stood on that toe, elevated one eyebrow, and twisted a finger here and there. His leading lady did the same. As a result, they were so busy pulling the strings of their anatomy that the impression was one of mechanical marionettes. The true emotion had been left out completely.

His performance convinced Nina that the only way to perfect stage work was to begin at the bottom and study long with a professional actor or actress. Gimmicks such as Marcus's memory system or MacKay's acting mannerisms could not possibly replace hard work and experience.

Sitting in her favorite chair beside the fire in her Bank Street home, Nina stared at a handbill she held. It was a notice she'd picked up at the theater for acting classes to be held by Matilda Herron. The actress suffered from ill health that prevented her from taking the stage any more, and she supported herself by teaching acting. Nina believed Matilda Herron to be a genius, one of the best actresses who ever walked the stage.

Taking classes, though, was another step closer to becoming an actress. Her mother had been delighted to hear of her happiness in teaching, but Nina knew how her mother felt about actresses. Mother loved the theater, but had not progressed as far as Mr. and Mrs.

Warren in accepting the people involved in the plays. There was a clear line that a well-bred woman did *not* cross. For Mother, that was the edge of a stage floor. Nina couldn't deny the attraction, though. She'd felt powerful onstage, accomplished in a way that swelled her heart with pride. When she wasn't onstage, Nina longed for the applause of the audience. She knew that acting classes with Matilda Herron would make her a better performer, but performing would infuriate her mother.

Twisting the paper in her hand as she considered options, Nina felt the pull of the stage, here in New York, more strongly than the specter of Mother's disapproval from California. Mother had overcome much in her life, proving her to be resilient. Although Nina didn't want to cause her mother grief, she refused to let Mother's expectations shackle her like Marcus's had. She rose from her chair and went upstairs to write a note to Mrs. Herron. After she'd sent it off with the butler, she wrote to Emma.

Dear Emma,

The Beach farm in Peekskill sounds like a lovely place to paint and spend time with family. I hope your friendship with Kate continues even if she has to travel to the country to visit. I wouldn't worry about your sister's lack of independence. She has many years yet to develop an awareness of herself separate from her mother and from you. Maybe she'll paint, or maybe she'll follow your mother to her various charities. Maybe Alice will discover something completely different that she is passionate about.

My brief stint as an actress has lit a fire within me. I strive to improve my dramatic skills every day. I have begun acting classes with the wonderful Matilda Herron. Her lessons are a delight, her method refreshingly natural. Mother encouraged me to teach, but she is too old-fashioned and strict to allow an actress in the family. Miss Herron has said that personal satisfaction will always triumph over family expectations. I propose that the same is true for you and your sister. You will find your personal satisfaction somewhere, and so will Alice. If such a goal truly triumphs over family expectations, it seems worthwhile to wait for the path to reveal itself.

Yours truly,
Nina

10

E mma Beach
     Peekskill, New York, June 1872

"An occasional compliment is necessary to keep up one's self-respect."
- Mark Twain, Notebook, 1894

Emma sat beneath her favorite gnarled apple tree, tucked away in a quiet corner of the family farm. It all must have been part of a thriving orchard belonging to some long-dead Hudson River Valley settler, overlooked when the orchard had been replanted. Kate had told her it was a Northern Spy tree, saying, "When baking a pie, use a Spy!" Emma smiled at the memory.

From this spot under her tree, Emma couldn't see the river. She loved the farm and the village of Peekskill, but she still wondered what had possessed her father to buy right next door to Reverend Beecher. He could have bought elsewhere in Peekskill, or in any one of the towns along the Hudson River. No doubt Mama had more influence over Papa than Emma could see. She had tried, and failed, to imagine what it would be like to love someone so much that you moved your entire family to live even closer to the person who completely disregarded the sanctity of marriage even as he preached it.

Emma returned to the farmhouse with a few wizened apples from last year's crop that she planned to paint. She heard voices in the parlor as she came in the kitchen door. Her mother hurried in to greet her. "Guess who's here for the weekend? Your old *Quaker City* favorite, Sam Clemens."

Emma winced. Sam had referred to *her* as his favorite, not the other way around. And he was here? Not alone, surely.

Mama let her into the parlor. Sam and her father sat in the large chairs near the fire. Livy Clemens sat on the couch with an arm around their son Langdon, who was a year and a half old. Mama had said the boy was sickly, but Emma thought privately that he was just indulged. In Livy's lap, the infant Suzy napped. Emma did as expected and went to see the baby first.

"Oh, Livy, she's adorable. Looks just like you," Emma said. "How old is she now?"

"She was born in April. She's two months old." Livy beamed with pride.

Emma turned to Langdon. "Hello, Langdon. Do you remember me?"

The boy stared at her with glassy eyes. His breathing sounded odd. Emma frowned. Maybe he really was sick. He burrowed into his mother's skirt.

"It's all right, Langdon," his mother said, "you don't have to speak." She looked at Emma. "He has a very sore throat."

Emma nodded. Her mother began to chat with Livy about motherhood and babies and things Emma had no knowledge of or interest in. She wandered to the window with her favorite view of the orchard. Despite her recent apathy about her painting, Emma found herself visualizing layering colors to create a landscape that would do the view justice.

Sam approached. "Hello, Emma. It's been awhile since I've seen you," he said. "How is your painting going?"

Every time he'd seen her over the last two years, Sam had begun the conversation exactly the same way. She turned to face him with a flash of irritation. "Just fine." She kept inside the words that would snap—there's more to life than painting, is that all you care about, what if someone asked you about your writing every time they saw you? Sometimes she wished she could be Nina, who never kept inside the sharpness of her feelings. Emma always had a humble smile, not a witty comeback.

Sam said, "Glad to hear it. A talent like yours shouldn't be wasted."

His words echoed in Emma's head, layering on top of all the previous times they'd talked. Normally she responded by saying, "Neither should yours," but today she just smiled and tried not to grit her teeth.

"Have you heard my next novel is to be published later this year?" Sam asked. "It's called *Roughing It,* a prequel to the first one about our cruise. It includes my time in Hawaii as well as the time I spent in Nevada."

"That's where you met the Larrowes. Do they feature in your novel?" She hoped he would say no. His words would infuriate Nina if he even hinted at her family.

He laughed and said, "You'll have to read it! I'll send you a copy."

Sam looked no different to Emma's eyes, with his rakish smile, tousled hair, and bushy mustache. To her heart, however, he was a different man. Emma explored this notion. She felt no pang of jealousy when he looked at Livy with love in his eyes. Instead, she compared Abbott Thayer's warm smile to Sam. Both were creative men, charming if not handsome.

"And you must show me what you're working on," Sam said.

"I don't have anything ready to show," Emma said.

Sam said, "I don't want to wait until your masterpiece is completed." He flashed his smile, making Emma wonder if he was teasing or serious.

She was about to demur again when her mother said, "She'd love to show you her latest piece, Mr. Clemens." Mama sent a footman to fetch it.

Emma twisted her hands in her lap as her stomach danced. She told herself Sam was an author. He knew no more about art than she knew about writing. Sam could enjoy her finished work like she enjoyed his. Why was she so nervous about what he'd say?

Mama beamed, the quintessential proud mother. Olivia talked quietly to Langdon, next to her, and glanced up at Sam every now and then. Papa stood at the window, obviously wishing to be somewhere else. They all turned when the footman returned with a painting, holding it facing his body. Emma wasn't sure which one he'd selected, but she was relieved it was a finished piece at least. He propped it on the piano keyboard and stepped back into the anonymity of staff. It was an innocuous picture of her apple tree in spring—not her best work, but satisfactory. Everyone in the room looked at her painting, then at Emma. Emma writhed, wanting to disappear into another room. Being the center of attention, with everyone's eyes on her, made her skin crawl and her voice freeze in her throat.

Sam walked over to the piano. He put his hand up to his chin and tilted his head as he examined Emma's painting. "The most effective encouragement a beginner can have is the encouragement which he gets from noting his own progress with an alert and persistent eye. You must have many versions of this work. Save them and date them; as the years go by, run your eye over them from time to time, and measure your advancing stride. This will thrill you, this will nerve you, this will inspire you as nothing else can."

Emma thanked him automatically. Inside, she fumed. Couldn't he have used a bit of tact and said he liked it? No need to expound as if he was New York's foremost art teacher.

Sam crossed the room to stand before her. His eyes pierced her heart. "I'm pleased to see that you are painting, Emma. You must not long for compliments. I can live on a good compliment for two weeks with nothing else to eat." He paused to allow her father to chuckle. "But compliments make me insolent and overbearing. I never wish to put that on you."

Anger pushed away all of Emma's nervousness and embarrassment. What a twisted way to tell her he liked her work. She'd have to come up with something equally obscure when next she read a book of his. Now she clenched her hands in her lap and arranged a proper society smile on her face. "Why thank you, Mr. Clemens," she said, as if she hadn't a brain to figure out his dissembling.

He looked surprised, but turned away to engage her father in conversation. Emma quietly asked the footman to remove the painting. The whole incident served to remind her how terrible it could be to put yourself at the center of attention. She sat quietly smiling and nodding, fuming on the inside, for the rest of the visit.

On his way out the door, Sam said, "I can be a bit caustic when speaking in generalities." He shrugged. "Some people find it funny. Keep painting, Emma. I keep writing, and not all of it is good. Some of it, though, some of it sings." He tipped his hat and followed his family out the door.

Just for a moment, Emma caught a glimpse of the man she'd idolized on the cruise. A glimpse, though, wasn't enough to pine for him.

Barely two weeks later, Emma's mother looked up from a letter with an ashen face. Looking at Emma and Alice, seated with her in the parlor, Mama announced that young Langdon Clemens had died from diptheria even as *Roughing It* had successfully been placed upon bookstore shelves. Emma gasped. She couldn't imagine Sam and Livy's pain even as she ached for their loss. Understandably, Sam forgot to send a copy of his book to Emma.

Dear Nina,

I find myself exploring the vagaries of love. Have you ever felt the pain of looking into the eyes of someone you love, waiting for them to proclaim their affection, and they turn away? Sam broke my heart, and I was certain it would never heal. Now his heart is broken and I feel only empathy.

Kate's beau, Abbott Thayer, may not be as handsome as one of your leading men, but his smile is one that lingers. I see them falling in love even as my heart beats faster at his smile. Please distract me with tales of the New York theater.

    Yours truly,

    Emma

11

N ina Larrowe
Greenwich Village, December 1872

There is no suffering comparable with that which a private person feels
when he is for the first time pilloried in print.
- Mark Twain, Life on the Mississippi

One day Nina arrived at acting class and found a man standing
with Miss Herron. She recognized John Brougham, a well-known
actor and director she'd run across a couple of times.

Mr. Brougham announced to the class, "I have written a drama
called *Lily of France*. It is based...loosely based...on the life of Joan of
Arc. Booth's theater on Twenty-third Street has an empty week in
December and will book *Lily of France* if I can make it ready. Because
we are short of time, I will be casting this play today. Rehearsals
begin tomorrow!"

He spread his arms wide to include the whole class. "Booth has
booked a society play starring Adelaide Neilson for the week
following us, so we must be top-notch."

Several members of the class laughed at his constantly changing comedic facial expressions. Nina just smiled and let him continue.

"The wonderful Frank Bangs will play the part of Durand, the male lead. I have yet to cast the female lead." Mr. Brougham peered at Nina.

Nina held her head up high and met his eyes. Her inexperience would never show in her face. Mr. Brougham smiled. But would she have the courage to audition for the lead? Frank Bangs was the Mark Antony of actors.

The members of the acting class nodded and chatted softly amongst themselves. Some came forward to inquire about the roles, and some drifted away. Nina remained. She needed the work. "Mr. Brougham?"

He beamed at her. "Yes, Mrs. Larrowe?"

"I'd like to audition for your play." She mentally chastised herself for using such a mousy tone. Lifting her chin, she continued in a stronger voice. "I am an accomplished speaker with onstage experience."

Mr. Brougham looked her up and down for a moment. "That's a fine thing, my dear." He looked at Miss Herron.

"Mrs. Larrowe just completed a New England tour with *Othello* so she has a bit of experience."

His gaze returned to Nina. "I'll try you as Jane tomorrow to see if you work out." Mr. Brougham clasped Nina's hands in his and squeezed.

"Jane?" she asked.

"Why, the female lead. Someone strong has to stand up next to Frank Bangs, otherwise he can dominate the stage and the plot is lost." He waved his arms to indicate disaster. "You seem to have a strong personality since you took it upon yourself to approach me with so little experience."

Nina smiled. "I would love to take the part of Jane." Her stomach flipped as terror belied her words. How could she be considering a major part with so little experience?

"Be at the theater promptly at nine tomorrow morning." He turned to another actor.

Nina walked back to Greenwich Village in a daze. She didn't know if she was proud or foolish to take a lead role beside such a vaunted leading man as Frank Bangs. Either way, she was terrified.

REHEARSALS BEGAN THE NEXT DAY. Nina stood for a moment in the middle of Sixth Avenue and stared at the theater. Only a few years old, the Booth Theater was already one of the finest theaters in New York. It had been designed by Edwin Booth, brother of the despicable man who assassinated President Lincoln, her father's friend. This most modern of theaters boasted electric stage lights.

"They can be turned off all at once, plunging the theater and stage into complete darkness," John Brougham had told the actors. Nina felt sure her heart would stop if that happened while she was onstage.

She entered the building, enveloping herself in the chaos of actors scurrying to and fro. Mr. Brougham pulled Nina aside. "Have you considered a stage name, Mrs. Larrowe? Other women find it comforting to protect their identity."

To ward against social slander, Nina realized. She no longer cared about that, but lately she'd been thinking about distancing herself from the Larrowe name just as Marcus had distanced himself physically. It seemed the next step to becoming a woman who could be her own person. Besides, with the number of Lockwood relatives in town who had her mother's ear, it might be best to stay anonymous. "I see that's a good idea. Let me think about it."

She continued practicing her lines in her head while she considered names. Deciding Helen was a dignified name, she thought about her aspirations to the temple of fame. A short time later, she told Mr. Brougham, "Temple. I'll be Helen Temple."

Mr. Brougham nodded and made a note on his script. "Helen Temple it is."

When Mr. Bangs graced them with his presence, Nina was already trembling from nerves. The actor turned his smile on her. Something about his curly dark hair, thick mustache, and light eyes emphasized charm rather than handsome good looks. He kissed her hand, focused on her for a scant minute, then moved on. For a moment, Nina was a fan, clutching the kissed hand to her heart and vowing never to wash it. But then the actress surfaced. After all, she was starring in a play alongside Mr. Bangs and must behave accordingly.

For three weeks, Nina alternated between joy and terror. Rehearsals gave her confidence and courage, but she fretted as the specter of opening night loomed. She'd be playing a lead role for a week in one of New York's finest theaters! Eating and sleeping became impossible.

Two days before opening, Mr. Brougham asked Nina to stay after rehearsal. "You poured your heart into the performance," he told her. "During the emotional scenes, tears ran down my face. Truly wonderful, my dear Helen Temple. This play is very dear to me. It may be my best one yet. If it doesn't do well, it certainly won't be your fault."

Nina floated home on a cloud of delight.

The stage manager greeted her warmly when she arrived at the theater for the opening night performance. She smiled at him and calmed herself backstage with the breathing exercises she'd learned in her elocution classes.

Nina's first scene had her entering with a howling mob that she had to quiet with a stirring speech once the priest protected her from the onslaught. Nina took her place at center stage and could not remember a word of the speech. Sweat beaded on her brow as the lights blinded her. Were they brighter tonight than they'd been at rehearsal?

The confusion and noise of the peasant mob surrounding her gave Nina some breathing space, and all the words came back. Her confidence returned, and she went all the way through the speech and never missed a line. After that, Nina blossomed onstage, loving the lights and playing to the audience. Her co-star, Mr. Bangs, showed his true colors, though, as he mugged for the audience during the most climactic scenes. He had a habit of moving and speaking slightly slower than the other actors. It drew attention and made him the center of every scene. Nina couldn't afford to be irked, though, since being billed with him would cause her own star to rise. Thankful for the fencing lessons she'd had growing up, Nina danced through the combat scene that ended Act Three with a glorious tableau where she stood with one foot on the prostrate foe and her sword held aloft.

The curtain came down, and backstage erupted in excited chatter.

Later at home, Nina ran through the play in her head, glowing at the applause. A passing thought made her wonder if Marcus would hear of her success despite the use of a stage name. Too wound up to sleep, she wrote an overdue letter to Emma.

DEAR EMMA,

I'm aware of Sam Clemens' new book, but I will not read it. Even if my family is not mentioned, no doubt others will be slandered in the name of humor, and I cannot abide that. I do have empathy for the man over his son's death. No matter how much I dislike him, I cannot wish that sort of pain on anyone. That's all I will say of Mr. Samuel Clemens.

Besides, I have news for you. I've done it. I've become an actress! I cannot describe the thrill of being onstage before a live audience, playing the leading lady to an actor of Frank Bangs' stature. It's satisfying to carry the audience along with you as the real world drops away. I imagine you feel the same when you've finished a painting that comes out the way you planned. Creative expression can be very fulfilling.

Don't believe everything you hear about Mr. Bangs, by the way. He can be quite arrogant. I'm writing this before I see the reviews that will come out tomorrow. I'm sure at least one of the critics despised the play. Isn't there always at least one? Tonight, however, the performance was perfect and I was its star. You mentioned you'd like to come see me in a play. I've enclosed a ticket for the closing night performance. It's short notice. I hope you're free.

    Yours,

    Nina

12

E mma Beach
       Peekskill, New York, December 1872

"Consider well the proportion of things. It is better to be a young June-bug
than an old bird of paradise."
- Mark Twain, Pudd'nhead Wilson's Calendar

Dear Nina,

Just a quick note to say that yes, I will be at your play tomorrow night.
I've seen the playbills for Lily of France. *I'm delighted to be able to say I*
know the leading lady! I don't care what you say about Mr. Bangs. I've
enjoyed him in every role I've seen him play. I will bring Kate with me,
since I'm staying overnight in town with her, but I'll pay for her ticket. I've
wanted you to meet her anyway. How delightful it will be to have my two
best friends together with me in the same room!

Kate has written me long letters this summer about the wonder that is
Abbott Thayer, so they have resumed their courtship. Was I so single-
minded when I was smitten with Sam? Her letters are filled with words
that are not her own. For example, she writes, "The ideal woman has an
innocent soul. She is poetic and graceful, fond of philosophic reading and

discussion." Those must be Abbott's words, not hers, but she acts like his description is tailor-made for her. It's so general, though, that I could find myself in it! So I wrote back to Kate that an ideal is an aspiration, something to strive for but never reach. She would do better if he thought of her as a friend. At least she'd be on the same ethereal plane.

I'm sure you've heard of Mrs. Victoria Woodhull running for president of the United States. She will not win, of course. She claims to be a Free Lover, one who can take whatever lover she desires and change lovers frequently with no interference from the law. Now she has come out in a blaze of hypocrisy and accused Reverend Beecher of similar behavior. She aired his current affair with Mrs. Elizabeth Tilton, a married member of the congregation. Reverend Beecher's behavior is a matter best discussed behind closed doors. Nothing good can possibly come of someone seeking attention like this. I can only thank God that it was not my mother that Mrs. Woodhull chose to showcase.

Yours truly,

Emma

13

N ina Larrowe
Greenwich Village, December 1872

"Pay no attention to the papers,
but watch the audience."
- Mark Twain, "Answers to Correspondents," Californian

On the chilly December morning after her opening night, Nina rose early and was already dressed and in the parlor when the maid appeared with the morning newspaper. Still glowing from the previous night's applause, Nina picked up the *New York Herald* to read the review.

Of Miss Ada Ward, who was Cornelia, and Miss Helen Temple, who represented the amorous widow, we can only say that they looked very pretty in very elegant costumes, and there our praise must end.

Nina closed the paper and slumped into a chair. The clocks chimed around her as if sounding a death knell for the first spark of her career. A weight settled in her chest, but she forced a deep breath and opened the paper once more to read the rest of the article.

And for Miss Temple to undertake the impersonation of Joan of Arc at

Booth's Theater last night was as bold and perilous a venture as when the simple peasant girl sought the command of the armies of France.....The traditional acting of the 'stars' of the sensational drama is almost as ridiculous as Miss Temple urging forward her forces on the ramparts of Orleans.

Nina swallowed hard. She'd been billed as "Introducing Miss Helen Temple" so theater critics knew she was green. Anger began to burn in her as she continued reading.

Miss Temple may have genius, but she certainly has not art. A more thoroughly uncultivated actress never undertook a leading part on the New York stage. Her voice is hollow and without a pleasant tone in its entire range, which sometimes reaches even the boisterous. Her acting is scarcely deserving of the name. She has not studied her profession except under the most unfavorable auspices and she brings to the part no peculiar quality except a lack of cultivation, which seems as inherent in the artist as in the heroine.

At the same time Miss Temple may improve and become at least a fairly trained actress. The only positive attribute which she evinces is force, and it is upon this that she will have to depend for whatever future progress she may make. The greatest obstacle to success, as we have already indicated, is in her voice, but thorough instruction in elocution may overcome much of the inherent weakness she now exhibits.

"Instruction in elocution!" Nina's incredulous exclamation burst forth at an unladylike volume. She'd always believed elocution to be her strength. After lampooning several more aspects of the performance, the review ended on a positive note.

The exception in the acting to which we referred is Mr. George Beck's Court Jester. The clown's conversation with his little white dog was an exquisite bit of acting and it was heartily recognized by the audience.

She'd initially thought the notion of a Court Jester and a dog to be ludicrous for the play, but she was neither the playwright nor the stage manager. And it was true that Mr. Beck had made the scene humorous.

She refolded the paper and set it aside. Taking a deep breath, she tried to marshal her resolve to show up again at the theater for the rest of the week's run. But she'd invited Emma to be there on Friday. Nina stiffened her back and squared her shoulders.

That night at the theater, John Brougham was waiting for Nina to arrive. He drew her aside. Nina wondered if he could sense the butterflies once again fluttering in her stomach.

"Miss Temple, I don't wish you to be dismayed by the *Herald's* review. The seasoned players will tell you that an actor has not truly arrived until he or she receives a scathing review. By that standard, you have arrived as an actress!" In true dramatic form, he swept his hand wide as if indicating the entire world.

Nina tried to smile at his effort to make her feel better. "That critic used quite a few lines to describe how bad I was. Miss Ward will go back to the London stage and think no more of her New York experience, but I live here."

He patted her arm. "Bravery, my dear. Make sure anyone who looks at you sees strength. Keep the doubt on the inside."

"Thank you, Mr. Brougham, I will." His words cheered her.

The normality of the backstage chaos surprised Nina. None of the other actors mentioned the review even though Nina was sure they'd all seen it. Were any of them troubled by it at all? Mr. Brougham's support had eased Nina's doubts, and the camaraderie of the troupe helped, too. She forced the *Herald's* words out of her mind and basked in the thrill of being onstage.

BY FRIDAY NIGHT, Nina felt like a professional. As long as the play was well-attended and the audience clapped and cheered, she could laugh at the reviews critics posted to make themselves appear knowledgeable about theater. Her confidence surged, and she looked forward to seeing Emma and her friend after the closing show.

When the curtain came down after the final performance, sadness tinted Nina's pride in a part well played. What would she do tomorrow? Next week? No, she'd take it minute by minute and fully enjoy what everyone but the critics said was a successful run. The curtain call brought the loudest cheering she'd heard all week. Mr.

Brougham brought flowers to her dressing room. To Nina's surprise, Mr. Bangs gave her a kiss on the cheek before he took his leave out the front door of the theater into a crowd of his adoring fans.

Nina changed out of her fancy costume gown into normal clothes and left her dressing room. She hurried toward the lobby, where she'd agreed to meet Emma. It had been five years since they'd met on the *Quaker City*, on the cruise Nina refused to call Mark Twain's. She spotted her friend across the lobby. Emma's hair still shone like fire, but Nina had forgotten how tiny the younger woman was. Kate looked much like Emma in stature, but with dark hair to Emma's red-gold. Force of habit had Nina suck in her stomach in the presence of the petite women. Kate saw Nina coming toward them, and her face lit up with a smile as she stepped forward. Turning to Emma, she said, "This must be your actress friend."

Emma said, "Nina! You were wonderful! This is my friend, Miss Kate Bloede. Kate, this is Mrs. Nina Larrowe. Or Helen Temple, as she is billed."

No one could ever resist Emma Beach. Nina basked in the warmth of her regard. "Pleased to meet you, Miss Bloede."

Kate clapped her hands. "Such an amazing performance! I'm delighted you invited us to attend."

Nina preened at their compliments for a few moments before she said, "Shall we get supper together at Delmonico's?"

Delmonico's was elegant enough to be the proper culmination of her first show. Unfortunately, they would never allow three unescorted women to dine there. Nina waved to a young actor who'd played escort for her before if she paid for his meal. Without introducing himself to Emma and Kate, or even speaking to Nina, he led them out to the street. They took a carriage to the corner of William and Beaver Streets, where Delmonico's sat upon its triangular plot of land and dominated Manhattan. The four of them were seated quickly at a circular table covered with a snowy cloth. The dining room was over half full. Murmured conversations, together with the clinking of silverware against good china, provided a pleasant background. The floral wallpaper and heavy draperies added to the grandeur of the room. The young man instructed the waiter to take the women's orders, then excused himself to the bar.

"Your friend Samuel Clemens dines here," Kate said.

Nina stiffened. "You must be speaking to Miss Beach," she said.

Emma hastily said, "Yes, Mr. Clemens does eat here when he's in Manhattan." She turned to Nina. "Do you have any other acting jobs lined up? I'd love to see you in another play. I enjoyed tonight very much."

Nina softened. "I'm not sure what else I will find."

"Theater requires the actor to bring the playwright's vision to life," Kate said. "I'd rather paint my own vision than rely on someone else to interpret it."

Nina bristled. Actors worked hard to bring life to the written word, much harder than a painter slapping paint on a canvas and calling it art. She felt Emma's hand on her arm, halting her impulsive response.

"Kate," Emma said quietly. "Are those your own words or Mr. Thayer's?"

Kate sat across from Nina, on the other side of Emma, staring into the distance with a dreamy expression.

Nina took a breath and shifted the subject. "Tell me of your own painting, Emma. Are you still painting the flowers of Peekskill?"

"I'm applying techniques learned at school with my dear friend, Kate." She laid her hand on Kate's arm, taking her friend out of her reverie.

Kate's laugh rang out like silver chimes. Nina could understand how the girl drew the attention of everyone around her. Kate said, "You should see her work, Mrs. Larrowe. It's quite good. I'll never master the tricks of light that we were taught. Abbott, now, has mastered painting the light. You should see his paintings!"

Nothing was more tiresome than a young woman in love. A waiter brought consomme and hors d'oeuvres to the table. To Nina's relief, conversation ceased as the three of them ate. Their accompanying young man remained in the bar, and his bowl sat untouched until it grew cold.

When the bowls were removed and the salmon course served, Kate spoke. "I can't stop thinking about your performance tonight, Mrs. Larrowe," she said. "In my humble opinion you were better than Mr. Bangs."

Nina gave a small laugh, as if discounting the adulation she loved. "He definitely has been a role model to me."

"I'm glad we were all able to attend together," Emma said.

"I'm so sorry Abbott wasn't able to join us," Kate said.

"Yes, I wondered," Nina said, leaning forward. "I looked forward to meeting your young man as well."

Kate flushed. "He's not my young man, not really. He's an artist. I exist in the glow of his talent. It's an honor to be near him."

"He seems to have his moods, from what your letters say," Emma said.

Kate shrugged. "An artist's moods. We all have them, do we not? I'm sure actresses are the same." She turned to Nina.

"One is never the best person to discuss the perception of their own emotions," Nina said. "Too often our mood is determined by what other people think of us. It's much better to believe that the whole world is on your side so long as you are true to the best that is in you."

Nina took the opportunity to speak extemporaneously on the topic of acting, actresses, and their place in society in order to keep the absent Abbott Thayer from dominating the conversation.

Their escort returned to the table as the waiter placed desserts of violetta cake on the table. He had the waiter leave his salmon and said nothing and he ate his dinner. Nina enjoyed his company more than that of Kate. Silence truly was golden.

14

E

mma Beach
Peekskill, New York, January 1873

"Mr. Beecher is a remarkably handsome man when he is in the full tide of sermonizing, and his face is lit up with animation, but he is as homely as a singed cat when he isn't doing anything."
- Mark Twain, letter to the San Francisco Alta California

Dear Nina,

I hope your holiday season went as well as your run in The Lily of France! *I so enjoyed having supper with you after, and introducing you to Kate. It made me smile to see my letter friend and my art school friend together. I know I said this over supper, but I truly enjoyed watching you onstage. Knowing you personally, I can see what a change in character you were able to portray, and I'm impressed.*

Remember I told you about Mrs. Tilton having an affair with Reverend Beecher? It's inconceivable to me that Plymouth Church has withdrawn Mr. Tilton's membership in our congregation. It has become a scandal larger than the horrific behavior of the Innocents while they were Abroad. Truly, if you cared to attend Mrs. Astor's next ball I'm sure that not one society maven would even notice. *I find it curious that Reverend Beecher is so involved with worthy causes such as abolition of slavery and women's suffrage, yet society continues to shine light on his indiscretions. Not that I think they are in error, not at all! At least the gossip centers around Mrs. Tilton now and not Mama. I still believe it's easier to remain in a position that doesn't attract such attention in the first place.*

I am looking forward to painting at the farm this summer. The majesty of the natural surroundings is such an inspiration, and my heart sings when I complete something that resembles the ideal in my head. I have a goal to paint the view in every direction from our front porch—probably the most ambitious project I've attempted. I dream of creating a painting that is alive, that brings the beauty of nature into the heart of the observer. It won't be easy to accomplish—I will have to think creatively about ways to achieve what I envision. I'm in no hurry, though.

Yours truly,

Emma

15

N ina Larrowe
Greenwich Village, February 1873

*"I have seen your Wild West show two days in succession, and have
enjoyed it thoroughly."*
- *Mark Twain,* Following the Equator, *Pudd'nhead Wilson's New
Calendar*

Nina returned to Matilda Herron's acting class in February of 1873, knowing she still had much to learn about her craft. Miss Herron told the class about upcoming auditions for a new show. She said, "It's about the western frontier. Have you read *Buffalo Bill, King of the Bordermen?*"

Several of the actors nodded. Nina knew the dime novel was popular, but she'd never read it. The author had written made-up adventures for the popular cowboy as they might have occurred. She could see where a play based on those stories might go over well.

Miss Herron continued. "The author, Ned Buntline, has put together a stage show called *The Scouts of the Prairie,* based in Rochester. The stars remain the same—Buffalo Bill Cody himself,

Wild Bill Hickock, and Texas Jack—but they are casting the smaller parts for a run of Hudson River towns."

A run of Hudson River towns. Nina's imagination burst with fantasies of life on the road. She was too smart to think it would be idyllic, but if she could get some kind of role it would solve a few pressing financial problems. Her absent, some-kind-of-uncle land-lord had sent a few notes hinting that he knew Nina was living on Bank Street alone, without her husband. The tone of the notes implied he found this unacceptable. Nina wondered what he would think if he knew she was entertaining actors and actresses in her parlor. Maybe a tour would give her enough financial independence to find another place to live.

A few actors walked away, uninterested, but Nina and several others took down the information Miss Herron gave them.

"Good for you, Mrs. Larrowe," she said. "Your skills are coming along nicely. I'll put in a good word for you on this one and point out your recent leading role."

"Thank you, Miss Herron."

WHEN NINA TOLD THE STORY in her head, she thought of herself as the leading lady of *The Scouts of the Prairie*. In reality, she played many parts in different scenes—a matronly woman, an Indian, a barmaid—all in the background. It was true she was onstage for almost every scene. That's why she referred to herself as leading lady.

She met Mrs. Anna Pomeroy, the other woman-of-all-parts, during the first rehearsal at Niblo's Garden, a popular Manhattan theater. Mrs. Pomeroy acted under the name Miss Goodrich, and Nina continued to be Helen Temple. The company embraced Nina. She wasn't the only one with little onstage experience. They all worked together to banish novice mistakes and become profes-sionals.

The Scouts of the Prairie was a good melodrama. Buffalo Bill Cody was a hero in New York, and his name was expected to draw crowds.

He sauntered around town in cowboy costume, telling about his experiences cavorting after Indians in the West. Men loved the Wild West aspect of the show, but it was Buffalo Bill's incredible good looks that attracted the women.

Opening night at Niblo's Garden was everything Nina had ever dreamed. As the audience took their seats, the animated chatter made Nina both nervous and excited. Be professional, she told herself.

Buffalo Bill Cody, Wild Bill Hickock, and Texas Jack took their places in front of the painted forest backdrop. The curtain came up. Someone in the audience coughed. Other than that it was silent.

"Hickock forgot his line again!" Nina hissed to Anna Pomeroy. The two women stood backstage, waiting for their entrance.

Texas Jack ad-libbed a line that hinted at Wild Bill's line.

Wild Bill turned on the charm and delivered his line. "Why, that's a fine kettle of fish."

The audience cheered.

"He's a showman if not an actor," Nina said. The show depended on Buffalo Bill's good looks, not Wild Bill's acting ability. Ned Buntline predicted sold out shows and enthusiastic audiences as they went up the river. She was grateful for the job and decided to relax and enjoy it.

"Buffalo Bill says he will perform like this in the winter and keep scouting for the army in summer. He escorts hunting parties, too. He's remarkable. He can do it all."

Nina looked sharply at the other actress. "You sound half in love with him."

Anna grinned. "No more than any other woman in the building." She nodded her head toward the audience.

The rest of the play went well. Critics, of course, did not agree. The next day, one of the *New York Herald* critics wrote, "Everything was so wonderfully bad it was almost good." The other newspapers agreed, but their readers did not. They loved seeing Buffalo Bill Cody and Wild Bill Hickock in their boots and chaps, and they treated them like heroes. They filled Niblo's Garden night after night to watch the handsome cowboy and the one who stumbled over his lines.

As the show began its winter tour in February, shopkeepers, factory workers, and their families filled theaters to see the story about Western characters starring the men themselves.

On the tour, Ned Buntline secured cheap hotels for the troupe. At one of them, the room was about six feet by nine feet, with the ceiling only six feet above the floor. Nina and Anna giggled when they heard Texas Jack complain to the front desk.

"I will not abide in a dog kennel room," he thundered in his best stage voice.

"You are welcome to bed down in the barn," the clerk said.

Texas Jack muttered and mumbled, and ended up with a room to himself.

Nina and Anna shared a bed in a room with four other beds full of troupe members. "I wonder who got the bed with the most bed bugs," Anna said, scratching her arm. She pulled Nina after her as she left the room. "Come with me. I need to use the outhouse and it's probably full of snakes and spiders and bats and whatever else hides in the dark."

"Bats?" Nina laughed. "Would a hotel called the Grand Riverfront have bats?" They'd made fun of the hotel's grandiose but inept name since they arrived.

"Maybe not," Anna conceded. "But you'd think they'd have better food."

Nina wrinkled her nose. The bread and corn mush they'd been served before the performance seemed to have been designed to keep them all lean and hungry, ready to work. It was a very different life from that of New York City, but she enjoyed it. On the road, she had no money worries, no marriage worries, no social worries.

BY THE TIME THEY REACHED ALBANY, the actors were friends as well as respected colleagues. Nina and Anna often shared a joke by catching the other's eye and smiling. Then they'd break into laughter, causing consternation among the others. The melodrama continued to sell out, and Wild Bill Hickock never managed to get through a performance without forgetting a line. It didn't matter, though. His name was all that was truly required from him.

After the Albany show, Nina changed out of her costume and sat in her dressing room removing her stage makeup and brushing her hair.

An usher darted in and handed her a business card. "An audience member, Miss Temple. He says he knows you."

Nina took the card. The name on it was unfamiliar. "Give me a few minutes and send him in." She rose and slipped on her day dress, urging one of the other actresses to quickly button her up, and turned to greet the visitor right on time.

A well-dressed man entered. He was older than Nina and possibly familiar. When he saw her, his face lit up. "Miss Churchman! I thought it was you!"

Nina's stomach dropped even as she drew herself up. "I haven't been a Churchman for almost ten years. Who might you be, sir?"

"Thomas Baine. I knew your family in Nevada." He tapped his forehead. "Yes, I remember. You married Marcus Larrowe, that political fellow." He squinted at her.

Nina felt that he was examining her, looking for the girl he'd known, considering what to do with his newfound knowledge about her. She wondered what Mr. Baine would say if he saw Marcus now. Marcus was no longer a political force. Instead, he spoke to crowds much like an actor might. "Mr. Larrowe is in New York," she said.

Thomas looked confused. "And he allows you to act with a traveling troupe? Does your mother know?"

Nina's defenses crumbled as she realized how easily this man could destroy her career and her newfound independence. As much as Mother advocated living a life parallel to her husband, and even teaching, Nina knew Mother would never approve of her acting. "Please, Mr. Baine, you must not tell my mother. I've had a reversal of fortune, you might say. Acting is the only profession I am prepared for. Please don't tell anyone you recognized me." Her acting skills failed her as she tried to keep the pleading tone out of her voice.

He took both her hands in his and squeezed them. "My dear Mrs. Larrowe, I promise to forget I saw you." He made a grand gesture of crossing his heart. "I shall not say a word to anyone."

Nina knew gallantry when she saw it. The thing about gallantry, though, was that it often faded when one was removed from the situation. But what could she do? "You have my eternal gratitude, Mr. Baine."

THE REMAINDER OF THE TOUR wrapped her in bustling activity, enough to banish the incident from her mind until they returned to New York early in March. The players in the troupe made tearful farewells to each other, promising to stay in touch, promising to follow each other's careers. Nina did the same, fully realizing she probably would never see any of them again. That was the nature of traveling troupes. Nonetheless, her parting from Anna Pomeroy was bittersweet.

Arriving at her home on Bank Street on a chilly spring morning, she entered the house and dragged her valise into the hall. The silence of the house pressed on her. No one had wound the clocks. A stack of letters awaited her on a tray near the door. An envelope with her mother's familiar handwriting topped the stack. She opened it with a smile, but as she read it her face drained of color.

Dear Nina,

I received a telegram from Mr. Thomas Baime this morning. I know I encouraged you to find something for yourself to enjoy, but acting? Properly brought up young ladies may enjoy the theater, but actually becoming an actress exposes a lady to a world of corruption that can destroy even the staunchest morals. The great majority of people are completely nefarious at heart no matter how hard they struggle to overcome or disguise their basest tendencies. The theater represents life as it truly is, and exposes the worst of a person. In the audience, one can remain detached from the lowest parts of the characters. Onstage, the players must embrace the immorality, to the detriment of their own souls.

It is clear to me that you must come home. Only then can you distance yourself from the depravity with which you have surrounded yourself.

Mother

NINA CRUMPLED THE LETTER. Retreating upstairs, she found an unopened box of chocolate caramels. She opened it, put a caramel in her mouth, and closed her eyes to savor it as she contemplated her mother's words.

DEAR EMMA,

While on tour in Albany, I had a scary moment when a longtime friend of my family recognized me. He promised not to tell my mother about my acting career, but must have sent a telegram to her the next day. Even though she and Father both loved the theater, Mother never expected me to partake in the sinfulness of the stage and its people. I suppose I was deluding myself to believe she'd never hear of it, but whoever would have guessed that an old family acquaintance would turn up in Albany, of all places! As an obedient daughter, I should hurry home to Mother as she's demanded. As an actress who has achieved a bit of success, I should push my mother's objections aside and secure my next role. I know many actresses who have done exactly that, but I cannot conceive of severing my maternal relationship so completely. If she would just let herself listen to me, I'm sure I could make her understand.

Let me share a humorous anecdote from my tour. The advertising posters, sent ahead of the troupe to announce the show, all had a picture of a buffalo on them even though there was no buffalo in the show. One night, during the curtain call at the close of the performance, a man's voice rang out from the back of the audience, demanding to know where the buffalo was. Other voices joined in, and the dissatisfied grumblings drove us from the stage. The posters were all destroyed after that, and new ones made without the buffalo. The cast and crew all laughed about the whole thing. This camaraderie and mutual respect what draws me to the stage.

The theater is a great field for the exercise of talent and self-support. What a shame if someone born with talent took my mother's view! I encourage any young person I encounter to act if they were inspired to do so, and persist until recognition is secured. No one has the right to kill a budding acting genius any more than they would take a paint brush from a young painter or a bow from a promising violinist. In whatever direction talent flows, it should be encouraged for the betterment of all.

Yours truly,

Nina

16

E mma Beach
Peekskill, New York, March 1873

"The first gospel of all monarchies should be Rebellion...against Church and State."
- Mark Twain, Notebook, 1891

Emma tucked Nina's letter behind a jar of paint brushes in her studio and stood staring at the painting on her easel without seeing it. Such bad luck that Nina's mother had discovered her daughter's acting. Nina should have been the one to tell her. Emma understood that Nina wanted to share accomplishments rather than struggles, but surely her mother would object no matter the level of her daughter's success. Recently society was reaching out to actors and actresses, sponsoring them and inviting them to dinner. Older women, however, like Nina's mother, still held the belief that a theater's players were for entertainment from the stage, not for mingling socially. Nina had spoken of her mother on the cruise and in letters. Emma had pieced together a picture of a woman who had overcome mistakes of her choosing. No wonder Nina was desperate to have some success to show her mother.

Emma wondered what it would be like to be driven by the need to succeed in your mother's eyes. Her own mother had married happily and had four living children. Mrs. Beach had never tried to hide her affair from her husband, and never denied that her youngest child wasn't his. Emma had hidden in the shadows and watched controversy swirl around her parents for her entire life. Her mother had made choices that turned out badly, as had Nina's mother. Mrs. Beach never admitted she'd done anything wrong. That omission poked holes in the very values she expected her daughters to espouse. As a result, Emma had never felt the need to please her mother with her own success.

That afternoon, after a morning of pushing paint around on canvas—she would not call the result painting—Emma joined her mother and sisters in the parlor for tea just as a visitor arrived. He was a nicely dressed man, unknown to Emma.

Her mother greeted him with a smile, and indicated he should join them. "Girls, this is David Livingston. His mother is a member of the congregation of Plymouth Church." She turned to the young man. "David, Welcome to The Beeches. These are my girls; Violet, Alice, and this is Emma."

Emma smiled, recognizing that this was an attempt by her mother to find a husband for her eldest daughter. "Mr. Livingston," she said, nodding at him. If Mama had intended to select someone as unlike Sam Clemens as she could, this man would be it. His dark hair was slicked back along his head more neatly than she'd ever seen Sam's. David was nervous, twisting his hands until Mama handed him a teacup. Then he balanced it precariously on his knee.

Alice leaned toward him. "Enchanted to meet you, Mr. Livingston. What business are you in?" She sounded just like Mama in her intonation and phrasing.

David beamed. "I'm working at my father's bank, just learning the ropes right now. Soon I'll have a position of responsibility, though."

A banker. How boring. Emma fixed her smile on her face between sips of her tea and watched her fifteen-year old sister conduct a perfectly proper afternoon tea. Mama must be so proud.

As they finished their tea, Mama said, "Alice, will you play for us?"

Emma almost laughed. Had Mama decided to focus her matrimonial efforts on Alice? It was true that David seemed closer in age to her sister, maybe eighteen. Too young, too dull, too nervous for Emma.

When Mama rose to walk David to the door, Emma caught Alice's eye. They both burst into giggles. "Horrors," Alice said. "How many more of those will we have to endure?"

"If you married one, it would take the pressure off," Emma suggested, half serious.

"No, you're the oldest," Alice said. "You marry one of them."

The idea held no appeal for Emma. She scrunched up her face. Alice laughed.

Dear Nina,

You've told me many times to step out of the shadows and find my own path. You did so, and you've begun to have some real success. I'm proud of you and sorry your mother is proving to be such an obstacle. Achieving dreams seems so impossible, even when family is supportive. I cannot imagine openly going against my parents' wishes, but then I have never longed for a career that would horrify them. Family is the rock of my world. Are you sure a career as an actress is worth the damage it would do to your relationship with your mother? Even the best theatrical careers thrive at the whim of the public, often dissolving in flames after only a few years. Family is forever.

I do not presume to advise you. You are strong enough to do whatever is right in your own heart. I just want to say that there are worse things than a life in the shadows. It can be quite fulfilling to help someone else achieve their dreams, except maybe for a mother who dreams of your marriage.

Yours truly,

Emma

17

N
ina Larowe
Greenwich Village, September to November 1873

"It is curious that physical courage should be so common in the world, and moral courage so rare."
- Mark Twain in Eruption

All summer, letters arrived from her mother. They alternated between demanding and pleading that Nina come home to California. Home to California? Nina hadn't lived there since before her father moved the family to Austin, Nevada, over ten years ago. She'd married Marcus and they'd left for New York only a year later. If anywhere was home, it was New York. Besides, she was twenty-nine years old, not some child who came running when her mother was upset.

After the death of Nina's stepsister, her brother-in-law, Edward Williams, had remarried and moved to San Jose with his new wife and four children. Her mother had gone with them. At any rate, Nina had never been to San Jose and could not contemplate it as a place to go home to. She hadn't told her mother about Marcus leaving for good, but she suspected Mother somehow knew or at least suspected.

She'd heard nothing from Marcus or about him. If his memory business was doing well, she should see notices of his lectures or classes. She searched the papers for articles or advertisements, telling herself it was only curiosity. It wasn't until September that she saw something in the *New York Daily Tribune*—a list of passengers departing New York for Liverpool aboard the steamship *Baltic*. One of the passengers was M. D. Larrowe. Nina stared at the words with momentary incomprehension. Marcus had finally left for London.

Setting the paper down, she paced the parlor. Sensing she was at a crossroads, she searched for the inner strength that had never failed her. Marcus had not filed for divorce, so in reality she was still married to a man she hadn't seen in three years. The idea galled her. She couldn't file herself because the law allowed women to divorce their husbands only to escape life-threatening cruelty. Her husband wasn't even in the same country.

Unable to disregard her legal husband's name totally, she decided to drop an 'r' from her last name and become Mrs. Nina Larowe. It was the best she could do to distance herself from Marcus. A minor victory, but it would have to be good enough.

The letters from San Jose kept coming. Clearly Nina's three nieces and a nephew were not enough to keep her mother busy. Mother's constant pleading sent Nina into a frenzy. She tore the letters in half before burning them. It wasn't long before she burned them unopened.

USUALLY NINA LOVED the buzz of anticipation that settled over New York as the holidays approached. This year, however, her reduced circumstances threw a pall over the season. Determined not to sink into the doldrums, Nina sent a note to Emma asking her friend to join her for a holiday shopping day on the Ladies' Mile. She was thrilled when Emma immediately accepted.

On a cold November day, Nina hired a carriage to take her to

Union Square. She pulled last year's coat closer around her stomach, and watched the residences and businesses grow more opulent as they approached Fifth Avenue. She didn't have enough money to shop on the Ladies' Mile, and she had no one to shop for, but for a few hours she would live vicariously through the other shoppers and enjoy the season. The street was festive, with Christmas tree stands on the corner, and wagons selling all manner of wreaths, stars, and evergreen decorations.

Disembarking in front of Tiffany's, Nina looked up at the massive cast-iron building known as the palace of jewels.

"Nina!" Emma's call was not a shout—that would be too common in the rarefied air surrounding the store. She had disembarked from a hired carriage before calling to Nina, and now she walked toward Tiffany's. Emma wore a forest-green coat and dress ensemble that set off the red hair peeking out from under her matching hat.

"Emma, so nice to see you," Nina said. And it was. She took both of Emma's gloved hands in her own and squeezed. This woman's letters were a light in the darkness of Nina's thoughts. In person, Emma's warmth enveloped her in a hug.

"I have so much shopping to do!" Emma said, her eyes bright with anticipation. "It's so much better to do it early in the season. This was a good idea, Nina."

"I've been looking forward to it." Nina felt the dark shawl of her recent mood lift. Yes, it had been a good idea.

They entered Tiffany's. The showroom was a marvel of black walnut and ebony display cases where shoppers perused items in leather, silver, cloisonné, enamel, bronze, and rosewood. Nina watched women glide through the store, acting as if shopping at Tiffany's was not out of the ordinary when the entire effect was designed to impress shoppers with its opulence.

Emma asked to see men's watches, explaining to the sales clerk that she needed a gift for her father. Nina had once been able to buy her mother a bracelet from Tiffany's, and she'd never appreciated that ability. Now she couldn't even afford to send a gift to California, much less buy one. She pushed away the negativity and tried on three bracelets, frowning and finding something wrong with each of them. The very patient sales clerk pulled out a fourth, but Nina shook her head.

"Ready to go or still shopping?" Emma asked, tucking a small turquoise bag under her arm.

"I haven't found anything here," Nina said. The sales clerk's smile never dimmed.

The women left Tiffany's and walked up Fifth Avenue. Whenever Emma saw a store she wanted to visit, they went inside. When they reached 19th Street, Emma stopped.

"Do you mind if we go to Gorham's? Mama lost one of her silver spoons and I'd like to replace it," Emma said.

"Of course," Nina said. She followed Emma up 19th to another store she could no longer afford. But she had a smile on her face. It was almost easier to look at expensive items when you knew you couldn't buy any of them. It was much harder to have an unlimited budget and have to find the perfect gift.

By the time they neared 23rd Street, Nina was hungry. "Shall we stop at Maillard's?"

Emma laughed. "Of course, but you must have something to eat before you start eating the chocolate caramels!"

Nina pretended to look shocked. It lightened her mood greatly to laugh with a friend.

They entered the Fifth Avenue Hotel and approached Maillard's.

"They say the Prince of Wales visited this hotel, and that is what started Fifth Avenue's appeal to the wealthy," Nina said. "I wonder how many boxes of chocolate caramels he bought?"

Both were smiling as they were seated in the lunchroom at a table covered with a white linen cloth. By this time, Emma had several shopping bags, and she set them under the table. The dining room was full of women. The Ladies' Mile was so safe that women shopped and dined in large numbers without male escorts. Nina and Emma ordered sandwiches and salads, then settled in to enjoy conversation.

Almost immediately, Emma's expression became serious. "I'm worried about Alice," she said. "Mama takes her to everything she attends, be it a ball or a charity event. Alice has no choice in the matter at all."

She'd been saying similar things about Alice in her letters for quite a while. Nina said, "Would Alice choose something different?"

Emma shrugged. "I don't know. She should at least have the option."

Nina watched Emma's face as she tried to smile. "Your sisters mean a lot to you. I'm sure you are as much of a role model as your mother."

"That's not much better," Emma said. "I'm a failure at relationships." She tried for a light laugh but failed.

The waiter brought their meal, and Nina took a bite of her egg and watercress sandwich while Emma poured tea.

"What do you mean, a failure at relationships?" Nina asked.

"Look at my life. I have no husband, never had a serious beau. My best real-life friend won't introduce me to a man she's passionate about. And my correspondent won't tell me about the tour of her play." Emma set down the teapot and sipped her tea.

Nina smiled. "I thought we were talking about you." She gave Emma a few details about the tour of *Scouts of the Prairie*, focusing on the highlights. Emma laughed at the tale of the man wanting to see a real buffalo because it was on the poster. "My relationship with the other cast members seemed solid when we were touring, but we've been back in New York for five months and I've seen and heard nothing of them. In a way, it reminds me of the relationships I had with my friends before our cruise to the Holy Land."

"Oh, Nina, what do you mean?"

"I thought I had friends, but they were quick to abandon me over rumor and innuendo. Except for you, all my friends have been so only for the duration of a social season or the run of a play. And don't assume that since I was married I had a close relationship there." Nina shook her head.

"How can you bear to keep going?" Emma said.

Nina looked at Emma in confusion. Here was a smart, pretty girl who had never really tried to have a serious relationship with anyone outside her family. She valued a notion that was completely in her head, that didn't exist in the real world. Nina gripped her teacup with both hands. "You can neither be a failure nor a success if you've never tried."

"Pardon?" Emma's voice was barely a whisper.

"You're a dear, Emma, please don't get upset. But you've always been the sort who preferred to hang about in the shadows and watch others get all the attention."

Emma nodded.

"Do you expect love and friendship to find its way to you? That somehow the perfect man will navigate his way past all the obligations you hide behind?"

Emma's face had gone pale, but Nina couldn't stop.

"Anyone can withdraw from something that makes them uncomfortable. It takes courage to push forward alone, with no help from anyone, and continue to work toward a dream." Nina's voice cracked at the end of the sentence. To her dismay, her throat closed up and eyes filled with tears. She focused on sipping her tea and hoped Emma wouldn't notice.

Emma noticed. She leaned across the table and put a hand on Nina's arm. "Fate hasn't been kind to either of us, my friend. But we can cling to each other. We can always be honest with each other."

Nina swallowed and took a deep breath, giving Emma a tremulous smile. "You're a good friend, Emma. Writing to you has saved me more than once."

Emma squeezed Nina's arm. "As it has me. Shall we get some chocolates now?"

18

E

mma Beach
Peekskill, New York, January 1874

"The proper office of a friend is to side with you when you are in the wrong. Nearly anybody will side with you when you are in the right."
- Mark Twain's Notebook

Dear Nina,

I hope your holidays were pleasant. The best thing about Christmas at the farm was watching Alice and Violet, in shades of delight over the presents under the tree. Violet, at seven, holds nothing back. Alice is sixteen, though, and tries so hard to act grown up and beyond childish joy. I can see it in her eyes, though, and it makes me smile.

I told my family about your triumphant entrance onto the New York stage and subsequent tour. My sisters are thrilled for you. Mama was noncommittal, saying something about scandal. I tried to point out to her that you are beyond being affected by scandal, having been drowned in that well already. I'm sure my tone was incredulous at her effrontery. She expects propriety even when she chose not to act within its rules herself. It makes me wonder how my sisters and I are expected to know which rules are sacrosanct.

At any rate, Happy New Year. I hope to hear soon about the next stage in your acting career (pun intended).

Yours truly,

Emma

In March, Emma's parents left on a tour of Norway, Sweden, and Russia. This meant Emma and Alice could look forward to half a year without Mama's attempts to find them husbands. Emma spent more time in her studio, painting from sketches she'd made the previous summer of flowers at the farm. This year she would be in charge of her sisters at the farm until her parents returned in September. Her brother William, now fourteen, planned to spend the summer with an uncle in Connecticut, so it would be just the three sisters at the farm. Luckily, Emma thought, the household staff would be there, too.

Emma stepped back to critically assess the bouquet of wild-flowers on her canvas. She'd made a few finished touches to the shad-ows, enhancing the cheerful hue of the daisies. A clatter outside her studio announced Violet moving quickly down the hallway.

"Emma! Kate's here!" Violet called, as if Emma were forty miles away instead of on the other side of the door. She enjoyed visitors, and Kate was more fun than the people who came to visit Mama and Papa.

"Violet, tone control, please," Emma said as wiped her hands on her smock.

Violet opened the door, grinning and stepping back to let Kate enter Emma's studio.

"Oh, a new one?" Kate asked, walking over to the easel. "Have you finished it?"

"I think so." Emma wrinkled her nose. "I don't think art is ever finished. I wonder if the masters see their work hanging in a gallery and bemoan a bit of missing shading or sloppy line work?"

"Emma, this is really good." Kate came closer to inspect the paint-ing. "Lovely colors, so bright, and the detail is amazing."

Emma bit her lip. She never knew what to say to compliments about her work. "The daisies don't look right. I should have stuck to the dahlias. They're decent."

"You should've painted a bunch of violets," Violet said. Then she laughed and scampered off to find something more interesting to do than talk to adults.

"The dahlias do look nice," Kate said. "Lovely soft yellows and pinks. The daisies are good, too, though." She paused, still examining the panting. "You know, Abbott has a show coming up in a small gallery in Brooklyn. The show includes local unknown artists. I'm sure he could recommend you."

"Oh, no," Emma said. Her tone was casual, not reflecting the panic welling up inside her. She could accept her art being on display, but galleries usually wanted artists to be there, too, to talk to patrons about their art and their methods. She'd rather die.

"Emma," Kate said, "you have to get over this shyness that paralyzes you and learn to accept compliments. It can be lovely to have people admire your work."

"But so upsetting if they don't like it."

"Abbott likes to imagine critics spouting off about how terrible something is without realizing they are speaking to the painter's best friend. The best friend, of course, roundly objects to the critic's views. Let them hang your picture, Emma. I'll be that best friend."

Emma looked again at the painting she'd just finished. It was one of her best pieces. She'd love to show it to people, but that was taking a big risk. What if no one liked it? She imagined a gallery full of people frowning at her work. Then in her mind she saw Kate and Abbott smiling and praising it. Their support would make it bearable. "All right. I'll do it." Even as she said the words, she felt bile rising in her throat. No, she was determined to take this step.

"You won't regret this!" Kate crowed in delight, drawing Alice from the parlor.

"What's going on?" Alice asked, peering into the studio.

"Your sister has just agreed to hang this picture...what are we calling it, Emma?"

Emma shrugged. "*Wildflowers?*"

"She has just agreed to hang *Wildflowers* in a show." Kate swept her arms wide, as if welcoming the world into Emma's studio.

"Emma, that's wonderful!" Alice exclaimed. "And about time," she said to Kate.

"We'll make an excursion of it," Emma said, "and bring you and Violet along, too."

"How exciting! I've never been to a real art exhibition," Alice said.

"You're in charge of corralling Violet," Emma warned.

Kate and Alice left to go tell Violet of the plans. Emma stared at the painting again, then away. She refused to do any more to it except framing.

TRUE TO KATE'S WORD, Abbott procured an invitation for Emma to hang *Wildflowers* in a small show at a gallery in Brooklyn. So two weeks after agreeing to the plan, Emma and her sisters went to Brooklyn and stayed at the Bloede residence. Kate came into the room Emma shared with her sisters.

"No," Kate told her friend, "you are not going to wear gray or brown. Surely you have something more alive." Kate went through the dresses Emma had brought and found a soft blue one. It wasn't as bright as something Kate might wear, but it was better than the dress Emma had selected. "And here, put this on." Kate handed Emma the brightly colored pansy scarf she'd given her as a gift.

Emma, already nervous about the show, didn't have the energy to protest. She had to admit the blue dress and pansy scarf looked nice. Kate left, planning to meet Abbott before heading to the show.

A few minutes later, Emma and her sisters set off in a hired carriage to the opening of Emma's first exhibition.

Emma knew that the best galleries were hard to find because they were so discreet in outward appearance. This one wasn't one of the best. Nonetheless, several people had gathered to see the artwork. Emma swallowed, trying to quiet the butterflies in her stomach, and pasted a smile on her face as she got out of the carriage. She spotted Kate and Abbott almost immediately.

Kate waved, but Emma's eyes were on Abbott. He looked very nice in a blue suit Kate must have made him put on. When Emma had seen him before, he always managed to look a bit disheveled. Not today.

Kate said, "Abbott, I don't think you've met Emma's sisters, Alice and Violet."

Abbott reached for Violet's hand and bowed over it like an old-fashioned gentleman. His eyes, however, remained on Emma. "Pleased to meet such a beautiful young lady," he said.

Alice said, "We're glad to meet you, too, Mr. Thayer."

"Let's go see where my paintings, and Emma's, of course, are hanging, shall we?" Abbott took Violet on one arm and Alice on the other, leaving Emma and Kate to follow.

Inside the galley, the artwork dominated the space. The glow of low gaslight gave an ethereal look to the room. People mingled and shared low conversation, glasses of wine, and hors d'oeuvres.

Violet took a cucumber sandwich off a butler's tray while Alice accepted a glass of punch from another tray. Emma didn't trust herself to eat, or to hold a glass of something. She followed Kate and Abbott into the center of the room. There, by itself on its own wall, hung a magnificent landscape painting. Emma recognized Abbott's style. "Abbott, it's wonderful," she said.

He beamed. "Turn around," he said.

Wildflowers hung directly across from his masterwork. Two women stood before it, heads together, talking softly. Emma leaned closer, trying to hear what they were saying. Kate wasn't so shy. "A lovely first work, is it not?" she asked.

One of the women smiled and turned toward Kate. "It's so lifelike. I feel like I can take that vase home and put it on my parlor table." The other woman nodded agreement.

Emma sucked in a breath. They liked it. She tried to step back, but Kate gripped her arm. "This is Emma Beach, the artist," she said.

Emma felt her face flame as the two women regarded her.

"I love your style," one said. "Do you have any other works for sale?"

"Other works?" Emma asked.

"It appears, Emma, that this one has already been sold," Kate said. She nodded toward a gallery clerk who was taping a Sold sign to the piece description below the painting.

Emma felt a rushing whirl of wind take control of her head. Dizzy with shock, she was unable to respond. She felt someone take her arm in a no-nonsense grip and lead her to a quiet corner of the gallery. A few deep breaths and she was calmer.

"You look pale," Abbott said. "Are you alright? You almost passed out."

"Thank you for taking me away," Emma said. "I never know what to say."

Abbott leaned closer. "First, you say thank you to the buyer."

"Buyer. It's real?" Emma said.

Abbott laughed. "Very real. Congratulations."

Kate found them. "Abbott, you have a buyer for your painting who wants to speak with you." Her eyes shone with excitement.

Abbott squeezed Emma's arm. "My fans are calling. Be well, Emma."

Alice arrived, with Violet in tow. "You sold your painting, Emma, congratulations!" Violet bounced in time to Alice's words. Then Alice's face lit up. "Oh, it's David Livingston!" She scurried off to greet him and give him a tour of the artwork.

Warmed by her sisters' approval and her friends' support, Emma was able to step out from her corner and glide in the direction of her painting. For the rest of the evening she found it easier to talk with patrons about Abbott's work, but she did manage to converse with her own admirers without choking up and embarrassing herself. Maybe she could learn to enjoy this world as much as Kate and Abbott did.

. . .

AFTER THE EXHIBITION, Emma returned to her studio at the farm, vowing to focus on her art and not be distracted by her first sale. She found herself staring out the window, though, not seeing winter-bare apple trees but visions of her paintings being sold at public venues. Oddly enough, the thought thrilled her rather than scared her. At least in her imagination.

Alice came into the studio one morning. She walked around the small room, examining paintbrushes and pots of paint as if she'd never seen them before. She perused the finished paintings leaning against the wall, then stood staring at the new work on Emma's easel.

"Alice?" Emma asked. "Are you looking for something?"

"You really do paint well," her sister said.

"You could learn to do so, too, I'm sure," Emma said.

Alice picked up a brush and looked at it dubiously.

Emma pulled out a second easel and a blank prepared canvas, indicating Alice should use it. "Here, let me show you." She proceeded to demonstrate on her own canvas some of the very first techniques she'd learned at Cooper Union, blending colors for the background. "You always start with the background no matter how much you want to paint the subject." She continued working on a corner she'd started before Alice came in.

Alice watched for a moment, then began mimicking Emma's work. Alice was uncertain at first, but Emma kept painting without offering encouragement or criticism. She wanted to believe Alice was interested. After a few minutes, Alice stepped back and tilted her head, comparing what she'd done to her sister's. She laughed. "It's not as easy as you make it seem."

"You've made a wonderful start," Emma said. "Do you want to do more?"

"You have the painting talent in the family," Alice said. She gave Emma a warm smile and patted her arm. "I'd rather grow the roses for you to paint."

Emma smiled through her disappointment. She'd been trying to interest Alice in painting for a long time. "Whatever intrigues you."

"When is your next show?" Alice said, putting down her brush.

Her eyes were bright, her smile hopeful as she turned away from the canvas and faced her sister.

"I don't have one planned." Emma narrowed her eyes. "You seem more interested in art shows than in painting."

"Did you see David Livingston at your show? I think he wanted to buy your painting, but that older man got it first. I commiserated with him." Delight filled her face as she related her experience. "He's really quite nice, you know. It was easier to talk in a relaxed setting than it was when Mama had him for tea."

Emma told herself she shouldn't have been surprised that Alice was interested in a man Mama had picked. "I didn't get an opportunity to talk with him."

"We talked about the Smallpox Hospital on Blackwell Island."

Emma stared at Alice. "Why? That place is where people go to die. It's not a hospital."

"David says the Board of Health is taking control of it. They need money to change the way it's run. David is helping his mother raise money for it."

Emma frowned, but said, "That seems worthwhile." She was surprised by Alice's sudden interest in health care.

"David says the Board of Health is trying to improve conditions. Did you know smallpox killed over a thousand people in New York last year? The Sisters of Charity at St. Vincent's Hospital are helping to improve care of patients."

Emma shook her head. "I'm sorry, but how is David involved exactly? And I thought that hospital was being closed. Aren't they making a nursing school there?"

Alice's face shone. "His sister, Emily, is one of the Sisters of Charity. They are marvelous women, devoting their lives to this cause. David's mother is Clara Livingston. She's hosting a musical soiree at her house next Tuesday afternoon. Proceeds will go to the Charity. David invited me."

"And you'll go?" Emma was impressed with the poise Alice showed. "You shouldn't go alone."

"Nonsense, Emma. The Livingstons are acceptable people, and

they live right in Brooklyn." Before Emma could protest further, Alice left the room.

So much for painting. Alice had clearly found a cause. Emma was proud of her sister for finding her own passion, be it a nursing hospital or David Livingston.

19

Nina Larowe
Manhattan, New York, July 1874

*"Since a hundred million dollars in New York
and twenty-two fish-hooks on the border of the Arctic Circle represent the
same financial supremacy, a man in straitened circumstances is a fool to
stay in New York when he can buy ten cents' worth of fish-hooks and
emigrate."*
- Mark Twain, "The Esquimau Maiden's Romance"

Shortly after the new year, a messenger delivered a note from some-kind-of-an-uncle Lockwood, the owner of the house. It was a terse note, asking Nina to vacate the premises because he'd found someone to purchase the property. As a concession to her status as a relative, he left her date of departure open. She'd been dreading this day for three years. Had he discovered that Nina was an actress? It didn't matter. She'd have to find a place in one of the women's boarding houses that were springing up all over New York. Assuming she could find enough acting jobs to pay for it, of course.

For six months, Nina searched for a place where an actress

without a husband could live. Her uncle, although polite, was getting more frustrated that Nina was still living on Bank Street.

A leading role as Mercy Merrick in *New Magdalen* took Nina on the road for another month. It was a play based on a novel by Wilkie Collins. Ironically enough, the character was a fallen woman trying to put her past behind her despite being thwarted by the prejudices of respectable society.

The *New Magdalen* tour visited many of the same towns Nina had played with *Othello*. This time, though, the tour was a series of one-night stands. After every performance, the troupe had to catch a midnight train, or sometimes a five o'clock in the morning train. Upon arrival at the new town, they slept all day to restore energy for the night's performance. For Nina, the mixture of fatigue and audience approval sank her into restful sleep. And no matter how tired she was, when the footlights went on so did she, coming to life and shining in a life she loved.

Returning to the empty house in New York brought Nina's spirits down. Nina wanted to keep her souvenirs from the cruise, and she knew she'd have to move, so she carefully took each item off its shelf and wrapped it in paper before nestling it in a trunk. She found a folded piece of paper that had been tucked under the carved canoe she'd bought for Marcus. Nina opened it to find an address for Anna Pomeroy, the friend she'd made on tour with *Scouts of the Prairie*. They'd intended to stay in touch. Nina had forgotten she even had the address.

Nina went upstairs to her bedroom and got paper to write a note to Anna. Maybe her friend knew of a boarding house for actresses. Nina had nothing to lose. The plate next to her bed that the maid had kept full of chocolate caramels was empty. Nina sighed.

ANNA'S RESPONSE CAME QUICKLY. As it turned out, one of her roommates had left to get married. Nina was welcome to move in. With a surge of hope, Nina went to visit her.

The house wasn't new, but it looked to be in good repair. It had rooms for a couple dozen boarders that weren't fancy. Her bed, one of four in Anna's room, would cost $1.50 a week.

"We have a couple of women in the theater business here," the boarding house keeper told her. "I keep a strict house, though. No men and no wild behavior." She punctuated her words with a sharp glare.

"No ma'am," Nina assured her. She paid the deposit and entered the room she would share with Anna and two other women. It was the first time she'd lived in a house full of strangers. Rather than a sad commentary on her life, she vowed to make it a positive experience. Sparsely furnished but clean, the room was not what she was accustomed to but serviceable. She had an iron bedstead, wash basin, and small bureau for herself. A vase of flowers would make it livable.

Nina packed up the rest of the house on Bank Street quickly. She sold everything in the house, keeping only her clothing and personal items, and the trunk of souvenirs. Finally, she dashed off a note and sent the keys to her uncle. When she left the house for the last time, she didn't look back.

Dear Emma,

Here is the address of the place I am living now, with Anna Pomeroy. It's a temporary solution, I fear. How did I not realize how much Anna enjoys drinking? Her current boyfriend takes her every night to a beer garden in Lower Manhattan that has a side entrance for ladies. When I get a longer-running role, I can find a better place. So far, the highlight of the year has been selling Marcus's clocks.

Despite the grim reality of the place, I remind myself that the happy ending to my marriage is that I am moving on, freeing myself for a more positive future. If I stay true to my heart, I'm sure my own path will reveal itself soon. I've played leading roles onstage, and now it's time for me to stop playing an extra in my own life.

Yours truly,
Nina

20

E mma Beach
      Peekskill, September 1874

"Start any rumor, and if the public can go with its curiosity unsatisfied for three days, something else will spring up which will make the public forget all about the first one."
- A Bibliography of Mark Twain, Merle Johnson

Dear Nina,

I loved painting the bounty of summer's roses at the farm almost as much as I love watching the apples ripen and dreaming of autumn's apple cider cake. All summer, my sisters and I have enjoyed the quiet life I love so much. Life can be complicated, but at the farm my mind can realize the beauty of the world and the boundless treasures it contains.

I'm not going to ask if you've read Sam's latest novel, The Gilded Age. *It's different in that he wrote it with another author. I can't imagine an author writing with Sam Clemens. It would be like me being asked to paint alongside Leonardo Da Vinci or Rembrandt!*

Sam is involved in a new venture, too. He's investing in a revolutionary invention by James Paige that he tells me will replace a human typesetter with a mechanical arm. I learned about it in a letter Sam wrote to Papa, hoping my father would also invest. Papa laughed at the idea, calling it a foolish dream. My father has good instincts for inventions, so I am nervous for Sam about the amount of money he is putting into this venture. He says he is investing the profit from his books. That must surely be a significant amount. I don't feel it is my place to caution him, however.

As much as I enjoy the peace of the farm, I do look forward to seeing my parents upon their return from Europe next week.

Yours truly,

Emma

ON A BEAUTIFUL AUTUMN DAY, Moses and Chloe Beach got out of the carriage and walked up to the front door of their farmhouse for the first time since early Spring. Emma and her sisters waited on the porch.

"Mama!" Violet cried, running into her mother's arms.

"Welcome home, Mama," Alice said, handing her mother a bouquet of fall flowers. "Welcome home," Emma said. She was glad to see her parents, but a little sad to see the end of her freedom from her mother's scrutiny. She'd enjoyed a summer without being pushed to meet another eligible man, to participate in one of Mama's charities, or to fill her days in a manner Mama approved.

Papa stepped forward to lead his family into the house just as a horse and rider came up the drive. Emma recognized Reverend Beecher just as he called out, "Welcome home! I couldn't wait any longer to see two of my best congregants!"

Papa frowned, but Mama blossomed. "Hello, Reverend! It's nice to be home," she said. "Would you join us for tea?"

Emma went inside to tell the staff there would be one more for tea. She didn't want to share her parents' homecoming with Reverend Beecher, but she was no longer in charge. Emma wanted to tell her parents about selling her first painting, and encourage Alice to talk about David Livingston, who was an increasingly important part of her life.

In the parlor, the family gathered in their usual seats. It felt good to be together again, even if Reverend Beecher didn't belong in her brother William's place.

As if reading her mind, Reverend Beecher said, "Moses, where is your fine son?"

Papa said, "William will attend boarding school in Connecticut under the watchful eye of relatives."

"So tell us what we missed this summer," Mama said, looking at her daughters.

Violet came alive, relating in animated detail every walk on the farm and every animal and flower she'd seen.

When Violet ran out of words, Alice said, "I've spent some time at the Livingston house, working on fundraising for the nursing school."

"Nursing school?" Papa asked, wrinkling his brow in confusion.

"Livingston? Was David there?" Mama asked.

Alice smiled, the sweetest smile a sixteen-year-old young lady had ever given her mother. "He's been very attentive." Her cheeks flushed pink, and she dropped her eyes to her teacup.

"What's this about David Livingston?" Papa asked, clearly unaware of Mama's matchmaking attempts.

Mama's gaze swung to Emma, one brow raised.

"We saw him at an art show where I sold a painting," Emma said.

"Art show? Sold a painting?" Papa raised his voice, trying to understand what he was missing.

Mama said, "Clearly I need to hear the whole story of your summer, girls." Her tone, however, dismissed the subject. "Reverend, tell us of the church."

"I've asked the church members to investigate the scandal. We need to put it behind us," Reverend Beecher said.

"You mean to clear your name," Papa said.

Mama glared at him. "Elizabeth Tilton does not deserve to have her name dragged through the mud by that liberated woman," she said.

"Liberated woman? You mean Mrs. Woodhull? She is not liberated simply because she advocates free love and ran for president." Alice's words raised every eyebrow.

"Alice, you don't know all the details, I'm sure," Mama said.

Emma's attention shifted from her mother to her sister and back again. It was the first time she'd heard her sister state her own position on anything. Alice must have gotten her ideas from David Livingston. Had they discussed Mama's affair with Reverend Beecher as well as Elizabeth Tilton's?

"What about Ted Tilton? He shouldn't have sued his wife over adultery and made the entire affair a public one. Plymouth Church was right to suspend his membership," Papa said.

Reverend Beecher nodded. "Thank you, Moses. Not everyone agrees."

Emma stared, dumbfounded, at her parents and Reverend Beecher. Mrs. Tilton's alleged affair with Reverend Beecher had been made public by Mrs. Woodhull, and Mr. Tilton had sued the reverend. Was Reverend Beecher saying that the same thing would have happened to her parents had Papa spoken out? Emma shook her head. All of this should have remained out of the public eye.

THAT SUNDAY, Mama insisted the family travel downriver to Brooklyn for services at Plymouth Church. Emma didn't want to admit that all summer she and her sisters had attended church in Peekskill. She'd enjoyed the freedom from perusal by other members of the congregation, especially when they looked at Violet. She'd developed some confidence from a summer in charge of the family, and from the sale of her artwork. She donned a new dress made of turquoise silk, a fabric that Violet had insisted she buy because it complemented her red hair. Adding her pansy scarf gave Emma even more confidence. If Emma's bright appearance surprised Mama, she gave no sign of it.

At the church, Mama took Papa's arm and walked through the gathering congregation into the massive church. Emma, head up, followed with Alice and Violet. Emma ignored the whispers behind their hands as women noticed the Beaches.

Alice spotted the Livingstons and slowed her pace until they came up beside her. "Hello, Mrs. Livingston." She smiled, but brightened even further as she turned to David. "Mr. Livingston."

"Miss Beach, I'm delighted to see you," David said.

Mrs. Livingston greeted Alice and her family politely, but walked away from them a bit quickly as she guided her family to another pew. Alice didn't notice. Emma did.

"Mama," Emma whispered. "Why do we put up with this talk? Why not go to another church?"

Papa overheard. He said, "Plymouth is our church. We will not run away with our tails between our legs." And that was that.

Emma fluffed her bright pansy scarf and straightened her shoulders. Trying to hide from public attention had never worked. She refused to hide any more.

21

Nina Larowe
Manhattan, September 1874

"It's human to like to be praised;
one can even notice it in the French."
-Mark Twain, "What Paul Bourget Thinks of Us"

It took every ounce of Nina's energy to move through the days with grace and elegance. She struggled to maintain the air of a successful actress even though her situation didn't live up to her aspirations. Nina wasn't the only one. The Panic of 1873 had resulted in a depression that still shrouded the country from New York, where fewer people attended the theater, to Nevada, where silver prices were depressed. She was thankful that her brother, Ney, now living in Virginia City, Nevada, was not involved in silver mining.

Nina nursed her tea in the parlor that was used by all the women in the house. The front door opened and Anna came in with several morning newspapers. Her eyes were bleary, and she still wore last night's clothes.

"Here's another one, Nina," she announced, tossing a copy of the *New York Daily Times* onto the couch beside Nina.

"Do I want to read it?" Nina asked. She and Anna watched the papers for reviews of each other's performances and kept a good-natured tally of who had the most positive ones.

Anna just smiled.

Nina found the review and read it aloud. "The qualities in Miss Temple's personation which most deeply impressed us were imagination, profound earnestness, and symmetry of treatment. The ideal in her thought was wide, clear, and perfect; she threw her whole soul into its expression, and she made that expression harmonious." She puffed out her chest in exaggerated pride. "They were deeply impressed."

"And they said you were peerrrrfect," Anna said.

"They love me at the Times," Nina said. "Their review of my last performance said I was heartily applauded."

"Yes, and a curtain call at the end of every act," Anna said. "You wait, my next role will bury me in such reviews."

Nina smiled, but would have willingly traded the newspapers' good reviews for one good review from her mother. The words from Mother's last letter haunted her. She had again asked Nina to come home so she could help her daughter repair the damage done to her reputation. In Nina's previous letter, she had said that it was becoming more acceptable for women of good families to enter the theater world. Mother had responded that it wasn't true in California, and that it pained her heart to think of her daughter traipsing through New York as an actress. "Anna, does your mother support your acting career?" Nina asked.

Anna said, "My mother passed several years ago. She never approved of anything about me."

As much as she loved her mother, Nina thought having no mother might be easier. She could continue the career she loved without the pangs of guilt that she felt every time she received a letter from California.

"Here," Anna said, "this will cheer you." She folded another paper to the review page and tossed it to Nina.

Nina peered at the paper. "Well, well. The *Boston Globe*. Their New York correspondent says, 'Miss Temple possesses qualities of a very high order, mental power, intensity, pathos. Her acting in the trial and death scenes were most admirable.' Another good one for me." She grinned at Anna.

"Well, it's off to bed for me," Anna said.

"I'll sit here a bit and bask in my reviews," Nina said. She grinned when Anna wrinkled her nose.

When her roommate had gone, Nina's smile faded. She picked up a letter she'd been rereading when Anna came in. She read it yet again, hoping the words from an old friend had changed or the nuances shifted.

Dear Nina,

What a delight to connect again with your lovely mother! She gave me your address and mentioned you are acting. Do you remember the plays we attended together in Nevada City as girls? We had such fun replaying them in our yard! As much as I would delight in seeing you in a New York play, though, you need to come home. Your mother is elderly now, and desires you to be near her. I am happy for your success, really I am, and so proud of you making it on your own in New York. I just don't believe anyone is being completely honest with you about your mother. She is aging daily and needs you badly. Her health is not what it used to be, and sorrow follows her. I would go so far as to say that living with the Williams family in San Jose may not be in her best interest. My husband and I have purchased a lovely vineyard in Glen Ellen, which is not far from San Francisco. You are welcome to at least come for a long visit. It will give your pride a reason to come west. She needs you, Nina. Please come.

Have you ever done any dramatic readings? I mean, apart from a full play? Miss Angela King, sister of the Unitarian minister Thomas King, has made quite a financial success of giving readings all over California. I know you could do so, too. It would give you a way to showcase your speaking skills without entering the dark world of theater that your mother abhors. I mean, Miss King is a minister's sister so it must be acceptable, right?

Yours very truly,
Polly Overton Warfield
Glen Ellen, California

SHE REMEMBERED POLLY WITH A SMILE. They'd had fun as children, before Father moved the family to Nevada. Hearing from her warmed Nina's heart, but what she said about Mother broke it. For once Nina couldn't find the core of determination her mother insisted all women of the family possessed. Marcus was gone, taking all hope of home and family with him, taking everything but his name. She pictured Emma celebrating the holidays embraced in family support that made Nina fiercely jealous. Top all of that with Mother's need for her, and Nina's life as she knew it was over.

Actresses who had broken from their family and gone on to star onstage filled Nina's thoughts. Had Matilda Herron felt the pull of an aging mother who needed her? Had Fanny Kemble ever thought about how her absence from the heart of the family had affected them? Nina marveled at the resolve it must have taken to leave family behind. Maybe they'd had angry fathers banish them, making it easier to stay away. She hadn't been banished. Instead, her mother was desperate to enfold her wayward daughter in the embrace of family once more.

If she did go home, what would she do? She knew how to be a daughter and stay at home doing whatever Mother wanted. She also knew how to be a wife and visit her mother. Nina did not, however, know how to be an independent woman of her own means while under her mother's roof. And she didn't know if an actress could make a living in California.

Nina remembered her mother's comment that Fanny Kemble had been of a social class that considered divorce to be worse than being an actress. Nina hadn't tiptoed over the line of social indiscretions, she'd leaped over it with both an acting career and a failed marriage. None of that mattered. She'd successfully lived an independent life for three years, and she'd enjoyed it. She wasn't the type of woman who could turn her back on family, however. Her mother, especially, had always been an important part of her life. To imagine Mother alone and unable to care for herself brought tears to Nina's eyes. As much as she may wish away her mother in order to be on the stage, Mother had loved Nina and cared for her without question for her entire life. It was only fair that Nina be with Mother now. Her head knew it to be true, but her heart bled at the prospect of leaving behind what she'd fought to build.

Nina let Polly's letter drop through her fingers. It sailed to the floor, arriving there as soon as despair enveloped her, and the tears began to fall.

DEAR EMMA,

I am besieged on all sides by friends and acquaintances telling me to go home to Mother. I know I have never been a parent, but a sermon I heard at the First Presbyterian Church resonates with me. The pastor advised the congregation that they should educate children, reason with them as they grow, tell them of the pitfalls that await them, then let them go forth into battle. My parents accomplished this. I suppose a parent's job is never done, though. Even though I hover on the brink of turning thirty, my mother strives to guide my life. And disappointing her still dismays me.

So many actresses come from theater families that it is difficult for those of us with no prior connections to be successful. I have worked so hard for what I've achieved. Why can't my mother be proud of that? She offers to forgive me. That angers me and strengthens my resolve to stay. I've done more to deserve pride than forgiveness.

I know actresses who have shaken the dust of New York off their feet and left for London to continue their career. That option is not open to me since Marcus poisons the very air of that city. Moving closer to him appalls me even more than slinking home to Mother in disgrace.

Guilt pricks me, though, when I read that my mother needs me. I know Mother is too stubborn to tell me herself that she is struggling and needs my help. If that is the true situation, however, how can I turn my back?

Yours truly

Nina

22

E mma Beach
Peekskill, April 1875

"Human life is maliciously planned with one principal object in view: to make you do all the different kinds of things you particularly don't want to do."
- Mark Twain, letter to William Dean Howells

Emma stirred the batter in the farmhouse kitchen, helping her mother make a cake to celebrate Violet's eighth birthday, as she mentally composed her next letter to Nina.

Alice rushed into the kitchen from the outside. "There's a carriage coming up the drive," she said. "Are we expecting anyone?"

Mama wrinkled her brow. "Not that I know of." She untied her apron and followed Alice into the parlor.

Emma greased the cake pans and lined them with parchment. It was Cook's day off, so her mother had seized the opportunity to take over the kitchen and bake her daughter a cake. Emma heard voices in the parlor, but was more interested in getting the cake in the oven than learning who was visiting. She poured the batter into the waiting cake pans and turned toward the oven. To her surprise, Kate Bloede stood in the doorway, attractive in a cream-colored gown with bold pink silk stripes to the hem. Her overskirt was decorated in bows from the same pink silk.

"Kate! What a wonderful surprise!" Emma hurried to put the cake in the oven before wrapping Kate in a welcoming hug.

"I knew you wouldn't mind us coming without invitation," Kate said. "Abbott's here, too. He's talking to your mother in the parlor."

Emma untied her apron and wiped a swash of flour off her cheek. "Let's gather a tea tray, shall we?"

Kate helped collect a tray and glasses while Emma made tea.

"You're in luck," Emma said. "We have fresh apple cider cake."

"Oh, I'm glad. Abbott will love it!"

Emma stacked plates and forks on another tray and added the cake. They picked up the trays and headed to the parlor.

Mama sat on her favorite walnut ladies' chair near the fire while Abbott made himself comfortable on the sofa. He wore a respectable dark frock coat and trousers, lending him a sober air, but his face lit up into a smile when Kate entered the room. Alice sat near Mama. Emma and Kate set their trays on the sideboard. Kate poured the tea while Emma cut the cake. Violet slipped into the room, cut herself a piece of cake, and perched on a chair, trying very hard to balance the cake plate on her lap as she ate.

"You're in for a treat," Kate told Abbott as Emma handed him a plate of cake.

He took a bite and closed his eyes, making appreciative sounds as Kate settled next to him on the couch with her own cake.

"These are last year's apples," Alice said. "You'll have to come back after the fall harvest. The cake's even better then."

Emma sat in a chair near her mother with tea. She'd eat her share of cake later. Right now, she was too curious about their visit. "So you came to Peekskill for the day?" she asked. Her words were directed at Kate, but her eyes were on Abbott. He was the sort of man who seemed comfortable no matter where he was, art gallery or parlor.

His eyes lit up when his gaze fell on Kate, and Emma wished someone would look at her like that.

"Yes, we did." Kate smiled at Abbott. He smiled back. To Emma, it seemed as if her friends had forgotten the rest of the world existed. Kate turned back to Emma. "Abbott has asked me to marry him. I said yes. We wanted to tell you together." Another shared smile.

"Congratulations!" Mama said.

Alice echoed the sentiment.

Emma said, "Oh, I'm so happy for the both of you."

Mama and Alice directed the conversation to wedding plans, asking about the church, the dress, the date, and the cake. Emma was happy for her friend, but she also felt a wave of jealousy that she tried to brush away. What would it be like to love and be loved like Kate? To glow with happiness like that, knowing you've made the right choice for your life?

When they'd finished their cake and tea, Emma offered to take Kate and Abbott on a walk around the farm. They set off through the apple orchard. The sun shone through the new leaves on the trees, making them glow with life. Emma considered how she would paint the leaves and still show the glow of the sun.

Abbott said, "What stunning light. I love the colors and vibrancy of the country. I grew up in New Hampshire near Mt. Monadnock. Someday I'll live there again and paint every day." He walked beside Kate, his hand straying toward her as if he wanted to hold her hand or tuck it under his arm.

"It must be lovely," Emma said. Abbott's smile was a ray of sunshine. It dazzled Emma as she imagined someone smiling at her in that way.

Kate said, "Tell Emma what we're going to do first, though, before you have a chance to paint your mountain."

Abbott stopped walking and faced Emma. "We are going to Paris. I will study portrait painting there, at the École des Beaux-Arts. There's more money in portrait painting than landscapes."

Kate laughed. "Abbott's even been painting pet portraits. Can you imagine someone paying for a portrait of a pet?"

Emma smiled, but noticed that Abbott's demeanor dimmed. "I think Paris sounds wonderful," she said, and was rewarded with a smile that made her heart leap as she imagined it was for her alone.

They walked back to the house, Abbott between the two women. Kate chattered about Paris. Emma felt her gaze drawn back to Abbott again and again as he responded to Kate's comments about Paris. There was such affection in his smile.

When they reached the house, Abbott turned to look out over the orchard toward the Hudson River. "When I visit such a beautiful place, I am glad for the main function of my life—my painting. Art is a land of immortal beauty where every step leads toward God." He turned away from the view to face Kate. "And I am the luckiest man in the world to have met my feminine ideal, an innocent soul—poetic and graceful, and so fond of philosophic reading and discussion. We shall be perfect together."

Kate's face glowed when she looked at Abbott. Emma fought jealousy. She was happy for her friend, but it couldn't be wrong to want such devotion for herself, too.

"My dear," Abbott said to Kate, "would you mind if I made a few sketches?"

"Of course not. It's what you do, after all." Kate sent him scampering off, pulling a sketchpad and pencil out of an interior coat pocket.

Emma and Kate settled themselves in the garden chairs. "Tell me everything about him," Emma said.

"It's interesting to watch Abbott paint," Kate said. "He works for three days on a painting. He claims if he works longer than that, he ruins it. On a good day, he takes a break after that and heads for the woods, or anyplace in nature, anywhere to get away from the painting itself. His students come in the afternoon, so he has them copy his work-in-progress while he's gone. Do you remember doing that at Cooper Union?"

"I do," Emma said.

"When Abbott gets back, all refreshed from his walk, he spends another three days or so working on the painting. He calls it his three-day shove, and he usually he ends up with multiple copies of the same painting, all in different stages of being finished."

Kate stopped talking, and Emma considered her words. "Is he teaching the students, then?" she asked. "Or is he unsure of his talent?"

Kate frowned. "We all question ourselves, do we not? Abbot has periodic moods he calls sick disgust. Nothing is ever good enough at these times." She looked off into the forest as if speaking to the trees. "He had a landscape painting hanging in a gallery and contacted the gallery owner directly to ask him to bring it back to the studio because Abbott had a few ideas how to make it better."

"That's odd," Emma said. "Can you imagine Sam telling the publisher to return copies of *The Innocents Abroad* because he wanted to change a few things? Creative works are never finished. I'd expect a master painter to know that."

Kate nodded. "He does. Most of the time. This time, though, he became obsessed. The painting had already been sold and shipped to the customer. Abbott went to the railroad station and found it, opened the crate, and fixed the painting right there on the platform!"

Emma stared at Kate, unsure what to say.

Kate flushed at Emma's stare. "He says he must paint when God inspires him. He has dark moods, Emma, and needs me to support him through them. Abbott's truly a gifted artist. The creative ones are most susceptible to periods of oddness, you know."

Emma thought of Nina with her stated goal of supporting her husband's career. Being needed was all Emma had ever wanted, but could she survive a neediness like that? And if she let go of that dream, what was left for her? She thought of Sam Clemens, the most creative writer she knew. He'd certainly been depressed when his son died, but that was understandable. His daughter, Suzy. was now two, and Livy had just given birth to another daughter. Maybe it was Livy who kept Sam grounded. Even so, Abbott exhibited much more alarming behaviors than she'd ever seen in Sam. "Kate, he sounds like he might need more help than you can give him."

"He can be lovely, funny and charming." A private smile, not intended for Emma, lit her face.

Emma's brow furrowed as she worried for her friend. Kate had always been the life in the room, the one everyone wanted to be around. Emma ached that she was so eager to tie herself to a man like Abbott Thayer. "So you are so dazzled by his greatness that you agreed to marry him?" She tried for a light, teasing tone, but even to her ears it sounded sarcastic.

Kate's eyes widened. "I love him, Emma, and I know that marriage is not all roses. At least I'm aware of what the dark times will entail, and I know we can work through them together. After the wedding, we'll go to Paris for four years." Her words trailed off.

"Another setting might help his moods? Is that what you think?" Emma tried for a neutral tone but sounded like a disapproving parent to her own ears. Surely Kate must have doubts. Otherwise, she would still be gushing about marrying Abbott.

"It's his decision to go to Paris. He's quite excited about it. I'm happy for him to have this opportunity, and thrilled that he's asked me to be part of it."

Emma nodded, trying to swallow her misgivings. "I'm happy for you, Kate." Something in her tone or expression must have revealed Emma's doubt.

Kate sat up straight. Her eyes blazed. "I don't need your approval. Do you believe we came here because we need your blessing?"

"Kate, you're my dearest friend. I only want you to be sure."

Kate's eyes narrowed. "I've chosen him." Her chin jutted like a recalcitrant teenager.

Emma said, "You talk more of his erratic behavior during his mood swings than you do of the happiness that you share. I'm concerned. When something that no one will speak of gets in the way of a relationship, it can end badly for all involved."

"You have no idea what you're talking about."

Didn't she? Her parents had seemed a loving couple, united in their affection for each other. Until Violet's birth, the birth everyone knew about but would not discuss. For eight years now, her father's face had been locked into a grim expression. It seems that in his eyes her mother had done nothing right since long before Violet was born. Her mother's cheery words seem forced. Everyone ignored the truth that lurked beneath them all, ready to break the family apart. What would it be like for Kate when she had children? What kind of a father would Abbott be?

Her silence lasted too long. Kate stood and brushed at her skirt. "I've done what I've come here to do. I have no reason to remain."

"You came to tell me of your marriage in person, at least. Thank you for that." Emma rose and followed Kate into the house. "I will miss you while you are in Paris. We'll have to see each other as much as possible before then."

Spoken as they were, tossed at Kate's retreating back, Emma's words rang of desperation.

Kate walked right through the house, past Emma's mother's startled face, and out the front door. Abbott stood in the yard, madly sweeping his pencil across the page. Kate took his arm and directed him to the waiting carriage. He climbed aboard before she did and bent over his sketch. Kate whirled to face Emma.

"Who do you think you are to comment on a relationship like this? You've never been married or had anything more than a school-girl crush on a man much older than you. You pronounce judgment on a fine man without getting to know him." Hurt and fury battled in her eyes.

"Kate, please. What kind of a friend would I be if I didn't voice my concerns and it all went very wrong?"

"What kind of a friend assumes failure when she doesn't have all the information? Oh, maybe one whose own relationships are safe?"

Emma recoiled. "Safe?"

"You stay here with your parents and your little sisters, hiding in the country all summer. Then you hide in your studio all winter. You profess a close relationship with Mrs. Larrowe, who lives in the same town but never visits you. What do you know of the passion between a man and a woman? Of what that passion can overcome?"

Emma felt her face blanch and her head grow dizzy. "I only tried to be a friend."

But Kate stormed to the stage and climbed in, slamming the door before the driver could get to it. He jumped back up to his seat and clucked at the horse to start him moving out of the yard.

Emma stood and watched until the dust had settled as if no one had ever come.

The front door opened. Mama said, "Emma? They're gone? What happened?"

"I only tried to be a friend," Emma repeated, agony twisting the words.

EMMA'S WISH TO SEE more of Kate before her wedding proved to be nothing more than a wisp of thought. Kate wrote, but filled her letters with vindictive words that made Emma cry.

DEAR NINA,

I've not needed your sage advice so much since Sam Clemens married Livy. My heart is bereft. Kate fought with me in person, then hissed and spat at me in letters for a month. In the end, I was not invited to her wedding. I read about it on the society page and wept. Once again, proof that I am completely inept at relationships, starting with misreading Sam completely. The most important relationships in my life are in ruins. My parents fight with each other and ignore me. Kate spurned me and is gone. My siblings are more interested in friends and school than in a sad older sister who will never be married. I have such a hole in my heart. Pull myself up, I can hear you say. If I only could. I swear I will lock myself in my room and never attempt another friend. You say I can't succeed if I don't try. I say I won't feel pain if I don't fail.

Someday you can say you knew Emma Beach before she hid herself away and became a painter of reckoning. You can stand in for me at gallery shows and tell everyone how my broken heart unleashed my talent. Such tragedy tugs at people's hearts and inspires them to buy. My tears will elevate the value of my painting faster than any class.

   Emma

23

N ina Larowe
    To California, June 1875

"It is hard to make railroading pleasant in any country. It is too
tedious. Stage-coaching is infinitely more delightful."
- Mark Twain, The Innocents Abroad

The train chugged west out of Omaha a year later, leaving white
clouds of steam behind like a dotted line against the endless blue sky.
Prairie stretched to the horizon on both sides, bisected by the tracks
that ran hundreds of miles without a curve, as if Nina's mother had
created it for the specific purpose of bringing her thirty-two-year-old
daughter home efficiently and in comfort. The Transcontinental Railroad would have her to California in four days. Four days of capitula-
tion after a year of stumbling in the dark, trying to find a way, any
way, out.

Even on her darkest day, Nina never said the words aloud, but
they hammered her brain over and over as they had since before
Christmas—It was better for everyone if the actress abandoned by

her husband returned to her mother where she could be hidden from public view.

The velvet upholstery cradled her in the most comfortable train seat she'd ever experienced. When Mrs. Sara Leppincott, an acquaintance who was an actress and women's rights advocate, approached Nina about sharing a Pullman section on the westward route, Nina had agreed. Sara had traveled the route before, and told Nina that if she didn't have a prearranged travel companion by the time they reached Omaha, the porter would assign one to her. No one wanted to share a section with a stranger, especially when the seats were transformed into a pair of curtained berths, one above the other, at night.

Sara, though, spent her first hours of the trip in the parlor car, chatting and having tea as if she were royalty deigning to honor the Union Pacific Railroad with her presence. Nina remained in her seat, preferring to be alone with her thoughts.

With a copy of Louisa May Alcott's *Little Women* open on her lap, Nina stared out the window. The luxury of the Pullman car freed her mind to consider topics other than her comfort. Thus she fixated on her failed marriage, damaged reputation, and stalled acting career.

Sara Leppincott slid into her seat, facing Nina. "Nina, dear, they'll call us for supper soon. You'll be amazed by the dining car." Sara affected the demeanor of an experienced traveler, but Nina knew she'd only traveled by Pullman once before.

"I'm sure it's marvelous," Nina said.

"Are you reading?" Sara waved a hand at *Little Women*. "You know, Louisa May Alcott wrote her first children's story for the magazine *The Little Pilgrim* that my husband and I started."

It wasn't necessary for Sara to impress Nina as if she was just another passenger, but Nina didn't say so. She picked up the book. "I met Louisa at a gymnastics school I attended one summer. I've never read her book, though." She tapped the page. "Jo and Meg have both refused offers of marriage. Very smart of them."

Sara uttered an unladylike snort. "I don't disagree. Writing about rights for women alienates most husbands, and mine is no exception. Yours disliked your career so much he actually left the country.."

Nina returned to looking out the window. "It's true he's in London." Gossiping about her failures held no appeal.

The porter came up the aisle, telling passengers it was time for supper.

"Thank you. We'll be right there." Sara waved him away without looking at him. The Black porter tipped his hat and turned to the men across the aisle.

"I'm not hungry at the moment, Sara. You go ahead." Nina waved her companion away in much the way Sara had dismissed the porter. Ignoring the book in her lap, Nina stared out the window as Sara walked down the aisle to the dining car. Dusk fell over the prairie with glorious colors fading to purple and black. The problem was that she enjoyed the stage too much. The variety of people associated with the theater gave spice to life and provided a myriad of interesting experiences. She missed it.

THE NEXT DAY, the route ran alongside the Platte River as it cut its way through the green of the plains. Nina spotted an occasional antelope and a small flock of plovers. By the time the train stopped at Cheyenne just before supper, her heart lifted to see the Black Hills above Cheyenne, and the Rocky Mountains in the distance. New Yorkers didn't know mountains, and the Sierra Nevada was still to come.

The train resumed its journey before supper service was complete. Nina left the dining car as soon as she finished eating, and let Sara chatter to the other passengers. Monstrous boulders crowded the tracks and huge chasms yawned beneath. Snow-capped peaks stood sentinel over it all, darkening as night fell with mountain swiftness. Nina closed the curtain around her bunk and Sara's above her. For the first time since she'd accepted the idea of returning West, she felt at peace.

. . .

TUESDAY BROUGHT STILL A DIFFERENT LANDSCAPE. For the whole day, the train steamed through a vast barren basin with nothing to see but sagebrush and alkaline dust. The melancholy feel of the view wasn't helping her mood, so she once again opened *Little Women*. The character of Jo felt the pressure to be like her mother, and Nina identified with that. Jo also desired her own career.

"Don't do it, Jo," Nina whispered. "Don't try a career." After all, personal happiness was fleeting. A mother's expectations will always win. Better to accept that and move on.

Before noon, the train passed the rocky ridge that designated the Continental Divide. All the rivers from now on would flow ahead of them to the Pacific Ocean instead of behind them all the way to the Atlantic. It felt like progress.

Nina once again laid her book across her stomach and found herself smiling over snippets of memories from her childhood. She remembered her first kitten, saved from a litter the servant girl had been instructed to drown in the river. That same servant girl had dressed up a couch pillow to serve as a doll for Nina, until her father bought her a proper one. One time Nina had asked her aunt to button her apron. The aunt refused to do so until Nina said, "Please." Nina found someone else to button the apron and crowed about it later to her aunt. Her mother had not been pleased.

By the time the view outside her window changed to green hills, then mountains, then narrow rugged canyons, Nina's memories had skipped over her marriage and turned to her brief acting career. She slept deeply that night and dreamed of the New York stage.

THE NEXT MORNING Nina awoke as the train passed Promontory Summit, where the great Transcontinental Railroad had been completed. Passengers had to disembark and change trains since this was as far as the Union Pacific Railroad would take their Pullman cars. Porters moved their luggage to the Central Pacific Railroad train, with Sara complaining the whole time about how slow they were. The Central Pacific's silver palace car wasn't as nice as the Pullman, but Nina knew she'd have thought it grand had she not just come a thousand miles in a Pullman car.

AT BREAKFAST ON THURSDAY, the train passed the old mining town of Humboldt City, Nevada. Even though it was abandoned and falling into ruin, it reminded Nina of her time in Virginia City, two hundred miles to the south. To everyone else, passing through Nevada meant only that they were entering the mountains. After a time, they entered the valley of the Truckee River, flowing below the majestic snow-covered peaks of the Sierra Nevada. To Nina's surprise, the familiar vista brought tears to her eyes. These mountains held some fond memories. Sara affected exclamations of delight as if she'd never been through these mountains before.

Nina realized she'd come a long way since leaving the West of her childhood, and not just in miles. When she and Marcus had traveled to New York as newlyweds, she'd been dazzled by dreams her mother had created for her—mostly of marriage and children. But her mother's view of a happy marriage with children was not to be Nina's fate. Nina would hold her head up high and make her own way as she had for four years since Marcus took his leave. She refused to sponge off relatives or so-called friends who might smile at her in public and complain behind the door. That didn't mean she couldn't enjoy visiting her mother.

Mother had restrained herself when it came to Nina's marriage. She'd never blamed Nina for Marcus's departure. Acting was different. It didn't matter to her mother that Nina was thirty-two years old. A daughter was never too old for scolding. She must make her mother understand how important it was for her to continue to be independent.

The train passed Truckee at noon, chugging heavily as it passed through tunnels and emerged at the Summit. Passengers were rewarded by the wondrous beauty of Donner Lake, nestled under lofty peaks amidst the soft whispers of the pine trees.

"It's all downhill from here," Sara said with a wink.

Nina smiled at the joke. It was, indeed, all downhill as the train swept through the foothills into the Sacramento Valley. She and Sara chatted about acting and people they both knew as the day lengthened. At sunset, they arrived in the city of Sacramento.

The passengers disembarked from the Central Pacific train for the last time. "One more night before we go our separate ways," Sara said, brushing the train's coal dust from her skirt. Tomorrow would see them in San Francisco, where Sara would stay. Nina would continue to San Jose to join her mother.

First thing in the morning, Sara and Nina boarded a Western Pacific Railroad train for the short jaunt to Oakland's Long Wharf on the San Francisco Bay. From there, they took a ferry to the city. San Francisco Bay looked nothing like it had when Nina had sailed into it in 1863 as her family returned from Valparaiso, where her father had been American consul for four years..

On shore, Nina hugged Sara. "Goodbye, my friend. I couldn't have made this trip without you."

"I enjoyed it," Sara said. "Let me know if you want to attend any of my readings."

They exchanged addresses before Nina turned away and directed the porter to move her luggage to the train bound for San Jose. One more train. Scarcely an hour left in a journey that had taken four days physically and an eon emotionally.

The train stopped in San Jose in a cloud of steam and hissing. Nina disembarked. Standing alone on the platform, she inhaled deeply.

"Nina!" Her mother's unmistakable shout of delight made Nina smile.

She turned to see her mother for the first time in seven years. She saw a sixty-nine-year-old woman with gray hair and sadness in her eyes. Her dress was an old one, softened by wear and washing. Mama leaned heavily on a cane and moved slowly toward her daughter, wincing as she did so. Then she smiled.

Guilt washed over Nina. How could she have been so selfish as to consider leaving her mother to handle the last years of her life alone?

Mother was family, and family would have to fill the hole in Nina's heart where the New York stage had once lived.

"I've missed you, Mother," she said, closing the distance between them.

Her mother folded Nina into the embrace that had always soothed everything from a scraped knee to a broken heart.

mma Beach
Peekskill, September 1875

"We should be careful to get out of an experience
only the wisdom that is in it...."
- Mark Twain,, Pudd'nhead Wilson's New Calendar

Emma paced the art gallery, focusing on appearing relaxed and confident while her stomach roiled with nerves. The show had been her idea, she reminded herself. All summer she'd immersed herself in her art as a way to stop missing Kate and Abbott, to stop thinking of Abbott's smile. As a result, she'd accumulated a good stack of finished paintings, mostly of flowers Alice had brought her.

As if summoned by her thoughts, Alice came up to Emma. She held a spent rose that had dropped a petal. "I'm picking a few sad ones out of the vases," Alice said. Her eyes shone as she scanned the colorful bouquets, set on tables in front of the artwork that depicted them. "Beauty in two mediums. This was a great idea, Emma. I'm glad the gallery owner remembered you. It's been well over a year since you sold that painting at Abbott's show."

"I'm memorable, I guess," Emma said with a smile. Alice sparkled naturally, like Kate did. Emma fingered the colorful pansy scarf Kate had given her. Her new green dress set it off perfectly, like leaves in Alice's garden.

"I wish David could have come," Alice said. "He wanted to, but he's been feeling poorly for a couple of weeks."

"He'd be here if he could, Alice. I'm sure he's imagining you enjoying the moment."

People milled around the gallery, admiring Alice's flower arrangements and Emma's paintings. They'd already sold a few of each, too. Emma didn't tell Alice that it had taken some effort to convince the galley owner to include flowers in the show. Emma had been determined to give her sister something of her own. During the six months their parents had been in Europe, Emma and Alice had let their creativity loose—Emma on canvas and Alice in the garden. Upon Mama's return, however, the focus had returned to marriage. It was a testament to David's feelings for Alice that he'd endured Mama's relentless pressure for the last year.

Emma's thoughts had been far from marriage, far from pleasing her mother. She'd been close to her mother before the cruise to the Holy Land, and grown closer to her father while they were on the cruise without Mama. Since then, though, Mama would only talk about marriage or Reverend Beecher. Neither subject appealed to Emma.

Reverend Beecher had been cleared of all charges in two church proceedings and civil court over the summer. Emma was just glad it was over. Now, though, her parents lived behind a wall of formal coldness. Papa spent as much time as possible traveling or visiting friends, leaving Mama to keep up the illusion of a happy home, which would be easier if she didn't spend so much time next door at the Beecher's. Emma hated it, and hated the heated words that were captured behind tight lips when she entered the room. By harvest time, public interest in the Beecher-Tilton affair had faded, but Emma still spent many days sitting beneath her ancient apple tree, watching blossoms slowly turn to fruit.

Mama hadn't even come to Emma and Alice's art show. She'd claimed she had to stay at the farm with Violet, who was too young to attend such an affair. Violet had been insulted. She loved spending time with her sisters.

"I wish Violet was here," Emma told Alice.

"She'd love all the flowers, wouldn't she?" Alice said.

Emma also wished Kate and Abbott could be there. It had been three months since they'd married and left for Paris. Three months without a letter. Emma knew they were in love and busy setting up their life together, but she didn't even have their address to write to them.

A noisy urgency broke the serenity of the show. Emma turned toward the door in time to see a disheveled man gesticulating wildly to the gallery owner, whose look of disapproval changed with the man's words. The gallery owner scanned the room until he spotted Alice and Emma. The gallery owner headed in their direction. Emma's heart plummeted. It must be bad news.

"So sorry, Miss Beach," the gallery owner said. "I hate to interrupt your show, but this man says his message is urgent." The messenger reached out, handing an envelope to Alice.

Alice's hand shook as she took the envelope. "It's from Mrs. Livingston. It must be congratulations? Why isn't it from David?" She opened the envelope and unfolded the note inside. Letting out a loud cry, Alice slumped to the floor.

Emma reached for her sister, but it had happened too fast. Alice knelt on the floor, consumed with sobs. Emma grabbed the note.

ALICE, *my dear, I'm sorry to ruin your gallery exhibition, but you need to hear this from me first. Our darling David died this morning. He didn't want you to know he'd caught smallpox, so he just said he wasn't feeling well. He was going to tell you after the show. I told him he was working too closely with that Smallpox Hospital.*

No, I won't dishonor him by speaking ill of his cause.

Yours in grief,

Clara Livingston

EMMA REELED IN SHOCK. David had been at the farm just two weeks ago. She remembered him talking about slow progress with fundraising for the nursing school, and about helping with the patients. She hadn't considered the risk to his life. But now she had to help Alice. She whipped off her pansy scarf and handed it to her sister. Alice buried her face in it. A nearby bouquet featured a spray of lavender. Emma seemed to remember Alice mentioning the calming properties of lavender. She took the spray out of the arrangement and wrapped Alice's fingers around it.

The patrons in the gallery began to leave, confused by the display of emotion from the flower artist. The gallery owner stood by the door, thanking them for coming and apologizing for the swift conclusion to the evening. He locked the door behind the last patron and turned the shop sign to *closed*. Stopping by the refreshment table of tea and cookies, he poured a glass of water. "Is she going to be alright?" he said to Emma, putting the glass of water on a table near a chair.

"In time," Emma said. She helped Alice up, but her sister seemed unable to stand on her own. Emma led her to the chair, where she slumped, still sobbing. Emma offered her the water. Alice folded the lavender and scarf into one hand so she could take the water. Emma knelt beside the chair with her arm around Alice's shoulders. It was several minutes before Alice could control her breathing.

"Take your time," Emma murmured. "You've had quite a shock."

Emma's mind reeled. Should she take Alice to the Livingston's house? Or home to the farm? Maybe they could stay in the city tonight.

Alice dried her eyes with Emma's scarf. "I want to go home."

"Home?" Emma asked. "To the farm?"

Alice nodded. "To Mama." She took a deep, ragged breath.

"That's what we'll do," Emma said.

The gallery owner called them a carriage. "You can catch an

earlier train than you originally planned," he said as he helped them into the carriage.

Emma nodded. She poured cold water on the scarf and used it to dab Alice's red eyes. It was a quiet train ride to Peekskill. Alice broke into tears several times, controlling herself only with a great deal of effort. Emma held her hand and said nothing.

Every disappointment in Emma's life paled. Losing Sam to Livy seemed trivial. Abbott and Kate moving to Europe was nothing. Alice's loss of David would devastate her forever.

THE NEXT MORNING, Alice stayed in her room. Emma went outside, where the brilliance of fall seemed oblivious to her sister's pain. Her mother came out the kitchen door.

"How's Alice?" Emma asked.

"She wouldn't eat breakfast, but she's stopped crying. Poor thing, her eyes are so red." Mama sighed. "Poor David."

"She'll recover," Emma said. "Right?"

Mama nodded. "It will take time."

Dear Nina,

My sister's fiance has died, and her heart with him. I'm sure she will heal with time and rebuild herself around her loss. She will never be the same, though, having loved so deeply and lost. I know a bit about that, although in my experience the love was one-sided and he didn't die. One day I hope that she is more glad than grieved that she had David's love, and I hope she will once again find solace in her garden.

Her grief echoes in my heart, and my painting shows it. None of this recent work will ever see a gallery, but it is the medicine I need to support Alice.

Yours,

Emma

25

N ina Larowe
San Jose, California, January 1877

*"When people do not respect us we are sharply offended; yet deep down in
his private heart no man much respects himself."*
- Mark Twain, Following the Equator

Dear Emma,

*I am embarrassed that it's been so long since I've written to you. I've
missed your letters and hope to rekindle our correspondence now that I am
settled. The past few years have been a turmoil for me.*

I'm not sure where to begin.

*Maybe how I got here isn't important. Suffice it to say that I am now a
resident of California. My mother and I currently live in the house of Ed
Williams, husband of my late sister Emily. She says she's here to help Ed
with Emily's four children. Ed, though, married Fanny four years ago.
Fanny dotes on their sickly son and leaves Emily's children to Mother. But I
don't want this letter to be a diatribe about Fanny.*

*My darkest days descended as I thought about reuniting with my
mother. I had failed at marriage, motherhood, and career. How I dreaded*

the disappointment and disapproval in my mother's face, but when Mother spoke the words welcoming me home, I knew she didn't mean to San Jose, where I'd never been before.

I once thought to leave my family upon marriage and start anew with my husband. My efforts to make that new life happen tainted my self image as well as my relationships. Upon my return to the land of my childhood, I am able to see this with clarity and realize how much I am like my mother.

Please write soon and tell me what is happening with you.

Yours truly,

Nina

"I'll SEE you in a few days," Nina said to her mother as she left the Williams house on Third and Reed. She could hear Fanny's footsteps headed toward the front door from somewhere deep in the house, and she didn't want to miss her train. Nina swiftly closed the door and descended the front steps.

The vision of her nieces and nephews on those steps when she first met them had stayed in Nina's mind. As she walked to mail the letter to Emma Beach, she recalled how Fanny had lined them up on the steps to meet Nina, as if they were household staff. Nina had stopped at the foot of the steps to gaze at her late sister's children. Edith, the oldest, was thirteen and her next sister, Nina's namesake, a year younger. They stood on the top step, their faces carved from stone. Nina's heart ached for these girls who had lost their mother so young. The twins, Emily and Ed, were seven and wouldn't remember their mother well. Their faces, though, were as somber as their sisters'. Fanny stood on the bottom step with her son, Waldo, in her arms. He seemed small for two, obviously the apple of his mother's eye.

Fanny said, "Welcome to San Jose, Mrs. Larowe." The children with the hollow eyes murmured polite greetings.

"Delighted to be here. Can Auntie Nina get hugs from her nieces and her nephew?" Nina smiled and opened her arms.

The four children stepped forward and gave her the most dutiful hugs she'd ever received.

Mother said, "Your auntie has traveled all the way across the country to stay with us."

Fanny had made a tsking sound that Nina had chosen to ignore. She handed Waldo to Edith and dismissed the children, who disappeared inside the house. Nina and her mother followed Fanny into the parlor.

"Your bags will be taken to your mother's room," Fanny told Nina. "We have no other place for you."

"That will be fine," Nina said. Mama had begged her to come. Clearly Fanny had not been as enthusiastic.

They sat on the parlor chairs. Nina would have loved a cup of tea, but was not comfortable enough to ask.

"So Mrs. Larrowe, did you know your husband has changed his name?" Fanny asked.

"He's still in London, as far as I know," Nina said. "He hasn't contacted me." She fought to hide her reluctance to speak of Marcus.

"He calls himself Alphonso Loisette now." Fanny's smug smile waited for Nina's reaction.

Nina said, "What a ridiculous name. I suppose it's no different than my acting under the name Helen Temple on the New York stage, but at least I didn't choose such a pompous sobriquet. I suspect he is hiding from those who disapprove of him plagiarizing much of what he spouts to audiences. At any rate, I refuse to call him Alphonso just like I refuse to refer to Samuel Clemens as Mark Twain." She met Fanny's eyes with a steely glare.

"We don't need to speak of him," Mother said. "Why don't we go upstairs to freshen up, Nina?"

They left Fanny in the parlor and went upstairs. Nina marveled at her mother's ability to live in the same house with such an unpleasant woman.

Mother must have known what Nina was thinking. With a shrug of apology, she said, "My grandchildren live here."

"They look miserable," Nina said. "Maybe we can take them on a picnic."

Her mother fidgeted, and her eyes dropped to the floor. "Fanny makes the plans for them."

Since that day, Nina had been largely unsuccessful in her campaign to cheer the children. This afternoon, to her relief, she would escape the Williams household for a few days for a visit with her friend Polly at Ten Oaks Ranch in Glen Ellen.

Polly picked Nina up at the train station, and they drove through picturesque vineyards, their grapes ripening in the sun, to the Warfield home among the oak trees.

"I'm so glad you're here, Nina," Polly said as the horses plodded along the road. "Jacob spends most of his time in his medical practice or in Sacramento. He's the State Assemblyman from Sonoma County." Her voice rang with pride in her husband.

"So who takes care of the ranch?" Nina asked. The stunning view reminded her of Emma's description of the Peekskill farm.

"Why me, of course," Polly said. "Right now I'm working with rootstock to resist phylloxera in the grapes, and experimenting with varietal wines. It's fun."

Nina nodded. "Sounds like you've learned a lot." Polly's independence and pride in her work reminded Nina of her mother saying she needed to have something of her own. Polly had certainly managed that.

They pulled up in front of the house, and Polly turned to face Nina. "I have one more surprise for you."

Intrigued, Nina followed her friend into the house. In the parlor, a familiar face waited for them. Polly bounced with excitement as she led Nina inside. "It's Sara Leppincott!"

Nina smiled at her travel companion. "Sara! Nice to see you again."

Sara squeezed Nina's hand. "Polly has been gracious enough to offer her parlor to plan a speaking tour for us."

Nina remembered their conversation two years ago on the train and flushed with guilt at her eagerness to plan anything that would take her away from San Jose. "That's wonderful, Polly, thank you."

Polly waved to a servant to bring in a tea tray. The three women sat down to plan a tour of dramatic readings. Sara and Nina debated pieces to be included, and Polly helped plan a route. By the end of the afternoon, Polly had already composed letters to send to various venues in the chosen town to set up the tour.

"I will have to find somewhere to store my things," Nina said, thinking of the trunks crowding her mother's bedroom. "My current situation is not ideal."

"Why not here?" Polly said. "I have plenty of buildings that could house a few trunks."

Nina nodded. It would be a relief to have her trunks safe from Fanny's complaints. "Thank you," she said.

THAT SUMMER, Nina engaged a theater in San Jose so that she and Polly could practice the readings they would do on tour. Polly spread the news of the event, so a large and interested audience attended. Polly even brought Nina's mother. Fanny declined to attend.

Stepping onstage in front of an audience again felt like coming home to a house full of family that smelled of gingerbread. Nina's heart hurt from being so full of joy. She and Sara were of a similar mind about performing. Both individual pieces and those they performed together generated appreciative applause. When the curtain came down, Nina's euphoria carried her through a celebratory dinner at the home of one of Polly's friends. By the time she and Mother arrived home to the Williams house, though, her heart was heavy.

"I hate leaving you here, Mother," Nina said.

"My grandchildren are here," Mother said. "I am content."

So in October, Nina kissed her mother goodbye and got on the train. She met Sara in San Francisco, and they embarked on their tour.

26

E

mma Beach
Peekskill, October 1877

"Independence...is loyalty to one's best self and principles, and this is often disloyalty to the general idols and fetishes."
- Mark Twain's Notebook

Emma read Nina's letter sitting under the apple tree, its laden branches full of ripening red fruit with pale pink stripes. She tried to maintain her anger at Nina's long silence, at her lack of detail about that lost time, but relief and pleasure at receiving the letter over-whelmed her. Nina had accomplished several successful roles.

Over the past two years, Emma had spent many troubled hours watching Alice's new independence crumble under grief. Alice had nearly worn out every dark dress in Emma's closet as she walked the farm alone in all weather. Violet, now ten, was becoming a miniature version of Alice before David, following Mama everywhere and mimicking her actions.

Recently, Mama had resumed discussing possible husbands for Emma and Alice. Alice left the room whenever the subject was raised, and Emma refused to believe her happiness and fulfillment lay with someone else, especially a man. After all, Sam had broken her heart and Abbott couldn't have it. Nina had done better for herself without her husband. Emma would do so, too. In order to manage that, she'd need to accomplish something worthy of respect. Not something her mother told her was good, but something Emma felt good about. She'd made a beginning, with two successful art shows. Now she just needed to keep at it.

Stuffing Nina's letter in her pocket, Emma went inside the house. Her mother and sisters had gone to visit Mrs. Beecher, and William was off with Papa somewhere. The only sound came from the kitchen, where Cook hummed and rattled pans. Emma made her way to the studio.

Looking through her unfinished pieces, Emma found one of the grassy area near her apple tree. She remembered the day she'd painted it. The August sun had browned the grass, and a small brown rabbit hid there. The similar tones in grass and rabbit made it hard to see the animal and hard to paint it so that a viewer could both see the rabbit and appreciate its ability to hide. Emma had given up in frustration.

She pulled it out and put it on her easel. Ignoring the problematic rabbit, she painted in the sketched apple tree, backlighting its late-summer leaves to highlight the burgeoning fruit that appeared as bright spots of warm color against the cooler tones of the foliage. The tree drew the viewer's eye to the side, away from the rabbit, but its branches curved down, bringing the eye back to the rabbit. Her teachers at Cooper Union would have approved of the composition. Emma added depth to her work by painting foliage behind the tree, but kept the tree the focus of the work. The brush in her hand flew with confidence across the canvas as she recalled lessons in texture and tone. Emma firmly kept her mind on the lessons, and shut out the people she'd experienced the lessons with. She wasn't ready to open her heart to that extent.

Lost in her work, she didn't realize how much time had passed until she heard Violet's clattering footsteps in the hallway. Her mother's and sisters' voices were indistinct as they walked past the studio toward the parlor. Violet paused outside the closed studio door. Emma smiled.

"You can come in," she called.

The door opened and her wide-eyed sister entered. "You're painting." Her tone was one of awe, not a question.

"I don't know if it will be any good." Emma winced. She needed to strive for a positive attitude. "I'm working on it." It was the best she could do with that blasted rabbit staring at her.

"I like the colors in the apples," Violet said. "Coming to tea?"

"No, I'll stay and work on this a bit longer." The door closed behind Violet as Emma turned back to the painting. Violet's compliment made her heart sing. It was so important, a few nice words from someone you loved.

When Emma's back began to ache from standing, she cleaned her brushes and put away the paint. She felt better than she had in a year. Painting with cheery colors helped, as did Violet's approval. She left her studio with her head spinning, full of ideas for subjects to paint.

LATER THAT MONTH, Emma and her family went to the Beecher's cottage for a small party. It was a time for celebrating the harvest and for saying goodbye to summer friends before the Beechers and the Beaches returned to Brooklyn for the winter. Emma picked up an apple pie she'd baked without waiting for the Northern Spy variety from her tree, which didn't ripen until November. "Alice? Are you bringing the cake?"

Alice had asked Cook to teach her how to make apple cider cake, and she was pleased with the results. "I've got it right here," she said, patting a cloth-covered plate.

"I don't need to carry anything," Violet declared. "I helped with everything." A wave of her hand indicated the entire kitchen.

The sisters walked uphill with their parents and brother, passing the massive mansion Reverend Beecher was building to replace his current cottage. "It'll be quite the marvel," her brother William said.

"Quite the eyesore, no doubt," Papa said. Mama glared at him. He rubbed the back of his neck like he always did when he wanted to say more but didn't dare.

Outside his barn, Reverend Beecher had placed baskets of apples, potatoes, and corn. Vases of flowers grown by Reverend Beecher graced the tables set up inside the barn. A vase of pink roses caught Emma's eye. She lost herself for a moment in mentally choosing shades of paint to replicate the colors. About a dozen people chatted about the weather, past and upcoming, and the harvest, completed and yet to bring in. Alice nudged Emma out of her reverie, and they put their food on a table already heaped with the specialties of Peekskill's women.

Alice, clad in drab brown, returned to her mother's side. Violet sailed across the room and inserted herself into the group with a laughing comment. It made Emma proud to see her youngest sibling so confident. She would do everything in her power to help Alice interact easily without Mama in attendance.

Emma picked up a glass of apple cider and returned to the vase of roses that had caught her eye when she came in. The vase was orange glass, a garish pairing with the pink roses. If she painted these, she'd make the vase more subtle so as to showcase the beauty of the roses. Was there anything more majestic than a full-blown rose just as it began to wilt? It reminded her of women she knew who kept their elegance intact long after Mother Nature attempted to rob it from them. It reminded her of Mama, but not of Mrs. Beecher, who was more of a wizened apple refusing to fall from the tree.

"Such a perfect example of a damask rose," Alice said. She had followed Emma to the table, and picked up a glass of cider. "They look better than moss roses, which have an almost furry look to the stems that make them appear unkempt. Personally I prefer the tea roses for their fragrance. Reverend Beecher has given me a cutting of his purple Noisette rose, and I can hardly wait to plant it."

Emma swelled with pride in her sister. "You've really learned a lot about roses."

"I've been talking with Reverend Beecher. He knows quite a bit about flowers and trees. It's something to focus on." Her voice trailed off. "I feel as if the past two years are boxed inside of me and I don't have the key." She took a deep breath and gave her sister a small smile. "Flowers ease that feeling. Maybe they are the key."

Emma watched her sister walk away, hoping her sister's interest in flowers had become a passion that rekindled her interest in life.

Mama approached Emma with a purposeful stride. "There are a lot of eligible men here," she said.

Emma managed to keep her groan inside.

"A tea party might be in order soon. Or a dinner party." Mama's words trailed off.

Emma realized Mama was already deep into plans for an event. "We will no longer entertain single men for tea," Emma said firmly. "If you invite them, I will leave the house. I'm not interested in your matchmaking."

Mama's face registered shock.

Emma felt a weight lift from her back. She'd endured Mama's unwanted efforts for too long. It felt good to say what she felt.

THE NEXT DAY, Emma spent the morning in her studio, working on her rendition of Reverend Beecher's pink roses. Afterwards, she settled in the parlor to read Sam's new book, *The Adventures of Tom Sawyer*. The main character's actions reminded her of her brother when he was younger and made her laugh.

Violet picked up the mail from the table on the entry. "You have a letter!" she said, holding it out to Emma. "It's from Paris! Maybe it's a handsome Frenchman who wants your paintings for his gallery." Her eyes widened and brows raised as she teased her sister.

"Paris?" Emma's heart fluttered as a stone hit her stomach. She only knew one person in Paris. She took the letter. Her hand began to shake as she recognized Kate's handwriting. Violet seemed to sense her sister's mood change and left the room without any more joking. Emma stared at the letter until she could hold it steady and breathe normally.

For two years, Emma had imagined Kate in Paris, married to Abbott, living a life very different from her life in Brooklyn. Kate had never written, so Emma had no idea where to send a letter. She'd missed them both very much, although her grief over their absence didn't approach Alice's grief over David. Emma smoothed the envelope, then opened it.

EMMA,

How I wanted to write Dear Emma, or To My Dear Friend, but I fear I might have lost the right to do so. I'm sorry. Necessary words, but so very inadequate. How can I put into words the depth of my regret for not writing sooner to my dear friend. I'm so sorry, Emma.

Rather than repeating myself even more, let me tell you about the miracle that finally inspired me to sit down and write to you. Our daughter, Mary, was born in March of this year. Abbott and I are besotted by this little angel. I can hardly wait for you to meet her. I hesitate to write that, but I must continue this letter as if you want to hear from me.

Abbott's muse has been inspired by his studies at the Ecole des Beaux-Arts. *He's focusing on composition and the human figure, taught by the master Jean-Léon Gérôme. Nature is his first love, though, and he painted* Landscape at Fontainebleau Forest *soon after Mary's birth. I know she will continue to be an inspiration for his art. He just needs to learn that an infant can't sit for hours to have a portrait painted of her!*

We are happy, my little family and I, but I miss you. You were the other half of my soul. I long for you to be my friend again. Please write soon.

Kate Thayer

EMMA TREMBLED with emotion as she reread Kate's words. She'd imagined Kate was angry at her. She'd imagined Kate had moved on and no longer needed the friendship of a spinster on a New York farm. Now she asked if Emma would be her friend again. It was all Emma had wanted since she'd seen the newlyweds off to Paris two years ago. Of course she'd forgive Kate. It was the right course of action, and her sisters would be proud of her. Emma tucked the letter inside *The Adventures of Tom Sawyer.* and looked up at her family.

Mama sat in her usual chair, knitting needles clacking, her face a mask of pointed silence. She still hadn't said anything to Emma about the statement she'd made the previous day, but she hadn't gone forward with party plans, either.

Alice sat next to Mama, embroidering. Her silence felt more serene.

Violet stood by, eyes on Emma. "What's in the letter?" she asked.

Emma smiled. "Kate is a mother. She has a little girl now."

Alice looked to Mama, who dropped her knitting into her lap and frowned. Emma felt a flash of irritation at Alice. Did she have to wait to see what Mama would say before she formed an opinion?

Violet smiled. "Oh, that's nice. I hope we get to meet her someday."

"Is all well with Kate?" Alice asked.

It was a masterfully worded question. It asked about Kate, but also inquired about Emma's relationship with her friend. "All is well," Emma said. She smiled, and for the first time in a long time, the smile actually warmed her inside.

The next morning, Emma sat at the tiny desk in a corner of her studio. She loved the quality of light from this window in the morning. It was a perfect time to paint, but today she had letters to answer.

DEAR KATE,

My dear friend, you have always been in my heart. Your letter delighted me. Congratulations on the birth of your daughter! I can hardly wait to meet her.

After a long time, I've started painting again. It's going well. I will share the pictures with you when I see you again.

EMMA DAYDREAMED in the sunbeams from her window. She'd hold Kate's baby daughter and laugh with Abbott over how adorable she was. Violet and Alice would come with her to see Kate and little Mary, and the visits would expose her sisters to something different than Mama's world. Kate had written of her daughter and husband. Emma drew a blank. What could she share of her own life that would interest Kate, so far away in a world of Paris, marriage, and children? She decided to simply end it.

Please write soon.
Your friend,
Emma

NOT THE BEST letter she'd ever written, but it said what it needed to. She folded the letter, sealed it in an envelope, and addressed the envelope. Then she pulled out a fresh sheet of paper and started again.

Her letters to Nina had always been chatty, several months worth of daily happenings large and small. This letter had to be sent now. It had already been four months since she'd received Nina's. Her friend must think Emma was angry.

DEAR NINA,

It was lovely to hear from you at last. I'm sorry the entire summer has passed since you sent it. I meant to answer you immediately but got distracted by summer at the farm.

My painting is going well. I've started to paint animals, but not just any animals. Have you seen how a bird's coloring hides it in the leaves of a tree? Or a deer's coat blends into the shadows? It's challenging to paint something hidden in plain sight.

My sisters are filling my mind, too. Alice is twenty now, and Violet is ten. Violet is sunny as a puppy. I know that will temper as she grows up, but I long to preserve as much of that enthusiasm for life as I can. Alice is so quiet, Nina. I worry that she will forever seek the shadows of others at the expense of her own life experiences. I know, I can hear your laugh. My stated goal when I met you was to find someone like your Marcus to support while he took the spotlight. I've seen how rich your life has become, though, when you took control of it for yourself. And I see how bland Alice's life is without that strength.

Have you read Sam's latest book? The Adventures of Tom Sawyer *is truly his best, yet. Don't let your grudge against him prevent you from enjoying this novel!*

Please continue to write to me. I value your friendship and appreciate you 'listening' to my woes.

Yours truly,

Emma

27

N ina Larowe
San Jose, California, February 1878

Some of you remember (Anna Dickinson's) determined lips and those indignant eyes, and how they used to snap and flash when she marched the platform pouring out the lava of her blistering eloquence upon the enemy."
- Mark Twain, Who Is Mark Twain?

Dear Emma,

It was more difficult to post letters while traveling than I anticipated. Every day I was enduring the travails of travel, or rehearsing, or simply too exhausted to write. Please forgive my silence over the last five months. I enjoyed being on tour again. For the first time in a long time, I felt complete. The physical break of moving across the country has shorn any ties to my husband and marriage. Now I am my own person, making my own decisions and choosing my own path. I am divorced by distance if not by law.

Sara Leppincott and I left San Francisco by steamer and returned by train, visiting towns all the way—San Luis Obispo, Santa Barbara, Los Angeles, Santa Monica, and San Diego. In Riverside, we saw men laying out land to plant orange groves. In Santa Barbara, I was astounded to encounter a hotelkeeper at the Arlington Hotel who knew my parents. The hotelman at the St. Charles in Los Angeles was a gallant military man who refused to let us pay for our room. We even spent a week at Yosemite Valley viewing all of Mother Nature's treasures. We rode precipitous paths on muleback, turning corners so sharp that the animal's head would be over the path and his hind quarters pressed up against the bank. It was a pleasant time to rest and recover from being on the road, which is not like being at home.

Sara and I arrived in Nevada City and many of the residents of my hometown remembered me. They showed their loyalty by embracing me and shaking my hand and complimenting my performance. It greatly strengthened my confidence as well as my determination to make this tour a success.

For most of the mining towns, however, our planned readings proved too intellectual for the audience, so we had to add more comedy. I'm not good at dialects, but luckily Sara is, especially with Irish. She does a comic portrayal of Hood's "Lost Heir." At one point an Irish woman runs out of the house with a frying pan and a huge piece of meat. It's quite funny. Even so, audiences apparently expected a minstrel show. Usually they were respectful, but one time an entire audience left during the performance. They slipped out one by one. Every time I looked out from backstage, fewer people were in attendance. Sara and I are seasoned troupers, though. We laugh at these experiences on the road and don't let them discourage us.

We next went to Truckee, a rough border town full of people who have fled from justice. Sara kept our money from the Nevada City performance in an ornamental waist bag hooked to her belt. While we slept, the bag was stolen. We awoke to an open window in our room, missing our money as well as our train tickets to Virginia City. It seems a symbol of my life, going from highs to lows in an instant.

Leaving Truckee, we rode on the top of the stage because if I sat anywhere else I would be as sick as I ever was at sea. At night, we crawled down into the boot and slept on the mail sacks. Our next stop was Lake Tahoe.

We performed at several resorts around the lake, encountering nice people wherever we went. At McKinsey's, we presented Mr. McKinsey with a letter of introduction that Sara had acquired. He said nothing, just walked away and left us standing there. We thought it rude, but he came back, smiling, and made us comfortable. He couldn't read or write, you see, and had to find someone to read it to him.

One night a man approached us and identified himself as the manager of a logging camp. He asked permission to bring his men to our performance, and we agreed. It would give us a guaranteed audience at the very least. My first piece that night was a tragedy, and the men laughed. The manager later apologized, telling us his men thought their laughter showed how much they liked it. The next night, we performed a comedy and the men dared not laugh. They completely did not understand the protocol of theater. At least they enjoyed the performances, and it gave Sara and me a good story to tell once we returned to San Jose.

We traveled all over California and ventured into Arizona and New Mexico. We paid all our expenses and enjoyed ourselves for a year. Now we have returned to San Francisco with a large amount of travel knowledge but scarcely any money. I find it difficult to accept that touring is not as lucrative as I was promised. The time for traveling dramatic readers has passed, I'm afraid. Once more I'm at a point in my life where I must reinvent myself to find a way to finance my independence. It doesn't help that throughout this trip I was overcome with guilt at abandoning Mama to Fanny's vitriolic machinations. While I dread returning to San Jose and the Williams household, I must rescue my mother.

Yours truly,
Nina

28

Emma Beach
Peekskill, August 1878

"That is the way with art... you start in to make some simple little thing, ... and you fetch out something astonishing. This is called inspiration."
- Mark Twain, "How to Make History Dates Stick"

Under the apple tree, a cool breeze softened the summer sun and made the shadows of the leaves dance across the ground. Emma read Nina's letter and looked up into the tree's canopy, pleased to hear of her friend's tour even if it didn't turn out as well as Nina wanted it to. As much as she enjoyed Nina's letters, though, she had something more pressing to consider.

Kate was coming home to New York for good.

Kate and Abbott now had a one-year-old son, Harry, as well as their daughter Mary, who was now three. They had steamed into New York Harbor and settled into the Bloede home in Brooklyn with Kate's father. Now they were all, except for the father, coming to Peekskill for a visit.

Emma kept walking past the parlor window, checking for an

approaching carriage. It was warm and muggy outside, with clouds covering part of the sky. It had rained overnight, and the leaves of the plants glistened.

She was eager to see Kate, but nervous too. They were old friends who hadn't seen each other in four years. Kate was a wife and mother now. Letters couldn't express how completely her life had changed. Emma had changed, too, if not as much. She no longer kept to the shadows as much as she had before. While she still didn't seek to be onstage, she could manage it when she needed to. In her letters, she'd told Kate she was painting, and about Alice's growing knowledge of the local flora and fauna, and that Violet was growing up. Emma was afraid she'd see Kate face to face and have nothing to say.

Finally the carriage pulled up to the house. Emma went outside and waited on the porch, clasping her hands so she wouldn't twist them. The driver helped Kate out first. Her dress, slim cut in the fashionable princess style, was dyed a purple bright enough to compete with Alice's roses. Kate's hat matched, of course, and was perched upon a tight chignon of dark hair. Kate helped her daughter out, picked up her son, and looked toward the house. Her luminous dark eyes shone in her pale face as she spotted Emma and waved.

Emma swept down the porch steps and greeted Kate, who introduced the children and nudged them forward. They shied away, looking around them with eyes as large as their mother's. Abbott Thayer stepped out of the carriage, moving with as much energy as the children. The tableau of a happy family caused a momentary pang in Emma's heart.

Abbott's face was narrower than she remembered, and his broad forehead was furrowed by frown lines. A mustache filled out his face a bit, and set off his aquiline nose. He took Emma's hand and gave her a quick nod. "Delighted to be here, Miss Beach," he said. He held Emma's hand a bit longer than necessary and fastened his eyes on her. Something about his manner reminded her of a puppy or a child, something sweet that needed care. Her heart responded immediately. Surprised, she pulled her hand away and turned to Kate.

"Come inside and have some tea," she said. "We have a lot of catching up to do." Emma tucked her hand under Kate's arm and turned toward the house. Kate laughed, sounding exactly as she used to. Emma relaxed.

In reality, they had very little catching up to do since they'd done that by letter. This visit was more about soaking up the very presence of each other. Emma had made sure Mama and her sisters would visit the Beechers today. Papa and William were working on the farm. Cook had prepared a tea tray, and she brought it into the parlor as Emma and her guests settled in.

"Look, Mary," Emma said to Kate's daughter. "Cook has made spiced butter cookies for you. And do you like lemonade?" Emma handed the girl a cookie. Mary took it and nibbled.

Kate reminded her to say thank you as Emma poured the tea. Emma liked children, especially little girls that reminded her of her sisters.

Emma turned to Abbott and offered him the plate of cookies. "When you visit after harvest, we'll have a variety of apple delicacies for you to try," she said.

Abbott took two cookies with a smile as eager as the children's. He took a bite and looked skyward. "These are wonderful. They would be at home in the finest Parisian cafe."

"Tell us about your painting, Emma," Kate said. She sipped her tea, keeping an eye on her children.

Emma glanced at Abbott, who also waited for her response. "I'm painting scenes around the farm, trying to apply techniques from school." Oh no, she didn't want to create the image of a schoolgirl dabbling in art. She took a deep breath and said, "I love the natural light in the morning. It gives a glow to the colors."

Abbott nodded. "The beauty of this area reminds me why I love landscape painting."

Kate and Emma shared tidbits of their daily lives. Abbott listened and ate several more cookies.

"So you're living with your father in Brooklyn?" Emma asked.

"For the moment," Kate said. "He has a big house and no one to share it with." Kate went on to share plans for Abbott's painting studio far enough away from the children's nursery that he wouldn't be disturbed. "You have no idea how hard it is to marshal a husband and two small children through a move between continents," she said with a laugh and exaggerated eye roll.

"I'm sure," murmured Emma, confused. It seemed such a permanent move would be planned well in advance, but she knew the children's nanny had chosen to stay in France. "I'll make sure you both are invited to my next art show."

"Your painting must be going well, then," Abbott said. When he spoke to her, his eyes never left her face. It made Emma feel that for this moment at least, she was the only person in his world.

Dear Nina,

I have finally been reunited with Kate and Abbott Thayer. Kate loves him and he loves her. Their children are well-behaved. During their visit, I talked about my art shows and Alice's grief, and about my venture into painting animals. That took about ten minutes. Then Kate and Abbott filled the afternoon with tales of Paris, of the children, and of his portrait painting. I don't feel as if I have nothing to offer, really, but rather that I am just starting on a journey where they are far ahead of me. I am content to include the Thayers in my life. I can be useful to them, and they will delight me. My art and my friends provide a full life.

Yours truly,

Emma

29

Nina Larowe
San Jose, September 1878

*"...when we want a thing, we go to hunting
for righteous reasons for it...whereas privately we know are only hunting
for plausible ones."*
- *Mark Twain, No. 44, The Mysterious Stranger*

Nina returned to San Jose with brilliant memories and drab aspirations. Much to her dismay, she slipped back into Fanny's household as if she'd never been gone. Every morning she walked her nieces to San Jose Normal School on Washington Square. She listened to fifteen-year-old Edith and thirteen-year-old little Nina talk about becoming teachers while eight-year-old Emily trudged along, clearly not wanting to be there.

"You don't want to be a teacher?" Nina asked.

"Oh, Auntie Nina," the girl said, "I want to draw houses. Someday I'll be a famous architect!"

Nina didn't think she'd known what an architect was when she was eight. "If that's what you want, you work toward that dream."

"She'll become a teacher like us," Edith said. "Miss Fanny will expect it."

All three girls fell silent. It angered Nina to see them so cowed by their stepmother that even thinking about her drained them of enjoyment. Not for the first time, she wished she could spirit them away to New York, to take them shopping and to the theater, to show them the Statue of Liberty and the Brooklyn Bridge that was finally under construction. They were lovely, smart girls. They deserved more attention than they were getting. Fanny spent most of her time coddling Waldo, and Ed spent most of his life running the water company.

Later, when Nina brought up the girls to her mother, Mother said, "Don't interfere. It's hard to bring up another woman's children. We should be glad that our Emily's children have two parents again."

So Nina made an effort to converse politely at dinner, when everyone gathered. "And how was your day, Fanny?"

Fanny's smug smile should have warned Nina. Fanny produced a newspaper clipping and handed it to Nina. "You do know I have a friend in London, do you not? She sent me this advertisement when I expressed an interest in Marcus Larrowe's memory classes."

Nina frowned. "You did what?"

Fanny waved off her question. "She wrote that the man has changed his name to Professor Alphonse Loisette because his father doesn't approve of his profession."

"That's true," Nina admitted, "but his father has been gone for twelve years. It's hardly necessary to adopt such a foolish moniker at this date."

"That doesn't matter. It's this advertisement I wanted to show you." She handed the clipping to Nina. "Apparently these have been distributed all over England. Professor Loisette claims to have discovered the natural laws of memory."

"What a bunch of nonsense," Nina said. She barely glanced at the advertisement, putting it away to look at later.

After dinner, Nina and her mother sat alone in a small morning room that gave them the illusion of privacy. Nina read the ad and told Mother, "He calls himself a French teacher. He claims to be able to teach a student French in a quarter of the usual time. I didn't even know he could speak French. No doubt he memorized the entire language in an hour to impress an audience. His notices also proclaim his passion for memory. He is now giving classes, privately and by correspondence. His Loisettian School of Physiological Memory teaches the Instantaneous Art of Never Forgetting, recommended by the high Scientific Authority. Lost memories are restored, the worst made good, and the best better, a Cure of Mind-Wandering. Have you ever heard anything more ridiculous, Mother?"

"He is certainly not the man we knew in Nevada, is he?" her mother said.

"No, he is not." Nina tucked the newspaper clipping into a book and forgot about it.

When the tensions in the house grew too much, Nina took the train to San Francisco for the day, or to Glen Ellen to visit Polly. When she was in San Jose, she gritted her teeth and tried to ignore Fanny's treatment of her nieces. Her entire life felt like it was in limbo, waiting for something to happen.

Three months later, it happened. Nina woke her mother one morning, concerned that Mama hadn't gotten up at her usual time.

"Nina? My right arm feels funny," Mother said, still sleepy.

"Funny how?" Nina asked. She took her mother's arm. It felt cold, so she rubbed it.

"I can't feel it." Mother's eyes widened. "I can't move it at all."

"Let's sit you up." Nina assisted her mother to a sitting position, discovering that she was unable to move her right leg either.

"Nina, what's wrong with me?" Mother said, anxiety coating her tone.

Nina tried to keep her voice calm. "I'll go call the doctor. I'll be right back."

Nina found Fanny ordering the kitchen staff around. She asked her to call the doctor. "I would do it, but I haven't learned how to use your telephone yet." Nina winced. She hadn't thought she'd need to call anyone. Now she was glad that Ed was involved in so many city affairs that Fanny agreed a telephone in the house was necessary.

The doctor arrived, and quickly proclaimed, "Mrs. Churchman has suffered an apoplexy." He proceeded to apply dressings to her paralyzed arm and leg, and perform bloodletting. Then he turned to Nina and said, "She will require constant care for quite some time. I can recommend a nurse for hire."

Nina said, "I'll care for her." She listened carefully to the doctor's instructions, but even so she felt helpless when he left.

Nina went downstairs where Ed and Fanny were waiting to hear the doctor's verdict. Nina stood for a moment in the doorway and looked at them. These people were not related to her. The Ed that her late sister Emily knew was a failed gold miner who sold water in mining camps. Fanny's Ed was a prominent city official. She told them what the doctor had said, and they stared at her as if they didn't know her at all.

"I can't have an invalid in my house," Fanny said. "There is already too much to manage with the family and staff."

Nina wanted to ask what she expected Mother to do, but bit back the words. "I need to write to my brother." She returned to the room she shared with her mother and poured out her heart to her brother. It helped to release the fear and anger that had built up within her.

By the time Ney's answer arrived, however, Nina was once again walking on eggshells. Fanny and Ed made no effort to make her feel welcome, much less like family. Ed spent most of his time working or meeting with important men who were shaping San Jose into a city. That left Fanny to sweep through the house in a superior manner, giving supercilious direction to servants, stepchildren, mother-in-law and Nina alike. Nina spent most of her time in her room, reading to Mother, who had not regained movement in her limbs, or sewing, or napping. Ney's letter was a welcome change.

DEAR NINA,

You must bring Mother home to Nevada. I've rented a large furnished house in anticipation of your agreement and look forward to seeing you. I've started practicing law in Virginia City, which isn't the lawless place it used to be, thank God. Money is tight, but you and I together will do what we need to do for Mother's comfort. First, we need to get you out of San Jose. Please send me a telegram with the date and time of your train arrival.

 Ney

Relief flooded Nina. She'd expected Ney to offer to help, and she wanted more than anything to move Mother out of this house, but she hadn't expected her brother to act so quickly. It did surprise her that Ney was a lawyer. That had been Father's dream for him. Her brother had always wanted to be a dentist. She shook her head. There would be time to learn all about his decision once they completed the move. She went downstairs to inform Fanny that she and Mother would be leaving on the next train.

It wasn't that easy, of course. The doctor had to clear Mother to travel, and arrangements for her travel comfort had to be made. Little Nina had a piano recital that her auntie must attend, and Nina also had tickets to a play in San Francisco.

Adelaide Neilson, who had met Nina in New York, sent the tickets to her. It was for her performance at the Baldwin Theater. Nina was thrilled to see an actress of her stature and had eagerly accepted. Mother had planned to attend with her, but now that was impossible. Nina took a train into the city anyway.

In spite of her anticipation, Nina sat in the darkened theater with tears filling her eyes. She had seen Miss Neilson in New York, when her own career as an actress was beginning, when she'd dreamed of entering that temple of fame herself. Now her struggle to enter it was over. Nina now had responsibilities that required her to have regular employment, responsibilities for more than her own independence. She must turn her mind to practical matters. Her mind accepted the notion, but her heart ached. She bade a sorrowful adieu to her stage name and left it in the empty theater.

Dear Emma,

I'm glad you have reunited with your friend Kate. You have a loving heart and have apparently taken the Thayers in. That's admirable, but don't let their lives subsume yours.

I am pleased to read of your continued commitment to your art. Painting is a creative endeavor like acting. It takes devotion to the art and persistence to overcome setbacks in order to be successful. I suppose your friend Mr. Clemens realizes this, too. After his novel The Gilded Age, it took three years before The Adventures of Tom Sawyer was published. How can he expect to live off a career like that?

I know a bit about sinking to the darkest levels. Let me share what I've learned from the theater. If you preserve your self-respect, nobody can harm you. In a company with coarse people, you can remain aloof and nobody will care to infringe on your privacy. No one, not even stage people, can lead you astray if you don't want to go. This is true of all work.

Please write soon,

Nina

30

E mma Beach
        Brooklyn, October 1878

"The holy passion of Friendship is of so sweet and steady and loyal and enduring a nature that it will last a whole lifetime, if not asked to lend money."
- Mark Twain, Pudd'nhead Wilson's Calendar

As fall colored the landscape, Emma's family harvested their apple trees. Emma wrapped up an apple cider cake and took a train to the Bloede house in Brooklyn. It may be full of Thayers now, but it would always be the Bloede house to Emma.

The butler answered the door and showed her in. Emma stepped into the parlor to wait for Kate and struggled to hide her dismay. She recognized furniture and artwork that had always been in the room, but now clutter filled all the spaces with items that could only have been acquired on Kate and Abbott's Parisian adventure. An ottoman, richly decorated with tufted upholstery and tassels, tussled for space with heavier footstools from Mr. Bloede's family. Chairs covered in French brocade sat next to larger, undecorated American pieces. A huge kentia palm dominated the room. A rickety plant stand in the corner held a collection of dracaenas, dieffenbachias, and caladiums. Emma stood where she could find a space. There certainly was no seating available.

Kate entered the room. Her smile lit the room as it always had when they were in school. "Emma! Delighted to see you!"

"As promised, I brought an apple cider cake." Emma held it out and Kate took it.

"Looks wonderful," Kate said, peeking into the box. "I'll have the cook cut it for us." She left the room but returned almost immediately.

"Looks like you are still settling in," Emma said, looking around the jumbled room.

"I know it's a mess," Kate said. "I just can't seem to manage it, and Abbott is no better. Let's find a spot to sit."

Kate led Emma into the hallway and toward the back of the house. In a breakfast room off the kitchen, they sat at a table that must be where the family dined.

"Are the children upstairs?" Emma asked.

"They are napping. Both at the same time, for once." Kate nodded. "I'm busy and exhausted, but Abbott is painting."

Emma nodded, but before she could say any more, Abbott came in. His knee-high leather boots needed polishing, and his knickers were rumpled. Paint splotches decorated his Norfolk jacket. Emma wondered if Abbott preferred to look so rumpled or if Kate just couldn't manage him. She greeted Abbott, who looked up in surprise.

"Hello, Emma, I didn't see you there." He turned to Kate. "Was it George Cable or Henry James I'm supposed to see this afternoon?"

Kate said, "Wasn't Mr. James next week?"

"I'll send a note 'round to Cable and tell him I'll be a bit late. That will give me time to figure out when I'm supposed to be there." Abbott hurried from the room, too preoccupied to take his leave of Emma.

"He seems to have a lot on his plate. You both must be exhausted," Emma said. As she said it, she remembered times when Kate couldn't find something she was looking for, or had forgotten a date.

Kate sighed. "I'm not much better. Thankfully, he has agreed to hire a nanny. I'm afraid it's all too much, with his appointments, and the children, and the household." Kate's voice trailed off.

"Nonsense," Emma said. "You can handle this. You just need some help getting on your feet. Let me help you get your house and affairs organized. I'm sure you can manage it after that."

"Oh, would you? Emma, I'd be so grateful." Kate's smile seemed to take a weight off her shoulders. "Let's have our apple cider cake now, then we can help Abbott look for his calendar."

The friends chatted while they ate. As they finished, Abbott came in brandishing a crumpled bit of paper.

"I found it! This afternoon at 4:00!" The sonorous tones of a grandfather clock began to chime. Abbott held his breath, listening. "Three! I've got an hour. Now where did I put the address?" He rustled in his pockets, coming up with several papers he looked at then discarded.

Kate's face took on a look that made Emma's heart ache. Her friend was overwhelmed. Emma stood up and said, "Abbott, your dear wife and I have decided that I might be able to help you both get organized. And keep track of your appointments."

"She's so good at it," Kate said.

"Do we need this?" Abbott looked genuinely confused.

"I think we do," Kate said, giving him a gentle smile.

"Then we'll do it! I'm going to gather all my bits of papers for you, Emma." He dashed from the room with new energy.

"Will he remember his appointment?" Emma asked.

"He has a decent memory," Kate said, "but he gets distracted easily." The friends laughed.

EMMA SPENT SEVERAL HOURS EACH DAY at the Thayer house. She'd always liked Kate's father, and made a point of taking him afternoon tea and chatting for a few minutes before tackling the detritus of Kate and Abbott's day. Over the next few weeks, she wondered more than once how two people could possibly create such chaos on a daily basis. Abbott kept track of his appointments by keeping scraps of paper in his pocket. Emma shuddered when she discovered this, and brought a leather-bound Excelsior diary for him. She got it from her father, who hadn't kept an appointment diary since he sold the newspaper. With only a few months left in the year, it was a good way to start keeping Abbott organized. The artist was hopeless, however. He would write down a client's name on the right date and forget to put a time and place. He always assumed he'd remember, and he never did.

Kate was no better. At least she could claim distraction from two small children. Emma began by transferring information from Abbott's paper scraps to the diary. She coordinated interviews with nannies. To Kate's relief, they found one within a few days. She moved into the house and began organizing the nursery and children the way Emma was organizing the downstairs and parents.

When she realized Abbott and Kate would never look in his calendar, relying on her to remind him, Emma added Kate's obligations into the calendar, not the least of which were reminders to water, prune, and mist Kate's growing collection of houseplants. Emma knew people who had more than the traditional kentia palm or aspidistra in their parlor, and Alice certainly loved plants. Kate, however, had become obsessed with houseplants in Paris. Unable to ship them to New York, she'd been shopping for them all summer in New York.

On one of Emma's first days with the Thayers, a delivery arrived with the largest monstera she'd ever seen. The plant stood six feet tall. She thought Kate must have lost her mind. Emma smiled and said, "Oh what a lovely specimen!"

Kate clapped her hands and beamed. "What a statement piece for the entryway! I'm so pleased!"

The butler moved the hatstand out of the way as the delivery man wrestled the monstera into place. Its large leaves waved like monster paws over the man's back as he pushed it into a corner next to the doorway into the parlor. Spotting the fronds of the kentia palm in the parlor, Emma imagined the monstera waving at the palm in order to let it know who was now in charge. She laughed at the image until Kate gave her an odd look.

For the rest of the day, every time Emma walked through the entryway, the monstera brushed her sleeve, and she jumped. "I'm going to cut off your leaf," she threatened.

Abbott didn't notice the monstera. At least he didn't acknowledge it. Emma kept waiting for him to crash into it, but it was placed far enough into the corner that a preoccupied artist didn't notice getting brushed by a wayward leaf.

That evening, Emma sat in her home studio as the light faded to dusk. She held a paintbrush in her hand, but it was already too dark. Smiling, she thought about Kate and Thayer, Mary and Harry, and Mr. Bloede.

Alice walked by the doorway. Spotting Emma, she turned back. "Painting in the dark?"

"No," Emma said. "Just thinking about my day. I'm glad I can help Kate take care of her family during this difficult time for her."

"Difficult time? You mean caring for children? Or dealing with a crazy husband?" Alice said.

"Abbott's an artist," Emma said. "He's got a creative temperament."

"You're creative, but I don't see you forgetting to wear a coat outside on a cold day."

Emma wished she hadn't told her sister that story. At least she hadn't mentioned what Kate had told her about Abbott's woolen long johns. She said he put them on in the fall and wore the same ones all winter. As the weather warmed, he cut off the legs until they were short pants. Alice would have a field day with that tale.

"She's my friend, Alice. I enjoy helping her."

Alice entered the studio and put a hand on her sister's arm. "I love you, Emma. I just don't want to see them take advantage of you. It seems to me they could hire a housekeeper to run the house and a personal assistant to manage the calendar. That way you could get back to your painting."

Emma looked at her sister's earnest face and nodded. She appreciated her sister's words, but Alice should understand how much she liked to be of service. Painting all day was pleasant, but it felt wonderful to be able to help the Thayers. "And you? Are you happy, Alice?"

"Are you? Truly?" Alice countered.

For a frozen moment, they stared at each other. Then the awkwardness of unspoken feelings rose between them. Alice left the studio. Emma stared at her painting, not seeing it.

Dear Nina,

Happy New Year! May 1879 bring you all the happiness you desire. I am completely involved in Kate and Abbott's family, and loving it. This year, I hope to find more time to paint, though. I wonder if Abbott would notice if I set up an easel in his studio? No, I jest. His studio is sacred. It's the only room in the house that I cannot (will not) organize. I understand that the creative mind craves chaos sometimes.

Kate always liked having people around her, and she enjoys spending days with me at her house. She and Abbott seem well suited, although I have trouble imagining how they managed to keep their lives orderly when they lived in Paris. I suppose there are many people that live disorderly lives, but I shudder to imagine it.

Alice says I spend too much time with Kate and her family. She thinks I need to do more about creating my own family. Maybe the very public nature of my parents' disputes has put all their daughters off the notion of marriage. Did I tell you that William married earlier this year? I am to be an auntie in 1879, even though he took his wife to Connecticut and I am unlikely to be the doting aunt I might want to be. At least Mama will have a grandchild to spoil.

Virginia City sounds rather wild to me, but then I've only been out of New York to a small farm in the country (besides our cruise, of course, but that was a long time ago and I was with my father). In your letter before the holidays, you wrote that Ney is becoming more disgruntled with his profession as a lawyer. I hope he is able to find a way to happiness there in Virginia City since I know how important it is to you that your family is together again.

Yours truly,

Emma

31

N ina Larowe
Virginia City, Nevada, 1880

"When I was a boy, there was but one ambition among my comrades in our village on the bank of the Mississippi River. That was, to be a steamboatman.
We had transient ambitions of other sorts, ...but the ambition to be a steamboatman always remained."
- Mark Twain, Life on the Mississippi

Dear Emma,

I've been back in Nevada for a year now, and I'm sure you will be delighted to learn that Mr. Clemens is held in high esteem here. His Tom Sawyer book is everywhere. I suppose I will read it someday. The Christmas holidays in Virginia City are celebrated very differently than in New York, but I enjoyed the time with my mother and brother. When last I lived here, the gold had lured cultured and brilliant people from the East. Now the city is full of tillers of the soil, people who work with their hands not their brains. The Comstock mine still produces millions of dollars of silver every month, but the only people getting rich off it are the four Irishmen who own it.

Mother does take the train to San Jose to visit her grandchildren, as you suggested in your letter. I accompany her, but we don't make the trip as often as she would like. Fanny is never welcoming and makes it difficult to visit with my nieces.

Write soon and tell me of your sisters' doings as well as your own.

Yours truly,

Nina

NINA FOLDED the letter and put it in an envelope. Would Emma notice much was missing about life in Virginia City? Nina had thought of telling her friend all about the city's recovery from the devastating fire five years ago, and the new International Hotel that was six stories tall and boasted Nevada's first elevator, or that Virginia City had two hospitals. If she'd gone on to that length, though, Emma would have known something was wrong. No, not wrong, just missing.

Nina had arrived in Virginia City exhausted from the journey. Mother had not traveled well. She'd been embarrassed by the lingering paralysis in her arm and leg, and by the amount of assistance she required because of it. "One more trip, Mother," Nina had told her. "After this, you can settle in one place with your children beside you."

Mother smiled and said, "How long has it been since you and your brother have lived in the same town, much less with me?"

Nina had answered that question the first time her mother asked it, but just smiled and shrugged when it became the theme of the trip. At seventy-four, Mama's memory was no longer sharp. It had gotten to the point that when she referred to "you and your brother," Nina wondered if she remembered their names. It had been a relief to arrive at the house Ney had rented, to be done traveling and to have another adult to help with Mother.

"Are you ready to mail that?" Ney asked when she sealed the letter to Emma. He'd been sitting at the same table working on his own correspondence. "If so, I'll take it to the post office for you on the way to the office."

Nina laughed. "So kind of you to offer." She knew he had an ulterior motive.

Ney smiled. "I can't help it if Miss Kendall's dress shop is next to the post office."

She handed him her letter. Ney's delight in Louise Kendall brightened Nina's day almost as much as it did his.

When he'd left, Nina sighed and went to check on her mother. She peeked in the bedroom and was relieved to see her napping. The relief flooded her with guilt. It was hard to keep up the household when she had to entertain Mother, especially when she was too confused to carry on a conversation. Often Nina recited long passages from readings she'd done on the road, hoping to soothe Mother to sleep.

Downstairs, Nina took stock of the state of the house. The parlor needed to be swept and dusted. In the kitchen, the remains of breakfast needed to be put away and preparations for the evening meal begun. Now that she no longer had a household staff, Nina had never appreciated them more. When they'd arrived, Nina had laughed with Ney about the adventure of learning to do the work itself instead of just ordering it done. It hadn't been an adventure for long.

It wasn't just the recurring chore of cleaning, laundry, and cooking that gave Nina the feeling of being trapped. She was no longer free to take a trip anywhere. In San Jose, it had been possible to take a trip to San Francisco for a night at the theater, or visit Polly in Glen Ellen. Going anywhere from Virginia City was a major endeavor. As long as she was responsible for Mother's care, Nina could not take an eight-hour train ride to San Francisco. Even errands to shop for groceries or go to the post office had to be undertaken when Ney was home. As his law practice grew, that became more and more difficult. But she no longer had the idle time to wallow in bad thoughts.

Outside, the huge kettle of water had begun to boil. Nina sent a mental prayer of thanks to Ney for hauling the water from the creek to fill the kettle. She was equally thankful that it was only the three of them in the household. How did women with several children keep up if they weren't wealthy enough to have a staff? Nina put three sets of bedsheets in the kettle and stirred it with a stick. She wrestled the first sheet out of the kettle and into the wash tub, leaving the other sheets tangled in a mass on one side of the kettle. The sheet she held was so heavy that it sloshed hot water from the kettle onto the fire, almost putting it out. Nina stuffed the sheet into the wash tub and grabbed two fresh logs. She shoved them under the kettle into the active part of the fire. In doing so, she unbalanced the kettle even further. It began to tip, and she cried out, reaching to catch it which, of course, she couldn't do. She pulled her hands back just as the kettle fell. It landed on its side, splashing hot water on Nina's shoes and dumping the wet sheets into the mud.

From inside the house, Nina could hear her mother calling. Abandoning the laundry disaster, she went to check on Mother. By the time she removed her wet shoes, dried her hands, and went upstairs, her mother had fallen back to sleep. Nina collapsed in the chair beside the bed, dreading returning to the yard. But she had no savior to deliver her from chores.

Nina returned to the yard and rekindled the fire. Using towels to pad her hands against the hot metal, she righted the still-warm kettle. For what seemed like the next five hours, she hauled water to fill the kettle. As the water heated, she went into the kitchen to make herself a cup of tea.

When Ney arrived home for supper, Nina was still sitting at the kitchen table, her teacup as empty as her motivation. "Kettle's boiling," Ney said. "May need to add more water?"

"Probably," Nina said. "I'm just resting a bit." She looked out the window and sighed.

"I have news. I've picked up enough clients to hire an assistant to help me."

"That's wonderful," Nina said. Her voice sounded flat to her own ears. "Can I hire an assistant, too?"

"I see that today's laundry isn't going well." Ney laughed so hard he had to grip his sides.

Nina glared at him.

"You take the laundry to the Chinese laundry ," he said.

Mollified, she fixed him a cold supper of sliced meat and cheese. When he returned to the office, Nina stormed into the yard and stood with her hands on her hips watching the kettle boil. She used a hook to tip it, dousing the flames completely. Then she bundled all the laundry, dry and dirty as well as wet and muddy, into a large basket. Nina put the basket on a hand cart and dragged it to Chinatown east of downtown. Breathing hard, she approached the first laundry she found.

Inside, Nina greeted a slight Chinese woman with a nod of her head. "I have laundry," she said.

A serene smile lit the woman's face. "We do for you." Her demeanor spread a blanket of calm over Nina, who smiled in relief and hurried home to Mother.

THE NEXT DAY, Ney had an hour in the middle of the day to stay with Mother. Nina stepped outside the front door and took a deep breath as if she was escaping to freedom. She walked to Piper Opera House, her favorite place in the city. It was a three-story building built into a gently sloping hillside, with a wooden walkway on one side and a balcony around the second floor. Inside, though, it was truly magnificent. Nina walked into the mammoth auditorium and sat to the side, partially hidden. The ornately painted walls and frescoes both distracted the eye and focused it on the stage. She came to watch the soloists rehearsing for the next performance. It didn't matter what opera they'd be singing. Nina was only there to soak up the presence of the theater and dream of being on the stage.

Nina returned home refreshed but with tears on her cheeks. She took a deep breath and wiped them off before entering the house. Removing her coat and hat, she went into the parlor, where Ney was sitting with a handful of papers.

"Feel better?" he asked with a knowing smile.

Nina nodded. "What do you have there?"

"I've been investigating a legal matter that concerns you."

Nina's eyebrows rose. "Concerns me?"

"I've been looking into Marcus Larrowe." When Nina began to protest, Ney held up his palm to stop her. "There is precedent for divorce on the basis of abandonment."

Nina collapsed into a chair. She'd mentioned to Ney several times that she'd love to sever the legal bond with Marcus. She hated even that much connection to the man. "Go on."

"Marcus Larrowe is living near the Pelman School in London. His 'Memory and Success' training is almost exactly what the Pelman School teaches. It makes sense that Marcus probably studied there, but it doesn't make sense that the school allows him to market their course of study as his own."

"You wait and see. Someday his blatant plagiarism will cause him grief," Nina said.

"Since he has no stated intention of resuming the marriage, I can put a notice in the newspaper summoning Marcus to appear in court to answer a complaint of desertion. He's not in the country, so of course he won't do so. As a result, the court will declare the bonds of matrimony dissolved. There's no property or children to consider, so it should be routine."

When did a woman divorcing her husband become routine? Nina nodded. "Let's do it."

"I suggest we use the *San Francisco Examiner* because it has a much wider reach than the Virginia City papers. We can show due diligence that way."

Nina nodded. "Thank you, Ney."

Ney left the next day for San Francisco. He was back in three days, striding in the door and saying, "The court was quick to declare since it's been ten years since you've seen Marcus. You are a divorced woman, Nina Larowe. Or will you resume using Churchman?"

Nina took a moment to let the rush of delighted victory wash over her. "I will once again reinvent myself and become Nina Churchman

Larowe." She stopped to consider the reality of her situation. "In New York, this would be yet another scandal. In Virginia City, no one will notice. Let's not tell Mother, though." She turned back to the book she'd been reading before Ney arrived.

Ney, however, remained standing in front of her. Nina looked up. Ney said, "One more thing. I've asked Louise Kendall to marry me and she said yes."

Tears sprang to Nina's eyes. She didn't believe in the longevity of romantic love, but he was happy, and that made her happy. "All my congratulations to both of you."

32

Emma Beach
Cornwall-on-Hudson, NY, 1880

"I have been born more times than anybody except Krishna."
- Mark Twain's Autobiography

Emma stared out the front window of the cottage Kate and Abbott had rented in Cornwall, on the side of Storm King Mountain, up the Hudson River from Peekskill. Spring was a time of renewal and rebirth. Renewal for Nina, who finally found herself free of Marcus Larrowe. Rebirth for Kate—her friend had just shared that she was expecting another child in the fall. Livy Clemens, too, was expecting another child in the summer.

Emma stood in the jungle that was Kate's parlor. She pushed the fronds of the kentia palm aside and paced between the plants, restless. She didn't want a child of her own, nor did she long for a husband. Kate and Abbott had enfolded her into their world, and Emma loved them. All three of them anticipated the new baby's birth. Emma had mastered her role as majordomo of the Thayer household, and basked in Kate and Abbott's appreciation. If anything was missing, it was her painting. She had all but given it up to spend time at the Thayer's. Emma loved her friends, but missed her art with a pain that threatened to send her back into a world of loneliness. Better to stay in the Thayer's world.

Just then the nanny came into the room. Her face was pale and she wrung her hands. "Oh, Miss Emma, you must come. Miss Kate... oh it's terrible." Tears began to flow.

Emma's heart flipped. Whatever could be so terrible that it rocked this paragon of efficient serenity? She rushed after the other woman and asked, "What is it?"

Nanny shook her head. "It's Master Harry." She choked up and could say no more.

Emma picked up her skirt and ran upstairs, following the wailing she could now hear from the nursery. A horrifying tableau greeted her. Kate knelt on the floor, her arms and upper body draped over two-year-old Harry's bed. Sobs wracked her entire body. Emma could see Harry's head on the pillow, his face pale and eyes closed, more still than she'd ever seen him. Dread gripped her heart.

"Kate? What happened?" Emma knelt beside Kate and took her friend in her arms.

"He's deeeaaaad," Kate wailed, drawing out the awful word as if to make it false.

Emma gulped, straining to control her own tears. Nanny had followed Emma upstairs and stood just inside the doorway. Partially hidden behind the nanny's skirts, four-year-old Mary, her eyes wide and solemn, tried to take in the adult's grief. Emma could find out what had happened later. Right now she had to manage the living. "Take Mary downstairs," she instructed the nanny, who immediately complied.

Emma heard heavy footsteps running down the hallway. Kate's wails must have pierced Abbott's concentration. He reached the doorway and stopped short. Slowly he approached his son's bed. Emma watched as shock drained the color from his face. Abbott pulled his son's body into his arms.

Emma stood up and led Kate from the room, heavily supporting her. Kate tried to resist, but Emma was firm. "You can't do anything more for Harry. You must see to the one you are carrying." Her voice cracked on the boy's name, but Emma could cry later. Now she had to support the grieving parents. She took Kate into her bedroom and encouraged her to lie down.

She went back to the bedroom and gently took Harry from his father's arms, laying him back on his bed. "Come with me, Abbott. You must be strong for Kate." He followed her reluctantly.

In her bedroom, Kate had curled into a fetal position, still crying. Abbott took a deep breath to still his sobs, but tears still streamed down his cheeks as he lay on the bed and put his arms around his wife.

Emma hurried downstairs and asked the butler to send for the doctor. Over the next few hours, the doctor arrived, examined Harry's body, and ordered laudanum be given to the parents. When Emma asked what had caused the boy's death, the doctor shook his head and said Harry had probably been suffocated by his pillow or blankets.

Emma's mother and sisters arrived the next day to help bathe the body, dress him in all white, and lay him out in the parlor. Alice brought a bouquet of her most fragrant roses. Mama hung a laurel wreath with a black crepe bow on the front door. Violet stopped the clocks and draped the mirrors in black. Emma greeted neighbors as they came to find out who had died, and gave them funeral biscuits prepared by the cook.

The upheaval in the house distressed four-year-old Mary, who insisted on seeing her brother and parents. In desperation, Nanny put a drop of laudanum in Mary's milk so she would sleep.

Over the next few days, the bustle of funeral arrangements, and family and friends coming to give condolences, kept the household busy. Emma encouraged Kate to get out of bed and sit in the parlor. People came by to grieve with her, but Kate stared at the tiny coffin without blinking. Abbott stalked the upper hallways as if pursuing a ghost. Emma left them both alone except to insist they eat something. She marshaled Kate and Abbott through the funeral, allowing them to wallow in grief while she took care of everything except allowing her own grief to surface.

THAT SUMMER, Emma visited the Thayers often in Cornwall. On one of those visits, she was thrilled to find Abbott in his studio.

"I'm glad to see you painting," she told him.

"Portraits are a living," he said.

She knew his reputation as a portrait painter was growing. He'd even exhibited some of his work at the National Academy of Design and the Society of American Artists. Emma walked closer to the portrait in progress. "She's a beautiful woman."

"Capturing a subject's inner beauty is what makes the portrait work," Abbott said. "Pairing an introspective expression with her natural beauty gives the picture a satisfying spiritual dimension."

Translating vision was difficult in all creative endeavors. Emma remembered Sam struggling to find the right words and imagined Abbott doing the same with paint colors. She knew from personal experience that her own inner vision was not always portrayed on the canvas correctly. She wondered if Abbott and Sam felt the same about their finished works.

"You started out painting landscapes, though," she said. "Will you go back to that?"

Abbott stilled his paintbrush and looked out over his easel as if peering through the walls into the forest surrounding the house. "Nature is my muse. I will absolutely return to depicting her glory."

Emma retreated and left Abbott to his dreams. Sam had written *The Innocents Abroad* and creatively interpreted the people he encountered. Abbott did the same thing with his portraits, but worked to give his subject a more positive aspect. Sam tore down his subjects in order to find a joke. Neither portrayal was an ultimate truth, but Emma preferred Abbott's method. Through Nina, she'd seen what pain Sam's method could cause.

The nursery door opened as she walked down the hallway. Nanny came out and closed the door softly, but not before Emma caught a glimpse of a wan face with huge solemn eyes. "Miss Emma? Can I say something?" Emma nodded. "Mistress Mary needs her mother, ma'am. She doesn't understand the grief in the household." The woman's eyes teared up.

Emma had been so worried about Kate and Abbott that she, too, had forgotten about Mary. "I'll speak to her mother." The nanny nodded and returned to the nursery.

In the parlor, Kate sat among several new lily plants that had been brought to Harry's wake a few months before. Alice had identified them as madonna lilies and calla lilies, but to Emma they were all the same, all mourning flowers. Kate's black dress enveloped her. It was designed to keep her stomach hidden as it burgeoned with new life in direct contrast to the specter of death that hung over the household.

"Feeling alright today?" Emma asked.

"As well as can be expected," Kate answered. The exchange had become their usual greeting. "I felt the baby move today."

"How wonderful. Are you going to spend the rest of the summer in this room?" The words came out harsher than Emma intended. "Someone besides your unborn babe needs you. When was the last time you hugged your daughter?"

Kate sucked in a breath. She raised a shaky hand to her forehead and closed her eyes for a moment.

"Mary needs you to show strength and mourn on the inside," Emma said. She felt horrible for pushing her friend, but that glimpse of Mary's pale, lost face wouldn't leave her mind. Poor little girl. Not only was her little brother gone, her parents were acting strangely. She didn't understand and didn't deserve this treatment. Emma was sorry it had taken the nanny's word to remind her. "I'll give you a few minutes, then I'll bring Mary downstairs." She waited until she received a reluctant nod from Kate.

Emma went upstairs to the nursery. She found Nanny sitting on the floor with a doll, trying to entice Mary into playing. Mary sat and stared straight ahead, not unlike how Emma had found Kate when she arrived at the house. "Mary, your mother would like to see you. Will you come downstairs with me?"

The girl nodded and stood up. Nanny scrambled to brush down the girl's dress with her hands and straighten the bow in her hair. Emma held out her hand, and Mary took it. Emma led her downstairs, saying, "Your mother is very sad right now. Can you make her feel better?"

The little girl nodded.

Emma wondered if she'd lost the ability to speak.

They entered the parlor. Kate sat where Emma had left her, but she smiled at Mary. "Come here, my darling, and sit with me," she said.

Mary climbed up on the sofa and nestled next to Kate, whose arm came around the girl in a hug. There may not have been much gaiety in the room, but Emma sensed contentment. It was a start.

IN OCTOBER, Kate was due to give birth, and Emma didn't think her frail friend could manage alone. Emma hoped the birth of a new child would help. She prayed daily that the birth would be a joy rather than a tragedy, then chastised herself for letting the notion enter her mind.

Mary was an expert in all things baby. She'd felt the baby move in Kate's tummy and laid claim to it as *her* baby. Kate was still subdued, but not quite so deep in her melancholy. Mary's natural exuberance helped cheer the entire household. Abbott finished two commissions, portraits of ugly society women that he'd subtly made younger and more pleasant looking. He'd basked in Emma's praise. So when Kate's labor began in late October, all was in readiness. Nanny occupied Mary in the nursery, and Abbott paced the downstairs hallway. Emma held her friend's hand as the midwife exhorted Kate to push. Kate screamed.

"Now, missus, remember that the pain is a reminder of Eve's original sin. When the babe is born, the pain you feel now will make you love it even more," the midwife said.

Emma kept her thoughts to herself, but doubted a mother's love could be increased with pain. If that were true, Kate's pain over the last few months would suffice to envelop this new person in love. She gripped Kate's hand tighter and whispered her own prayers. She focused on Kate's face, soothing her breathing and talking of their shared past. Let the midwife handle the important part.

Kate's groans and screams increased until finally the midwife announced the baby was coming. Another push and the baby slid into her hands, crying almost as soon as she touched it. The midwife expertly cut the umbilical cord and tied it off. "Here," she said to Emma. "Take him."

"Him?" Kate said.

Emma took the infant from the midwife. "You have a baby boy, Kate." Her eyes filled as she looked at the perfect new person in her friend's life. She cleaned the baby with the warm water and towels laid out for that purpose, then swaddled him in a blanket before laying him next to Kate in the bed. The midwife pushed on Kate's uterus until the afterbirth was expelled. With great efficiency, she gathered up the sheets and blankets under Kate. Emma arranged pillows and helped Kate sit up.

"I'll be on my way, then," the midwife said. "I'll tell the father before I leave, if that's alright?"

"Please," Kate said. She reached for the baby, and Emma placed him in her arms. She brushed Kate's hair because she knew Abbott would want to come right in. He arrived before she finished.

"A boy?" he asked.

Kate beamed with the glow of a very tired new mother. "A boy," she confirmed.

Abbott looked down on his wife and his son. "Ralph Waldo Thayer," he said.

"Ralph Waldo?" Emma said. She knew Ralph Waldo Emerson was a good friend of Abbott's, but why name the boy after that friend rather than any other?

"Ralph," Kate said, looking at her son in her arms.

Emma left Abbott and Kate alone with their son. She went to the nursery to tell Mary she had a baby brother named Ralph, then went downstairs to send someone to tell Kate's father, still living in Brooklyn.

THE CHRISTMAS HOLIDAYS THAT YEAR sparkled with love and warmth at the Thayers. Emma made the trip upriver to visit the new family just after celebrating the holiday with her family. Once again, laughter was heard more often than crying.

Emma stepped into a perfect holiday when she entered Kate's home. The house smelled of pine and cinnamon. In the parlor, several of Kate's plants had been relocated to make room for a conifer decorated with colorful glass ornaments and candles whose flames danced. Strings of cranberries gave the tree its bright Christmas color. Christmas cards filled the mantel over the fireplace, where a fire warmed the room.

Kate welcomed Emma with a smile. "Come in and get warm." She rocked two-month-old Ralph in her arms and gazed at him with sparkling eyes.

Mary ran in to show Emma the doll Santa had brought her. Abbott greeted Emma with a smile and asked after her mother and sisters. The happiness in the house made Emma smile, too, and tugged at her heart. Ralph was just the angel Kate had needed to bring her back to her family.

After supper, Mary danced while Kate played the piano in the parlor. Emma held Ralph and inhaled deeply his scent of baby powder. Abbott spoke about his new painting, waving his hands in animated explanation. "I want to show people symbolically, with their true natures revealed behind them."

He was so excited about his vision, Emma let him talk even though she didn't quite understand his concept. She loved his passion.

She stayed overnight and rocked Ralph to sleep, enjoying the deep contentment of holding a sleeping baby and knowing nothing else in the world was as important right now as that little life.

The next morning dawned clear but cold. Emma bundled up and took her leave of the Thayer family. As she sailed downriver on the ferry, the wind chapped her cheeks but the smile never left her face. For the next week, Emma painted and hummed as she recalled Kate and Abbott's happiness.

One morning, a month after her visit to the Thayers, a telegram arrived for Emma just as a savage winter storm attacked New York. Emma retreated to the parlor to read the telegram in her favorite chair by the window overlooking the East River. Snow swirled outside in a mad tangle of opposing winds that screamed and howled.

Ralph Waldo dead. Kate distraught. I don't know what to do. Abbott

The telegram slipped from Emma's fingers. She tried to recall the happiness of Christmas but could only picture unlit candles and broken ornaments. The snow covered rooftops and ship decks alike and froze the edges of the river. Tears rolled down Emma's face as she realized the storm meant she could not go to Kate immediately. Kate would survive this. She must. But she'd have to do it without Emma. She prayed Abbott would just take her in his arms and hold her. The thought brought Emma some comfort, at least.

Visions of baby Ralph looking up at Kate with adoration filled her head. She could almost feel the soft warmth of his sleeping body. The notion that he was gone devastated her. Kate and Abbott's grief would overwhelm them. Poor Mary wouldn't understand losing another brother. Emma covered her face with her hands and wept.

Dear Nina,

February 1881—I am consumed with grief for Abbott and Kate. Their three-month-old son died two weeks ago. That's two sons lost within months of each other. I wasn't able to visit until the snow storm abated and the river trip became feasible if not comfortable. Abbott paces the house and rages at God. Kate sinks into melancholy and spends her days staring out the window. She blames herself, I know not why. Abbott says the very air inside the house is full of germs and the only healthy place to be is outside, embraced by nature. I cannot imagine that being out in the middle of a storm is healthier than being inside with your family.

Their daughter, Mary, will be five years old next month. I cannot imagine there will be much of a celebration. I will bring her a present and maybe a little cake.

Mama feels bad for Kate and her family, but she tells me I spend too much time at the Thayer house. She accuses me of living Kate's life instead of my own. How can she imagine I want Kate's life with all its tragedy?

Abbott needs a distraction, if such a thing exists. I've written a letter to Sam Clemens, hinting that he should have Abbot paint his portrait. A portrait of such a well-known figure would no doubt help Abbott think about something other than this monstrous tragedy.

It's winter, so Alice's beloved flowers are sleeping until Spring. She and Violet spend their time embroidering and discussing issues of the day. Both are staunch advocates of women winning the vote. Papa spends his time closeted in his study with a stack of newspapers that he reads front to back every day. I think he misses the time he was in charge of the Sun.

I would like to spend more time painting, but I cannot leave Kate to grieve alone. We'll see what the rest of the year brings. I hope your days are spent in happier pursuits.

Emma

33

Nina Larowe
San Francisco, August 1882

"Death is the starlit strip between the companionship of yesterday and the
reunion of tomorrow."
- on monument erected to Mark Twain

Dear Emma,

Every time I think of you, I remember your devastating news about
Kate's sons last year. I have only known a mother's love from the daughter's
point of view. I cannot imagine Kate's pain at losing two children. You, I
suppose, are acquiring a taste of motherhood by helping Kate with Mary.
That includes the pain of loss as well as the joy. Does the joy truly outweigh
the pain? It must, or women would refuse to have children at all.

I do understand grief. Just this past spring, Mother succumbed after
suffering for a long while. As a child, Mother was my world. Everything I
did, she was there to accompany me and encourage me. She laughed with
me and cried with me, guiding me according to her life experience. I am a
different woman than my mother. She knew it and loved me for myself. She

was a proud, strong woman who lived life to the fullest. That is the best eulogy I can give to my mother, Samantha Lockwood Churchman.
  Nina

NINA WAS glad that Ney and Louise had married before Mother passed away. Her eyes had shone when she saw Ney's happiness, even if it wasn't clear whether she understood who Louise was. Ney's happiness also eased Nina's guilt over her relief at her mother's death. She'd been caring for an elderly woman who didn't resemble her mother at all, and the role had chafed.

She'd written to Ed and Fanny after Mother died, but only out of a sense of duty to Mother's grandchildren. Her niece, Edith, wrote back. Nina shared her letter with Ney and Louise over dinner.

"Edith says both her sisters are teachers now," Nina said. "She says that Fanny has a new baby, another boy." She scanned the letter. "Paul. They named him Paul. Apparently he's the apple of everyone's eye. Edith helps Fanny with the baby. All three sisters dote on their brother Edward and spoil Fanny's children, Walter and Paul, rotten— my words, not hers."

"What a lovely large family," Louise said.

"I wish our sister Emily had survived to see her daughters grown," Nina said. "Edith says her father is very disappointed in Edward, and Walter continues to be sickly. No doubt Paul is the hope of the Williams family."

Ney shrugged. "We'll probably exchange letters with them infrequently until someday we stop and realize we haven't corresponded in years and wonder what happened to them."

"No," Nina said. "I feel connected to my nieces after my time with them. Edith reminds me of Emma Beach in that she seems made for a life of service to someone else. If my support can help either of them find their own path, I'll be content. Little Nina, my namesake, will marry and have beautiful children. It's all she's ever wanted, and it seems perfect for her. Emily wants a career her father doesn't support. I pray her distress ends when Ed passes away. So I will continue to write to the three of them, at least."

"They sound like lovely young women," Louise said. She looked at Ney and reached for his hand.

Ney met her glance and smiled. "We have news, too, Nina. I've been accepted into the dental school at the University of California in San Francisco. It's the first dental school west of the Mississippi!"

Louise said, "I'm so proud of him."

Nina's eyes widened. "Oh, Ney, I'm so happy for you! I never understood why you became a lawyer anyway. Now you can pursue your own dream instead of Papa's."

"It means we will move to San Francisco, Nina," Ney said.

Louise hurried to add, "We'd love you to come with us."

"Oh, no, I wouldn't want to intrude on your married bliss," Nina said. She smiled, but inside her stomach churned. What would she do without Mother to care for, and without Ney and Louise? If there was one thing she'd learned by returning west, it was that family was important. She never wanted to live in a city without family again.

Ney said, "I don't want to lose touch with you the way we are losing touch with Emily's children. Please come with us."

Nina's heart opened and she embraced both of them. "You are my family and I would hate to be without you."

THEY MOVED TO SAN FRANCISCO with glad eyes to the future. Ney busied himself with school while Louise happily set about creating a home for them. Nina found herself the odd one out, with no clear function in the family dynamic. To contribute to the household and keep herself busy, she looked for a job. She didn't want to pursue acting right away, not relishing any conflict it might create with Ney and Louise. Instead, she wracked her brain to remember the names of her late father's connections in San Francisco. James Churchman had been a prominent lawyer in the city before he moved the family to Nevada. Surely someone would remember the Churchman name.

She learned that Mr. Burton, an employee of the United States Mint, had known her father and sought an interview with him. She spoke to his secretary about her father's early Republicanism, and his service to the government, but only received the standard reply, "I will take your name and address in case a vacancy should occur." Such a maddening phrase. It was as difficult to get an interview with the superintendent as it ever was to win a role in a New York play.

At dinner that night, she spoke to Ney and Louise about her idea of getting a job. "You don't need to do so," Ney said.

"It's not a bad idea," Louise said. "Our money won't go far if we're paying for school and have no income. I'm exploring the idea of taking in laundry or offering seamstress services."

Ney laughed. "Nina won't be doing laundry."

His sister wrinkled her nose. "From an acquaintance, I've learned that the mint needs to have bags made. I am not a seamstress, and have no idea what sort of bags are required, but if others can make them I can certainly learn. So I returned to the mint but found that making bags for Uncle Sam requires as much influence as being presented at Court!"

"These bags are made at home?" Louise said.

Nina nodded. "They send you a shipment of stiff canvas and a sample bag."

"I could help you," Louise said. "We'd have to hire a sewing machine. I can teach you how to use it."

"That sounds promising. I will persevere!" Nina said.

She continued to follow up, and before long she received her canvas and instructions. The bags were required to be large enough to contain a thousand silver dollars each. They had to be sewn with coarse linen thread, then turned and sewn again. Nina struggled to cut the canvas straight, even with Louise's help, and she broke several needles on the sewing machine. It took her a week to use up the first shipment of canvas. She was paid eight cents a bag but had to furnish her own thread. Nina would have quit but for Louise's encouragement.

Then came the day when Mr. Burton was appointed superintendent of the mint. Nina introduced herself and secured a job as one of the mint's employees. That gave her the right to walk up the steps of that massive granite building each day with pride in its stalwart strength.

"Those of us who work there call it The Granite Lady," she told Ney and Louise. "She's built on a granite and concrete foundation that was designed to prevent tunneling into the mint and to withstand earthquakes. So far, it has succeeded in both areas."

"I'm going to continue making bags," Louise says. "That works best for me, what with the household to run."

"And I will continue to be the best future dentist I can," Ney said.

The women laughed. Nina loved that Ney enjoyed dental school so much. She likened it to her first steps onstage after a lifetime of admiring the theater. She shook her head, refusing to mourn something long gone. She said, "There also is a legend that the cornerstone of the building was laid during a Masonic ceremony and filled with gold coins that were struck at the mint. The drama of that possibility intrigues me."

"Don't go snooping around looking for treasure," Ney warned.

"At least take some of my bags with you if you do!" Louise's eyes lit with laughter.

LATER THAT YEAR, a friend of Nina's was appointed head of the mint. She promoted Nina to a position of filing gold blanks down to the proper weight to be stamped for coins. Handling all that gold was a thrill at first. She imagined grand scenarios where it was all hers. After a while, though, the novelty fades and it was just work. They were shut up all day in a stifling room, clad in leather aprons attached to their drawers. Before leaving, they brushed every particle of gold into the drawer. It was interesting work, but it wasn't performing, which Nina missed as much as an amputated limb. She didn't know what was in store for her in the future, but she didn't believe it would be a long career with Uncle Sam.

34

E mma Beach
Keene, New Hampshire, 1887

"Nothing that grieves us can be called little... a child's loss of a doll and a king's loss of a crown are events of the same size."
- Mark Twain, Which Was the Dream?

Emma spent as much of the next six years as she could with the Thayers in Keene, New Hampshire. The rural town of Keene had been Abbott Thayer's birthplace, and after the emotional upheavals of the past couple of years, he wanted the familiarity of surroundings he knew. And Kate wanted Emma. Kate and Abbott now had three children—Mary, nine; Gerald, four; and Gladys, who had just passed her first birthday. Abbott had hoped the children would cheer Kate, but she once again struggled through each day, even with a good friend, a husband, and three children surrounding her.

Abbott had painted the portrait of Sam Clemens in 1882, not long after little Ralph's death. He'd left Kate at home, nursing her grief, and gone to Hartford, Connecticut, for the author's sittings. As Emma had hoped, that commission drew him back to painting. Kate, however, remained locked in grief. Emma longed to help her friend as much as a bug in Sam's ear about a portrait had helped Abbott.

Every day, Emma took Mary and Gerald outside. Sometimes they played near the house, and sometimes they walked. At nine, Mary enjoyed playing with her yoiunger brother, but she liked watching her father paint, too. Abbott loved the outdoors and never minded when Emma and the children followed him to whatever spot he set up his easel. He fell into what Emma called an artistic trance as he painted, with nearby Mt. Monadnock as his favorite subject.

One day, Emma took a picnic dinner on a walk in the forest with Abbott and the children while Kate napped. A thunderstorm had drenched the area the night before, but today the sun bathed the foliage. Gerald kept darting off into the brush and returning with sticks, rocks, or leaves he found interesting. Nanny followed a few steps behind. Kate had risen from bed and dressed, but declined to join them.

Mary tried to participate in the adult conversation. "Will we see Miss Turner and Miss Gorse today, Papa?"

Abbott bounced Gladys in his arms and grinned at Emma. They didn't often see his painting students while out walking. "Maybe we will."

"Will Arthur Carey visit later?" Mary said.

"He's expected today or tomorrow," Abbott answered. "He will sit for his portrait in the mornings then walk with us in the afternoon."

"He's rather a favorite of yours, isn't he, Mary?" Emma said.

Mary nodded, but seemed anxious. Her eyes darted to the tiny trail Gerald had taken. They could hear Gerald crashing through the foliage, returning with the treasure of the moment. Mary swung her arms at her sides and stared at the ground.

"Mary? Are you all right?" Emma asked.

Abbott leaped ahead in an exaggerated trot designed to entertain Gladys. In the next moment, he'd fallen into a hole that had been covered with brush. Emma cried out in surprise and hurried forward to make sure they were alright. The hole was almost hip deep on him, deep enough to jar him but not enough to injure him. Gladys cried at the unexpected jolt, and the nanny came forward, leaning down toward Abbott, who handed her the crying girl. Abbott climbed out of the hole and brushed the dirt and twigs off his clothes.

Mary had frozen, her face a mask of horror. Gerald bounced back into the group and stopped cold. "Papa? Did you fall in the hole?" He couldn't hide the glee in his voice.

Emma turned to Mary. "Sweetheart? Are you all right?"

Mary's eyes teared up. "We're sorry, Papa, we didn't mean to hurt you."

Gerald said, "Nanny was supposed to fall in the hole." He looked so crushed that Emma had to hide a smile.

Abbott roared with laughter. "You two scallywags dug this hole to trap Nanny? And covered it so cleverly!"

Nanny hid her own smile by burying her face in Gladys's dress for a moment. She looked down at Mary and said, "We'll have to have a discussion about what is funny and what is not."

Emma didn't envy her that discussion. For all that someone could have been hurt, the adventure of digging a hole trap was a creative use of the children's time. Abbott would appreciate the planning and teamwork it took to carry it out. Emma took Gerald's hand and Abbott took Mary's. The rest of the walk passed without incident, but when Emma caught Abbott's eye, they both grinned. As it always did when he smiled at her, Emma's heart skipped a beat. These family walks with Abbott and the children were Emma's secret delight. They all loved her, and she loved them. If sometimes she imagined loving Abbott in a different way, she shut down those thoughts right away. Abbott belonged to Kate.

THE NEXT DAY, Emma and Kate went for a walk together. The two women left the house on Washington Street and walked toward the reservoir in the park. Emma had learned not to walk the other direction down Washington, past the cemetery toward downtown. Kate always fixated on the cemetery and spoke of nothing but dying for the rest of the day. So Emma guided her friend the other direction, looking for a peaceful respite from the chaos of the Thayer house.

"What a beautiful day," Emma said. The sun illuminated trees that were just beginning to flame into fall colors. By the time they were at their most gorgeous, Emma would be back in Peekskill to spend the winter with her family. The time with her family felt more like a visit now than the time with Abbott and his family.

Kate said nothing.

"Maybe later we can bring Mary and Gerald to the park with us," Emma said. The children had been almost totally in Emma's care all summer. Nanny cared for Gladys, but if it weren't for Emma, Kate wouldn't have noticed the baby's first birthday in July. She'd worry about them when she was away, and she'd worry about Kate. And Abbott. She frowned. "Has Abbott said anything about school for Mary?"

Kate replied in a flat voice. "Abbott needs them at home. Besides, schools have germs. And school will corrupt them."

Emma remembered Abbott saying his children's youth would not be corrupted by a formal education. He taught them in a home full of music and books. "That's fine, but Mary will need a tutor at least, don't you think?"

"I can't love them too much, you know," Kate said. "I loved Harry and Ralph, and they died. If I try not to love the others, they will live."

"Not so," Emma said. "They need their mother's love." Abbott took a walk most days with Mary and Gerald, sometimes coming back with a little snake, or a toad. The children had learned their mother didn't leave the house very often. "Kate, your love didn't cause your sons to die. It wasn't your fault." According to Abbott, the doctor said if they kept repeating to Kate that it wasn't her fault that Kate might eventually believe it.

"You need to come visit me this winter," Emma said. "We can go to the city and shop for Christmas. The Statue of Liberty stands in the harbor now. It's been almost a year since she was dedicated. She's truly a wonder, Kate, you should see her."

"Maybe someday," Kate said.

"You know I'm leaving tomorrow," Emma said. She sighed, wanting to stay where she was needed. Her family expected her to join them for the winter. She'd extended this visit with the Thayers too long as it was. "I will miss all of you."

"The children will miss you," Kate said with a detached voice.

Her words stung Emma. Kate wouldn't miss her? Then she shook her head. Kate would miss her, as would Abbott. Kate just didn't think of saying it out loud.

They reached the park and turned back with only the sounds of birds and the wind in the trees. Entering the house, they were greeted by a paint-covered Abbott, smock and hair awry. "Ah! You've returned!" Abbott said. "Isn't *Angel* lovely? Don't you think it seems promising for my peculiarities that I did the wings and background first before I put Mary in at all?"

Kate nodded, but Emma enthused over the portrait of Mary, dressed all in white with large white wings spread behind her. The girl's dark hair was pulled back from her face, and her large dark eyes looked out of a pale face. The image tugged at Emma's heart. Abbott had been fixated lately on melding his image of purity and perfection with a symbolic portrayal of afterlife. At least he'd found an outlet for his grief. Mary looked like her mother, just a bit younger than when Emma had met Kate in school. Mary didn't have Kate's fiery sparkle, but then Kate no longer had it, either.

Kate settled herself in the parlor, and Abbott went to sit with her. Emma missed the long conversations she used to have with Kate when they were in school. She didn't know how to help Kate other than to help with the children.

IN THE MORNING, Abbott helped Emma load her valise onto the wagon and drove her to the train station in Harrisville.

"I wish I could stay," Emma said.

"So do I. She's better when you're around. Nanny does a good job with the children, but they really perk up when you visit. Please say you'll come back soon," Abbott said. "I'll miss you."

Emma's heart raced. "I'll be back when the snow melts in the spring."

"I'll hold you to that."

After he'd driven away from the station and Emma boarded the train, she was free to wallow in sadness. To keep herself from falling into melancholy herself, she started a letter to Nina.

DEAR NINA,

I am returning to Peekskill now to spend the snowy months with my family after spending all summer with the Thayers in New Hampshire. It pains me to see Kate so subdued. I remember her as the life of any gathering. Everyone wanted to be in the sparkle of her presence. Some days I want to shake her and demand she snap out of it, but I end up being gently supportive. I understand her grief, but after six years shouldn't she be able to push past it to lead a normal life? It sounds rather callous to say that, and I'd never voice it to anyone. After all, who knows how I would react in a similar situation. I tried to keep Kate engaged with the children, who are lively and smart. Mary already shows talent for art, and Gerald for making mischief as any young boy will. Gladys is a happy baby being raised by her nanny.

I never even told Kate that Mr. Henry Ward Beecher passed away last spring. I didn't want to bring up another death, even if it is one that affects my family more than hers. Mama grieved for Reverend Beecher maybe a bit more than necessary, but who am I to regulate how much (or how long) a person should grieve?

This winter I will distract myself from my friend's problems by reading The Adventures of Huckleberry Finn *and focusing on my painting. I may even take up the nagging problem of that painting with the rabbit hidden in the grass. I'm looking forward to seeing my sisters again, too. It's been a long summer without them. I hope they saved me some apple cider cake.*

Yours truly,
Emma

35

Nina Larowe
    Portland, Oregon, February 1888

"Perseverance is a principle that should be commendable in those with judgment to govern it."
- Mark Twain, "The Enemy Conquered; or Love Triumphant"

Dear Emma,

Recent years have been a struggle for both of us. You're spending time with Kate and Abbott Thayer, and I'm sure they're glad of a friend like you, but please make time for your own painting. It's not selfish to make a bit of time for yourself. I have not read The Adventures of Huckleberry Finn *yet, nor have I read the one before it,* The Prince and the Pauper. *I formed a negative impression of the author on the cruise and afterwards, and he has done nothing to change that opinion. I've read two of his works and found them full of inaccuracies, embellishments, exaggerations, and utter untruths. Yes, I am aware they are purported to be novels, but anyone who writes so close to the truth should include more of the truth in his work.*

I'm living alone now in San Francisco. Earlier this year, Ney's beloved Louise passed away. Distraught, he couldn't remain in the city. Having spent so much of his life in dry, sun-baked Nevada towns, he decided to find a place among flowing rivers and greenery. He chose Portland and set up his dental practice there. So he lives alone with his personal tragedies and practices his dream job. I live alone with my own tragedies and failures, looking back over my life with a mixture of pride and pain but no regrets. I'd love to get back on the stage, but at this point my path forward is murky. I just can't see it.

Excuse my maudlin tone. I am feeling the lack of family keenly at present. When you're alone, it's very difficult to keep spirits up. It's human nature to assume the worst and choose the darkest path. My most recent setback is yet another slump in my fortunes. Since the election of President Cleveland, a Democratic furor has resulted in all Republican employees at the San Francisco Mint to be fired. Therefore, I am without income.

Family is the constant in one's life, is it not? I am the only family Ney has, and he is mine. Therefore, I've decided I must move to Portland. I will write again from the Pacific Northwest.

Yours truly,

Nina

GLANCING out the window of Ney's house in Portland five months later, Nina watched the snow that just would not stop falling. The *Oregonian* claimed that this storm had buried the entire West Coast, dropping almost four inches of snow in San Francisco. Portland was no better. In January, the temperature had averaged twenty-two degrees. Shivering, she returned to her couch by the fire.

Ney had welcomed her into his home when she arrived with only two hundred dollars to her name after a rough four-day steamship voyage from San Francisco. She found Portland to be a small city, still somewhat primitive, full of rivers that cried out for bridges but were served only by antiquated ferries and horse cars. The new Portland Hotel was nothing but foundation walls and actually looked like an old ruin, so she'd moved in with her brother. They were content—the widowed dentist and the divorced actress—but Nina had never anticipated such a brutal blizzard.

"I hate snow and ice," she said. "I will never even hang a picture of it in my home." She turned back to the room, where Ney was preparing to brave the storm to go into his office. "I came to Portland to live, but I might go home."

Ney came up behind her. "Portland is home now, Nina. It's never this cold, though. Usually in January it's a full fifteen degrees warmer."

Nina gave him the dirtiest look she could manage, but then laughed.

He laughed back at her and thrust a copy of the *Oregonian* into her hands. A short article was circled. "Look!"

"Dr. Churchman Instructs and Amuses," Nina said. "What a great headline. Is this about your trout thing?"

"Trout thing?" He widened his eyes. "I'll have you know it was an important talk to the Oregon Fish and Game Association. They loved it. Mark my words, I'll be president of the organization someday."

"You might well be. The paper says your talk was 'instructive as well as humorous' and 'received amid considerable mirth.' Congratulations for making a fish funny." Nina laughed. "No, really, Ney, good for you."

He must have heard the misery beneath her words. He said, "When the storm clears we'll go for a sleigh ride and watch the kids skate on Guild's Lake."

Ney always made her smile. "I look forward to that, brother dear."

When the snow gave way to Portland's usual mud, Nina set out to find a way to teach elocution or gymnastics, determined to both keep busy and not to be a financial burden on her brother. At one school for young ladies, the headmistress said, "People don't need elocution unless they are going to recite or go on stage."

Nina told her, "Mastering elocution makes one graceful, one's speech clear and distinct, one's voice mellow and pleasing, one's walk and poise elegant, one's conversation refined. In fact it covers a much larger field in the way of general culture than anyone dreams."

The headmistress fixed her with an icy glare, and Nina left without the job.

At a large house with a room to let, the landlady told her, "I can't have elocutionary work in my parlor." She went on to explain that the sort of program Nina wanted to run would make too much noise. But later Nina found out that she rented to a singer, who sang all day from base to top notes, then still higher into shrieks.

Nina bemoaned the situation to Ney. "I could play the piano all day long and it would be fine. If I properly recite one piece in a private house, I would be asked to desist."

Ney considered the situation. "You need a few speaking engagements to show what a good elocutionist can do. Let me see what I can arrange."

Nina nodded. "Public performances as a way to get my name in front of people. Just like I used to help Marcus do. I can also teach gymnastics. Young ladies with speaking skills and physical strength can do far more than act on the stage."

"Let's concentrate on your readings. You can demonstrate your elocution skills and create demand."

Nina nodded but didn't let her hopes rise far.

A week later, Ney had set up a short series of engagements. "Your first one is at the City Barn on Thursday night," he said.

Nina laughed. "A barn is hardly a New York stage, but it's a good place for a crowd to gather."

On Thursday night, Nina donned her performance dress, being sewn of stiffer silk than a day dress, and decorated with heavier brocade and buttons. She melted wax and fixed it between her two front teeth, to fill the space there, laughing to herself when she remembered the letter from an audience member in Reno who suggested the wax as a way to improve her looks.

Wooden sidewalks had been placed over the muddy streets, but Nina took a horse-drawn streetcar to her speaking engagement. She traveled from downtown to the northwest section of Portland, where the barn was located. The barn itself was a plain wood plank structure that didn't even have a sign out front. A few people milled about out front, and that gave Nina hope that the evening would be well attended.

Inside, the stage was a roped-off section of the floor where someone had placed a platform for Nina to stand. The roof soared above like the best New York theater, and chairs filled the room. She loved performing, and this was a place to do so. Nina stepped up onto the box and waited for the audience to settle into their chairs. Nervous anticipation settled over her, as it had for every performance she'd ever given, but a confident smile remained on her face.

When the spotlight shone on her, Nina blossomed. She performed artistic renderings of standard authors as well as blank verse. She even sang two songs. In every piece, she modeled tonal changes as well as projection of her voice. The result was a fair approximation of a professional New York production. Nina stepped down from her platform, well pleased.

"That went well," Ney told her. "I wish I'd seen you perform in New York. You must have been amazing."

"Thank you," Nina said. "I value that, coming from you."

Her first review appeared in the *Oregonian* a few days later.

The reading given by Mrs. Nina Larowe, at the City Barn, on Thursday night of last week, was not a decided success from a financial point, and only moderately so in the way of entertainment. Had it been a burnt cork minstrel show, or something of the "can-can" order, the attendance would probably have been larger and the applause louder. Those who did attend got their money's worth in the way of very fair renditions of popular pieces, some of which were "elocutionary chestnuts" but good nevertheless. Her character sketch of the backwoods school-girl's essay was inimitable and worth the price of admission.

Ney said, "It's not a glowing review, but it's not entirely bad."

"Not the worst review," Nina agreed.

Despite the reviewer's lukewarm view, people continued to attend Nina's readings. She taught elocution and acting classes focusing on Shakespeare. When spring finally arrived in the Pacific Northwest,

Nina took her students outside to improve their voice and strengthen
their lungs. In her mind, she imagined her students performing readings of Shakespeare to an appreciative audience.

36

Emma Beach
Keene, New Hampshire, May 1889

"A dream that comes only once is oftenest only an idle accident, and hasn't any message, but the recurrent dream is quite another matter—oftener than not it has come on business."
- Mark Twain, "3000 Years Among the Microbes"

In the spring of 1889, Emma once again headed to Keene, New Hampshire, to join the Thayer family. This time, though, she found herself anticipating long walks in the woods with Abbott rather than gloomy one-sided conversations with Kate. The feeling seemed disloyal to Kate, and guilt almost overcame her. Then anger washed the guilt away. Emma was entitled to enjoy her summer, too. There was only so much wallowing in grief with Kate that she could take.

Emma arrived at the house only to find a black wreath on the door. Terror drove her inside, where the hall mirror was covered. She ran to find Abbott, or Nanny, or Cook, afraid Kate had died. But Kate sat in the dark parlor in her usual place. Emma took a deep shuddering breath to calm her racing heart. "Kate? Has someone died?"

Kate didn't look up. "Papa has passed away."

"Your father? Oh Kate, I am so sorry." Emma ran to wrap her friend in a warm hug even as she knew that grief could not be hugged away.

An untouched meal lay on the low table beside Kate's sofa. "Have you eaten anything?"

"She's touched nothing this week at all." Abbott's ragged voice reached Emma from the doorway.

She turned toward him. His sunken eyes were full of despair, his rumpled hair showing how restless his nights had been. "I'm so sorry," Emma said. She walked over to Abbott and hugged him.

Abbott's arms came around her automatically, warm against Emma's arms and back. He buried his face in her hair and sobbed. Emma felt his tears trickle down her head, as if Abbott's very life drained away. She held him and swallowed hard to control her own sorrow in order to comfort him.

Abbott gained control and pulled away. After a few deep breaths, he took Emma's arm and led her out of the parlor. "Her melancholy is worse. I can't help her." He stopped.

Emma waited. Abbott clearly had more to say.

"The children don't know." He stopped again. This time, once he'd started, the words tumbled out. "I have to take Kate to Blooming-dale's. Not the department store. The sanatorium in Boulevard City. The doctor says she has nervous exhaustion. I can't help her here. No one can. It's my fault, Emma. It's my fault she's in this dark state. She has to go to a sanatorium."

"You have supported her as best you could," Emma assured him. Her heart ached for him, for Kate, for their family. How difficult it must have been for him to make this decision. "Does the doctor say she'll get better?"

"They can't say."

"Oh, Abbott." Emma wondered when grief would stop attacking this family she loved as if it were her own. Abbott and the children would have to adjust to life without Kate. Emma brought herself up short. Kate hadn't been an active part of the family for eight years.

Her grief over the loss of her sons was too great, and now she'd lost her father. Gladys and Gerald had no memory of their mother as the vivacious presence Emma had known in school. Mary had been five when her brothers died, so only the earliest memories of her mother were different from the morose woman sitting in the dark parlor. It was Abbott who would need the most comfort, and Emma would continue to be the reliable friend.

The rest of the day Emma greeted the staff, played with the children, and settled back into the guest room she called hers. Everyone treated her like a savior, coming to save the Thayer family from darkness. If only she could.

The next morning dawned gray for a spring day, appropriate for the adults' emotions as Emma prepared Kate for her trip. She dressed her friend in a good dress, combing her hair and pinning her hat in place, all while talking about inconsequential things. When emotion threatened, Emma grew quiet. Kate said nothing.

Nanny kept the children inside as Emma led Kate outside. Emma was surprised how unresponsive Kate was, even worse than a year ago. As much as she didn't want to admit it about her friend, the doctor was right. Kate needed to be somewhere they might be able to help her. She needed more than Abbott and Emma could give her.

Emma stood by the front door as Abbott took Kate's arm and led her to the horse and wagon he'd borrowed from the neighbor. A trunk of Kate's things already waited in the wagon. Abbott helped her in and climbed in beside her. The physical evidence of her friend leaving devastated Emma. She wasn't sure Kate even recognized that she was leaving her children, possibly forever. As the wagon rolled away, Emma let the tears fall.

In the years since her babies died, Kate had been quiet. Emma didn't understand how her absence now made the house even quieter. She refused to let her sorrow affect the children. Taking a cue from Abbott's belief that fresh air healed everything, Emma went to find Mary who, at eleven, was the unofficial leader of the nursery.

"Mary, it's warm outside even if the sun isn't out. Should we take the children for a walk in the woods?" Emma knew that she couldn't tell the girl what to do. It was best to suggest an activity by asking permission.

"We'll take Nanny to carry Gladys when she gets tired," Mary said.

With the decision made, Emma was able to make sure they all put on their sturdy walking shoes. She arranged with Cook to pack a picnic hamper with dinner for the two adults and three children.

Nanny tried to take Gladys's hand as they left the house, but the three-year-old snatched it away, insisting on walking by herself. "At least we can still catch her if she toddles off," Emma said. Nanny smiled and picked up the picnic hamper. Emma slung a satchel over her arm, but refused to say what it contained. Gerald lost interest almost immediately, but Mary gave the satchel sidelong glances for quite awhile.

Gerald seemed to have two goals on the walk—to find a stick to poke everything he passed, and to stomp in every puddle left by the rainstorm earlier in the week. Nanny assured Emma this was normal behavior for a five-year-old boy.

Mary alternated between her childish and grownup personas. She started out walking with Emma behind the rest of the family, but every time Gerald exclaimed over something he'd found, Mary ran ahead to see. In this way, they found a patch of wild strawberries and gathered some to add to their meal. Emma enjoyed the children's wonder at their discoveries. Their delight in the woods lightened Emma's sorrow but didn't dispel it.

When the children got hungry, Emma spread a blanket on the ground under a tree, and Nanny set out the simple meal on wooden plates. Each person received a ribbon-tied paper package that contained a sandwich of chopped ham and mayonnaise. Emma sliced pound cake for dessert. When Gerald snuck bites of cake before finishing his sandwich, Emma sipped her glass of cold lemon tea and pretended not to notice.

In the space of time between eating and resuming activity, when even the children were at peace, Emma opened her satchel. "I brought a few painting things in case you wanted to paint," she said.

Mary leaned toward her to see what Emma had brought. Gerald appeared to be more interested in something he spotted in the dirt.

Emma set up a small easel and put a blank canvas on it. Handing Mary a brush, she instructed the girl to paint shapes and colors as she saw them. Emma busied herself setting up another canvas for herself and let Mary experiment. She knew Abbott had given his daughter some direction with paint and brushes, but didn't know how much. Emma chose a medium green to wash the canvas before adding tree detail.

Nanny occupied Gladys with a rag doll and kept an eye on Gerald as he collected rocks.

Emma resisted peering over Mary's shoulder. She worked on her own canvas for a while then put down her brush. Emma exaggerated peering at Mary's work, turning her head, then sitting back and stroking her chin. She was rewarded with a rare giggle. In truth, though, Mary's instincts for composition and color were very good for her age. "It looks good. You've done a wonderful job with the tree-line." Mary beamed.

They worked until Gerald became so bored he was a nuisance, running around the painters like a wild animal. Nanny packed up the lunch and Emma packed the paints. She slung the satchel over her shoulder and picked up her painting. "A painter carries her own work," she told Mary.

"I'm not a painter," Mary said. "I'd rather write stories." Nonetheless, she proudly picked up her canvas, careful not to smudge the wet paint. As they walked home, Emma's mind spun with ideas to help Mary write her stories.

ABBOTT RETURNED THE NEXT MORNING. His clothes and hair were more rumpled than usual, and he had dark circles under his eyes. Emma suspected Mary noticed her father's condition, but the girl didn't say anything. Gerald and Gladys were just glad to have him home. After they'd greeted their father, Nanny took the children upstairs.

"How are you, really?" Emma asked their father.

Abbott crossed the room and stood awkwardly in front of her. As naturally as if he'd been one of the children, Emma took him in her arms. He laid his head on her shoulder and cried as if Kate had died. Emma swallowed her tears. She must be strong.

When he'd cried himself out, Abbott pulled back and ran his hand through his hair. "I'm sorry," he said.

Impulsively, Emma reached out and took his hand. "Oh, Abbott, you don't have to be sorry. Kate is where she needs to be." She wanted to add reassurance that Kate would be coming home, but she didn't want to hold out false hope.

He gave her a faint smile in return and squeezed her hand. "Should we walk in the woods?" he asked.

"Always a good idea," Emma said.

Emma inhaled deeply as they walked among the pine trees. She didn't want this walk to end. The woods restored Abbott's spirits. He walked a little straighter, with a bit more spring in his step. Emma showed him a bank swallow's nest she and the children had found. He leaned closer to her for a better angle to see the egg. She placed a hand on his shoulder, and he turned toward her, laying his head against hers.

Although she wanted to soothe him, Emma felt uncomfortable with this closeness. He belonged to Kate. Emma would not be the one to take her husband the minute she was gone. When they returned to the house, Emma kept away from Abbott.

For the next few days, Emma kept the children busy. They walked with their father every morning, sometimes going quite far up the slope of Mt. Monadnock. Later, they often paddled the canoe with him on Dublin Pond. Emma brought her satchel of painting supplies a few times, and Abbott seemed happy with Mary's progress. When Abbott brought his own canvas, Emma's heart sang. She loved to see him painting. It was a good way to move beyond grief.

"Late spring is a good time to paint the mountain," Abbott said.

"You like to paint the mountain in any season," Emma teased. He gave her a bigger smile than she'd seen from him in a long time.

Mary left her painting to join her siblings as they played a chase game with Nanny. Emma and Abbott painted side by side. The birds sang, and the breeze rustled the trees. It was the most peace she'd ever found in unspoken companionship with another person.

The feeling lingered as they finally packed up their things and headed back to the house. Nanny took the children inside to wash their hands and faces, and to let them have a short rest before supper.

Emma followed Abbott to his studio. "Can I store my painting things in here? Do you have a spare corner?"

Abbott's face lit up with humor. "If anyone can manage to find a spare corner, it's you."

Emma laughed.

He took her canvas and satchel from her and laid them against a wall. Then he took both her hands in his and pulled her close so there was barely an inch between them. Abbott looked down at her and said, "Thank you, Emma, for being exactly what I need."

Looking up at him, Emma tried not to recoil. She wanted to be what he needed, but what was that, exactly? He leaned closer to her and set his chin on the top of her head for a moment before pulling back and dropping her hands. Emma was shaken by the nearness of him, uncertain of his intentions.

During supper, Emma focused on the children, and after supper she excused herself early. In the guest room, she sat on the bed and explored her relationship with her best friend's husband. She shook her head. No matter what Kate's condition, she would not be the woman who took advantage of a man's pain when his wife was away.

She hadn't had a relationship with a man since Sam, and that was a relationship only in the head of a silly young girl. Now she was a woman in her thirties, still unable to discern if a man meant friendship or something more with his nearness. She only knew she wanted to be with Abbott Thayer all the time. She packed her bag and spent the night restlessly pacing the room, weighing the children's need for her as a mother figure against the pitfalls of Abbott's potential need for something more.

In the morning, Emma asked Abbott to drive her to the train

station in Harrisville and tried not to react to the shocked anguish in his expression. She took her leave of the children and rode in silence with Abbott to Harrisville. When he pulled up the horses at the station, Abbott turned to Emma.

"What did I say? Are you angry with me?" he said.

"Of course not, dear Abbott." The confusion in his expression tugged at her heart, but she couldn't stay. She couldn't let her sorrow for the family allow Abbott to grow any closer to her, couldn't allow him to depend on her any more than he already did. If she said anything to him, he might laugh at her for misinterpreting his actions, much as Sam would laugh if he ever learned about the depth of her infatuation. Emma couldn't bear that.

Abbott lifted her valise from the wagon, saw that a porter loaded it, and stood next to the horse while she prepared to board the train. Emma managed to keep a pleasant face, if without a smile, only by clenching her teeth to prevent words escaping that she dare not say. But she couldn't leave without saying anything. She turned before climbing into the passenger car. "Take care of yourself and the children, Abbott." It was the best she could do.

Emma took a seat beside the window and watched the man, horse, and wagon grow smaller with distance. She tried to distract herself by sorting paint colors in her head that she might use to depict the scenery, but it didn't work. All the way to Peekskill, her jumbled thoughts tormented her. Abbott's entire face lit up when he was inspired, either to paint or take the children on an adventure. Emma loved those children almost as much as Kate did. But Kate deserved a loyal friend, and it wasn't loyal to dream of intimate moments with her husband. Abbott was a wonderful father. She wanted to assist him with the children. He didn't deserve to raise those children alone, for even though Kate was still alive, she was gone. But she didn't know how to prevent him from taking her hand or pulling her into his arms.

At the first stop, Emma left the train to send a telegram to her family. As a result, her sister Alice was at the station with a hired wagon to see her home.

"Rather a sudden return," Alice said as they left the station. "What happened? Last year you were a free household manager to the Thayers all summer."

Emma had kept her back ramrod straight, her expression neutral, for the entire trip. Alice meant home, though. Alice was her sister. "Oh Alice," she said. Her posture crumbled, and she covered her face with her hands.

Alice took her sister's hand and waited.

"Kate is in a sanatorium. Abbott is beside himself. I had to comfort him. The children don't understand," Emma said as the tears began to fall.

Alice squeezed Emma's hand and said, "Tell me more about comforting Abbott."

Emma knew Alice would pick up on the important parts of whatever she said. Alice would never judge her, though. Now that both sisters were in their thirties, their age difference didn't matter. Emma was no longer her sister's role model. She was Alice's confidante and Alice was hers. She told her sister about Abbott taking Kate to the sanatorium, and how distraught he was. Then she said, "He held me."

"He *held* you," Alice repeated, her brow furrowed. "What does that mean?"

"In his arms. Just for a minute. A couple of times," Emma said. She paused, then said, "I love the children. They need a mother."

"I'm sure that's true. But, darling Emma, you don't have to step in for Kate in all aspects of her life. You aren't Kate. I hope you came home to try and put Abbott out of your head. Now let's talk about something else. Violet has a friend in Peekskill who might as well be living on the farm with us."

"A beau?" Emma's interest piqued, even though she knew Alice was trying to distract her.

"No, it's a young lady. Lucy and Violet are so much alike I'm surprised they get along at all."

Emma smiled. "It's nice for her to have someone her own age. It's hard to be friends with sisters who are old spinsters like us." She laughed, and the grip of anguish around her heart lessened.

"She's only ten years younger than me," Alice said. "You are the old spinster of the family. After all, I'm just barely thirty, but you are pushing *forty*." She held a hand to her forehead as if she was about to faint.

Emma laughed. "It's so good to be home." Her words coincided with the wagon pulling up to the Beach farmhouse and Violet running down the porch steps, followed more slowly by their mother.

Once the women of the family had greeted each other, Violet introduced Lucy, who had waited on the porch. Lucy was a slender, hazel-eyed girl, politely gracious, who definitely looked comfortable with the Beach family, especially Violet.

Emma escaped to her room, pleading exhaustion from the trip. The emotional roller coaster of Kate going away, of Abbott's need for her, of her family's warm welcome, finally subsided. Emma could look out her window at her gnarled apple tree and be transported to a place of serenity.

Dear Nina,

I'm home in Peekskill now, and will be spending summer with my family for the first time in many years. It's not that the Thayers don't need me, in fact Abbott may need me more than ever.

I remember when we met on board the Quaker City *twenty-one years ago. You were determined to conquer the spotlight and focus it on yourself. I wanted only to assist from the shadows, to be of value to someone who needed me. Now it seems I have found that, but he is my dear friend's husband. Her illness changes that not a whit. My sisters are well launched on their own lives, so neither they nor my mother need me like they once did. Part of me misses that time, but part of me is eager to devote my life to painting. I can hear you now. You're saying you've heard that before. You're not wrong.*

Recent dreams have dazzled me, of helping Abbott Thayer to show and sell paintings of the natural landscapes he loves so much. He concentrates on his art so thoroughly that the children can get into all sorts of mischief if they are allowed to play unsupervised near him while he's painting. He needs someone to supervise them.

Abbott has begun to paint wings on his female subjects, beginning with the picture he did of Mary. The women he paints are elegant but not ostentatious, and he paints them with introspective expressions. The wings show how much he values women and children as connections to heaven. These are some of his most moving works. He often uses his children as subjects, but he has never painted Kate, and has not asked me to pose for him.

My going on about him reveals much, does it not? I cannot be with him for fear of encouraging physical closeness, and I cannot be apart from him without wondering how he is coping. So I am home with my family in Peekskill and will be painting flowers, not angels, this summer.

Yours truly,

Emma

37

N ina Larowe
Portland, Oregon, 1889

*"The primary rule of business success is
loyalty to your employer. That's all right--as a theory. What is the matter
with loyalty to yourself?"*
- Mark Twain- Speech

First Street was the business district in Portland. Ney's office was there, and the YMCA was right next door. Nina knew the YMCA provided services for community members to enrich their lives and reach their full potential.

"Do you know anyone at the YMCA?" she asked Ney one day at dinner.

"Only to nod a greeting to. No connections. What are you thinking?"

"They offer physical fitness classes. I wonder if they'd let me teach gymnastics to women?"

"To women?" Ney's brow furrowed. "Why would women need gymnastics?"

"Hmmm, obviously there is a need for education," Nina said.

Nina went in and spoke to Mr. Frost, the head of the organization.

"I am eager to share the work of Dr. Diocletian Lewis with women who were unable to travel to Boston to hear it before his death. Dr. Lewis was an advocate of temperance and physical activity. His exercise program came in the nick of time, for well-to-do women were either delicate or invalids. They spent most of their time lying on couches, since while standing they had to lace themselves to a 20-inch waist and weigh themselves down with some 20 pounds of clothing. Dr. Lewis prescribed a loose dress and low-heeled shoes. He then invented the light wooden dumbbell, the wand, and the bean bag."

"I am not in a position to offer lectures about the benefits of exercise," Mr. Frost said.

"I provide that information solely to convince you of the validity of Dr. Lewis's program, which I studied in Boston two decades ago. My intention is to offer a demonstration of the exercises, to be followed by classes if interest warrants."

"An exhibition I can do." He arranged an evening for the program.

When she told Ney, he said, "I'm proud of you! That took a great deal of insight and motivation to approach him. I'll be in the audience."

On the appointed night, Nina walked into the hall at the front of the audience, straightened her back and displayed her best posture. She wore a short dress over her bloomers, which were necessary to allow proper movement. At the center of the stage area, a small table held the implements she would use to demonstrate the exercises. When she spoke, her voice reached the far corners of the room even though the place was not full.

"A century ago," she began, "a respectable lady was expected to show her gentility by fainting now and again. She was not allowed to be healthy or engage in sports. The late Dr. Diocletian Lewis changed all that. The exercises required of athletic young men, however, did not meet the needs of boys, old, fat or feeble men; or girls and women. Tonight I will present an introduction to his program of light gymnastics for women and children."

Nina picked up a dumbbell from the table and held it aloft. "The weight is slight because the manner of exercise requires it. Most useful are exertions in which the lungs and heart are made to go at a vigorous pace." She proceeded to demonstrate the five positions, in the correct order, twisting the dumbbells rather than lifting.

She performed additional exercises with the wand before she picked up the bean bag. Nina had no partner with whom to demonstrate, so she just said, "Throwing and catching objects not only affords good exercise of the muscles of the arms and upper half of the body, but cultivates a quickness of eye and desirable coolness of nerve." She kept the bean bag in her hand, enjoying the tactile crunch of the beans as she squeezed it.

Nina concluded the performance with Dr. Lewis's admonition that women, invalids, and children could all benefit from regular use of these exercises. She thanked them for coming and bowed, a traditional homage to a respectful audience.

Rather than applause, a smattering of conversation and even a few laughs accompanied the people as they left. One woman said, "Imagine coming to class in such an outfit!"

No one inquired about exercise classes, and Mr. Frost didn't invite her back. Nina said to Ney, "The idea of women exercising is too new."

Dear Emma,

Disappointment has won again. I suppose it's better to be defined by how we progress after disappointment rather than let the disappointment itself do so. In trying new ideas, I sometimes form false impressions of people and how they will react to me. When reality strikes like a winter storm, it throws me off course. I resolve to teach myself to face future disappointment with cheerfulness and courage despite the pain. I remember once telling you that you cannot succeed without trying. I still believe that, even when it seems like every effort is failing.

Yours truly,
Nina

38

E mma Beach
Peekskill, New York, 1891

"...my dream-artist can draw anything perfectly."
- Mark Twain, "My Platonic Sweetheart"

For all of 1890, letters from Abbott Thayer wrenched Emma's heart. He blamed himself for Kate's dark state and claimed his wife's physical deterioration would not be so horrible if only her soul was visible. Emma empathized with him. The idea of her dear friend confined to an institution grated on her nerves. As the summer progressed, Abbott's pleas for Emma to visit had become more strident. *You are my dear fairy godmother, Emma,* he wrote. *The children and I miss you dreadfully.*

Emma carried his most recent letter in the pocket of her painting apron. When she received a new one, she put the old letter in the writing desk in her studio and the new one in her pocket. She felt connected to Abbott in that way, closer to the wife he never mentioned. Sometimes as Emma painted, the art required her entire concentration, but sometimes her mind was free to wander places she shouldn't let it go.

Emma found herself wondering what it would be like to be married to Abbott. When she was painting, she'd become aware of her hand holding the paintbrush and remember Abbott's hand as it deftly and confidently brushed the canvas. He always had paint on his hands. It made her smile to remember guessing to herself the subject of his painting according to the colors of paint on his hands. Then she would think of Kate and imagine the conditions at the asylum, based on the New York *World* articles by Nellie Bly. Bly had been admitted to the Women's Lunatic Asylum on Blackwell's Island for ten days in 1887. In Emma's mind, Kate's face overlaid Bly's vivid descriptions of the experience and filled her soul with dread.

Kate had been at Bloomingdale Asylum for a year when Emma could no longer endure the pain of wondering about her. On a sunny day that May, Emma took the train to Manhattan, then a ferry to Blackwell's Island, a two-mile strip in the East River. She hired a carriage that carried her along rural roads dotted with mansions. The carriage turned on to Bloomingdale Drive and continued through a lush, manicured campus complete with gardens and paths, groves of trees, playgrounds and greenhouses, and views of the River. It pulled up before a beautiful limestone building that looked more like a Victorian mansion than a state-run facility.

Emma sat for a moment and stared at a facade partially obscured by mature trees. She wanted to go inside and see Kate with her own eyes, but she also wanted to turn her back and drive away. Emma needed to reassure herself that Kate was being cared for. It was only possible to do that by going inside. She took a deep breath, got out of the carriage, and started up the wide front steps.

A hush enveloped Emma as she entered the building. The hall was empty. She hesitated, not sure where to go. An ear splitting scream shattered the silence and made Emma gasp. A man came out of what must be an office, looking expectantly at her. He'd clearly been drawn out by her gasp rather than the scream. Emma refused to consider what that might mean.

"Hello," she said. "I am here to visit Kate Thayer."

The man nodded, moving his head so far up and down that it was almost a bow. "I see. Might I ask who you are?"

"I am Emma Beach. She is my friend." Emma stood tall and spoke with confidence. She'd seen her father deal with obsequious staffers like this all her life.

He muttered an acknowledgement, and told her his name so quickly she didn't catch it. "Is this your first visit, Miss Beach, to our facility?"

She nodded. "I presume an appointment isn't necessary?"

"Oh no, ma'am, of course not. Please follow me." he started along the main corridor. "Our female patients are housed in the Green Building, named not for the color, mind you, but for John C. Green, whose widow donated the money to build it."

Emma said. "What is your treatment goal for your patients?"

"I can't discuss specific cases with you, of course," her guide said. "In general, we prioritize the humanity of people. Bloomingdale takes people who are disruptive and removes them from society so they can get back in touch with what makes them human. Here we go."

He stepped back and indicated Emma should precede him into a large room off the corridor. She stepped in and scanned the space. Women sat and stared out the window, or off into space. Others ambled across the space without looking at anything but the floor. A few napped. Emma had to look twice to recognize Kate. The guide followed her to Kate's side, obviously intending to stay with her.

Kate wore the same drab gray dress that the other women did. Her dark hair had lost its shine. It had been hastily brushed, if at all. She sat in a worn leather armchair near a window, but her gaze was directed just to the left of the view.

"Mrs. Thayer?" the guide said gently. "You have a visitor."

Kate didn't respond.

"Kate, it's Emma. I've come to visit you." Emma moved forward to perch on a leather chair that matched Kate's and had evidently been set out to encourage conversation.

Kate moved her focus from some undetermined point in the

distance to Emma's face. She showed no signs of recognition. Emma's stomach clenched at the hollowness in her friend's eyes. She was here now, though, and needed to make the best of it.

"Your children miss you, but they are doing fine." She searched her brain for tidbits to share, dismayed to find no current ones. "Mary is quite an accomplished writer. You would be proud. Gerald is learning to paint, but little Gladys just loves to make splashes of color."

Was that a hint of a smile on Kate's face? Emma continued.

"Abbott misses you, of course, and wishes he could visit more often." As she spoke the words aloud, Emma wondered if Abbott had visited at all.

Kate's faint smile didn't change.

"The grounds here are really quite stunning. Do you want me to bring your painting things?" Kate turned her head away from Emma.

"I'm sure when you return home, they will all be delighted to welcome..." Emma's words trailed off as the guide touched her arm and shook his head.

"We don't discuss home," he whispered.

Emma nodded and sat for a while in silence. The serene view of the East River belied the anxieties swirling beneath the empty eyes of the Bloomingdale residents. Emma wanted to scream, to run, to howl with laughter at something—anything that would ruffle the complacency of this place.

She stood and touched Kate lightly on the shoulder. "Stay well, my friend. I will come again." Emma felt like a traitor as she followed the guide back to the lobby of the main building. "How is she doing, really?" she asked.

"We don't discuss patient progress with visitors."

Emma nodded.

The carriage started off as soon as Emma was seated. She didn't need to look back. Every image of the facility and its patients was ingrained in her memory and tugged at her heart.nShe wanted to believe Kate was getting treatment, peace and quiet, whatever she needed, but she'd never come here again. It served no purpose.

Emma succeeded in convincing herself that was true until she was aboard the train back to Peekskill. She tried and failed to visualize Kate the way she'd been in art school. Tears slipped down her cheeks as she vowed to keep Kate's children whole. Abbott had been right. They didn't need to see their mother like this, and they didn't need to hear about her condition. Emma would focus on Mary, Gerald, and Gladys instead of whatever Abbott was or was not feeling. But to focus on the children, she must handle her feelings for Abbott.

To keep her mind busy, Emma began painting detailed studies of leaves. She'd choose a leaf off a tree or flower bush and examine it closely, painting every vein, every brown spot, every imperfection. As autumn brilliance transformed the leaves, Emma worked to duplicate the range of colors. Only then could she control her thoughts.

Alice seemed to know more of Emma's inner turmoil than she let on. She arranged bouquets of flowers from her precious garden for Emma to paint, flowers in various stages of budding, blooming, and wilting. "There!" she told her sister. "That should challenge you a bit."

Emma always smiled at Alice. "Put it over by the window," she said. "I'll paint it when I've finished this leaf."

Alice scanned the small canvases leaning against the walls of Emma's studio. "Why so many pictures of leaves? Flowers are prettier."

"That's true. I suppose I'm a bit obsessed with leaves at the moment." Emma's hand stilled and she stared out the window, admiring the many shades of orange and red and yellow Nature painted on her trees as summer turned to autumn.

"If you ask me, you're obsessed with more than leaves. Abbott's writing often, but I don't see any letters going out. Whatever's happening inside your head is crowding out your common sense. Your friend is unwell, and her children clearly need you."

Emma looked at Alice and frowned. "He hasn't mentioned the children specifically, only to say they miss me. He also hasn't mentioned Kate." A memory of Kate at the asylum intruded into her mind and she pushed it away.

"Whatever may have happened, or not, between you and Abbott, the children are no part of it. Their mother is gone, and they probably don't even know why. Think of little Gladys. For her entire life, her mother has been a dark, mysterious figure. You are the one who encourages her, exclaims over her achievements, and reads her stories. And now you're gone, too. And she doesn't know why."

Emma blanched at her sister's words as Alice turned and left the studio. How could she ignore the Thayer children she loved because of her uneasiness with their father? He'd done nothing improper. All improprieties were in her head. Her own cowardice kept her away from Kate's children. She was afraid to face Abbott, afraid of her own feelings.

Her heart had fluttered at every glance from Sam Clemens, every bit of attention. She'd been positively obsessed with Sam, and embarrassed when she'd matured enough to realize it. What was it that made creative men so attractive? Sam's writing and Abbott's painting dominated their lives. Their genius gave them accolades from the public but increased their self-doubt as well. Emma acknowledged Livy Clemens's skill at managing her children as well as the drama that was Sam. Kate had not done so well. Emma had never thought of Kate as a fragile person. She'd been joyful and effervescent, full of vitality.

Emma shook her head and stood up. Maudlin thoughts had no place on a warm autumn day in Peekskill. Even so, Alice had planted a seed. Emma couldn't get the Thayer children out of her mind. In late September, she broke down and sent Abbott a short letter inquiring after Mary, Gerald, and Gladys.

Abbott's response arrived on a cool autumn day that carried hints of winter on its breeze. Emma had painted all morning and now sat in a cast iron lawn chair at the back of the house. A copy of Henry James' *The Bostonians* lay in her lap, and a cup of tea sat on the round cast iron table next to her. Emma would alternate between reading a chapter, sipping her tea, and admiring the flowers in Alice's autumn garden. Alice brought Abbott's letter to Emma and dropped into the other chair, clearly waiting to see if her sister would share.

Emma opened the letter. After a minute, she said, "He thinks I'm wonderful and wants me to visit."

Alice said, "That's it? Nothing from the children?" Emma shook her head. "He's selfish, Emma. If he loved you, he would respond to your inquiry about his children."

"I don't know that he loves me," Emma said. "I don't love him."

Alice raised an eyebrow.

"I don't even know what love is, Alice."

Alice shook her head.

AT CHRISTMASTIME, Emma sent presents to the Thayer children. She selected painting supplies appropriate to their ages. For Mary, she chose a set of sable hair brushes. Watercolors for Gerald made sense. He could smear paint all over his paper to start. Gladys got a thick-handled inexpensive brush to start making circles and lines with her father's paint. Emma sent Abbott a painting she'd done of a caterpillar on a leaf. Alice accompanied Emma to the train station to send her packages.

"Have you noticed how giddy Violet has been?" Alice asked. "I think she must be in love."

"You can't convince me I'm in love so now you're focusing on Violet?" Emma laughed.

"Don't be silly. This isn't about you. Every time I see Violet and Lucy lately, they are giggling and whispering."

Emma said, "Maybe Lucy is in love."

"Maybe they both are. And with the same man!" Alice's eyes grew wide as they sparkled with mischief.

"Now you're being silly," Emma said. "They would hardly be giggling if they were in competition."

Alice's observation intrigued Emma, and when they returned to the farm she watched Violet more closely. Her little sister rarely left the farm. When she did, she was with Lucy. Emma supposed it was possible that Lucy acted as chaperone. Violet definitely bloomed with delight in life, but then so did Lucy. It could be their youth, Emma thought. None of her suppositions quite made sense, though.

Over the holidays, Emma and her parents, her sisters, and her brother and his family celebrated with dinners, gifts, games, and songs. Lucy was present for all of it, but there was no evidence of a gift from Violet's beau. Emma began to think she was wrong about Violet's young man.

Alice brought every missive from the Thayer home to Emma in her studio, accompanying each with a scowl or sigh of exasperation. Abbott's letters were sporadic.

Emma would receive two or three right after each other, then nothing for months. Shortly after Gerald's eighth birthday, Abbott wrote of his frightful mood.

My life is blighted by the Abbott pendulum, Emma. From tranquil all-wellity my sight turns inward and I have such a state of sick disgust at myself. My mother's influence manifests itself in me as a great ocean of hypochondria, and I have inherited my father's irritability. Nothing is good enough, not my painting, not the children's progress in their studies, not even the food served in my house. I am exhausted and anxious, plagued by bad eyes and headaches, and prone to fright fits that leave me unable to rise from my bed.

Emma's dismay focused on the children. Abbott was embroiled in his own mind and couldn't see himself or his art clearly. The children didn't deserve another parent lost to melancholy. Abbott hadn't said anything about Kate, and although she didn't agree with him, she respected his decision not to discuss Kate's decline with the children. She also hadn't seen any of Abbott's most recent work, but the work she remembered reflected his spiritual regard for nature. His richly expressive brushwork showed in pieces of abstract color, and his composition reflected the simplicity of the Japanese prints he'd admired in New York.

Emma didn't know how to answer him so she sent Mary a copy of *The Adventures of Huckleberry Finn*, autographed by the author. Since

Abbott had painted Sam's portrait, Sam was thrilled to autograph a book for Abbott's daughter. Mary sent a sweet note of gratitude.

Between these letters, Emma's focus shifted to her sisters. In response to Emma's interest in leaves and her questions pertaining to trees as art, Alice taught Emma to become a local tree expert.

They often had tea together in the garden, sometimes including their mother or Violet. On one of these days, Alice set a vase of flowers on the table, and Emma said, "I'll get the tea tray."

Alice nodded and wandered over to the flower bed. No doubt she'd spotted a weed or spent blossom she needed to take care of. Emma headed for the house, intending to fetch a book from her room before gathering the tray. She paused when she heard someone in a small room near the kitchen. It was a room Alice used for her plants, and she knew Alice was still in the garden. Alice's room was as sacred as Emma's studio. The door was ajar, so Emma pushed it open, just a little bit.

Violet's back was to the door, but Emma could see Lucy in her arms. They were kissing, and it wasn't a chaste peck on the cheek. Surprise and shock made Emma back away from the door. She stumbled into the kitchen. She had never been kissed the way Lucy was kissing her sister. Emma couldn't identify if she was jealous or angry once the shock dissipated.

Her sister had been so happy lately. Emma realized Violet didn't have a young man that made her happy. She had Lucy. Emma shook her head, contemplating that relationship with difficulty. It was certainly not what she'd ever dreamed of for her sister.

Violet and Lucy came into the kitchen, laughing and holding hands. When she saw Emma, Violet's face fell and she dropped Lucy's hand. Lucy's eyes slid to the floor.

Emma saw no reason to dissemble. "I saw you." She didn't know what else to say.

At twenty-four years of age, like Violet was now, Emma had still been moonstruck over Sam Clemens. She'd never had the calm certainty in Violet's eyes.

"We love each other," Violet said. Her tone was not belligerent or defensive but confident. She reached out to take Lucy's hand. The smile they gave each other spoke of profound happiness.

"I see how happy you are. I guess that's what's important." Emma's emotions were still in turmoil. She couldn't sort them, but she knew that Violet's happiness was foremost. There was time to worry about the ramifications later.

She took the tea tray out to the garden, where Alice waited. Alice poured the tea, nibbled one of Cook's seed cakes, and chattered about something Emma couldn't focus on. Her thoughts were on Violet.

Finally Alice poked Emma's arm and said, "Hello? Emma? Have you gone away into your mind?"

Emma smiled. "Sort of. Have you seen...I mean have you noticed..." She hesitated when she saw Violet and Lucy leave the house. They weren't quite hand in hand, but if you knew what you were looking at, they were very close. Emma waved in their direction.

"Oh, yes." Alice nodded. "I wondered if you knew. You've been distracted, that's all. They really aren't as discreet as they think they are."

Emma sighed. "She's happy, at least."

Alice said, "She is. And Lucy is wonderful for her. It truly is like having another sister. Their relationship may not be for me, but it's working for Violet. I wouldn't want to take that away from her."

"That's true." Emma sipped her tea and ate a seed cake. "Does Mama know?"

"Are you joking? Last week I heard her trying to interest Violet and Lucy into meeting the twin sons of a friend of hers." Alice and Emma both laughed. Mama would never change.

Over the next few weeks, as the apples ripened on the trees, Emma watched Violet and Lucy without saying anything to anyone else. She never again caught them kissing, but she noticed clasped hands, an arm around a waist, and one leaning into the other as they sat near each other. The two women's bodies clearly yearned for each other. Violet smiled, and her conversation was animated. She decided that Violet being a spinster with a special friend like Lucy was better than Alice being a spinster with only her garden. She didn't dare to compare either to being a spinster with her best friend's family.

Dear Nina,

I believe love means caring more about another person's happiness than you do about your own. That is why a person suffers so when a friend does. We cannot choose how those we love live their lives, but trust them to find happiness and be there to support them if they cannot. I have tried to shape my sisters' lives, but I never would have chosen the lives they have. It's really about them finding happiness in their own way, not living the life Mama wants for us more successfully than I have.

I remember you telling me to step out of the shadows. So I did, and now I have the need for cheerfulness and courage and a positive outlook that might hide turmoil inside.

Yours truly,

Emma

ina Larowe
Portland, Oregon, 1891

To be good is noble, but to teach others how to be good is nobler--and less trouble.
- Mark Twain, Doctor Van Dyke speech

Nina continued to give readings to demonstrate her elocution skills, but her list of students had stopped growing. One evening, Ney arrived home to find Nina sitting at the table, her shoulders slumped. "What's wrong?" he asked.

"It's not working," Nina said. It galled her to admit she was failing yet again, but she was not earning enough to support herself, and she didn't want to treat her classes as a hobby. She was not a dilettante dabbling in teaching. "There just aren't enough people in this town who want to pay me for what I can do."

"What's next?" Ney asked. They'd talked about her need to work, to show her independence. If Nina refused to be dependent on a husband, she surely wouldn't depend on her brother to support her.

"I want to teach dancing, which seems to be more popular than elocution. The problem is that Portland is not suited to the establishment of such an enterprise."

"What are you going to do?" Ney asked again.

"There's an article in the paper today about Gonzaga College. It's...let's see..." Nina picked up the newspaper lying on the table in front of her and paged through it. "It's in Spokane. Here, read this article."

Ney took the paper from her and put it on the table without looking at it. "Spokane? What does it have that Portland does not?"

"The article talks about the college. It's a Jesuit institution, so it shows promise. Surely they will need an instructor of elocution and gymnastics."

"Don't make a hasty decision," Ney said. Go for a visit and see if you like the college and the town. Personally, I don't think I could ever live without a family member close by again."

Nina smiled at him. She, too, had enjoyed having him near. His advice was good, though.

Packing a valise, she left on a train to Spokane in June. On the train, she read everything Ney had found for her about Spokane. Two years before, the city had experienced a fire not unlike the Virginia City fire. One year later, the city hosted The Northwest Industrial Exposition. The booklet extolled the city's beautiful new brick, stone, and terra cotta buildings as well as the energy of its citizens.

Approaching the city, Nina could see villages of the natives that still lived on the bluffs above the Spokane River. She passed a Methodist college that had a charming view of the falls before arriving at her hotel. Nina hid her shock at the price of a room, and walked through the downtown area which was so new she imagined a scent of sawdust in the air.

She met with an official of the college, which seemed as new as the rest of the town. Heart sinking, she could not imagine that this raw town would be able to support a robust dancing curriculum. In fact, she didn't think they'd need many faculty members, either.

Nina walked through the lush grounds of the school and imagined the glowing future that lay somewhere in the distant future. She had started from nothing before, pushing her program onto potential clients, with mixed success. She was nearing fifty years of age, though, and no longer had the energy of a pioneer. She wanted to teach dancing in a place that was established enough to appreciate it. Spokane was not that place.

Before she even met with anyone at the college, Nina boarded the train back to Portland. Ney picked her up at the station, and they drove to his home on Kearney Street in silence. When they entered the house, Ney said, "Are you going to tell me about it?"

Nina took off her hat and hung it on a hook by the door. She removed her coat, tugged at the bodice of her dress, took a deep breath, and turned to him. Disappointment at yet another failure filled her eyes with tears that she blinked away. "The newspaper made the college seem like an important affair. It was not. It was a small school, still finding its way, unable to support much of a faculty." She did not tell her brother that the room prices in Spokane were even higher than in Portland.

"Should I have the cook make a batch of chocolate caramels?" His eyes twinkled, and Nina laughed.

"It's true chocolate fixes everything, but I'm tired. I think I'll turn in."

A good night's sleep restored Nina. She woke to a dish of chocolate caramels on her bedside table and smiled at Ney's thoughtfulness. She couldn't lie in bed, however. That would lead to relying on Ney for the rest of her life. She popped two candies in her mouth and rose to perform the day.

40

mma Beach
Dublin, New Hampshire, July 1891

"Marriage -- yes, it is the supreme felicity of life...
And it is also the supreme tragedy of life."
- Mark Twain, Letter to Father Fitz-Simon

In July of 1891, Abbott wrote to tell Emma that an admirer of his, Mrs. Mary Amory Greene, had built a summer house for him on a piece of her rambling property in Dublin, New Hampshire. She was a wealthy philanthropist, a student of Abbott's, who was tired of taking the train to Keene to see his work. Emma was sure Mrs. Greene had been thrilled when Abbott and his family moved into the house to live there year-round. Emma wondered if Abbott was having an affair with the woman, and if so, who was watching the children. At any rate, Abbott was clearly coming out of his melancholy of the previous year and once more anticipated showing his paintings.

Emma stared into the cloud-dotted sky and imagined the Thayer children. Gladys was five years old. Was she as incorrigible as Gerald had been at that age? At eight, Gerald, no doubt, was still mostly inspired by dirt and rocks. Mary was thirteen. Emma hoped she was a demure young lady now rather than a shy girl. It would be wonderful to see them. Still, she hesitated. Her delight in the children would be equaled by her delight in seeing Abbott. How could she keep those feelings from spilling over?

By July of 1891, she could no longer ignore the Thayers. Images of Kate in the sanatorium had become more frequent in her mind than daydreams of Abbott, and Emma felt compelled to visit. She traveled to see the Thayer family in Dublin, New Hampshire. The road passed a small fruit orchard and approached a rambling complex of wood-shingled buildings. Most impressive, though, was the view of Dublin Pond and Mt. Monadnock. Emma could see why the location appealed to Abbott. When she stepped down from the wagon, Mary opened the door of the house and glided down the steps to greet her.

Emma was stunned at how Mary had changed in just two years. While eleven was still a child, at thirteen Mary was a young lady. She still had a somber air about her, but she moved with more grace than before. She'd filled out, too, and lost the coltish look of youth.

"Look at the kitten Mrs. Greene gave me," Mary said. She held out a tiny black kitten for inspection.

Emma exclaimed over the kitten as expected.

"Our house isn't painted yet," Mary said, "and the inside isn't quite finished. The carpenters are making a lot of noise, but they stop at supper time."

Emma was saved from replying by the arrival of Abbott in a paint-smeared smock. He walked across the road from a separate building that must have been his studio. The green and blue smudges indicated a landscape was on his easel, probably of his favorite mountain. Emma's heart warmed to see that he was painting, and her heart beat faster when his face lit up when he saw her.

His face wreathed in smiles, Abbott ran to hug Emma. "Our fairy godmother has returned, Mary," he said. Emma tensed, but his arms felt safe. He didn't hold her longer than a friendly hug, and Emma relaxed.

"I'm glad to be here," Emma said. And it was true. It felt good to be back among this family. She took a deep breath of fresh mountain air.

"Mr. Weatherby will get your valise," Abbott said.

A nondescript man stepped forward, surprising Emma by his very ordinariness. Abbott loved vivacity and color. Where had he found Mr. Weatherby? The man wore rumpled brown clothes. His hair peaked out under his trilby hat, which shaded his eyes, all brown. Even his skin was browned by the sun. He scurried to fetch Emma and Alice's things.

Emma hugged Gerald and Gladys, who were waiting on the porch. Gerald looked the same, only a bit taller. After all, a boy didn't change much between six and eight years old. Gladys, now five, was no longer a baby. She shyly took one of Emma's hands and led her past a Grecian bust by the front door and inside the house. A stuffed peacock stood in the entry itself. To the left, Emma could see a small room with bookcases full of books—art, literature, and texts obviously used by the children for their lessons. She followed Gerald and Gladys into the living room, which held a jumbled mass of Kate's plants. Their condition saddened Emma. Leaves drooped, with edges browning, and some looked too dry to revive.

"Can we put some water on those plants?" Emma asked.

"No indoor plumbing here. Just the hand pump in Mrs. Weatherby's kitchen," Abbott said. "Gladys can fetch it." The small girl scampered to help, disappearing out the back of the house.

From a cage amongst the kentia palms, a red, blue and yellow macaw squawked, the sound almost louder than the bird's colors. On the shelf behind the bird, a stuffed downy woodpecker perched on a shelf of black winter twigs and branches. As Emma crossed the room, the woodpecker seemed to disappear into its background. "Come see Josephine and Napoleon," Gerald said. He led Emma into a screened porch with a scuffed table that must be where the family ate meals. Emma started toward a large cage with several spider monkeys, but the boy led her to a smaller cage with two pet prairie dogs.

"Cute. Do they do tricks?" Emma asked.

Gerald shook his head. "We mostly just watch them." He indicated the monkeys. "They do the tricks. Sometimes they even get out of their cage."

Emma laughed. Gerald led her back into the living room, where Abbott stood in the middle of the room with his hands in his apron pockets. Emma wondered how many scraps of paper with important details were in those pockets. At one end of the living room was the fireplace, with a portrait of Mary and Gerald hanging above it. Emma walked over to look at it more closely. In contrast to the large eyes of Mary in the angel painting, this one showed the girl with heavy-lidded eyes, looking to the side. Gerald just looked lost. Emma's heart ached for the young lady who must be mother to her younger siblings. She turned back to see Abbott's eyes on her, imitating the lost expression in his son's painted eyes.

A rabbit hopped through the room. She must have looked curious because Abbott laughed. "Nature is welcome in our home. There's an owl that flies through the windows from the front of the house to the back. We've seen woodchucks and weasels, too."

"Has anyone thought of closing the windows and doors?" Emma was confused. She knew Kate had never allowed wild creatures in her house—other than the children, at least. "They must disturb your sleep."

Abbott turned to Mary. "Would you like to show Emma where we sleep?"

"Come with me," Mary said. She gave Emma a little smile and headed out to the front of the house. Emma followed.

A path led into the beginning of the pine woods. Emma could see a couple of three-sided Adirondack huts concealed in the bushes. Passing the first one, Mary l said, "This is where Gladys sleeps. I'm up ahead a bit. Gerald and Papa are on the other side of the house." She continued to her own sleeping hut.

Curious, Emma came closer. Although it was as tall as a regular room, the structure was barely big enough to contain a bed. The sides and back were wooden, but the front was open. The thatched roof extended over the front just far enough to keep the occupant dry during a storm. Mary's bed was neatly made, with a bearskin rug spread over it.

"Do you sleep here every night?" Emma asked.

Abbott joined them. "The fresh air is the best medicine of all. We sleep out here year round."

"It must be cold in winter," Emma said.

"Even in thirty below weather, our bearskins keep us warm. Besides, it's not much warmer in the house. It's a summer cottage, so it isn't winterized, and there aren't enough fireplaces."

"Don't you ever sleep in the house?" Emma asked.

Abbott's eyes darkened. "I must do what I can to keep my family safe from disease. The fresh air is invigorating and healthy."

Later Emma learned that the house also had no gaslight. The Thayers used candles and kerosene lamps instead. There was just the hand pump in the kitchen for water, and the well outside. The privy stood behind the house not far from the sleeping huts. Abbott did have two Irish maids as well as Mrs. Weatherby, the cook. The maids were very much alike with their red hair and freckles, and they giggled as they made up a guest room for Emma inside the house.

"Sorry, no guest sleeping huts yet," Abbott said.

Emma preferred to think he was joking and laughed. She went downstairs and ran into Mrs. Weatherby. The brown man's wife was heavy-set, as a cook should be. Her smile welcomed Emma as her words poured forth. "The children are so glad you're here. I'm sure Mr. Thayer is, too. There's been a lot of singing and laughing getting ready for your visit." She shook a wooden spoon at Emma. "You seem a tiny slip of a girl to be causing such a ruckus in the household, but you're a redhead. That means you're feisty. Or stubborn. I can never remember. Dinner at eight." She waved the spoon in dismissal.

That evening, Emma sat on the open piazza with a glass of lemonade and watched the sun set over the garden. The children were in various stages of bedtime, and Abbott was in the kitchen thanking Mrs. Weatherby for a wonderful meal.

Abbott came out of the house and laid his hand on Emma's shoulder. He squeezed it, then left his hand there. At one time, Emma might have been anxious at his touch. Now it was just a friendly hand on her shoulder. Abbott stood there in silence, then walked toward the sleeping huts.

Emma explored her feelings. She liked being here with Abbott. Although he could be odd, he was a wonderful father and painter. She enjoyed painting with him and talking about art. If her heart beat faster when he smiled at her, or leaped when he touched her, she could handle that. She walked through the parlor and headed upstairs to the guest room.

The next day, a telegram arrived for Abbott. He came out of the house to take it from the messenger, who rode off right away. Abbott read the telegram and crumpled. That was the only way Emma could describe it. He crumpled to the ground and wailed. The telegram fell to the ground. Emma picked it up. As she read it, the world around her seemed to fade so that only she and the words existed.

Mrs. Thayer has passed away due to a lung infection. Awaiting your instructions. Bloomingdale Asylum

On some level, when Kate first went away, Emma had believed she was caring for Kate's children until she came home. Abbott had told her that Kate's doctors had advised against family visits, claiming it would harm her medical progress. Emma didn't know if he realized that she had gone to visit Kate anyway. She knelt beside Abbott and took him into her arms, already planning to extend her visit. How could she return home and leave him even more broken?

She held his hand when he told the children their mother had died.

Gladys furrowed her brow and said, "Mama?" She looked at Emma in confusion. Emma didn't know if the girl wanted comfort or if she even remembered Kate was her mother.

Gerald shifted his weight from foot to foot. Emma suspected he was in the middle of some excavation in the woods that he wanted to get back to. After all, he hadn't seen his mother in two years, and she'd been a symbol of melancholy more than joy for his entire life.

Mary, however, lost all color in her face. She remembered her mother before the death of her baby brothers. She remembered joy and fun and laughter that wasn't coming back. Emma moved to hug her, but Mary turned to the younger children. She knelt to embrace Gladys even as she took Gerald's hand. "We must all be strong for Papa," she told them. Mary was their rock, their guide for how to feel.

"Thank you, Mary," Abbott said, his voice dull.

OVER THE NEXT FEW WEEKS, Emma instructed Mrs. Weatherby to make the family's favorite meals and turn away guests. Abbott had his wife's body returned to their home in Keene, New Hampshire, where she was buried in the Thayer family plot. The occasion was grim and private. Emma stood with an arm around Gerald and one around Mary. Gladys nestled into her skirt as Abbott stood next to the gravesite and cried.

Mere days later, Mrs. Weatherby sought Emma in the parlor. "Miss Beach, if I may?"

"Come in, Mrs. Weatherby. Say whatever you need to. You've been an incredible help to the family," Emma said, giving the cook a warm smile.

"Are you aware that Mr. Thayer has a showing of his paintings next month?" Mrs. Weatherby asked.

"Yes, I remember," Emma said.

Mrs. Weatherby frowned. "He's not finished the paintings. He says he's unable to, but the household needs the money. I think it's up to you to make that show happen," she said. Her message delivered, the cook returned to the kitchen.

Emma walked out the front door and crossed the yard to Abbott's studio. She found him dabbing at a painting that took her breath away. Blue sky behind the central figure's head set off the white clouds, angled like wings. The young woman, undoubtedly Mary, held her brother and sister by the hand and strode forward toward the viewer with confidence. Emma's heart twisted at the lost expressions on Gerald and Gladys's faces.

"A rendering of Winged Victory," Abbott declared. "Isn't she splendid? I call it *A Virgin*."

"Mary inspires your art," Emma agreed, "and this one is splendid indeed."

The man had real talent. No one could deny that. If he seemed obsessed with winged girls who looked like his eldest daughter, no one would question that as long as the work was this magnificent.

"Will this be hung at the Society of American Artists show?" Emma asked.

He nodded. "Yes, at the Fine Arts Building next month." He scratched his head. "If I can get it perfect by then."

"That's Helena de Kay Gilder's group. Have you told her about Kate?" Emma remembered Helena de Kay from Cooper Union. She'd been one of the talented group of artists that included Emma and Kate.

Abbott was quiet for a moment. "I should notify her before the show." He turned to Emma. "Could you do it?" His tone pleaded with her while his expression held hope.

Emma said, "I'll send her a letter today. You finish the paintings to hang in the show."

"What would I do without you, Emma?" Abbott said as he turned back to *A Virgin*.

Emma naturally took over the running of the household, allowing Mrs. Weatherby to remain in the kitchen she loved. Emma organized schoolwork for Mary, Gerald, and Gladys, focusing on building their strengths and exposing them to new ideas in their weaker areas that might inspire them to try harder. All three had strong artistic streaks. Gerald was becoming interested in science, and Mary loved languages. Gladys learned to love writing almost as soon as she'd mastered the alphabet. Emma also made sure Abbott ate and slept at regular intervals, and, as she always had, she managed his calendar. When it came to his art show, however, she put her foot down.

"At this show, everyone will know about Kate's death and be wondering who I am and what place I hold in your life. I want all their attention to be on your magnificent art, not on me. I'll stay here with the children," she said.

Abbott enlisted his patroness, Mrs. Greene, to accompany him to the show, and they set off early one morning in September. They intended to stay in Manhattan for the full week of the show.

A few days later, Emma received a letter from Abbott.

MY DEAR EMMA,

How bereft I feel with you apart from me. I have come to rely on you almost exclusively. I know Kate would approve of how you are caring for the children, and I'm sure she'd want me to take care of you. Please consider marrying me, Emma. I cannot live with the notion that you might need to leave for some familial commitment that doesn't include me. The children are thriving with you close by, as am I. You are a vital piece of our lives. Marry me, Emma. I hope you agree so we can be wed soon. We'll discuss it when I return.

Yours,

Abbott

IT AMUSED Emma that he would propose in a letter. It disappointed her that he didn't profess undying love, but she was too old for romance like that anyway. She knew he cared for her, and if she married him she wouldn't have to leave his side. Her love for him and for his children would be enough.

When Abbott returned from the show, he was excited by the attention he'd received and the sales he'd made. At first, Emma thought he'd forgotten about his proposal. It wasn't until well after dinner, when the children were sleeping and the Weatherbys retired to their cottage on the grounds, that Abbott took Emma's hand and led her out to the piazza. The summer sun had almost completely left the sky, but its heat still warmed the air.

"Darling Emma," Abbott said. He gathered her close until he held both her hands in his. "Have you thought about my proposal?"

Emma searched his eyes. She saw tired excitement from the art show and a faint trace of grief. Gradually, tension eased, leaving a soft glow that might be love. "I have," she said.

"I do love you, Emma. You are the only person who can fill this hole in my heart as well as the hole in my life. Please marry me."

Emma no longer had to deny her feelings. She could move forward as his wife, act as mother to his children, and love him. "I will."

His lips claimed hers, and the world disappeared.

ABBOTT INSISTED that he wanted to walk barefoot to the top of the mountain for the wedding ceremony, and he suggested a long, gradual trail that crossed bubbling streams and ascended through woodlands before reaching the summit. "The summit is a gorgeous place to tell the world how much I love you," he told Emma.

She was touched at his romantic idea, but shook her head. "My favorite trail, Abbott, but it takes three hours to walk up there. My mother isn't going to do that."

"I have an idea. How about if you and I leave at dawn and say our own private vows at the summit? We can join our guests on the slopes afterwards for a more formal ceremony, if you like, and a feast," he said.

Emma agreed, her eyes sparkling.

As dawn peaked over Mt. Monadnock and colored the sky orange, Emma and Abbott crawled from their sleeping huts and hurried into the house to dress. Emma put on her cream-colored linen dress while Abbott chose his cleanest trousers and shirt.

"Barefoot?" he asked. "It connects you to the earth even as you ascend to heaven."

Emma's heart was full. She took off her shoes.

They walked the familiar trail through stands of mountain ash and patches of sheep laurel and, near the top, mountain cranberry. They were alone in the world, just the two of them before God. At the bare rock summit, Emma and Abbott faced each other and clasped hands.

"I vow to love and cherish you all of my days," Abbott said.

"I promise to love you, to care for you and to obey you for all of my life," Emma said.

They embraced and kissed. When they drew apart, Emma raised her hands to the sun and laughed. She'd never been so completely happy.

They walked down the mountain to a clearing where Mr. Weatherby had set up two folding tables. He and his wife, together with the maids, had laid the food and drink on the tables. The wedding guests waited for the bridal couple to descend from the summit.

Alice spotted them first. She ran to give Abbott a sprig of stephanotis for a boutonniere, and Emma a bouquet of long-stemmed roses. Violet gave Emma her lace overcoat, and Abbott his best frock coat. "Now you're ready," Alice said to them.

Emma didn't say so, but in her heart they were already wed. This ceremony, though, was for the guests. Mary was the maid of honor, and Gladys stole the show as a flower girl. Both wore white muslin dresses with ribbon sashes that matched the green ribbons in their hair. Gerald wore short trousers and a round linen collar on his shirt. His job was to make sure the short train on Emma's dress didn't drag in the dirt. They looked so nice it brought tears to Emma's eyes.

Mama came to give the bride a hug. "You look lovely, Emma. That bridal glow? Hopefully that's happiness and not from the exertion of climbing a mountain." She rolled her eyes.

Emma laughed. Mama's disapproval couldn't touch her today. The reverend from the Dublin church blessed the couple and heard their official vows, then it was time to share food. Only Emma's family and a few of Abbott's painting students were there. When the guests left, Mrs. Weatherby handed each of them a small box containing a slice of rich, dark fruitcake with white frosting. The wedding festivities concluded in the early afternoon, so even Emma's family caught a train home. That night, after the children were tucked into their sleeping huts, Emma and Abbott celebrated.

Abbott and Emma spent their wedding night inside the house in the guest bedroom. On her first morning as a married woman, Emma awoke next to a snoring Abbott. She slipped out of bed, threw on a dressing gown, and went downstairs. It was her house now, after all. No need to get dressed to impress anyone, and she didn't want to disturb her husband. What a thrill! Husband!

"Good morning," she said to Mrs. Weatherby as she entered the kitchen.

"Good morning, Mrs. Thayer," the cook said with a smile.

Emma grinned. Mrs. Weatherby knew her preferences well, and poured the tea while the bread toasted. She took her breakfast to the screened in porch as she usually did in summer, but today she was a different woman. A married woman.

She was on her second cup of tea when Abbott came downstairs. "Good morning, angel."

Emma smiled. Angel? He'd never called her that before. "Sleep well, dear Abbott?"

Mrs. Weatherby brought him a teacup and put a fresh pot of tea on the table.

Abbott sat down and scratched his head. "Alright, I suppose. I'm really not comfortable sleeping in the house."

Emma had suspected this was coming.

"You know, human life is entangled everywhere by germs that cause diseases like tuberculosis. Extreme cold, like on the mountain, cleanses the air. The trees out there are a boundary of sorts between the bacteria of the cities and the pure air of the mountains." His agitation grew as he spoke, causing him to stand up and pace. "I need to walk in the woods and take deep breaths."

Emma had known Abbott loved nature. She also knew that his father believed the fresh air theory of health. This was not a new idea, not one she could change. She rose and said, "I'll go with you. Let me get dressed."

They walked in the woods surrounding the house. Abbott showed Emma his sleeping hut, which had a table as well as a large bed. "We can sleep here tonight, alright?" he asked.

Emma nodded. "Of course." She still wasn't sure about the snowstorms in winter, but a warm summer night outside seemed reasonable. The distance from Abbott's sleeping hut to the house worried her, though. It was close to Gerald, although Gladys and Mary were on the far side of the house.

That night, Abbott pulled out a violin when the children went to bed. He played Beethoven to lull his family to sleep. Emma was touched. She'd never heard him play before. He told her he only played when he was truly happy.

BY THE TIME FALL ARRIVED, Abbott was restless. In the evening, his agitation had him pacing the yard. Late in September, he told Emma, "I need to work late hours and get up early in the morning. Sometimes inspiration calls in the middle of the night and I must answer." He grasped her shoulders and leaned over to look in her eyes with a slightly manic look in his. "We must find a site for your own sleeping hut."

Emma stroked his arm to calm him. "I think I already have. Walk with me."

They left the house and crossed the piazza. Along the path to the West Garden was a small copse of brush. Emma stopped. "This is closer to the house and won't disturb anyone."

Abbott threw his hands up in glee. "It shall be done!"

Emma slept in her own hut for the first time three days later, snuggled under blankets against the cold night, with furs for winter stacked nearby. She slept soundly.

The following morning, Abbott was waiting when Emma arrived in the kitchen. "Today is ours!" he announced. "I'm having a picnic lunch prepared and we will row on Dublin Pond."

His enthusiasm was infectious, and Emma loved to see him smile. She put on a day dress with a floral pattern and walked hand-in-hand with Abbott down to the lake. The sun shone overhead in a blue sky that reflected in the lake.

Emma sat in the bow while Abbott rowed the length of the lake.

He paused a couple of times to point out birds, and when they were hungry he beached the rowboat and laid out their meal. Emma smiled to see the sandwiches, pound cake, and cold tea that Mrs. Weatherby always packed for days she spent in the woods with the children.

Emma lived for blissful days on the lake or in the woods, alone with Abbott or with the children, too. Mary very capably took charge of Gerald and Gladys's lessons when Emma was painting. In this way, the family floated through the first year of Emma and Abbott's marriage.

Dear Nina,

I can tell you that we were wrong. It is definitely possible to love a man so much that you ache when he is merely in another room. When challenges try to part us, I know we will always find a way to overlook each other's imperfections and come together again. I look forward to the rest of my life making him as happy as he makes me.

Yours in love,

Emma

41

N ina Larowe
    Portland, Oregon, 1893

"Nature knows no indecencies; man invents them."
- Mark Twain's Notebook

She walked through downtown Portland, looking for a job, any job, and almost passed the doorway to a small newspaper office. Over the door, a poorly painted sign said *Daily News*. A scrawled notice said "Society editor wanted," A daily paper she'd never heard of with a job? She shrugged and entered the office.

She asked for the editor. When he came out from his office, she said, "I'd like to apply for the position."

"We're a small paper and can't pay much, but I'll give you a chance."

Nina frowned. "You don't need to see a sample of my writing?"

The editor shook his head. "Nah. If you can't write you won't last long."

"Thank you so much, sir. You won't regret it." Nina tried to make her tone more professional than gushing. At home that evening, she asked Ney to help her list everyone of importance in Portland society.

Over the next weeks, she wrote about the Portland Woman's Union, a charitable and benevolent society, and their plans to open a boarding house for self-supporting girls. The topic touched Nina because if she didn't have Ney, she'd be one of the girls looking for a room at such a boarding house.

The Oregon Humane Society protected all harmless living creatures. Nina covered their annual contest looking for the best essay on kindness to animals written by a public school student. The secretary of the Society provided a framed engraving of Pharaoh's Horses to the winner, a shy, blushing girl who attended Portland High School.

Ney introduced his sister to Georgiana Pittock, a patient of his. Mrs. Pittock had founded the Portland Rose Society and was hosting a rose competition in her garden. Nina approached the mansion, nervous but too well-trained to show it. As a reporter for the *Daily News*, she had as much right to be there as anyone else, even if Mrs. Pittock's husband owned the *Oregonian*, Portland's premier newspaper, and a rival to the tiny *Daily News*.

Portland's women moved around the garden in colorful dresses that looked like even more flowers among the roses. Nina talked to them about their own roses as well as their view of the event and its founder. She recorded the names of the popular roses and made a mental note to tell Emma about the event so she could share it with Alice.

By the time she came face to face with Mrs. Pittock herself, she had a great deal of respect for the woman. She'd heard stories of how Mrs. Pittock had come west and been kidnapped by the Sioux, and how she'd brought rose cuttings with her. What impressed Nina most, though, was how active her host was in all sorts of charitable organizations.

"Such a pleasure to meet you, Mrs. Pittock," she said. "I am Mrs. Larowe, society editor for the *Daily News*. I also teach elocution, acting, and gymnastics, but I haven't been in Portland very long."

"Pleased to meet you, Mrs. Larowe. Thank you for coming to our little soiree." Mrs. Pittock gave her a gracious smile. "It seems you are as busy as I am myself. We'll have to get you involved in some of my organizations."

The fine lady moved graciously through the garden, greeting everyone.

Nina hurried back to the *Daily News* office so she could write up her piece. With each event she wrote about for the *Daily News,* Nina hoped the paper would take off and her salary increase. It did not. She typed up her story and took it to the editor's office.

The editor sat at his desk with his tie loosened and his shirt unbuttoned. An open bottle of whiskey sat on his desk. The scene looked like the Depth of Despair scene in a stage play. He didn't even look up as he said, "We're shutting down. Can't compete with the *Oregonian* like I hoped. I'm sorry, Mrs. Larowe."

Stunned, Nina handed him her article on the rose competition. "One last piece, I guess."

She turned away and walked out of the office with her head high and her lips compressed. Nina was good at accepting failure graciously. She'd certainly had enough practice. Undeterred, she set about reinventing herself yet again.

While reporting for the *Daily News,* she'd realized that people in the small towns surrounding Portland weren't able to make their way into the city very often, and their small towns weren't able to supply all their needs. An idea blossomed. She went to see Mrs. Pittock.

Seated in the society leader's parlor, Nina felt at home. It reminded her of New York, before her husband had lost or taken all their money. At her hostess's prompting, Nina said, "It can be diffi-cult for women in the surrounding towns to come into Portland to shop. I'd like to offer a service where I do that sort of shopping for them."

Mrs. Pittock nodded. "I can see where that sort of service would be helpful." She thought for a moment. "Say I needed three spools of thread, red, white, and black, as well as a packet of needles. Hardly worth my effort to get into town. You would purchase and deliver those?"

Nina nodded. "The customer would pay a small commission for the convenience."

"All right. Where would you find these women?"

"That's where I would need your assistance. My part is mostly an investment of my time. I would need to use your connections to get started. After a while, I hope my clients will speak to their friends about the service."

Mrs. Pittock nodded. "That I can do."

Elated, Nina headed home.

Like any business, it took time to get it started. One woman asked her to match a piece of ribbon. She spent hours on that job, looking in shops all over Portland and found nothing. By the fall of 1887, Nina realized her customers would come into the city to purchase large expensive items, and shopping for the small inexpensive items was more frustrating for Nina than lucrative.

Around this time, Ney introduced her to another patient of his. John Baltimore was a city editor for the *Oregonian*. His drama critic had retired, so he hired Nina to be a drama critic and write for the society page, much as she'd done for the defunct *Daily News*. Nina appreciated Mr. Baltimore's flowery writing style even as she cringed at his overuse of adverbs. Mostly, though, she appreciated the job.

Nina received occasional letters from her niece, Nina Williams. Now twenty-nine years old, the little girl she'd wanted to protect and nurture was a wife herself.

Auntie Nina, I can't find the words to tell you how wonderful my Henry is. He comes from a fine old New York family, and he runs a cattle ranch in Cholame, California.

The letter warmed Nina's heart. Her namesake niece had found a path that made her happy, and that made Nina happy. The letter continued, passing on other family news. Nina frowned.

My sister Emily is teaching school. She hates it. Emily should pursue her dream of becoming an architect even if Father persists in forbidding it. She's miserable doing anything else. Fanny says Emily should get married, but Em's friend Lil would object to that, I'm sure.

Nina looked up from the letter. She considered ways she might be able to help Emily Williams, but discarded them all. Her niece would have to persevere on her own. Nina said a silent prayer for her and continued reading.

Fanny says a man named Mr. George Fellows has published a book exposing your husband as a fraud. I know he's no longer your husband, but Fanny insisted I tell it that way. The book is called Loisette Exposed *and claims that the man you know as Mr. Larrowe does not own the copyright to what he calls the Loisette System. Mr. Fellows says that if the system works, then the world should have it free of charge. He includes it in his book. Mr. Larrowe will never earn another penny from it!*

Nina laughed so loud that Ney looked up from the newspaper he was reading. "What's so funny in your letter?"

"My niece says that Marcus has been exposed as a fraud. I'm delighted."

Ney laughed. "It's been a long time coming. He deserves it."

After a few more paragraphs detailing the merits of her young man, Nina Williams signed off. Nina folded her niece's letter. She'd said nothing about her older sister, Edith, or Emily's twin brother, Ed.

The following week, the managing editor of the *Oregonian* left, and Mr. Baltimore retired. The new editor decided he didn't need a drama critic and let Nina go. She went home, once again unemployed, and told her brother.

"Are you all right?" Ney asked, brows furrowed in concern.

"Actually, yes," Nina said. For the first time, being out of a job didn't make her feel worthless. "I think it's time I do what I was meant to."

"What does that look like this time around?" Ney teased.

Nina wrinkled her nose at him. "You're funny. I've wanted to open a dance studio, and I'm going to do it."

"Good for you. I'll help you look for a proper location tomorrow."

Decision made, Nina's dreams took wing. She imagined herself the queen of dance instructors in Portland, maybe in the entire Northwest. Dances would be held at her studio, and all of Portland would want to come. Everyone in town would know her name. Isn't that what it was all about?

DEAR MRS. THAYER,

I couldn't resist using your new married name. Congratulations on your happiness. I can't say from my own experience, but I know my mother would tell you that a lasting marriage requires hard work but reaps a fine reward. I wish you and Abbott a lifetime of love and happiness.

Although I am once again without an income, the situation no longer distresses me. I know I have the power to choose a path to change my future, maybe even to something I have not yet envisioned. I've hit rock bottom before, and this is not it. From that lowest point, I let go of who I thought I wanted to be and experienced the greatest spiritual growth of my life. Each time I must start over, I see myself becoming a greater person.

Yours truly,

Nina

42

E mma Thayer
Dublin, New Hampshire, 1894

"Architects cannot teach nature anything."
- Mark Twain, "Memorable Midnight Experience"

Emma wrapped her coat more closely around her. The calendar said spring was on its way, but the days were still cold enough to have extra furs laid out in her hut. Just that morning she had awakened there to a light dusting of snow. She liked the way even a light dusting of snow softened the hard edges of fences and stone walls and gave a purity to the landscape.

"Emma!" Abbott's shout broke the stillness of the forest.

Emma turned to meet him as he strode up the trail. His wispy hair stuck out from his head, and his eyes alight. Before she could discern if he was excited or manic, Abbott said, "I'm going to write a book!"

"Are you?" Emma said. For the three years of their marriage, she had tried to keep his moods on an even keel, but he soared to ecstasy for about six months, then crashed to despair for another six months.

As a result, she was familiar with her husband's Wild Idea of the Moment. She would believe in a book when she saw it.

"It will have lots of illustrations. You'll have to help me, and Mary, too."

"Gerald's twice the artist Mary is, and Gladys is quite good as well. Mary prefers her books, and her study of language. She's taught herself French and German. Did you know that she writes to Kate's relatives in German?" Emma said.

"She does?" Abbott only hesitated a moment. "The book will be about how animals use their coloring to hide in plain sight. They use countershading." He murmured the word again, trying it out. "Countershading."

Emma smiled. "Hidden animals will be easy to paint." She remembered her own experiments with the rabbit hiding in the grass. Where was that painting? She'd have to drag it out.

They turned to walk toward the house. Abbott chattered the entire way about ideas for his book. On the piazza outside the screened porch, Emma spotted Gladys with her easel. "Let's see what she's working on," she suggested to Abbott. Abbott's shrug told Emma that he would indulge her, but he really wasn't interested.

Gladys wore a blue woolen dress that looked like she'd plucked it out of a clear summer sky. A bit of lace on the bodice made the dress a bit fancy for painting outdoors, but even at eight years old Gladys was her own person. Seated at her easel, with a blanket over her lap and the gray-blue February sky above her, Gladys seemed posed for a painting herself. Her dark hair, swept up onto her head, reminded Emma of Kate. The daughter who never really knew her mother was the one who resembled her most.

Gladys exuded calm confidence, even when her father swept up like a tornado and peered at her work. Emma came up on the other side and laid a hand on Gladys's shoulder, pleased to see that the subject of the painting was a row of bushes with their scant winter covering. Gladys had chosen for texture and contrast rather than a recognizable subject like the mountain.

Abbott peered at the canvas. "Huh," he said, "nice work." He looked at his youngest child as if he'd never seen her before.

Emma smiled. "She's talented, Abbott. I've been teaching her about flowers, but she could use some help from you with landscapes and portraits."

Gladys flexed her fingers, which looked blue from cold, and looked up with the eagerness of the child she no longer was. "Oh yes, Papa. Can you teach me to paint portraits? Please?"

Abbott loved to teach more than anything besides painting. For a potential student to beg him for instruction puffed his chest out so he looked like a preening bird. "I would be honored, young lady."

Emma left him lecturing to his daughter about portrait painting. In the dining room, Emma was dismayed to see that one of the maids had left a bowl of vegetables on the table that hadn't been properly drained before bedtime. A crust of ice had formed around them overnight. Emma frowned. She wished that Abbott would let Mrs. Weatherby keep the house temperature above freezing. She crossed the room to put another log on the fire.

A new painting of Abbott's hung above the fireplace. Oil on canvas, it depicted snow-topped Mt. Monadnock, the view from her husband's studio. Abbott loved that mountain, and this was a fitting tribute to it. Emma would rather have the money from selling the painting than have it displayed in the house. Abbott liked it, though, so as long as he managed to sell enough paintings to keep the family fed, it could stay.

Emma walked to her studio, near the garden that would be planted with corn and squash when spring warmed the ground. She'd never found the painting she'd started of the rabbit hiding under the apple tree, so she'd started a new one, trying to use Abbott's technique of countershading. The cotton-tail rabbit's coloring mimicked the background where it needed to hide from whatever would hunt it. She called it *The Cotton-Tail Rabbit among Dry Grasses and Leaves* and hoped Abbott would include it in his book.

"Can I see, Emma?" Mary came into the studio.

Emma's face lit up. Mary had grown into a striking young woman with dark hair and large eyes like her mother. She didn't have Kate's sparkle like Gladys did, but the resemblance was there. Emma waved a hand to indicate permission, and Mary stepped up to look at the rabbit.

"What a wonderful example of *camofler*," she said, showing off her French.

"Yes, camouflage!" Emma said. "Your father prefers his own term, though. Countershading is what it will be called."

Inspired to work on pictures for the book he envisioned, Abbott worked for three days nonstop, painting himself into a tizzy as he sometimes did. Emma hovered nearby with food and drink, and encouraged him to sleep, which he did sporadically at best. At the end of the three-day painting binge, Abbott collapsed and slept for twelve hours. Emma paced, waiting to see if he'd wake up content with his progress or furious at his ineptitude. She could never predict his mood.

Gerald was there to support her when Abbott awoke. Gerald had the family coloring, dark hair and dark eyes, and at eleven he had begun spending more time with his studies than running wild through the forest. All three children looked more like Kate than Abbott. Luckily, they'd also inherited the even disposition of their mother's youth. Emma could only hope that they wouldn't develop their mother's melancholy later in life. Gerald had brought his father's notes about Abbott's theory of countershading. Abbott forgot about his most recent painting and dove into the notes. He wrote a scientific article on animal coloration to test reception of the idea in the scientific community. The article introduced his countershading as an important scientific discovery uncovered by an artistic mind, using scientific language to explain how animals blended into their surroundings.

After being published in *The Auk*, a journal of biology and medicine, as "The Law Which Underlies Protective Coloration," the article received widespread praise, causing Abbott's spirits to soar. He took more interest in the activities of the others—Emma's painting, Mrs.

Weatherby's garden, Mary's letters—and could be heard laughing at the antics of squirrels in the trees.

Abbott's premise stated that all animal coloration evolved to allow the animal to go unnoticed, especially by predators or prey. Some biologists, though, took great glee, in Emma's opinion, in pointing out that coloration also made animals *more* visible in order to attract a mate. She knew Abbott could be stubborn, but he would not hear any criticism. He refused to answer questions or acknowledge evidence that contradicted his work. He ignored his critics and continued painting animals. Emma answered correspondence intended for her husband, graciously putting off demands for acknowledgements of his errors, and even retractions, from the scientific world.

One of Emma's favorite illustrations for Abbott's future book was that of a peacock, his multicolored tail blending in with light-dappled foliage. It was a beautiful piece of art, but Abbott's article didn't mention that the peacock had not been painted in its native habitat in India. Emma, in fact, had helped her husband pose the stuffed peacock from their entryway on a wall outside in the garden. The bird's tail draped into the shrubbery, but the colors of tail and ground were blended on Abbott's palette, not in nature.

Sitting on the piazza one day, Emma asked Abbott about the peacock. "*Peacock in the Woods* is a nice piece of art, but why choose such a brilliant bird? Surely the cottontail I painted would illustrate countershading better."

"Emma, my dear," Abbott said, "are you looking for praise for your own work? You know I had to address Charles Darwin's frustration with the peacock when explaining his theory of natural selection."

He went on to talk of Darwin's theory and his own rebuttal, but Emma didn't listen. She knew Abbott was an artist, however much he pretended to be a scientist.

When his rush of words faded away, she said, "I still think my picture should be in your book."

He stared at her, his face twisted with confusion. She patted his hand, calming him, but the idea of her own work being part of his book didn't go away with the furrows in his brow.

ANOTHER PAINTING for the book that cast doubt on Abbott's premise was of a group of flamingos blending into a sunset. To duplicate the countershading effect in the flamingo painting, Abbott Thayer traveled to the West Indies in 1894 and located a flock of flamingos. He lay down in the swamp at dusk, mimicking the point of view of a hungry alligator.

Emma waited for a letter explaining how his experiment had worked, but received nothing. After Abbott returned, they sat on the piazza of their Dublin home, facing the West Garden. Emma poured tea and waited for him to speak.

Abbott said, "I wanted to see the flamingos disappear into the setting sun as they were lit from above to match the natural lighter coloring underneath their bodies."

"Did it work?" Emma asked. She sipped her tea and waited for him to gather his thoughts.

Abbott ran a hand over his bald head. Emma remembered years ago when he'd done that over thinning hair. "Did you know flamingos are active all day long? They are not preyed upon by alligators in saline ponds. In fact, seen against the sunset they stand out as dark spots against the sky."

Emma said nothing. She just took his hand. What was it about creative minds that just couldn't handle criticism? If Abbott had been willing to concede that some animal coloring was not used for concealment, his work on countershading would have been universally lauded. But he refused to compromise. As a result, all his work was mocked by the scientific community.

Despite naysayers claiming Abbott's trip proved he was a crackpot, Abbott needed to be right. He continued to dismiss his critics even as he hid inside his Dublin compound and allowed his mood to darken, reflected in the house's dark paneling and the dark forest outside. Emma struggled to encourage Abbott to paint, which always seemed to take him out of his negative contemplation.

For a brief time Abbott perked up when zoologist Hugh Cott, also a researcher of animal coloration, praised his work on countershading. When Cott went on to say he regretted Abbott's overenthusiastic attempts to explain away critics, Abbott subsided once more into melancholy.

Emma's best efforts to cheer him amounted to nothing against the depth of Abbott's self-loathing. Over most of 1894, Abbott's visage rarely lightened. Emma watched him deteriorate much as she'd watched Kate, and she was helpless. She encouraged Gladys to paint with her father, which amounted more to her painting in his presence. She asked Gerald to approach Abbott more often with questions about his research, even if Gerald knew the answers. She had Mary share her writing with her father. Nothing helped for very long.

Emma spent more time in her own studio, her guilty refuge. When she found herself painting with browns and blacks, and midnight blue, she forced herself to splash yellow and white on the canvas. She was the one holding Abbott together, and the one holding together a successful public image for him. She mustn't give in to her own despair.

To distract herself from her own dark thoughts, Emma took a more active role in selling Abbott's work. She'd been the organizer of his life since he and Kate first returned from Europe, but she'd always let him be the face behind his work. Now as he wallowed in despair, Emma handled all inquiries from dealers interested in acquiring Abbott's work. When he seemed capable, she discussed packing and shipping the paintings. When he wasn't able, she did it herself.

She always approached her husband cautiously so she could assess his mood. On this day he was in his studio, staring at a half-finished painting as if his glare would put paint on the canvas.

"Abbott? She touched him lightly on his shoulder. "Darling, where is *Winter on Dublin Pond*? The driver is here to pick it up."

He stared at the canvas as if she wasn't there.

"You sold it, remember? To that gallery in Pennsylvania?"

No response.

It wasn't the first time she'd had to search for a particular piece. Sometimes he destroyed canvases he decided he didn't like, or he hid them. Mrs. Weatherby served tea to the driver while Emma ransacked the house. She found *Winter on Dublin Pond* under the kitchen sink.

ONE DAY EARLY IN 1895, when Dublin Pond had barely lost its winter ice, Mr. Weatherby came running to find Emma. "Missus, he's not right!"

Emma cringed, automatically reacting to what Abbott would say about someone saying he wasn't right. "Where is he?"

"In the pond! He's taking a boat out by himself."

Emma hurried after him. They had always cautioned the children to row the boat on the lake only with each other, never alone. Even when they became adults, that had been the rule. With Abbott's dark mood, she suspected the worst every day. Would he try to slip away under the cold dark waters of the pond? Her heart in her throat, she ran out on the dock.

Abbott had climbed into the boat, and it began to drift into the cold, black lake. The oars remained on the dock. Emma called out to Abbott, "Abbott, dear, you've forgotten your oars! Sit still, and we'll bring them to you!" She couldn't keep the tremble of fear out of her voice.

Mr. Weatherby brought a long pole from the boathouse. He stood on the edge of the dock and reached the pole toward the boat. He poked it, but was unable to affect the motion of the small craft.

Emma shouted, "Abbott, I need you to grab hold of that pole right this moment!" She used her best angry stepmother tone, and he responded. Moving slowly, he reached for the pole. It took a minute for him to grasp it tightly enough, then Mr. Weatherby pulled him back to the dock and helped him out. Emma didn't know whether to shout at him or hug him. She opted for a hug and led him back to the house, telling Mr. Weatherby, "We must ensure he never takes the boat out alone."

"I can't paint unless it's cold," Abbott said as they walked toward the house. "I must take a bath and open the windows."

Emma knew he believed if he got clean enough and cold enough he could attain spiritual perfection. In that state, anything he painted would be divinely inspired. She told Mr. Weatherby to open all the windows in the house.

Emma led her husband into the living room. "Abbott, you must stay well. All your students love you and will want to continue classes."

Abbott brightened. "Of course they will."

She squared her shoulders and sat next to Abbott. "Tell me what you're painting."

Abbott's painting provided Emma time to connect with reality. While he was painting, she wrote letters to dealers in New York and beyond. She also worked on a book of his letters. It was important that she made sure the world saw Abbott's talents as greater than his eccentricities. Most importantly, she painted. In her studio, Emma could lose herself in the feel of the brush and the delight of colors blending to match what was in her head. Flowers cheered her by reminding her of Alice, so she painted more of them. The intense focus on something external and trivial, like a vase of flowers, banished her frustration and anguish over Abbott.

When one of the gallery owners in New York wrote to ask about her own artwork, Emma stared at the letter for a long time and considered what pieces she had completed or close to completion. The idea of an art show appealed to her. She hadn't done a show since before her marriage. Besides, the money from any sales would ease the constraints of the family budget. She wrote back to the gallery owner with a list of works she had available, indulging herself with dreams that were hers alone.

Dear sir,

Thank you for asking about my work. I know men who scoff at women who paint flowers, assuming such a pursuit is the epitome of femininity. I like painting flowers because it is impossible to capture the fullness of them —the geometry of their blossoms, the softness of the petals, the fragrance. A single flower can represent love or hardship, growth or decay, purity or darkness. When painting flowers, I can become a better artist and still remain humble. Enclosed please find a list of my current works for sale.

Respectfully,

Emma Thayer

Abbott's students continued to come to the house for lessons. Emma appreciated their loyalty but admonished them to say nothing of her husband's erratic behavior to anyone outside the compound. It was the students who gradually roused Abbott from his melancholy.

The next morning, Abbott stayed in his sleeping hut. Emma walked out to rouse him. "Time for breakfast, my intrepid artist."

"I cannot, my dear. I fear I am suffering from another fright-fit where I cannot conceive of rising from my bed."

He was slipping again into a dark mood. For two weeks, Emma brought meals to his sleeping hut and sat with him, chatting about the children, her sisters, the winter garden, the snow on the mountain, anything she could think of. Abbott didn't respond, but he listened.

Winter was just losing its grip on the mountain when a letter arrived from the gallery owner, offering to hang a couple of her pieces in his gallery. Emma, busy with the children and Abbott's whims, dashed off a quick note of agreement. She didn't tell Abbott or the children.

In late March, Emma took an early morning train to Peekskill, where Alice joined her. They continued to New York.

"I know how hard this is for you," Alice said, "to go in alone and have attention focused on you. But you've been too long in Kate's shadow, then in Abbott's. It's your turn to shine."

Emma's stomach was in knots. "Don't leave me," she said.

For two hours, Alice remained glued to her sister's side as Emma greeted patrons and spoke about her flower paintings. When Emma's

resolve weakened, Alice contributed details about the flowers themselves and anecdotes about growing them on the farm in Peekskill.
On the train home, Emma felt dizzy with relief, as if the entire world
had been lifted from her shoulders.

"I'm so proud of you," Alice said. "This whole situation with
Abbott has been hard for you." Emma nodded. "Come for a nice long
visit whenever you wish."

Emma's heart filled with warmth. "I will."

TWO MONTHS LATER, a letter arrived from an art collector in
Seattle. He was interested in purchasing two of Abbott's paintings
that he'd seen at an exhibition on a recent trip to New York. Emma
went to the studio and shared the letter with Abbott. "Seattle, Abbott!
Your fame is spreading."

"Will he come to pick up the paintings?" Abbott's brow furrowed.
He painted a swash of green across the canvas.

Emma swallowed and continued carefully. They needed this sale,
and she couldn't let Abbott nix it. "He can't come at this time. What
do you recommend?"

"I will *not* ship my paintings all the way across the country!"
Abbott's voice thundered the declaration.

Emma knew not to argue with her husband when he was so
adamant. She had traveled to Europe as a teenager, and certainly had
been no stranger to traveling since then, but she had never gone all
the way across the country alone. She took a deep breath. "I will
deliver them for you."

"Take one of the children along if you like." Abbott turned back to
the painting in progress.

Emma smiled, anticipating the reprieve a trip like this could
give her. At seventeen, Mary was a capable young lady. Emma
relied on Mary to manage the household whenever Emma was
away. Emma was proud of Mary, as she was of the other two.
Gerald was a big help with his father, and Gladys was just coming
into her own. Watching them grow gave Emma great satisfaction.

She knew Kate would be just as proud. No, this trip would be hers alone.

The more Emma thought about it, the more the trip excited her. She would add on a few days in Portland to visit Nina Larowe. And at forty-four years of age she could certainly manage the trip alone. In all honesty, Emma looked forward to the respite from worrying about Abbott. Their marriage had never been conventional, but what exactly did that mean? Her parents had stayed married despite a very public scandal about her mother's affair. Nina's marriage had broken up over a scandal. Society didn't approve of either one.

Speculation couldn't help her day to day existence with Abbott, though. She did what she could, but it was exhausting. After her trip to Seattle, maybe she'd spend time in Peekskill with her sisters.

JUNE 1895

Dear Nina,

I am coming west! There is an art collector in Seattle who is interested in a few of Abbott's paintings. He is unable to come east to fetch them, and Abbott will trust them with no one but me. I know, I can hear you say that he's shipped paintings before. Lately, though, they are as precious as babies. At any rate, I will deliver the paintings to Seattle at the end of July, then visit you in Portland for a few days before heading home. The train ride will go quickly, I'm sure, because I'm looking forward to seeing you.

I hope your dance instruction is going well, and I can hardly wait to see your studio and meet your brother. Portland has no idea what you can bring to them! What is your favorite modern dance? I'm quite sure I won't have heard of it as we are pretty remote here in Dublin. Our music is the song of the birds, and we dance to stay warm on chilly nights!

The travel bug seems to have gripped others, too. Sam Clemens is embarking on a world tour. His publishing house folded in the Panic of 1893, and he owes a lot of money. You have to admire a man who books a tour to pay his debts even when he hates to lecture. Sam will be in Portland on August 9. Shall we plan to attend his lecture together?

Yours,

Emma

43

N ina Larowe
    Portland, Oregon, 1894

"I was exceedingly delighted with the waltz, and also with the polka...You have only to spin around with frightful velocity and steer clear of the furniture...."
- Mark Twain, letter to Territorial Enterprise

Nina rented a hall and placed advertisements in all the Portland newspapers for students of dancing, listing dances such as "The Persian Vestal Dance," "The Minuet," and "Society Skirt Dance." She sewed a dance instructor's dress for herself with an Empire waistline and flaring skirt. It was cut to a shorter length so that students could see the steps.

Clients trickled in, but they kept coming. Nina offered gymnastics, acting, and elocution and asked Ney to help her find a bigger hall to buy rather than rent. It was the next step in her plan to become Portland's most popular dance instructor.

Ney found an old hall for sale on 23rd and Kearney that had

been vacant for some time. When he first took Nina to see it, she wasn't impressed. The downtown area had recently been paved with Belgian blocks, which were chunks of basalt shipped on barges up Lake River to Portland. The result was a wonderful respite from winter mud. The hall, however, was on a dirt road, which meant mud in the winter. It was too far out of downtown and surrounded by trees.

"It's owned by the German Savings and Loan Society," Ney told her. "They will give you a loan for the purchase price."

"And what is the purchase price?"

"They're asking $6,000."

"Six *thousand* dollars?" Nina's head spun. Her family had always paid cash for everything. She didn't know anything about loans.

"You'll have five years to pay it back," Ney said.

"How can I manage to earn that much money in five years?" The very notion put panic in her heart, but her brother reassured her.

"Your business is doing well. With a bigger space it will grow even more. You'll see. All of Portland will come to you."

Ney accompanied Nina to the bank when she signed the loan, and he was there when she opened the Esquire dance hall. "Portland only has one premier dancing teacher, and that's you," he said with pride.

"I do know what I'm doing," Nina said. "I went to dance school every year growing up."

"Mother would not approve," Ney teased. "A dancing teacher would never measure up to her expectations for you."

"I believe dancing is a fine art like music, sculpture, painting, architecture, and acting. Some people will coarsen and degrade it, but there are also those who elevate it." Nina had no wish to speak ill of her mother, but she felt strongly about this.

"You ennoble yourself by teaching the arts properly," Ney said, reassuring her.

Nina refinished the wooden floor in the hall for dancing and placed wooden chairs along the walls. The hall had a beautiful tall ceiling, with a viewing gallery accessed by a stairway. It even had a raised loft over the doors for a choir or orchestra. Nina envisioned bands playing there while the floor was full of dancers.

She worried that students would not travel so far from downtown, but they did. Nina greeted them all with a great show of confidence but inward doubts and fears. Pushing those negative thoughts away, she concentrated on her ingredients for success—punctuality, eagerness, conscientiousness, patience, and high standards. She gave students who struggled extra attention, and they blossomed.

Not long after the hall opened, a tall, thin woman came to see Nina with her shy daughter, a young lady on the verge of her social debut. Nina didn't trust tall, thin women. Slender was acceptable, but thin usually meant sharp tongue. She wanted to offer thin women some cake or chocolate caramels, wondering if fattening them up would soften their words. This one was tall, too, and that gave her the advantage of being able to look down her nose at everyone with little effort. Nina watched the other mothers in the room as they gasped and whispered to each other. The tall, thin woman ignored them all and walked right up to Nina.

"Mrs. Larowe? I am Eugenia Holman." She didn't bother to introduce her daughter.

Nina had heard of Mrs. Holman when she was writing for the *Daily News* but never met her. This woman was the font of all gossip in Portland, maybe the entire Pacific Northwest. She nodded. "Mrs. Holman, welcome. Did you want a class for yourself or for your daughter?"

"I fear you're too stout to teach dancing. You must be light enough so it's not such hard work for you."

The room fell silent as everyone listened. Nina drew herself up into her best leading lady stance and said, "If you don't believe your daughter will benefit from my instruction, you are welcome to go elsewhere." Her stare landed somewhere on Mrs. Holman's chin, but Nina didn't flinch. She was always at her best in roles that required a stiff back and steely glare.

"Oh don't take offense," Mrs. Holman said. Her tone slipped from scathing to supplication. "I hear you're the best, and that's what I want for my daughter."

Nina could hear the expelled breath of relief of everyone in the room. She felt as though she'd passed a test. Would all her students have walked out had she not been able to placate Mrs. Holman? She smiled at the young lady, who still had not been introduced, and relaxed her stance. "Miss Holman, why don't you come with me?" She focused her entire attention on her new student and led her across the room. From the reactions of the other women, she knew when Mrs. Holman left the room, but Nina forced herself not to look.

Not long after that, Nina hired musicians and hosted a dance party. The musicians played from the alcove above the door, just as she'd envisioned when she first saw the hall. Her students brought their families and friends for an evening of dancing. Mrs. Holman arrived with her husband and daughter in tow.

"This is a wonderful idea, Mrs. Larowe," Mrs. Holman said. "Portland needs exactly this sort of thing." She bustled off to find someone to dance with her daughter.

Mrs. Holman wasn't the only one who approved. The dance hall was full of smiling faces and good music.

Nina's success allowed her to make regular payments on the loan to the bank. If she arranged her studio as if it were a stage, and choreographed her dancers as if they were actors, no one knew but Nina. She planned recitals every few months to showcase the dances her students were learning. Each one was an elaborate stage production —for Portland, at least.

The *Oregonian* did a story on Portland's up and coming dance instructor. They interviewed her after a class where Nina was teaching the waltz to young people who would soon become the city's elite. Thrilled with the publicity opportunity, Nina sat with the reporter and waited for his questions. Ney joined them, perching on a chair nearby.

"Tell me about your dancing school," the reporter began. He scribbled on a paper as Nina spoke at length about her dancing school and its goals. When she finished, the reporter shuffled his papers and looked up.

"Are you related to Marcus Larrowe?" he asked. "Also known as Alphonso Loisette?"

Ney turned away, disguising a snort of laughter as a cough.

Nina set her lips in a tight line. "Why would you ask that?"

The reporter shrugged and looked at his notes. "Different spelling, but it's the same last name. He's returned to New York from a stint in London and is engaged to marry Miss Ida May Hough in Manhattan. She's thirty-seven and he's sixty-three. Is he a brother? A cousin?"

When Nina remained silent, Ney said, "That scoundrel! He's her ex-husband. They've been apart since not long after Nina returned from the *Quaker City* cruise with Mark Twain."

"Mark Twain?" The reporter's eyes lit up.

Nina was glad that the subject had moved on from Marcus but dismayed at how Ney went on to speak of her relationship with Mr. Clemens. He knew nothing about it. Most likely, he thought he was doing her a favor by distracting the reporter from Marcus Larrowe.

The resulting interview didn't mention her ex-husband or his child bride. She was certain, though, that in the future the paper would link her with the author. *Mrs. Nina Larowe, friend of eminent author Mark Twain....*

DEAR EMMA,

The twentieth century approaches. Can you believe it? I pray that the leaders of this new century are those who empower others.

I feel as if I'm on the forefront as the youth of Portland seem determined to learn the most unsavory modern dances. I'm still working to ban the "Turkey Trot," for example. It's like a turkey on a hot plate, constantly lifting its feet so that they won't get burned. When danced in the extreme, the dancers' heads are held very close together—too close together, I should say. Another dance is the "Bunny Hug," where the evil is all in the closeness of the position. I've already had mothers say I'm behind the times, and several have left my studio. I tell them I am happy to keep up with fashion or custom as long as they are right.

I'm impressed that you are coming all the way to the Pacific Northwest by yourself. I look forward to seeing you.

Yours truly,

Nina

44

E mma Thayer
Seattle, Washington, August 1895

"Broad, wholesome, charitable views of men and things cannot be acquired by vegetating in one little corner of the earth all one's lifetime."
- *Mark Twain*, Innocents Abroad

The excitement of making the decision to travel across the country by herself faded quickly. Emma wondered several times a day what she had been thinking. She'd never done any such thing by herself. The image that froze her inside was arriving in Seattle and approaching a stranger with confidence. She would be alone, and everyone would be looking at her—Her worst nightmare for her entire life. Why hadn't she suggested Gerald go? She could have accompanied him and organized everything from the shadows.

Emma remembered Nina writing about her trip west in a Pullman car in 1875. Twenty years later, the Pullman was still the epitome of luxurious travel but the duration of the trip had been sliced to three days. What a miracle—three days to cross the entire country to San Francisco. From there she'd take the *George W. Elder*

steamship all the way to Seattle. Rivers, roads, trains, and ships—
what a trip!

Emma settled into her Pullman seat and picked up her book, a
copy of Sam's latest, *Tom Sawyer Abroad*. It had been out for about a
year, but she hadn't had a chance to read it yet. As the train chugged
out of the station, she opened the cover. The story was a sequel of
sorts to *Adventures of Huckleberry Finn*, told from Tom Sawyer's point
of view. The novel promised to entertain her during the trip and take
her mind off what waited for her.

Morning saw them steaming through the Sierra Nevada mountains
on the last leg to San Francisco. Emma knew that a lot of Nina's life had
taken place in Nevada and California, so it seemed appropriate that her
thoughts turned toward her friend. Her friendship with Nina had seen
her through many doubts and despair. Her relationships, including her
marriage, had been stronger because she'd been able to think out her
options on paper, in her letters to Nina. Nina's advice had always been
given honestly, which made it more palatable when they didn't agree.

The bustle of getting off the train in San Francisco, taking the
ferry to Oakland, and boarding the steamship heading north occupied all of Emma's attention. Once underway on the ship, with only a
few hours left in her journey, she could no longer avoid thoughts of
what awaited her in Seattle.

Disembarking on a cold gray day, Emma tied her colorful pansy
scarf tighter around her neck. It was softened with age now, but still
gave Emma confidence when she needed it. That, and her vow to
emulate Nina's businesslike manner, gave her the strength to ignore
the butterflies in her stomach as she left the ship.

A rotund man in a trench coat and hat stepped forward to greet
her. "Mrs. Thayer? I am George Walker." He held out a hand to shake
hers.

She shook his hand and said, "Emma Thayer, Mr. Walker. I am
delighted to be able to deliver Abbott's work to you."

"I'm surprised and honored that you came yourself," he said. "My
truck is over here."

Emma directed the porter to load the two crates containing Abbott's paintings on George Walker's truck. The driver pulled away, and George turned to Emma.

"I will take you to your hotel, if you like?" he said.

Emma shook her head. She needed to get this over with. "I'm not staying in town. I need to leave for Portland as soon as we conclude our business."

George nodded and led her to his covered carriage. "I'm hoping Thayer's works will help bring cultural appreciation to Seattle," he said as the carriage started to move.

"I'm sure they will," Emma said. She talked about the inspiration of the two angel paintings George Walker had selected until the carriage pulled up at a large, comfortable home. The truck with the paintings had arrived and was being unloaded.

Inside, George directed a servant to bring a light lunch, and his wife joined them. "Let's visit a bit until the paintings are uncrated. Emma, this is my wife, Sarah."

"Good to meet you, Mrs. Walker." Emma had been too nervous to eat on the ship that morning, and she tried to nibble daintily rather than gobble the sandwiches and little cakes.

She'd been engaging in social small talk since she was a young girl, so that part of the visit felt comfortable. When a servant came to announce the paintings were ready, Emma's stomach turned over as she imagined George and Sarah frowning in displeasure and ordering her to take them away.

She needn't have worried. Sarah exclaimed with delight, and George beamed with pride in his selections. He drew Emma into his study to hand her an envelope. She wasn't sure of the protocol, but she had to make sure all the money was there. She opened the envelope, counted it and nodded to George. "Thank you for your business, Mr. Walker."

"I'm delighted to have discovered your husband's work, Mrs. Thayer. I will be in touch when I convince a gallery in the area to have a show."

"That would be wonderful. Thank you." Emma shook his hand and took her leave.

George Walker asked his driver to take Emma back to the train station, where she calmly purchased a ticket to Portland, Oregon. She settled into her seat on the train, proud of her ability to venture out in the world alone with confidence. To her surprise, she'd enjoyed it and looked forward to doing it again. She looked forward to laughing with Nina about Emma's journey from timid wallflower to confident businesswoman.

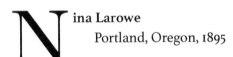

45

N ina Larowe
    Portland, Oregon, 1895

*"When we think of friends, ...we content ourselves that that friendship is a
Reality, and not a Fancy—that it is builded upon a rock, and not upon the
sands that dissolve away with the ebbing tides."*
- Mark Twain, Letter to Mary Mason Fairbanks

While Nina was pleased about Emma coming for a visit, she had
no interest in spending her hard-earned money to help Sam Clemens
out of debt. Nina had her own money problems to worry about. In
Portland, as in all of the Pacific Northwest, the economic depression
continued. Men who'd lost their jobs abandoned their families or
committed suicide. The abandoned women stole from markets to
feed their children and were kicked out of their apartments. City trea-
surers loaded bags with public money and absconded. The economy
of the Pacific Northwest, like the rest of the nation, came apart. Nina
had faced hard times before, but this time she owed money before
the economy even crashed.

All Nina could do was keep her head up and continue doing what she'd been doing. Ney's practice barely suffered since everyone needed a dentist, but Nina's students struggled to pay for lessons. She extended credit to many of them, but that meant she had difficulty meeting her own loan payments. She took to planning overnight trips through Oregon and Washington giving lectures and dramatic readings, then returning to her Portland dance studio. The irony wasn't lost on her that Mr. Clemens was also on a lecture tour to pay his debts.

Chatter and clatter echoed through the hall as students arrived for their next lesson. Nina folded Emma's letter and tucked it under a book on the table.

"Mrs. Larowe! There you are!" Mrs. Holman had come upstairs to find her.

Nina put on a smile. This was an important woman to keep happy even if she defined busybody. "Mrs. Holman, how nice."

"I just had to tell you myself. Mark Twain is coming to town!"

Nina closed her eyes for just a moment. "I've heard that is true." Once Ney had revealed that she knew Mr. Clemens, Mrs. Holman had taken responsibility for embellishing Nina's relationship with him to the point that most of Portland society no doubt believed she'd had an affair of sorts with him while visiting the Holy Land. She'd weathered worse gossip, though, and could no longer be ruined by it. Trust Mrs. Holman to know about the author's visit before the *Oregonian* had done more than list it in the back pages.

"I know you were previously acquainted with him. Will you see him speak? He'll be at the Marquam Grand. Maybe you'll have dinner with him after?"

Mrs. Holman clearly wanted fodder for the gossip mill. Nina didn't do gossip mills. "I have no plans to see him." She swept past the other woman and headed downstairs to begin the class.

Later that evening, she told Ney what Mrs. Holman had said. "How many people will assume I want to attend the event or have dinner with that scoundrel? How can I politely refuse?"

"It's been almost thirty years. Maybe you don't refuse," Ney said.

"I will never forgive him." Nina emphasized her words by shaking her head.

"I know that. But why protest? It just brings more attention to what the public will see as a rift."

Nina didn't say anything. There was no point arguing with her brother about something that might never happen. Either Mr. Clemens would slip into town unnoticed, or his talk would be sold out and no tickets would be available. There would be plenty of local luminaries wanting to get close to a celebrity, so Nina would not be expected to meet him.

Ney said, "You should attend the lecture with Emma Thayer as she requested. That way your clients see you there, but you can say entertaining your guest from back East prevents you from meeting with Twain."

Nina considered the idea. She would hate to be in the same room with the man, but Emma still admired him. Nina sighed. "Fine. I'll get tickets and try to summon some enthusiasm."

The next morning, Nina went outside, tying a scarf over her face. Wildfires had broken out all over the Pacific Northwest, and the smoke stung her eyes and roughened her throat. She walked to the Marquam Grand on SW 6th and Morrison. When the five-story opera house opened in 1891, the *Oregonian* had called it "one of the neatest theaters in the west."

In the window, Nina saw a small poster advertising Mr. Clemens' lecture. A banner across the poster screamed SOLD OUT. Nina shook her head. It was only mid July. The lecture was three weeks away.

She went home and told Ney she couldn't get tickets.

"Mrs. Holman could probably get them for you. Of course, the whole town would know about it, and you'd be indebted to her forever." Ney laughed.

Nina knew Emma would be disappointed if she couldn't go to the lecture. That meant more to her than Portland's opinion about its dancing instructor's attendance at the event. She'd ask Mrs. Holman for two tickets and hope there were none available.

As Ney predicted, Mrs. Holman was delighted to assist. She fell over herself assuring Nina she could get tickets. A few days later, she burst into the dance studio waving tickets. "Oh, Mrs. Larowe, I told you I could manage this! I got the dollar tickets, too, not the cheap ones." She beamed at Nina as if they were now the best of friends as she handed her the tickets.

"Thank you, Mrs. Holman," Nina said. "I will take the amount off next week's dance lesson."

"Oh no, no, no, you mustn't. I am happy to assist Portland's premier dancing teacher." Her gushing left no doubt that she was quite aware of the favor she was doing Nina. Mrs. Holman hurried out across the dance floor to the group of mothers waiting for their children's class to start, no doubt eager to brag to everyone that she had procured the tickets for Nina.

Nina shook her head. She needed the goodwill of women like that to keep her business growing, but she hated the gossip mill surrounding Mrs. Holman and her friends.

ON AUGUST 7, the wildfire smoke had worsened. Nina waited at the train station, scarf over her face, for Emma's train to arrive from Seattle. She hadn't seen her friend since Emma and Kate had attended her play in New York twenty years ago. At that time, Emma had been a vivacious redhead. It had always dismayed Nina that Emma tried so hard to hide her personality, to shrink into the shadows, when she had so much life.

Emma must have changed in order to make this trip on her own. Nina knew how much her friend had preferred to stay hidden. She never pushed herself forward. Now, however, she represented Abbott in the sale and delivery of his work on the other side of the country. That took courage and a willingness to step forward. It reminded Nina of the sort of thing she'd done to support Marcus's career. As long as Marcus appreciated her efforts, she'd been happy in the role. She wondered if Abbott was glad for Emma's support.

When the train came in and stopped amidst steamy hissing and squealing of brakes, Nina stood up. She removed the scarf over her face and pulled at her bodice to straighten it. Passengers disembarked, and then she saw Emma. Her friend was a little stouter than she'd been twenty years ago, but then who wasn't? She wore a smaller hat then she used to, and Nina could see a bit of red hair underneath. It wasn't as bright as it had been, but it was still red. Emma spotted Nina and her face lit up with a smile. Nina waved, her heart full.

"Oh, Nina it is good to see you," Emma said as she approached. She hugged Nina, who hugged her back.

"You are a sight for sore eyes yourself," Nina said. She sent a porter to gather Emma's luggage and led her friend to the waiting wagon. "Let's get home, and I'll fix you some tea. You can tell me all about your trip, and Seattle, and the children—everything."

Once underway, Emma chatted about the trip and the art dealer in Seattle. Nina made noises to indicate she was listening, but she watched Emma's face and mannerisms, which were carefully controlled. Emma exuded confidence and maturity, which made Nina smile as if she was the proud big sister. What a long way Emma Beach Thayer had come from the teenage girl on the *Quaker City*.

At the Kearney Street house, Nina introduced Emma to Ney and they sat down to tea.

"It feels nice to have arrived, even after the short journey from Seattle," Emma said.

"You are welcome in our home," Ney said.

"Tell us about your family," Nina said. She wanted to know about Abbott, about their relationship.

"Mary is quite the young lady." Emma laughed. "Gerald is twelve. He wants to help his father so much, but his help isn't quite valuable yet. Gladys is nine. I still think of her as the baby, but she's quick to point out she's not."

"And your sisters?" she asked.

Emma glowed. "Alice loves her flowers and has become quite an expert on Peekskill's best varieties. Violet and her friend Lucy are a delight. They support a few charities in the Peekskill area, and have lots of friends."

"And Abbott?" Nina said. Was he still as eccentric as Emma's early letters had indicated? Did she love him? She clearly loved the children.

Emma's smile slipped. "He's going through a rough patch. Some days are worse than others, but his future is bright."

Ney said, "I'm sure he appreciates your support."

"Husbands don't always express themselves well when it comes to gratitude," Nina said. Her heart ached for her friend. She remembered changing her own self to deal with Marcus and how dissatisfied she felt as a result.

"He's writing a book," Emma said, her smile bright again. "It's about what he calls countershading—how animal coloring helps them hide from predators."

"And he's painting the pictures?" Ney said. "That will be a nice book."

"Yes, he is," Emma said, but her smile dimmed again.

But what about you, Nina? Tell me about your dance studio."

"It's going well." Nina thought about the thousands of dollars she still owed on her loan, but forced a smile.

"The parent of one of her students got two tickets for Mark Twain's lecture," Ney said.

Nina wished he hadn't brought up the lecture. She still hoped that somehow she wouldn't have to go.

"Oh, you did get tickets! I'm so excited. I haven't heard Sam speak in years," Emma said. "It will be fun to see him together."

"His talk should be very interesting," Ney interrupted.

Emma said, "I rather feel sorry for him. We've all felt the financial pinch in the last few years, but the papers say he owes $70,000. That's a lot of money."

Nina nodded. "It is." And $6,000 was a lot of money to her. Everyone worked doing whatever they could to pay off debts. At least she was doing it without ruining the lives of people she knew by mocking them publicly.

On August 9, 1895, the people of Portland packed the Marquam Grand. Nina and Emma made their way to seats in the third row. As she sank into the seat, Nina was relieved to be out of the crush of the crowd.

Emma, of course, had talked to the ushers at the door and inside the theater. She said, "The first man told me Sam hasn't arrived yet. He spoke on the seventh in Spokane, but there was a problem with his ferry. He is on his way, though. The other man said Livy and their daughter, Clara, are on this trip with Sam. They are apparently under the weather and waiting for him in Tacoma, but he speaks at Olympia after here, and doesn't get to Tacoma until the twelfth. I hope they're all right."

Nina nodded. Emma's prattle couldn't touch her dismay at having to attend this debacle. She would put on her very best face, pretend to enjoy it, and pray Mr. Clemens didn't see them.

Mr. Clemens arrived at the theater at 8:22 p.m. for an 8:30 show. Nina knew that because of the cheers of the outside crowd. The theater was packed, with standing room only, and many left outside.

When the man himself appeared, Nina heard Emma's intake of breath. "Oh, it looks like he is sick, too. It must be so difficult to perform when you're ill."

"It is." Nina remembered actors on the stage and on tour who went onstage while not feeling well. It was what a professional did.

Nina inspected Samuel Clemens, close enough to get a good view, but far enough away to be hidden in the crowd. He appeared taller than she remembered him, but maybe it was her vantage point. He wore a plain dark suit and russet shoes, and he carried his trademark cigar. The snow white bushiness of his hair, eyebrows, and mustache were new to Nina. On the *Quaker City*, all that bushiness had been red, although darker than Emma's hair. He looked almost frail, with a pallor to his skin that indicated illness or exhaustion, maybe both. Nina remembered being on the road. It definitely took a lot of energy. Being onstage, though, was worth it.

"He hates lecturing so much," Emma whispered.

"One has to pay the bills," Nina responded.

When Mr. Clemens began to speak, the crowd quieted. "I've been told there are mountains in the Pacific Northwest, but I have yet to see them. Probably because the entire state of Washington is on fire. I don't mind. I'm a perpetual smoker." He waved his cigar. The audience laughed. "Really, the scenery here is wonderful. It's quite out of sight." The audience roared again. Mr. Clemens pulled on his mustache.

Nina sat stiffly, without laughing. She remembered how this man had flirted with seventeen-year-old Emma and stolen her heart. From the adoring expression on Emma's face, she still admired him. Nina remembered the pain of trying to live in New York under the shadow of scandal caused by Mr. Clemens' remarks about Americans and their ugly behavior in the Holy Land. It had been the trip of a life-time, but she'd been unable to share her joy of places they'd visited without seeing a ripple of disgust pass over the face of her listener.

She'd gone on to reinvent herself as an actress and divorcee, no thanks to Mr. Clemens. Nina wondered if his stories of Tom Sawyer and Huckleberry Finn contained bits as painful to people who'd known the author as a boy as *Innocents Abroad* did for those on the cruise.

Onstage, Mr. Clemens told the story of "The Jumping Frog," and over the next hour and a half, shared the original stories "My First Theft," "Character of the Blue Jay," "A Fancy Dress Incident," "Bit Off More Than He Could Chew," "Tom Sawyer's Crusade," "Fighting a Duel in Nevada," and "A Ghost Story."

Nina listened as an elocutionist, and had to admire the volume and sonorous tone of his voice. His quiet manner and drawl gave the audience time to see the point of his stories, and every one received thunderous applause.

At one point, he mentioned his debt, then said, "I cannot hope to build up another fortune now. I am getting too old for that. I shall be more than satisfied if within the next five years I can pay off my credi-tors. I believe I *can* do it, too."

As the crowd roared approval, Nina was struck dumb by the real-ization of the similarities in circumstance between the author and herself. She, too, had creditors to pay off was too old to build up another fortune. She'd reinvented herself many times over the years.

Mr. Clemens was an author, no one could take that away from him, but he was currently without a publisher and lecturing to bring in money. Both he and Nina had used every available talent to survive.

Nina watched the man on stage perform, looking for Mr. Clemens under the persona of Mark Twain. For almost forty years, she'd built up in her head the evil this man had done to her marriage and reputation. Was it possible all along that he'd just been trying to make a name for himself, to stand out among the writers of the day? She might have done much the same thing onstage as an actress had she not been called home to care for her mother.

If not for Mr. Clemens' articles about the *Quaker City* cruise, Nina would still be married to Marcus Larrowe, still be the supportive wife her mother trained her to be. Remembering that woman now, Nina hardly recognized herself. Only after her marriage dissolved did she discover the resilience that allowed her to become an actress, a lecturer, and finally a teacher. Her entire metamorphosis was the result of Mr. Clemens ruining her reputation, leading to Marcus ruining her marriage. It had taken those events to push her toward where she was today.

She'd learned that feeling fulfilled depended more on pride in her work than on the applause of a large audience. Today the good regard of her community meant more to Nina than praise from critics that she didn't know.

On stage, Mr. Clemens said, "Portland seems to be a pretty nice town, with some nice, smooth streets. Now Portland ought to lay itself out a little and pave all its streets. Then it ought to own all the bicycles and rent 'em out and so pay for the streets." The audience clapped and laughed, the murmur of conversation pleased at the author's categorization of their town. "Thank you all for such a cordial reception this summer evening. I am pleased to learn that the people of Portland are of such substantial and pleasing character." With a wave of the cigar, he left the stage and the curtain fell.

Stunned, Nina found herself laughing at his delivery. She snuck a look at Emma, beside her. Her friend's face was alight with pleasure.

It must be gratifying for her to see Mr. Clemens in all his glory, and she was probably congratulating herself on getting Nina to be there.

Sam Clemens had also been there when Nina met Emma. Since then, she'd had someone to listen, albeit via letter, to the vagaries of life. With Emma she'd shared the frustration with Marcus, the delight of the stage, the despair of her marriage ending, and the never ending struggle to present a more positive face than her heart experienced. The critics' reviews of Nina's private life might have darted from scathing to ecstatic and back again, but Emma had always listened without critique. Sam Clemens may have been the catalyst, but Emma was a friend.

The audience began to chatter as they filed out, but enough people kept clapping that Sam came out once more.

"Give us the 'Stammerer's Tale'!" someone shouted.

Sam nodded, and gave a most gracious rendition of the tale. Then he left the stage for the last time.

Emma insisted on going backstage to see Sam. Delight showed on his face when he saw them. "Two of my *Quaker City* favorites! It's a different world now, isn't it, ladies?"

"It's good to see you, Sam," Emma said. "I heard that Livy and Clara are ill. I'm sorry."

"They are waiting for me in Tacoma," he said. "They couldn't even make the trip to Portland. Tell me about your painting, Emma."

She grimaced. "Right now I'm imagining Abbott painting with Gladys and Gerald, reading what Mary has written, and maybe worrying about my trip home."

Nina smiled and reached out to grasp her friend's hand. "You have a family that loves and needs you. That's something to be proud of."

"I'm still painting flowers," Emma said, "and a gallery in New York has sold some of my pictures. I'm also helping Abbott with illustrations for his book. It's quite the undertaking. "

"Book illustrations. That's intriguing." He turned to Nina. "Tell me what you've been up to, Mrs. Larowe." Sam Clemens looked at her with a friendly smile on his face.

"I'm a dance instructor here in Portland," Nina said. "I also teach elocution and acting. In fact, I can use examples from your lecture tonight to show my students how to use their voice to impress a room."

Sam laughed. "As long as it's a good example, I approve."

"She's one of the best," Emma bragged.

"You're both keeping busy. That's good."

"And I have a lifelong friend," Emma said. She squeezed Nina's hand.

"I suppose you do." Nina smiled and squeezed back. No matter their differences over Sam Clemens or their choices in life, Emma had always listened to what Nina said with respect and responded honestly. Nina had tried to do the same. After all, that's what friends were for.

"What about your writing, Sam? Are you working on anything?" Emma asked.

He shrugged. "I have a few bits of new Huck Finn and Tom Sawyer novels. Nothing that will be a huge success, I'm afraid."

Emma chattered away to Sam like the old friends they were. Emma owed her current happiness to Sam, too, Nina realized. Because of the broken heart he'd given her, Emma knew what love was when Abbott Thayer came into her life. She, too, had learned about perseverance as a result of knowing Samuel Clemens.

If today was the day they disembarked from the *Quaker City*, Nina thought, Sam Clemens would have drawn more reporters than Moses Beach. Nina remembered telling Emma that connections built prosperity, that people knowing your name gave weight to your words. She'd been trying to refute Emma's claim that there was value in a quiet life well lived.

Come to find out, they'd both been right.

AUTHOR AND HISTORICAL NOTES

I like to say I write heritage fiction about my ancestors. For this one, however, it's more accurate to say it's about women on my family tree since neither Nina Churchman Larrowe or Emmeline Beach had children. To see that family tree, visit ulleseit.com.

This story was inspired by a family legend that one of my ancestors was told by her father that he would never let her marry the "Western roughneck" Mark Twain. It is true that Emma Beach remained lifelong friends with Mark Twain and his letters to her are available online through Project Gutenberg. Although the two women were only five years apart in age, I've chosen to portray Nina as much older since she's lived in Iowa, Valparaiso, Chile, California, Nevada, and New York. She's also married. Emma lived a more sheltered life in Brooklyn with her parents. Even her trip to the Holy Land was undertaken with her father.

I'd like to thank my family, my editor (Jenny Quinlan), my critique group (Jill Caugherty, Jennifer Olson, and Laura Beeby), and the Paper Lantern Writers. Without their unwavering support, both emotional and professional, this book would not have happened.

Any historical mistakes not mentioned here were my own, sacrificed in the name of creating a good story. For more historic details about these people, visit my website ulleseit.com.

Printed in the USA
CPSIA information can be obtained
at www.ICGtesting.com
LVHW051940080924
790210LV00020B/323